THE OLD GODS LAUGH

THE OLD GODS LAUGH

a modern romance by

FRANK YERBY

The Dial Press 

NEW YORK

Manufactured in the United States of America

FIRST NOTE TO THE READER

The writer sincerely hopes that no earnest reader will confuse the very real Republica de Costa Verde with those imaginary ones found on the maps of the geography books, scattered in multicolored profusion around seas of pale blue ink. Nor attempt to identify Miguel Villalonga with any of the swart, pudgy little strong men who have no being a priori in the Kantian, Hegelian sense, since we know them only a posteriori as created by those wonderful novelists, the Dostoevskis of the Public Press.

To continue this customary disclaimer: Peter Reynolds, Judith Lovell, Alicia Villalonga, Isabela de los Cienmilamores, Luis Sinnombre, Padre Pío, Tim O'Rourke, Jacinto of the Yellow Eyes, and the rest, of course resemble many people living or dead, with this difference: They are alive, while the persons to whom they may seem to have certain similarities, and you, Reader, and I—

> . . . Are such stuff
> As dreams are made on, and our little life
> Is rounded with a sleep.

SECOND NOTE TO THE READER

I have called this book a Modern Romance. Exactly what I mean by that, I do not know; except, perhaps, that it is *not* a realistic novel; and is hopefully dedicated to the old-fashioned reader, who reads for fun.

Madrid
December, 1963

Two Somewhat Irrelevant Quotations

Inside that mountain
My Lord spoke,
Out of that mountain
Came fire and smoke. . . .

—Negro spiritual

The Gods are dead. They all died laughing the day when one old Grim Beard of a God got up and said: "Thou shalt have no other Gods before me."

—Nietzsche, *Thus Spake Zarathustra*

Book One

THE MOUNTAINS

I

The wind came in from the sea so that the plume of smoke that had not left the top of Zopocomapetl for five years now bent inland above the tropical rainforest, and Peter could see the town. It was very white. The houses were hard-edged and clear even from where they rode, picking their way across the long slant of solidified lava seven hundred meters down from the snowline, and fifteen hundred, more or less, above Ciudad Villalonga. Except on the eastern side, the part of the town nearest the sea. There the heat waves coming up from the burning oil refinery the Castristas had dynamited the night before made the houses dance like stones seen under moving water. The sooty, black-capped orange flames stood straight up for two hundred meters. Then the wind took them, too, bending them over in the same direction as the smoke from the volcano, driving them westward toward the Sierra Nevadas, white-peaked and mist-blue beyond the town.

"I have heard," the guide said, "that the oil company is flying a man down from Texas to put out the fire. An expert in this business of putting out oil fires. They spend uselessly both their money and his time. Tomorrow, the exalted ones who would import the revolution from Cuba, whiskers and all, for our special benefit, will only start another fire. A bigger one."

"Then you are not of the Castristas, Tomas?" Peter said.

"*Hombre*—" Tomas said, "so much as that—no——"

"But neither are you for The Unconquerable, The Generous Benefactor of the people of the Glorious Republic of Costa Verde, The Father of the Country, The Supreme Head of the Everlasting State?"

The guide Tomas looked around him in every direction. At this level—because they were newly made and the wind hadn't had time to sculpture them—the slopes were gentle. They had been flattened by the lava flow from the last major eruption, the one that had buried the Pueblo of Chitimaya up to the bell tower of the church. On the surface of the slope lay a foot or two of volcanic ash. The horses hoofs sank into the ash. Sometimes they broke through the top crust of the lava, too, and the smoke came up around them. When that happened, the horses would snort and roll their eyes, and dance. The guide had warned Peter to expect that before they had started out. It was only a matter of holding the big-barreled, short-legged, shaggy mountain ponies hard between their knees and sawing at their tough mouths with the bits until they stopped it. Which didn't even call for thinking after the first time. But there was no vegetation at all, except here and there a clump of those white flowers that the Indians called La Flor de la Muerte, The Flower of Death. The flowers were very beautiful, but they weren't tall enough or thick enough for a man to hide behind. While he was waiting for Tomas to reassure himself of that fact, Peter Reynolds looked out over the white town to the bay where the two aircraft carriers, one British, one American, waited to take their respective nationals off, in case the revolution got beyond the stage of random bombings and nightly murders. The *Seaflower,* The Leader's yacht, wasn't in the bay at all.

The guide looked at Peter. What he was trying to make his mind up about now was another thing.

"Señor Reporter," he said, "is it your custom to write in your newspaper all things which are said to you?"

"Yes," Peter said. "But never the names or even the professions of those who say them in countries like yours, or in troubled times like these. It would pain me much to think that your teeth, your blood, and pieces of your skin might be splattered over the walls of one of The Unconquerable's Centers of Moral Correction and Social Re-education because of an indiscretion of mine. Hence I do not commit such indiscretions. Of that you can be secure."

"Good," Tomas said. "Then I will say it, since it is a thing which, if you have been down here even a day, you already know: Nobody is for Villalonga. Not even his great whore of a mother. Last week at a party at the embassy of your country, she said that if she knew with any certainty who the father of Miguel was, she would emasculate him to make sure he begat no more monsters. Of course she had been drinking the whiskey of your country to which she is unaccustomed. Someone who knew her in the days of her glory—when she was the star of those curious exhibitions performed at La Luna Azul, in which intervened men, women, creatures of indeterminate sex, horses, dogs, and even monkeys—remarked that to have any certainty she would have to geld the entire male population of Costa Verde above the age of fifty, in which the Castrated would outnumber the Castristas."

"And from then on could be distinguished from them by their lack of beards," Peter said.

"*Aiyi!*" Tomas laughed. "You extend the jest. I must remember that—"

They looked down at the city.

"Señor Reynolds—" the guide said.

"Yes, Tomas?"

"If this of the Fidelistas goes badly, what am I to tell Señorita Lovell?"

Peter looked at him. Said:

"The same thing I told her before we left: 'Gringa, go home!'"

"I do not understand this. You, Señor, it seems to me, are the luckiest of men, and . . ."

"Luck is various," Peter said. "There is the luck of winning a million pesos in the National Lottery; but also the luck of keeping them, once won. Or, to put it another way: You were once, in your youth, a killer of bulls, no?"

"No," Tomas said, "that is a lie I tell to the usual type of tourists. But since you are neither a tourist, and certainly not ordinary, speaking, as you do, our language like a Spaniard of Spain . . ."

"Which is where I learned it," Peter said.

"I find myself compelled to the truth. A rarity, no? I was a peon in the *cuatela* of the great Manuel. Manuel the Mighty. So I can talk convincingly of the bulls. I have, after all, run them. I was not bad with the cape. With the *banderillas,* excellent. It is probable that I would have become a torero if I had not been gored. But fear entered me along with the horn of that black enormity from Piedras Negras. Much fear. More than I could dominate. So I quit. But what has this to do with Señorita Lovell? *Dios mío!* How pretty she is! No, more than pretty—beautiful in truth! Why——"

"So," Peter said, "are those flowers over there."

Tomas looked at Peter.

"Do you know what they are called, Señor?" he said.

"Yes," Peter said, "The Flowers of Death."

Tomas went on looking at him.

"Many times I have had difficulty understanding the people of your country," he said, "but that was because my English is bad; or in the few cases where they believed themselves capable of speaking Spanish, what they spoke was of an incomprehensibility total. But with you, there does not exist this difficulty. What you say is perfectly clear. It is your meaning that is obscure."

"Perhaps I have no meaning," Peter said. "Perhaps there is no such thing. I sometimes think there isn't."

"*A iyai yai!*" the guide said. "Now you have lost me, truly. We were speaking of Señorita Lovell."

"No," Peter said, "we were speaking of luck. If that exists, either."

"*Sí, sí!* Clearly it exists! A man who can take nightly in his arms this blonde one with hair like sun on snow; eyes like those great blue flowers that open only in the morning; lips like . . ."

"Let us not enter into details over all the physical excellences of the Señorita Lovell. Nor indulge in speculations about the precise nature of my relations with her. I grant you that a man who knows her within any of the acceptable degrees of intimacy is lucky, surely. And when he speaks against luck, he blasphemes, no? But I do not speak against it, Amigo. I simply say it is various. That there is—say the luck of placing the *banderillas* side by side in the great hump of muscle that grows behind the bull's neck—power to power, you call that one, don't you? And the bad luck of having them fall out, once placed. There is the fine luck of killing cleanly with one enormous swordthrust; or dying well against the planks of the *barrera* with the horn in your guts and all the lovely girls screaming in horror and in anguish as you die, going out on the great wave of their wail of self-pity, for it is that, you know, Friend Tomas, because they individually and collectively have lost in a very personal manner all that maleness, all that valor, even—though they know it not—the sweet, night-long use of that mighty pair which gave you what it took to do this thing. But there is also the luck of living on after a horn wound of the gravest kind, when that hard black living spike destroys the femoral artery or enters between the cheeks of the buttocks. One lives on, after a fashion; but belly, groin, and thigh look like the map of Costa Verde, and all the natural functions are impaired—"

"You mean?" Tomas said.

"Nothing. Or everything. I knew Señorita Judith Lovell before. When she was nineteen years old and had played no more than secondary roles in minor Class B films. And again, five years ago, when she was twenty-two. In Madrid, where she was making the great spectacle picture about the Byzantine Empress Theodora. By then she was already between husbands, having divorced the first one and not yet acquired the second. Which might account for it. But then, it might not. Who knows?"

"What, Señor?" the guide said.

"*Hombre,* I talk to myself, posing questions which have no answers.

But no questions have answers, truly, do they? And there are no solutions to anything whatsoever in this world. Which is enough of this subject. More than enough. A repletion."

"As the Señor wills. Shall we go, then? It is still far to the place where casually, accidentally, and unfortunately, you take the wrong fork of the trail and lose yourself—"

"And you," Peter said, "what will you do then?"

"Report the unfortunate occurrence to the authorities, who will then immediately publish a report that the celebrated North American journalist, Mr. Peter Reynolds, has been abducted by the Castristas and is probably undergoing torture, in order to induce your Marines to land and your Navy to send the planes from those aircraft carriers out there to bomb and machine-gun the jungles at the foot of the Sierras."

"You mean Villalonga *wants* us to send in the Marines?"

"Naturally. Who else would be willing to save his hide? You North Americans are a strange people. You call yourselves democratic, and yet you support the enemies of the people, everywhere—"

"Say we support the less dangerous of the people's enemies against the more," Peter said. "Is there not in Spanish a proverb which goes 'Better the known evil than the unknown good'?"

"'*Mejor lo malo conocido que lo bueno por conocer . . .*'? *Sí.* We say that, yes. But in the case of Miguel Villalonga, the proverb is without meaning. For nothing could be worse than Villalonga. Nothing at all."

"You've got a point there," Peter said. "Come. Let us ride on while there is still light."

Now where they rode it was cold and the wind came down from the snow-capped peak of Zopocomapetl with a sting of fine flakes, and something else, too—they did not know what it was until they came around the shoulder of the volcano to the side where the lava spilled over the rim and melted the snow. Then the horses began to snort and buck; looking at Tomas, Peter saw the guide was crying blood. He put his hand to his own cheeks and his fingers came away sticky and red, but he saw it was a kind of wet red mud, mixed with steam vapor and the mist from the melting snow. They both started coughing at the same time, doubled over in the saddle while the vapor that was nearly three parts pure sulphuric acid to seven parts steam tore into them. The guide jerked his pony's head around, and they went down the slope very fast on the edge of the fresh lava flow that was too hot to cross, being cherry-red and blistering their foreheads above the snow goggles they had put on, even from five meters away.

When they were out of it and picking their way across the lower tongue of solidified lava that wasn't always even solid but was always so hot that getting across the narrowest part, twenty-five meters wide, was an exercise in horsemanship, they stopped and washed their faces in the rivulets of melted snow.

"Can one drink it?" Peter said.

"No," the guide said. "It is, like the smoke, of a poisonous nature. Better to use the water in the canteens."

Peter unslung his canteen, drank, but rolled the water around in his mouth without swallowing it. When he spat it out, it looked like blood, and some of it maybe was, the acid vapor had burned his throat so. But it made him feel better.

"Now," Tomas said, "we are past the bad part. From here on, it is all downward."

"Is this where I leave you?"

"No; not yet. In that place there is a definite fork in the trail which makes this of your getting lost plausible in case Our Glorious Leader investigates. Señor Reynolds, will you explain something to me? I do not mean to put my nostrils into your business, but I should be happier if I understood——"

"Understood what?" Peter asked.

"This of Padre Pío. What interest has your paper in saving him?"

Peter looked at the guide.

"You think he's alive?" he said.

"I know he is alive. The Castristas are not so stupid as to murder him. For, by doing that, they would lose surely what they hope to gain."

"Which is?" asked Peter.

"The Indians. You know that seventy-five per cent of the population of Costa Verde is of pure Indian race. Without them, the revolution has no chance. Yet so far, peons that they are, hungry, abused, almost slaves, with nothing to lose and everything to gain, they have not joined it."

"Because of Padre Pío?"

"Because of Padre Pío. And because they love the little brown Indian Virgin, and the Saints with the faces of Tluscolas he caused to be painted. Because they are by nature devout. You know they worship their ancestors and the dead? Until Padre Pío induced them to accept Christian burial, they used to keep their dead in a room with barred windows to keep the pumas and the wolves out, until they mummified. Then they would sit them at the table with the living at every meal, and do them honor, offering the first and the best of the maize and the goat meat and the *mescal* to them—"

"That must help the appetite," Peter said.

"It is macabre," Tomas said, "but it is also beautiful. Piety always is, no matter what its nature . . ."

"So the reason the Communists kidnapped Padre Pío is—?"

"To induce him to stop telling the Indians that the first thing they would do upon gaining the power would be to burn all the churches as they did in Spain."

"And how do they propose to induce him to do this? By pulling out his fingernails?"

"No, Señor. I have told you they are not stupid. They seek to make a bargain with him. It is said they propose to make him Archbishop of the State Church when they come to power."

"And he?"

"Is neither stupid nor for sale. He says that of cowardly archbishops of captive churches there is already an excess, that what is necessary in this world is faith, and the valor to die for it if need be. Besides, he says they are incapable of realizing that his priesthood detracts not one jot from his Spanish manhood but rather adds to it."

"Spanish manhood?" Peter said. "He is Spanish, then, your Padre Pío?"

"Vasco. Basque. Which is the same. Only stubborner."

"You," Peter said, "have much precise and detailed information on this matter, no, Amigo?"

Tomas shrugged.

"I am a guide," he said. "I go many places. And my hearing is of a sufficient keenness. Besides, when one has lived the number of years that I have under the rule of the Generous Benefactor of the People of Costa Verde, one automatically closes one's mouth to preserve one's teeth. With the Fidelites, I am a Red; with the Army officers, who alone support our Leader because they know that upon the day of the uprising the people will lynch them along with the Generous Benefactor and with equal justice, I am more rightist than Villalonga himself. Here it is only by being all things to all men that one stays alive."

"Yet Padre Pío—"

"Is safe from both sides, because his death at the hands of either would mean the ruin of their hopes. Now here we have a journalist! I ask him a question, which not only does he not answer, but in recompense for my impertinence in asking it, he digs out of me the replies to ten questions of his own. But I ask it still: Why, in a country of Protestants—"

"Like our President?" Peter said.

"All right. I will say it differently. Why, in a country with a majority of Protestants, does a newspaper interest itself so much in the fate of an obscure Basque priest?"

"There is not much news these days, Amigo. Or rather there is too much. All of it of a boring sameness: 'Shall we bomb them, or will they bomb us?' So this of the little Padre Pío, with his faith, his valor, his Spanish manhood, his heart, say. It tugs at the emotions—which, Amigo Tomas, is what sells papers. And that's all I am—a paper boy. '*Wuxtra!* Read all about it! PARISH PRIEST DEFIES REDS!'"

The guide looked upward toward the cone of the volcano. Above it now the sky was red.

"I do not permit myself the luxury of criticism," he said, "but it seems to me ugly, this thing you have said."

"What isn't?" Peter said. "In my lifetime, and yours, Friend, what hasn't been?"

And now, having passed that fork, he was alone. The trail went down very steeply, and the coolness went out of the air. In a little while he was going to be down to the level where the jungle growth started. He knew what that was like. He had been in tropical rainforest before. So he stopped where he was and made camp for the night. Here it was still cool enough for him to sleep comfortably. He was still above the level of the insects that came in stinging clouds and ate a man alive, above the height favored by the vampire bats, the scorpions and the snakes. He slept very well, being awakened only once by a puma who was trying to get at the horse. He shot at the puma with his carbine and missed it, but it went away. Farther down in the jungle it might have been a jaguar instead of a puma. And missing *el tigre,* as the Indios called the jaguar, would have been fatal. He cursed himself for a rotten shot, and went back to sleep.

One hour after he'd started out the next morning, half an hour from his prearranged place of rendezvous with the Castroites, Fidelites, Communoids, he saw the plane.

It was so high up that all he could make out about it was that it was a high-winged monoplane with gear that didn't retract. But even from that height they must have spotted him, because the next time it appeared it was only three hundred meters up and he could not only recognize the type but also read the markings. A Piper Cub, Civilian. Registered in Costa Verde itself. It lifted, went away. But when he hauled the mule-stubborn mountain pony around the next bend of the trail, it met him head on in a classic strafing run so low that the spinning sunlit disk of the propeller was directly in front of him, and he could see the pilot's eyes. But he kept on riding upright, not throwing himself out of the saddle as the pilot probably wanted him to, until the rate of closure was a sickening thing and even the sound of the eighty-five horsepower double-opposed Lycoming was no louder than the beating of his heart. It rose a little, lazily, negligently, went over at a distance so close that if he had had a knife in his hand he could easily have punctured one of the fat-low-pressure tires.

For the next half minute he couldn't see where it had gone; he was too busy trying to stay on the horse, amid the little tornado of volcanic ash and dust the prop had kicked up. By the time he had the beast quieted the Cub came over again, climbing now, and flew straight ahead of him in the direction he was going. Three kilometers away, or maybe five, it circled once, twice, three times. Then it went up again, headed back toward Ciudad Villalonga, climbing all the time; but when it got to Zopocomapetl it still wasn't high enough, so it banked vertically around the rim of the volcano just under the smoke. After that he couldn't see it any more.

Three and a half kilometers down the trail, he met the Communist guerrillas.

They came out of the woods on both sides of the trail. They had Czech-made machine pistols in their hands. The pistols had a twenty-five shot clip that stuck horizontally from the side of the gun, and slotted air-cooled barrels. They also had a rifle stock that was nothing more than an open lightweight metal frame that clipped into the back of the pistol grip so the gun could be raised to the shoulder and sighted like a rifle. But none of them was even starting to pull the damnfool trick of trying to aim one of those little squirters. They'd found out, or had been taught long ago, that holding the stock of a burp gun to your shoulder while in a standing position and trying to draw a bead on your target through the rudimentary notched sights had three absolutely certain results: The recoil raised the muzzle until you were spraying the treetops; the blowtorch spluttering blast at the muzzle thirty scant centimeters in front of your eyes left you blinder than a bat; and that nice, pretty, all-but-useless stock slammed back against your shoulder in a series of mule kicks that broke your collarbone.

From the easy way they held those lethally beautiful lightweight assault arms—hip high, cradled against one side, the muzzle pulled down low by the left hand on the forward grip, ready to swing in a flat, belly-ripping arc, Peter could see that some Red Army drill sergeant on the Island of Cuba had known his business forward, backward, and crosswise.

They were all very young. They all wore beards. They were all dressed in paratroopers' uniforms without insignia. Jungle uniforms, spotted with camouflage.

"*Hola,*" Peter said.

They didn't answer him. They stood there looking at him with the two eyes in their heads, and those other great dark final eyes that were the muzzles of the burp guns.

"*Buenas días,*" Peter said. "My name is—"

"We know who you are," the tallest one, clearly their leader, said.

"Look, Juan!" the second one said. "Kill him. There is no doubt possible. Or permit me that I do it, myself. Because, if not—"

"Shut up," snapped the one called Juan. "I give the orders."

The other said nothing. Peter noted that the one who had no possible doubt and wanted Juan to kill him had yellow eyes. They looked like the eyes of the puma he'd shot at and missed the night before.

"Señor Reynolds," Juan said. "You will throw down your carbine to the ground. Slowly. Without abrupt movements."

Peter eased the Winchester out of its saddle sheath, let it trail downward until the muzzle was almost touching the ground. Then he let go of it. The thud it made striking the earth didn't carry too far.

"Now your revolver."

"I have no revolver," Peter said.

Juan nodded. Yellow Eyes stepped up to the horse and ran his hands all over Peter, stepped back.

"He has no pistol, Chief," he said.

"All right," Juan said. "Now, Señor North American Journalist, you will dismount, remove your radio very carefully from your pack and hand it to Jacinto, here." When he said that he nodded a little in the direction of the one with the yellow eyes.

Peter swung down off the shaggy pony, stood there looking at them.

"Señor Jefe—" he said.

"Camarada Jefe," Juan said.

"Comrade Chief," Peter said, "I am of those who have no spiritual affinity with the twentieth century. Revolvers in my hand, refuse to shoot. Radios always have their batteries dead. Therefore I dispense with them, and with all things I am incapable of managing—"

"You lie!" Jacinto of the yellow eyes said.

"Shut up, Jacinto," Juan said. Then to Peter: "Your radio, Reynolds. Your walkie-talkie. The small apparatus with which you summoned that plane."

"I am here," Peter said. "There is my horse. You have many hands, all of which need not be occupied with those little machine guns. So find it, this marvelous radio of the black novels of espionage with which I have communicated with the air force of a man for whom I have no use at all."

"Why not?" Juan said. "Why have you no use for our sweet little Fascist?"

"I have a big nose. And a weak stomach. A bad combination, no? Say I object to Miguelito's smell."

"And how does he smell, Comrade Reporter?" Juan said.

"Of death," Peter said.

Juan stood there, looking at Peter. Then he turned to Jacinto.

"Search him," he ordered; "search the horse."

"He has no radio, either," Jacinto said, "at least, not now."

"What do you think I did with it, if I don't have it now?" Peter said. "Swallow it?"

"No," Jacinto said. "For that even an apparatus of transistors would be too big. You threw it, doubtless, into the brush before meeting us here. From the time the little aircraft descended close enough to touch your head until you reached us, you had time enough for that. We could not keep you in sight every moment."

"From here to there is three kilometers," Peter said, "all of it but the last hundred meters bare rock and volcanic ash. My beautiful radio will be in plain sight beside the road. I could not throw it far. I am not strong enough. Here, take my horse and go to get it. I am longing to have my radio back. I miss it. I want to call the White House. Tell our Irish President not to worry. That he need only shoot off a firecracker, and enemies of such imagination will die of heart attacks, thinking it the H bomb."

"A comic," Jacinto said. "A clown. But a clown of the bad death, making jokes of a fatal lack of humor. Jefe, with your permission I will make him another mouth—a little farther down, about the level of his windpipe, say. So that he may laugh out of them both . . ."

"Leave him in peace," Juan said. "He threw down nothing after this of the little plane. I was watching him through the glasses. Yet that pilot dived upon him like a hawk. Tell me, Comrade Reporter, how do you explain that?"

"I cannot explain it," Peter said. "I can only speculate."

"Speculate then," Juan said.

"I think that an officer of the Security Police must have been present in the saloon of The Blue Moon when I made the arrangements to ransom Padre Pío. In civilian clothes, of course. Or that one or more of the *chicas* there sells information as well as her perfumed flesh. From getting that information to hanging a tail on me was just a step. You will note that they did not send a big and powerful aircraft loaded with bombs and machine guns to wipe you out once I had located you and called them with the radio I do not have. Instead they sent that little yellow toy of an airplane which can fly almost as slowly as a horse walks and hence is useful in locating a single rider on a mountain trail. But this, I think, has no importance now. What does have importance is that we all leave this place with a certain rapidity."

"Why?" said Jacinto.

"Because, Comrade, while I admit that this skin my sainted mother gave me is no longer handsome, after having been burned and stung by thirty-seven years of sun and wind, and having been perforated with various metallic objects in various wars, the fact remains it is the only skin I have and I retain a kind of sentimental fondness for it. My desire to preserve it, more or less intact, is keen."

"I think," Jacinto said, in rare good humor now, "that the Comrade Reporter has nothing in his pants. And that he sits down to urinate."

"And I that you have nothing in your head," Juan said, "except your tongue, which is as loose and heavy as the clapper of a church bell—and just as meaningless."

He turned to Peter with a little smile.

"Shall we go, Comrade Reporter?"

They moved through the jungle on foot. Two of the soldiers went ahead, hacking out a trail with their machetes. Peter walked between Juan and Jacinto. All the rest, fourteen in all, followed. The last man led Peter's horse. He had taken advantage of the occasion to hang his machine pistol and his pack over the horn of the saddle so he didn't have to carry any weight through the brush.

It was hard going. Every plant had thorns. The insects rose up. The sound of their wing-drumming, long-tearing whine filled the heavy, hot, wet, stench-laden air. What little patches of sky were visible through the treetops, ominous and dark with the smoke from the volcano, they blotted out as they came down. They hit the horse first. He went crazy. Juan had to put another soldier at his head to help hold him down. Then they hit Peter. A hundred red-hot needles plunged into every visible, uncovered inch of his flesh.

"Here," Juan said. "Take this. Smear it over your face and arms."

This was an oily insect repellent. The insects loved it. They ate it up.

The lead guerrillas killed a python with their machetes. It was bigger around than the biceps of a wrestler, and a shade over fourteen feet long.

"How," Peter asked, "do you stay in this place, Comrade Chief?"

"We don't," Juan said. "We only use it for cover on our raids. Do not preoccupy yourself, Comrade Reynolds. We shall be out of it, very soon . . ."

They were. Two hours later they came out of the jungle at the foot of the Sierras. Started up them. Before they had reached the three-hundred-meter level, Peter was freezing. The wind blew through his clothes. They were soaked with the sweat that hadn't been able to evaporate in the steam wash of the jungle. But even after they had blown dry, he kept on being cold. His teeth chattered. His lips were blue. Something was happening to his eyes. They wouldn't focus. Juan, Jacinto, the guerrillas ballooned and shrank, towered into giants, diminished into dwarfs, elongated into a multiple lizard with hundreds of feet. He saw that some of the feet had hoofs, and laughed aloud.

Juan looked at him. Turned to Jacinto.

"We halt here," he said. "Get out the medicines. Call Pepe. As a doctor he is not much; but since we have no other—"

The one called Pepe slipped the needle into his arm expertly. Then the three of them, Juan, Jacinto, and Pepe, squatted around him in a circle until he began to sweat. The water poured out of him in rivers. Then it slowed. Peter opened his eyes.

"How long was I out?" he said.

"Two hours," Juan said. "Comrade Reynolds, do you think you could stay in the saddle?"

"I think so," Peter said. "Why?"

"It is too exposed for us to make camp here. Especially since Villalonga is equipped with the airplanes given him by your government to aid him in his fight against the Communist Menace, the Red Threat, the Fidelista Infiltration—namely us—a sum total of less than a thousand men, scattered throughout the Sierras with nothing heavier than mortars to use against his tanks—"

"Castro had no more," Peter said, "but look at Cuba now."

Jacinto lifted up his head and laughed aloud. It wasn't a pleasant sound.

"What diverts you, Comrade?" Peter said.

"A jest. A good one. This medicine, Señor Don Hireling of the Blood-sucking Capitalist Press, which we used to break the onslaught of your fever is part of the ransom Fidel forced you to pay for the stupid and clumsy sons of the oppressors of the Cuban people we took while they were trying to play Commandos at the Bay of the Pigs!"

"You took?" Peter said. "You were there?"

"And Juan. And two or three of the others. We were getting our training in guerrilla tactics under our valiant Cuban brothers at the time."

"You mean under the Russians," Peter said.

"No," Juan said. "From them we learned only mountain warfare. They have no experience of jungle fighting. There are no jungles in Russia. That we learned from the Fidelistas themselves, who are past masters at it. Will you try to get up now?"

"Yes," Peter said, and got up. He felt their hands come out and take him, holding him until the trees, the sky, the mountains stopped their slow and stately dance above his head. Stood still again. Rock-solid, there.

Jacinto was still laughing.

"Tell me, Comrade Reporter," he said, "is it true that the invasion was planned by the infant daughter of your President? Or did the plans come to him in a sealed letter from the Pope in Rome?"

"No," Peter said. "I planned it for him. I'm good at that sort of thing."

Jacinto lifted his head and howled.

"What sort of thing, Comrade? Planning invasions?" Juan said.

"No. Screwing up the deal," Peter said.

He was dog-sick now, but he hung onto the saddle horn with both hands. Juan came up to him. Gave him a canteen. Said:

"Here—drink this. All you can."

It was dark Cuban rum. It flowed through his veins, making a warmth, a singing. He could feel his strength coming back. But he knew better than to trust that feeling. In the twelve years he'd worked the Latin American beat—with four out of the middle of them when he'd covered Spain, meeting Judith again there, learning some things about himself that weren't pleasant to contemplate even now—he knew how hard it was to get rid of tropical fevers. He knew he was in for it, that he could count on four or five days flat on his back, delirious, raving, and twenty days to three months of palsied, trembling, half-alive existence before he'd be able to shake off the effects.

He took another pull at the canteen. The sickness receded. He felt great.

"Think you can walk a little now?" Juan said. "This part will be difficult to manage on a horse."

"Of course I can walk," Peter said. "Another shot of that black glory, and I'll flap my wings and fly."

"Walking will be enough," Juan said.

Peter climbed down off the horse. He went on feeling fine. They went up the steep rocky trail. Ahead of them, Jacinto was still laughing.

Peter leaned close to Juan's ear.

"Is the Comrade Jacinto always entirely well in his mind?" he said.

"No," Juan said; "he is a little crazy. But it is a type of craziness which makes him a clever and dangerous fighter. Besides, he has reason enough to be mad."

"I see," Peter said.

They went on climbing. Now the effects of the rum were leaving him, and he was beginning to be sick again. But he hung on, alternately freezing and burning up, forcing his eyes to focus, his feet to move.

"We are almost there," Juan said. "You can see the sentries now."

Peter looked up just in time to see the sentries bringing the muzzles of their burp guns down and around in the direction of the trail. At once he threw himself flat on his belly.

Jacinto laughed aloud, clearly, gaily.

"As I told you," he said, "the foreigner sits down to—"

"Shut up!" Juan said; then he called out: "Point those unnameable namelessnesses of machine guns in another direction! And slowly. I have no wish to be murdered by the trembling hands of cowards. We come!"

The sentries swung the machine pistols away.

"Comrade Reynolds," Juan said.

Peter heard his name being called from a long way off. A very long way. But he didn't get up. It was very comfortable where he lay at the very heart of darkness, the nadir of existence—the warm, soft, lightless womb of time. Only Judith's face kept coming in, breaking the night apart. It was distorted, slack-lipped, her mouth a little opened, her breath stirring against his face. He heard her voice, but his mind rejected the words. She was being tender with him, after her own peculiar fashion. Which meant that everything she said was totally unprintable.

"Pick him up. We'll have to carry him in," Juan said.

II

When he came back again it was morning and the sun was up, shining through the flap of the tent he was unaccountably in, and he was looking into an old man's face. The face was ugly. It was lined and seamed and crumpled and scarred until it looked like it had been accidentally eroded out of the bole of a tamarind tree by the sun and wind and decay and insects. It was so ugly that Peter didn't believe it. For one thing, it had been there before, fading in and out of Judith's in the midst of that furious torture that she called making love. And he, knowing all the time that Judith wasn't there, that neither her face nor that Zopocomapetl lava bath consuming his loins was real, figured that this ancient gargoyle's face wasn't either. Only it was.

He lay there studying it with some care. Then it smiled at him and the ugliness was gone. Which was a rare thing. Somebody, something, somewhere flipped a switch and it was gone. Like the darkness goes when a light snaps on. In no time, no interval, without transition. And what was there now? Not beauty, but something finer. What there was in that face were all the words you couldn't say in English any more because English belonged to the twentieth century, to the age of anguish, and they sounded phony as all hell. But you could say them in Spanish because Spanish hadn't got out of the thirteenth century and maybe never would. All those big, fat, round, sonorous words ending in *dad;* Tranquilidad. Serenidad. Bondad. Even—hell, yes!—Santidad.

He kept on watching it, and the light came through the tent flap and sculptured a body under it. A bent, wizened, old man's body, dressed in the cassock of a priest.

"Here we are!" the old man said. "By the grace of God and His infinite wisdom in permitting men to discover the wonders of His Science."

"Do not speak of God," Jacinto said. Turning on his cot, Peter saw him standing there in one corner of the tent, his young face, above the formless ink blot of his beard, orange-red in the sunlight that filtered through the canvas. "God does not exist, Uncle Pío. He is a myth, invented by the capitalists to enslave the minds of the people with superstition."

"And you," Father Pío said, "you are a myth, Jacinto, invented by Karl Marx and distorted by Fidel Castro: That you are a handful of chemicals which can be bought for a few *reals,* a few kilos of insubstantial flesh on brittle bones, deterministically determined by some mindless glands and economic forces. Such a sad little myth, my son! How it diminishes you!"

"*Ha!*" Jacinto said. "Do not call me son, Priest! Do you know what a priest is, little Vasco?"

"Yes," Father Pío said. "A priest is a servant of God."

"A priest," Jacinto said, "is a man who is called father by all the world, except by his own children, who call him uncle."

"This is a jest, Jacinto?" Father Pío said. "Hmmn—not bad. I must remember it so that I can tell it to the Archbishop when I go back to Villalonga City."

"If you would listen to reason, you stubborn old fool, when you go back to Ciudad Villalonga, you would *be* the Archbishop."

"Thanks, son! A thousand thanks! But are you not a little confused? What makes you think that you can make archbishops or even bishops? Her servants can only be chosen by the Mother Church, under the guidance of God."

"God!" Jacinto said. "Where is your God, Old Man? Show Him to me! I want to see Him, now!"

Father Pío got up from where he sat beside Peter's cot, walked over to Jacinto, and tapped him on the chest.

"Here," he said, "in here. And if you would stop shouting and firing off your childishly murderous toys, you could hear Him speak. He does, you know. To everyone, in the silence of his heart."

"Good, Father!" Jacinto said. "Good! You hear? I have called you Father. And I am going to go down on my knees like a superstitious peasant, like your cadaver-worshiping Indians, and ask you a thing. Even if your God exists, what good is He? What good at all?"

"My son," Padre Pío began, but Jacinto cut him off.

"What good! When is He ever there when you need Him? Where was He the day the soldiers of Villalonga took my father out of the house after beating him so that he was bloody all over and could not stand? Where was He when they sat my poor little father in a chair and stood my angel from heaven of a mother—she who had no politics at all but was in your fornicating church praying to your fornicating saints morning, noon, and night—up beside him, both of them without blindfolds, and shot them both? Shot my father who was sitting, through the chest, but my mother, because she was standing, through the lower abdomen, but in both cases badly so that it took them hours to die; and I, who was hidden in the stable under the hay with Guillermo the groom, with his hand which smelled of the dung of horses clamped over my mouth to keep me from crying out, and his whole body which smelled of sweat and tobacco and urine and the sickening stench of fear pressed down on top of me to prevent me from running out to help my parents, could hear them screaming until they could not scream any more and after that moaning until the moans themselves became less than silence. And when I at last broke free of Guillermo and ran to aid them and seeing them there like that, like slaughtered animals in their blood and being unable to stand that either, ran into the house where everything was smashed to bits, and tried to turn on the lights because it was growing dark by then; but there were no lights, because they had cut the wires. So I found my father's flashlight and went to look for my sister Teresa. Where was your monstrous obscenity of a God, Padre, when I found Teresa who was fifteen years old then, found my sister who was beautiful as a flower, pure as the snows on the Sierras, lying there naked in the shreds of the clothes they had ripped off her, in—this, too, Father!—a pool of her own blood on which their filthy semen floated like little white islands? Lying there staring into the beam of the lantern with her mouth and her eyes opened wide trying to cry without tears and to scream without voice?"

"Jesus!" Peter said.

"Do not blaspheme, my son," Padre Pío said. "Go on, Jacinto. I am glad you are telling me this."

"Glad!" Jacinto said. "He is glad! You hear this, Comrade Reporter? He is glad to know how the men, who on Villalonga's orders attend Mass daily, comport themselves when they are out of it! He is proud of his communicants of rapine and murder! You beg the question, Padre! Where was your God when my parents were dying that bad, ugly death? When my sister was praying to Him to let her die also, and He wouldn't even grant her that small mercy?"

"In His heaven, as always," Father Pío said. "Where, very shortly, with that special indulgence granted those who suffer much, your parents and your sister joined Him."

Jacinto raised his two fists to the sky. Threw back his head and howled with laughter. With that kind of laughter that is harder to listen to than crying ever is.

"Now I know!" he said. "I have suspected it a long time! For, if my sister is in heaven, Padre Pío, then heaven is located on the corner of Avenue Bolívar and the Street of the Fourteenth of June! Yes, yes! Your heaven, if it contains my sister, is in La Luna Azul! A whorehouse of a heaven! A heaven of heavenly whores! Oh, they take a man to heaven all right. Better than you do, Padre! Ah yes!"

"Son, you've had it rough, haven't you?" Peter said. "But, since you've told us this much—why not finish it? How'd your sister happen to end up in The Blue Moon?"

Jacinto frowned.

"I think," he said, "it was because after that she did not care. She hated her own body; sought, I think, to debase it. So she did the great act to which we are all born, with anybody. Stable boys, grooms, drunken sailors, Negroes; filthy, stinking Indians smelling of the stench of the dead bodies they keep in their beds. Being lovely still, she caught our Benefactor's eye. Soon she was installed in a palace. Soon she was the mistress of the Head of the State. For a while. For a very little while. Because, since Miguelito is not truly or entirely male, he tires fast. Soon he was—as is his custom—giving her to Luis Sinnombre, that unspeakable beast of all manners of vile practices, while he, Miguel, watched the performance, which is the only way, truly, he can enjoy—"

"So he is a voyeur?" Peter asked.

"I know no French, Comrade," Jacinto said.

"What you have said. One who watches."

"*Sí*. Among other things. Along with abusing small boys and little girls. And indulging in circuses with Luis and two girls. Or two queers. Or any other combination that excites his capricious nature. He is not the son of Isabela Cienmil for nothing."

"Isabela Cienmil?" Peter said.

"Isabela de los Cienmilamores. Isabel of the Hundred Thousand Loves. She owns The Blue Moon. Or didn't you know that, Comrade?"

"No," Peter said, "I didn't."

"Perhaps she doesn't now. For no one has seen her since she got drunk and made a spectacle of herself at the American Embassy. What a performance! There she was, waving the carving knife under the nose of your so very, very dignified Ambassador who had invited her along with the higher society of Costa Verde, because he, fatuous fool that he is, knew nothing more about her than that the Illustrious Lady was the mother of the Head of the State. And they, the high society who would not have been found dead with that foul-mouthed witch if they hadn't known that to refuse the invitation would be to end up dead indeed, because Miguelito of the French perfumes and delicate practices and ritual murders would be quick to resent the insult, had to sit there and listen to her long dissertation on the art of castration, starting, of course, with the father of Miguel, so that—"

"He could produce no more monsters. I know. I heard that one," Peter said. "But tell me one thing, Comrade Jacinto: If this of the revolution succeeds, what will you do about your sister?"

"Shoot her," Jacinto said.

"My son—" Padre Pío said.

"Shut up, Father! I shall shoot her, Comrade Reporter, with great tenderness, as one shoots an incurably wounded beast. With tenderness, Comrade. With love. Not because of stupid bourgeois prejudices, but to end her sufferings which are unthinkable because there is no pain equal to the pain of self-loathing. So now, Padre Pío, little Father Pious of the death-worshiping Indians, I ask you to bless this pistol with which I will shoot my sister in the back of the neck, ending very quickly and kindly her terrible life. An act of compassion, no? Of Christian charity. With sorrow and pity and tenderness and love. Come on, Father; bless it!"

"No," Padre Pío said.

"Then bless this knife with which I shall rip open the belly of the ugly Alicia once I have used her as her brother's men used my sister!"

"Alicia?" Peter said.

"*His* sister. Alicia Villalonga de Duarte y Marin—who has no more secure right to the name than Miguel has, since old Cienmil doesn't know who her father was either. But his half-sister, anyhow. Whom he adores, despite her ugliness, which is great. Who is now a young widow since Miguelito, having discovered that his brother-in-law was a member of the junta of conservative Army officers plotting to overthrow him, blew up the airplane in which Emilio Duarte was voyaging, killing fifty men and women and three children in order to eliminate Alicia la Fea's adored husband—to the great sorrow of all the chorus girls at the Teatro de la Comedia, all the whores at La Luna Azul, and even of Alicia the Ugly, herself, who, I'm told, loved him. But ugly as she is, I shall mount her. And make him watch it, since he is of this dirty French-named vice you said!"

Juan poked his head through the tent flap.

"All right, Jacinto," he said, "get out. Now—before your ravings attract the notice of the Dictator's Army. They must have heard you even in Ciudad Villalonga, you noisy fool. You heard me! Go!"

Jacinto stood there, looking at his Chief. Then, very slowly, he bent his head and went through the tent flap out into the sunlight, saying no word at all.

"Poor devil," Peter said.

"No," Father Pío said. "I have great hopes for Jacinto now. Do you not see, my son, that what he has said is a kind of confession? That his pain and his anguish are acceptable sacrifices in the eyes of God? I will save him yet—the day I teach him not to hate. You see that I am already gaining ground with him? Today he spoke sincerely, and from the heart—"

"How is your patient, Padre?" Juan broke in.

"Very well. Tomorrow he will be entirely well, fit for all tasks."

Juan smiled. "Have you performed another miracle, Padre? If so, you must be punished. You must know that miracles are against our Socialist concepts—"

"Do not speak of miracles, son," Padre Pío said. "I am not so presumptuous. I know only that I gave him medicine made from the roots of a certain plant the Indios told me about—administered, of course, with prayer. But el Señor Reynolds will be up, and entirely well, tomorrow. You may call it a triumph of Socialist medicine if you like, since it was first proved in your camp. Or, if you prefer, you may call it a miracle of the good God. As what is not, son? Even that we go on walking, breathing air. Or that the sun goes on rising in the mornings, and setting itself at night. Life is a miracle, son. So is love. Tenderness. Compassion. The condition of being human. *Vaya!* You have had your sermon for today!"

"And I go," Juan said, "lest you reduce me to counting glass beads, mumbling nonsense, and burning candles before silly, simpering images of painted plaster. You are in good hands, Comrade Reynolds. Tomorrow I shall look in upon you again."

"All right," Peter said. "But you won't have to. I'll be up. You heard what the good father said. And I believe him."

"Oh, so do I; so do I," Juan said.

"Son," Father Pío spoke. "I have a thing to say."

"Then say it, Father," Peter said.

"You are Catholic, are you not?" the old priest said.

"I was," Peter said.

"But now you are not?" Father Pío said.

"Now I am nothing. Now I am dirt. No, less than dirt. Garbage."

Father Pío laughed aloud. His laughter was young. Like the roaring of young bulls as they enter the arena.

"Why do you laugh?" Peter said.

"At the nonsense you talk, son! You think that God ever lets go of a man?"

"Padre—I have no skill at talking theology. I only know that too many have died who could have been saved. That too many brave, fine, valuable lives have been snuffed out. And by the bad, the worthless. That there is too much hunger, too much misery, too much sickness, too much pain. I was brought up in the Church, so I know the answers. All the answers. Only they don't satisfy me. Not any more."

"What a presumptuous one! He wants a private explanation from God!"

"No, Father. Because I wouldn't believe Him, either. He's cheated me too many times now. Father, pardon me, but couldn't we just skip this discussion? I am ill, and my head labors badly. It always does, even when I am well."

"Of course," Father Pío said. "It is skipped. No more theology. Tell me, son, are you going to marry Miss Lovell?"

Peter stared at him.

Father Pío smiled.

"No miracles. Not even one. You raved. On the basis of what you said, I could give you absolution, because you hate your sins. Of course, much of the time you were talking English, which I do not understand. But the things you said in Spanish were enough to convince me of your repentance. Now you must tell me consciously that you mean to give it up. Then I will absolve you. I'll make you say two hundred Pater Nosters and five hundred Ave Marias; but nothing more. If you will remove the sin by marrying her, I shall be glad to officiate when we return to the capital—"

"Padre," Peter said, "I can't."

"Why can't you, son?"

"I told you I was brought up in the Church. That part stuck. To me, marriage is just once, and for life."

"I don't understand you, son. Not at all."

"I do not wish to be Judith Lovell's fifth husband. Not while the other four are still alive."

"I see," Padre Pío said. "Now I understand. She is a star of the cinema, no?"

"She was; yes," Peter said.

"And not of our Faith?"

"And not of *your* Faith," Peter said.

"How stubborn you are, son! What you must do is very simple. You must leave her."

Peter turned his head away from the old priest. Looked out through the tent flap. The sun was very bright.

"Simple," he said. "Very simple—oh, very simple. Like falling off a log."

"What did you say, son?"

"That nothing is simple. Or everything is. I wouldn't know."

"All right. Your mind wanders. Sleep now, my son—while God and I watch over you."

"You watch over me, Padre. I trust *you*," Peter said.

The next morning he was still dog-sick but he got up anyhow. He wasn't going to let Padre Pío down. He didn't know why, but he couldn't.

"Can't screw up your miracle," he said in English, "you sweet, simple-minded old coot, you . . ."

"What do you say, son?" Padre Pío said.

"That I encounter myself great, fine, enormous," Peter said.

"You don't look it," Father Pío said. "You look like the bad death, son."

"No, of truth I am fine. Come, let us look for Juan. I have a thing to say to him."

"This of the ransom?" Padre Pío said. "He won't take it, Pedro my son."

"Why not?" Peter said.

"Because in his politics, Juan is very pure. They have replaced the religion he thinks he has lost but has not, truly. Neither he nor Jacinto, who is a little mad and hence will become a very great criminal, or a saint. I worry more about Jacinto. With Juan I shall have time."

They came out of the tent together, and the sunlight was a bundle of golden arrows piercing Peter's eyes. Fire stabbed into his brain under his skull. He reeled a little.

"Son—" Padre Pío said.

Peter straightened up.

"Come on, little Father. Let's go save sinners!" he said.

When they started across the camp under the trees, they saw the Indians. They were coming down from the top of the Sierras in a long double line, hundreds of them. They wore serapes over the ordinary baggy pants and shirts of peons. They had felt hats with big, floppy brims on their heads. Some of the men had a hole punched in the top of their hats with a condor feather stuck into it. They also wore bracelets and necklaces of hammered silver. When they were close enough, Peter could see that the workmanship was very fine.

"Excuse me, son," Padre Pío said, "but now I must attend to my children. They have come a long way—from Xilchimocha, likely—so that I can bless their dead."

"Who are they, Father?" Peter said. "What tribe?"

"I do not know truly. From their features, I should say they are Chibchas, come over the Sierras from Colombia many years ago. Their language is similar to that of the Chibchas, though it has many Toltec words; and others that may be Inca or Maya, since those words are lost. They call themselves Tluscola, which means only The Men. Or the Real Men. Go back to your tent. Or join Juan. This will take time."

And now, suddenly, Peter saw what the Tluscolas had with them. Saw those straw-wrapped figures in the thronelike chairs. Sitting there upright while four young Tluscola braves bore each chair aloft on long white birch poles set on leather cushions to save their shoulders over all the hundreds of kilometers they must have walked, climbing over the peaks of the Sierras, wading snowdrifts, winding through the passes with their sacred burdens.

And now the wind came down from the peaks, cold and sharp and with a sting of snowflakes in it, light and powdery and dry; but that didn't help that smell. He had smelled it first in Korea, lying in that cave with five of his company dead around him and the maggots moving in the great rent in his shoulder, eating his own hideously stinking flesh, which was why he still had his left arm and why it was only a little stiff in bad weather, because those fat white eaters of putrefaction had left the wound so clean that it healed almost perfectly, leaving only the enormous silver ridge of the scar. He had smelled it again in Hungary, his first big story, and after that in Algiers; and now and again in a hundred places where the thrust and probe of a relentless ideology ran hard up against the stubborn resistance of another that liked to call itself free. He had smelled that smell in Argentina, in Santo Domingo, in Guatemala, in Venezuela, in Colombia —all over Latin America, where fat, porcine little generals bought what they called order with the people's blood. And were maybe the lesser of the two evils, since what it took to strike a balance between thunder on the right and lightning on the left doesn't even exist in the Spanish-speaking world.

But he had never got used to it. It wasn't a thing you got used to: that sweet, sick, utterly vile odor of rotting human flesh. Smelling it now, with the fever still in him, his stomach turned over. He bent his head and vomited, noisily, terribly. Afterwards, he put his back up against a tree, and stayed there, like that, until he saw, five meters to his left, Jacinto lying on his belly, sighting a tripod-mounted Czech copy of a Hotchkiss 9-mm. air-cooled light machine gun, the kind that had the almost-semicircular shell clip mounted on top of the magazine, toward the Indians. Then he moved, crossing the distance that separated him and Jacinto in five long strides, got there, his right foot swinging back, his weight pivoted on his left, bringing that right foot forward, clad in and protected by his stout Alpine boots, to crash against the barrel of the gun, sending it over and to one side so that the short, ripping snarl of the burst Jacinto got off, either deliberately, or because his finger was still on the trigger when Peter kicked, cut a pine sapling in two and sent it crashing down.

Jacinto's expression didn't change. He simply put his hand to his belt and came out with his Commando knife, with which he could have shaved if beards hadn't become the latest ideological symbol. Then he kicked free of the overturned gun and got up without haste, looking at Peter with those flat yellow eyes without anger in them or hate or anything at all but that ice-cold mindless glare of the great predators to whom killing is neither an emotion nor a conditioned reflex but an instinct, requiring nothing more than opportunity.

Peter stood there in a great blaze of sunlight, his arms down at his sides, unmoving, watching Jacinto's arm going back in that smooth underhand swing, the light glinting on the blade and the smell of burned cordite in his nostrils now, the vile green taste of nausea in his throat, noting all his own sensations with detachment and curiosity, just as though he were going to be around to analyze them later, as if they mattered, which they didn't, any more than the act of dying did to him then, considering what his life was like now, and was going to be.

Father Pío's voice, when it spoke, wasn't even loud. It was, in fact, curiously gentle.

"Stop it, Jacinto," he said.

Jacinto looked at his knife. Then he put it back into the sheath. Bent and picked up the machine gun, put it right side up. Took an oily rag out of the toolbox beside it and began to wipe the dirt off the barrel, digging it out of the slots of the barrel with a part of the rag.

"Better dismantle it," Peter said. "It's surely got dirt in the magazine. Next time you fire it, it'll jam, or blow up."

Jacinto nodded. Then he dropped to his haunches and began to take the gun apart, laying each piece out on a piece of oilskin, very, very carefully.

"Go back to your tent, son," Father Pío said. "It has passed. He will not trouble you again."

But before Peter could move, Juan was there.

"Jacinto," he said.

"Yes, Chief?" Jacinto said.

"You were going to kill the Indians, no?"

"*Sí*, Jefe," Jacinto said.

"Why?" Juan said.

"Why not?" Jacinto said. "They love death. Why not give them what they love?"

"And Peter? Does he also love death?"

"Yes. When I came to kill him, he did not even lift a hand. He waited, and was glad."

"Jacinto—" Juan said.

"Yes, Juan?"

"You are not to kill, understand? Only those I tell you. Our enemies. The enemies of the people. Do you comprehend, Camarada?"

"Yes, Juanito. I understand."

"Look, Comrade Reynolds," Juan said, "there is no time to discuss this of your proposal to ransom Padre Pío. Because now we must break camp and move with great haste."

"Why?" Peter said.

"Because of the Indians. If they have not been seen by the airplanes of Villalonga—the ones with which the great democratic country of the United States so kindly supplied him—it is truly one of Padre Pío's miracles. Hundreds of them heading straight to this place. It is like a great arrow pointing, you know. This is the third time we've had to move because of them."

"How do they know where he is?" Peter said.

Juan frowned.

"I do not know," he said.

"They smell him," Jacinto said. "He smells as they do—of death. Stinking Indians! Hauling their dead across the mountains so Tío Pío can bless them, then hauling them all the way back home again. And, afterwards, he will have to go to Xilchimocha to make sure they have actually buried them instead of sleeping with them like the necrophiliacs they are! Ha! Perhaps he is, too! Ah ha, Uncle Pío! Do you like a little piece of dead tail from time to time?"

"Shut up, animal!" Juan said. "He makes a bad joke, Comrade Reporter. The Tluscola do not use the dead sexually, as this beast knows very well. That would be a heinous blasphemy to them, which they would punish by the most cruel death they could devise. But come, then, you are well enough to ride, are you not—after Father Pío's latest miracle?"

"Yes," Peter said.

"Then I will ride with you, as the Indios have brought Father Pío a horse as a gift to recompense him for his mumbling Latin and sprinkling water over their maggoty corpses. I think they mean for him to use it to escape. So I will forestall him. I will borrow it. Then you and I will ride out to find a new campsite—as inaccessible as possible."

"You want *me* to go with you?" Peter said.

"Yes. So that you can tell me about your interview with Fidel in las Sierras Madres—before he came to power. I can learn much from that," Juan said.

"You can. But you won't. At least not the essential," Peter said.

"And that is?"

"To call the whole thing off," Peter said.

III

When they found that place, it looked very fine, a wood of fir and balsam and pine growing on one of the shoulders of the mountain with a vertical precipice that dropped five hundred meters straight down on one side of it, of shale rock that even a fly couldn't have scaled, let alone a man, with no way into the woods except up a tongue of ancient solidified lava from the days when the whole Sierra had been as active as Zopocomapetl was now, over which an army could have marched single file without leaving tracks, and no way out of it, so far as Peter could see, at all. On the other side of the woods opposite the precipice, the peak of the mountain went straight up at an angle that—if it wasn't ninety—was at least eighty-five degrees.

"Like it?" Juan said.

"No," Peter said.

"Why not?"

"Because this is a campsite for heroes, and I am a coward."

Juan smiled.

"A rare sort of coward, Comrade," he said. "But, seriously, what is wrong with it?"

"As a base from which to attack, nothing. As a natural fortress, formidable. Give me a machine gun and enough ammunition and the food to last a year, and I personally could eliminate Villalonga's Army."

"So?" Juan said.

"I have already said it. Think about it," Peter said.

"I have thought. And it is perfect, Comrade Reporter! First they have to find us, and those trees make wonderful cover. Say they have found us. They have to make a frontal attack up a tongue of volcanic rock so narrow that only two men can walk abreast. What a slaughter! Why—"

"Juanito—" Peter said.

"What?" Juan said, frowning.

"They don't have to attack. They merely have to camp down there at the foot of that lava tongue, with jeeps bringing them food, hot food, every day, with the smell of it blowing up here to where you starve. Out of range of your knee mortars and your light machine guns. Then, when they have got tired of waiting, they will hitch a couple of those old French Seventy-fives from the first world war, which still shoot pretty good, son, behind their jeeps, bring them up to that nice flat little plateau down there at the foot of the lava tongue and start lobbing shrapnel in here. And incendiaries. And wait down there at the foot of that one-way street you're so proud of for you and yours to come out of the woods which will be burning by then. Or stay in them and roast. Or throw yourselves over that precipice. Because your choices will be reduced to that, Comrade—various highly unpleasant ways to die."

Juan sat there on the horse, looking at Peter.

"Of course I forgot something," Peter said.

"What have you forgot?"

"That Khrushchev and Castro will, of course, airlift troops and ammunition and food to you. That solves your problem of logistics. And our President, of course, will hide under his desk in the White House, and let them do it. He wouldn't dream of sending the Atlantic Fleet, or a few jet fighters, or even the Marines to interfere, now would he?"

Juan used the sharp, explosive Spanish word *"Mierda!"* which means fecal matter in English, but you can't translate it with English. You have to use Anglo-Saxon.

"Right," Peter said, "and you've had it, chum. You've been buried in it, up to the eyes."

Juan went on looking at those woods.

"Have you seen anything better?" he said.

"No," Peter said. "And this will do for a hiding place for a few days. Maybe even a week. But if they even start getting close, you'd better move on."

They hauled the horses' heads around, and started back down again.

"About Padre Pío . . ."

"No," Juan said.

"Look, Juan!" Peter said. "With the money my paper's paying, you could *buy* Ciudad Villalonga! Then you wouldn't have to—"

"No," Juan said again.

"And if I try to sneak him out of the camp one fine dark night?"

"I should let Jacinto handle it. That's his department."

"I see. You pass the buck. You delegate murder to other hands."

"Something like that," Juan said. "But seriously, Comrade, do you think even an ant could get out of our camp if I gave orders for him not to?"

"You've got something there. Your sentries are pretty nervous types. Still, I wish you'd let me bail Padre Pío out. He's too old to—"

"No," Juan said again.

"Why not?" Peter said.

"Because only he can deliver the Indians to us. They are essential. Without them we shall never prevail against the Spanish upper class, and the middle class, which is Mestizo. How can one have a Dictatorship of the Proletariat without the proletariat? Or a People's Democracy without the people?"

"Will you let them go on keeping Grandpa's corpus delicti in the living room?"

"*Hombre,* I will go them one better! I will teach them taxidermy and supply them with artificial glass eyes. I will teach them how to achieve a high gloss on Abuelito's mangy hide; how to stuff him with pleasant-smelling straw, perfume his gray plaits, coat the condor feather in his hair with a long-lasting insecticide, how even to stand him up in the foyer in a lifelike pose, with his arms extended so that he may be useful as a hatrack, say. Why, I'll even . . ."

It was then that they heard the plane.

They were below the forest by then, going down a well-marked trail. On both sides of that trail the slopes fell away in a long gentle curve of sheet rock, and old ash rotting now into soil. They could have gone down those slopes easily enough, except there was no reason to go down them since their nakedness, their total absence of cover, was now, under the circumstances in which they found themselves, not merely indecent but obscene.

For that bellow blasting the sky apart wasn't any eighty-five horsepower Lycoming in a Cub. That was a double-row eighteen-hundred-horsepower Pratt and Whitney, close-cowled into the nose of a cranked-wing Vought Corsair. Looking up, Peter could see the red and yellow markings with the thin purple cross like the letter *X* that Miguel Villalonga had copied with slavish lack of imagination, only reversing the order of the colors, from the Army of the Air of Spain.

"Blood, pus, and permanganate," he said. Then, seeing Juan digging his heels into the big-chested, finely built roan the Indians had brought as a gift for Padre Pío, he shouted:

"For God's sake, don't run!"

But he was too late because the big roan was already off and away, and he, sawing at the bit of his shaggy mountain pony, trying to hold him, saw those curious cranked, reverse gull wings which were the distinguishing feature of the World War Two-vintage fighter—the last propeller-driven pursuit in active service, having lasted through Korea before being retired, where, as now, it had proved itself on ground-support missions the jets were just too fast to manage—heel over in a vertical bank; peeling off, screaming down, that beautiful blue-painted image of sudden death, rocking level now, pulling up five kilometers behind them, but coming on, the prop a mist-silver disk scribed about with a perfect circle of orange; and he, that red-hot pilot, that authentic blue-flame boy, one of the twenty-five young Costa Verdian aristocrats, sons of landowners, manufacturers, coffee, sugar, and oil fortunes, trained at Keeler Field, Mississippi, at San Antonio, Texas, and in California, as a sort of technical lend lease to do effortlessly, perfectly, what he was doing now.

His run was straight out of the textbook. He cranked down full flaps, even lowered his landing gear to slow him down enough, and floated in, looking for all the world like a vulture headed for carrion; except that this particular group of four-footed and two-legged carrion was momentarily still alive.

Then, looking up and back, Peter saw the leading edge of the Corsair's wing start its acetylene blowtorch splutter in four separate and distinct places, the white line of tracers arching out, and the fifty-caliber Browning slugs throwing up a column of dirt and rock that came quick-stepping down the road behind him like a platoon of dancing, idiotic ghosts. And he, Peter, diving out of the saddle headfirst into a shallow ditch beside the trail, the breath going out of him and night coming down to lift only when he heard his pony scream, high and shrill like a woman in pain.

And, lifting his gaze, seeing the shaggy beast with its head down now, vomiting blood, and the red tide pouring out of it through a line of holes stitched along all its flank, watching that, unable to see Juan at all, hearing the rustling back washing wall of air from the prop going over and past and a shower of shells from the ejector chutes bounding and glittering on the road; and the plane banking, climbing, tucking its wheels up into the wing roots again, then screaming down in a shallow dive, but pulling up short, far short of the target, which he still couldn't see because he was too far down off the trail, but seeing what he could see easily enough, that the pull-up hadn't been short after all, because that fat, finned bomb continued the trajectory the plane had started it on, whistling down in a long, only slightly curving arc to end time, to stop the world.

He saw it. Saw that little black rag doll rise with both arms and the one leg it had left extended, flying now, borne up on the blast, hanging in midair in apparent defiance of gravity for a segment of time that could not have been more than the barest measurable fraction of a second, but which Peter's own pain, shock, horror extended unbearably until his arrested breath, life, heartbeat stared once more and renewed perception let that nothing blasted out of the middle of existence become something, become Juan's body arching downward, falling now, whistling earthward amid the thick showering shale rock amid the pieces of the horse.

And he, Peter, getting up, forgetting the plane that was already nothing but a blue crooked cross silhouetted against the dark plume of Zopocomapetl, and stumbling, falling, getting up again until he reached the place where Juan lay—miraculously but not mercifully alive, the life draining out of him through that shredded mass of red rags and splintered bone where his right leg ended just below the knee. And Peter bending, whipping off his belt, looping it around Juan's thigh, tightening it in ferocious jerks until the red tide slowed. Then, afterward, tearing off his own shirt and wrapping it around the stump in a clumsy bandage. And standing there, looking at Juan, but not thinking because there was nothing to think about now; only things to be done.

He went back to where his pony lay dead in the road and got his canteen from the saddlebag. He wasted five minutes searching for Juan's amid the chopped, splattered meat and the pink, slimy sausage rolls of horse guts. Then he gave it up. He lifted Juan onto his back by the arms and started down that trail.

In the first kilometer, he didn't fall even once. But in the second he fell three times. In the third, five. By the fifth, he was averaging a hundred meters between falls. In the middle of the sixth kilometer, he knew he wasn't going to be able to get up again, so he eased Juan off his back and tried to force some water between his lips which were swollen and black and oozing blood at the corners. He couldn't. So he took a drink himself, and lay there.

When the first shadow passed over his head he thought it was the plane come back again. But it hadn't made any noise so he looked up and saw that it was a forked-tail kite. Then another one passed over, and another and another until the air was black with them, circling. He moved his arms in a waving motion, and all the kites screamed and lifted. But they didn't go away. They only circled higher. Then a bigger shadow drifted across the road and dropped the trailing edge of its wings to an almost vertical position, stopping itself dead in mid-air. Its red, scaly feet came out of its dark belly and spread, gripping a rock. Then it sat there, looking at him, its eyes black and patient in the midst of its bluish-red, bald, scaly head.

Peter tried waving his hand at it, but it paid no attention. He clawed his fingers into the surface of the road for loose rocks, threw them one by one at the buzzard. He was too weak. They all fell short. The buzzard sat there looking at him. The kites circled lower now, screaming.

He saw the others coming in, but he was too tired and too sick to count them. The rocks on both sides of the road were covered with them now. When the last one came in, he was sure it was a plane, it was so much bigger than the others. But then he saw that red, turkey-cock comb on the top of its head, and knew it was a condor. The others made room for it. It sat in their midst, head and shoulders taller than the rest.

He lay there looking at them. From time to time he sipped the water in the canteen. He was beginning to feel a little better, enough, maybe, to make another five meters before he'd fall again. Then he remembered that Juan was probably wearing his sidearm. He groped for it, found it, dragged it out of the holster. He held it in his two hands, pointed at the condor. Squeezed. But the safety catch was on. He flipped it off, squeezed the trigger again. The Mauser-type automatic bucked and roared. The condor fell over in a sodden heap. The buzzards rose heavily, clumsily, found an updraft, soared.

Five minutes later, Jacinto and a scouting party were there.

Jacinto looked at Juan. He didn't say anything. He simply lifted his machine pistol toward where the kites and buzzards circled. He got five of them before it barked empty.

One of the others was working on Juan's leg. He seemed to know what he was doing, so Peter looked away toward Jacinto.

"How—" he said.

"Your shot, Comrade Reporter. Of course we heard that profanity of an airplane. We even heard it machine-gunning the road. When it dropped the bomb, we knew it had you. But we came anyhow. When you fired at the condor and the other carrion birds flew up, you pinpointed this place for us."

He turned to the other one who was working on Juan.

"Is he going to die, Pepe?" he said.

"Yes," Pepe said. "He has lost too much blood. If the Yanqui hadn't applied the tourniquet, he would be dead by now."

"Soon?" Jacinto said.

"How do I know?" Pepe said. "He might die in five minutes, or in five hours. I cannot tell. But it would be better if he died now, without regaining consciousness; or else we shall have to use up all our morphine on him. Because, Comrade Second Chief, that vileness of a leg is going to hurt with a vileness unspeakable, and if the pilot of that plane has told them to scout in this area, his screams well might give us away."

"You think it advisable to shoot him, then?" Jacinto said.

"Jacinto, for the love of God!" Peter said.

"God does not exist, Comrade Reporter," Jacinto said. "Do not speak idiocies; it distracts my attention. And now, I must think."

Peter lay there, looking at those yellow eyes. They were withdrawn and rapt. Then they cleared.

"We will take him to the camp. Perhaps he has orders to give us. And, in any case, if he screams too much, we can always shoot him there."

Peter let out his breath, slowly.

Jacinto looked at him. Then he roared with laughter. It sounded like the howl of a timber wolf.

"You see?" he said to the others. "He still has fever! Now will you cease to speak of the miracles of the ugly little Vasco? Or would you say the Yankee has no faith?"

"He is a heretic. A Protestant," Pepe said.

"No, he is Catholic," Jacinto said. "I heard him say so to Uncle Pío."

"Look, Jacinto," Pepe said. "With this of the revolution, of accord. There have been many abuses which we can only remedy by killing the abusers. And I am a Communist. I do not believe in God—not any longer. But I have seen the little Basque Father do too many things for which there are no reasonable explanations. So, as practical men, why take chances? Look at the vile vileness of the luck we have been having lately. So, Comrade Chief, may I respectfully suggest that you cease to fornicate with their fornicating God?"

"And I," Jacinto said, "may I suggest, with no respect at all, that you cease to gamble upon the fact that you are the only one among us who has any knowledge of medicine? Considering the equally important fact that you were suspended in all your examinations at the Medical School, your domination of medical science is insufficient to make me think overlong about whether or not I should shoot you, Comrade Doctor! Now pick up poor Juan and march!"

Nobody bothered to pick Peter up. But with a shot of rum in him from the canteen of the young third officer called Federico, who made sure Jacinto was not looking when he offered it, Peter found that he could walk. Slowly, stumbling along, but upright. By the time they got back to camp, he was bone-weary and aching all over. But Father Pío was right; the fever was gone.

And now the three of them—José, called Pepe as all Josés are called in Spanish by their friends for some long forgotten reason, Father Pío, and Peter—watched over Juan. Pepe was a better doctor, or at least a better surgeon, than Jacinto gave him credit for. He boiled his instruments, cut away the shredded flesh, sawed off the splintered bone, leaving a neat flap of skin which he sewed over Juan's knee to make a stump. He dusted the wound with sulfa, shot a million units of penicillin into Juan's veins. Stood back, watching. Said:

"He is in shock. What he needs is a transfusion. But we have no plasma."

"Blood," Peter said, sitting there with the sweat pouring out of him from having watched it. "Take mine."

"Or mine," Father Pío said.

"No," Pepe said.

"Why not?" Peter said.

"I do not know his blood type. Nor yours. Nor Uncle Pío's. Nor mine. You know what happens when you give the wrong type blood?"

"Yes," Peter said. "It kills the patient. But, since he is going to die anyhow, why not gamble upon it?"

"I prefer him to die. I do not wish to kill him," Pepe said.

"Son," Padre Pío said, "it seems to me that you are wrong. If you make no effort to save him, the guilt is in part yours. If you do make the effort, and he dies, then clearly his death is the will of God . . ."

"God does not exist," Pepe parroted. "*Mierda!* Do not tangle me in your Jesuit sophistries, Padre! I have done what I could. But if he dies in convulsions as the result of a transfusion, Jacinto will shoot me, surely. Jacinto loves him much."

"I don't think Jacinto loves anybody," Peter said.

"Oh yes, he does," Pepe said. "You saw that back there on the trail he gave up the pleasure of shooting him? And if you knew how Jacinto enjoys shooting people! It is his greatest delight——"

"I gathered as much," Peter said.

"Son—the transfusion," Padre Pío said.

"No. I am sorry, Padre; but I am not that much of an altruist. I want to live," Pepe said.

They sat there, watching Juan. He was very quiet. Father Pío put out his right hand and bathed Juan's forehead. Peter saw that round, deep sunken bluish scar in the middle of his right hand.

"This," he said to the old priest. "How did it occur, Father? Or is it that you bear the stigmata of Our Lord?"

Father Pío laughed softly.

"I am not worthy of such an honor," he said. "No, son, a bullet made that. In Spain, during the Civil War. I was blessing the firing squad who shot me."

Peter looked at him.

"You were blessing the Red execution platoon who—"

"Not the Reds. The others. But apart from that minor detail, yes. I was blessing the soldiers who were trying to kill me."

Pepe stared at him.

"You mean to say, Uncle Pío, that it was the Fascists who shot you? You, a priest?"

"But a Basque priest," Father Pío said. "That made a difference."

"How?" Pepe said.

"Because in Vasconia we did not spend our time moaning over the terrible crimes of the Reds—and they *were* terrible, son; more terrible than you imagine—we simply asked ourselves what it was the Church had done, that Spanish men, unquestionably the most loyal of all her sons, could come to hate her so."

"And what had the Church done?" Peter said.

"Neglected them, followed the age-old, blind policy of siding with the rich, the powerful. Advised them to submit, to be patient, to be humble. To work fourteen hours a day for wages too small to feed their families. For in Vasconia we knew even then what all Catholics have learned since: that social justice *is* the business of the Church. That if we do not insure it, the Reds will use the misery of the poor as the lever to overthrow us."

"Let us not speak of politics," Peter said, "or even of religion, which are subjects of insupportable heaviness. But, speak of your execution, Father. I have seen many men shot as spies, and they do not survive. Twelve men in a firing squad are unlikely to miss. This was another of your miracles, then?"

"Son Pedro," Father Pío said, "I have not the power of miracle-working. If I had, do you think I should permit this slaughter between brothers? Or the traffic in women that goes on in Ciudad Villalonga?"

"Yet," Peter said, "they shot you, and you live."

"Three of them shot me, son. The rest fired over my head. And even those three did it badly. You see, they were from Navarra. Royalists, and the most devout Catholics on earth. It upset them to have to shoot a priest. Even a Red priest, as they called us. Afterwards, I'm told, with the other twenty-four of us they shot for the crime of lending spiritual comfort to those Republican soldiers who wanted it—and there were many such, Son Pepe, despite their exposure to your Marxist nonsense—they got used to it. But I was the first, and it upset them. They were very young, as they were all crying. Even the lieutenant commanding them was crying. When he approached me to give me the shot of mercy, he saw at once that I was not badly hurt. So he whispered, 'Father, can you hear me?' And I said: '*Sí, hijo.*' He said: 'Can you hold out two hours until I can come back?' I had much pain, but I told him I could. So he straightened up and shouted 'No need to waste a shot on this filthy Red! He is already buzzard food!' Then they marched away."

"And?" Pepe said.

"I crawled away from there into another street. A woman found me. A woman whose son had been murdered by the Reds. She took me in. I spent the rest of the war as a woodcutter by day and a priest by night. At the end I escaped over the mountains into France. That's all."

On the cot, Juan stirred, moaned. They all bent over him. But he was still again. They sat there, watching him. An hour later he woke up and started to scream.

Peter held him while Pepe prepared the needle. Shot the morphine into him. But it didn't take effect. He kept on screaming until Jacinto came into the tent with his pistol in his hand.

Father Pío got up, stood between Jacinto and the cot.

"No, son!"

Jacinto slammed him to the floor with the flat side of the pistol.

Pepe edged toward the door.

Peter came upright then, slowly and carefully and quietly.

"Jacinto—"

"*Mierda!* Screw you, Gringo!"

"Your mother," Peter said. Spanish profanity is an art. You don't have to be explicit. You simply pick out your opponent's closest female relative. He'll know what you mean. As Jacinto did now.

He whirled upon Peter, those yellow eyes luminous as sparks. Then, slowly, he stopped. Began to laugh.

"You want to provoke me, Comrade? Then try something else. I am past all the notions I was born to—even that one. A woman is only an animal for breeding. Any woman—even my mother. So go on, curse me! Speak of it. This you will do in the bad milk of that. This was done by my mother, by my grandmother, by my great grandmother. My father was perverted, my grandfather the Queen of the Fairies. Go on! Speak of it!"

"No," Peter said.

"Why not?"

"I do not waste breath. We have too little. I say only this: If you so much as point your Czechoslovakian toy toward Juan, I shall take it away from you and break your teeth out with it. By the long route. By shoving it up you till it protrudes. Is this entirely clear?"

"*Vaya!*" Jacinto said. Then his mood changed. "Look, Comrade Reporter, I have no wish to shoot Juan. We have been friends since we were little boys. It would pain me much to hurt him. But I am commander now, and the whole band cannot be sacrificed for one man!"

"Wait," Peter said. "Pepe!"

"Yes, Comrade?"

"Bind up his mouth. With gauze. Tape it shut. It will not make him suffer more; and it will keep our valiant Chief from having to shoot him."

"That is intelligent," Jacinto said. "Do it, Pepe. I order you to do it." Then he turned and marched out.

Peter helped the old priest up from the ground. He was bleeding from a cut above his right eye. Pepe finished gagging Juan, got up, came over and attended to that, too. Cleaned the blood and dirt out of it. Dusted it with sulfa.

"He is a savage, Jacinto!" Pepe said.

"He has suffered much, son," Father Pío said.

Peter lifted his hand suddenly. Pepe and the old priest stopped talking. Stared at him.

"Juan," Peter said. "Look at Juan!"

Juan's eyes were wide open. They moved slowly. He was looking into their faces. His eyes focused properly. They were clear.

"Juan," Peter said, "can you hear me?"

Juan nodded his head. Very slowly. With immense effort.

"You want me to take the gag from your mouth?" Peter said.

Juan nodded. More slowly now.

"And you will not scream?"

The movement of Juan's head was barely perceptible.

"Take it off, Pepe," Peter said.

Pepe hesitated.

"Take it off!" Peter said.

Pepe removed the pad of gauze he had taped over Juan's mouth.

"Thanks," Juan said. The word was hushed, death-dry, and rattling. "Peter—" Juan said.

"*Sí*, Juanito?" Peter said.

"You—it was you who brought me in, no?"

"No," Peter said. "Pepe and Jacinto and the rest found us."

"After you had made five kilometers with him on your back," Pepe said. "Perhaps I retrogress to bourgeois morality, but I prefer truth. He saved you, Juanito. The Comrade Gringo saved you. And now I wonder—"

"What?" Juan said.

"If they will work, our revolution, our new Socialist state. If they ever can. Do we not need, maybe, even this ancient monkey of a Basque, and his superstitious mumbo-jumbo? When a man is alone and surrounded on his last hill, what then, Juanito? You are near death. And the dying speak truly. Tell me, Comrade, whether—"

"No," Peter said. "He is too weak. Do not make him talk."

"Then you, Comrade," Pepe said; "you who have traveled much, and lived in many lands. Are we right? Or do we merely replace one evil with another?"

"Do not ask me these things," Peter said, still watching Juan. "I am not wise enough to answer. Ask Father Pío. That's his department."

"No," Pepe said. "He is of a prejudiced point of view."

"You think I'm not?" Peter said.

"No. It seems to me that you generally speak justly. Juanito, does our talking disturb you?"

Juan shook his head.

"Water," he said. "I have thirst. Give me water. Then talk."

Father Pío held the canteen to his mouth. He drank painfully. Moved his head aside.

"Talk," he said.

"We had better not," Peter said; "perhaps—"

"Talk!" Juan said. "I want to hear—to know——"

"And I," Jacinto said, coming into the hut. "Yes, Comrade Reporter, talk! Let us determine whether we already have a Titoist movement of deviationists upon our hands."

Saying that, his voice had changed. And now it came to Peter why. He was consciously trying to talk like the Chief of a Communist guerrilla band. But using the ponderous and meaningless shibboleths of Marxists' jargon which had been imposed upon him from without—during his training in Cuba, probably—and which had penetrated neither his mind nor his heart, Jacinto was merely ridiculous. No—pitiful.

"Which you will then settle by shooting everybody?" Peter said.

"No, not everybody," Jacinto said, "just the ones with the stink of corruption in them, like our Pepe here. But do not let me interrupt you, Comrades. This is a democracy, no? And free speech is permitted, is it not? At least while the speaker lives . . ."

Pepe's head came up.

"Look, Jacinto," he said, "your jokes are not diverting. Nor your half-hidden threats. It seems to me that your mania for killing people will one day cause your own death. And I will speak. I will say what I think. Principally I think that you are mad and a danger to our cause!"

Jacinto laid his machine pistol down on the ground at the foot of Juan's cot. Took out his Beretta automatic and put it beside the burp gun and his knife.

"Now," he said, smiling out of his flat yellow eyes rather than with his mouth, "I am unarmed. I can kill no one. Speak."

"All right," Pepe said. "Comrade Reporter, do you think we shall prevail?"

"Yes," Peter said.

"And afterwards, what?" Pepe said.

"Afterwards, nothing," Peter said.

"You mean we will not end the abuses?"

"I mean you will substitute others."

"Why?" Pepe said.

"Because you are not Anglo-Saxons. Or Danes. Or Swedes."

"You mean we're no good?" Jacinto said.

"I mean you're Latinos," Peter said.

"And hence no good?" Jacinto said.

"No," Peter said, "I do not mean that. You have virtues enough, God knows. Let us say you are not sufficiently slow of thought or cold of blood. Which is why you are of such rare political ineptitude."

"*Ha!*" Jacinto said.

Peter looked at him.

"Have you ever heard of any country where a man of your race has set foot that has not had twenty-five revolutions and fifty dictators by now?"

"I will accept that," Pepe said. "Will you accept our contention that these are the things that *we* will remedy?"

"No," Peter said.

"Why not?" Jacinto said.

"Because," Peter said, "I was in Russia. And in Hungary. And in Cuba."

"You, Comrade Reporter," Jacinto said, "are the classic reactionary."

"Will you shut up, Jacinto?" Pepe said. "Look, Comrade, according to the Party theoreticians, the things we do now: the shooting of deviationists—"

"The torture of prisoners. Brainwashing. The extermination of thousands, even millions when it seems necessary . . . ."

"Lies!" Jacinto said.

"I was there," Peter said; "I saw."

"Let me finish," Pepe said. "Let me present the orthodox Leninistic point of view—about which, frankly, Comrade Yanqui, I have my reservations. But, for argument's sake, let me present it. Those things, Comrade Reporter, great as they seem to you and me because of our bourgeois intellectual background, are, in the scale of history, very small. And temporary measures only, until true peoples' democracies can be established everywhere. I confess this theory does not sit well on my overly sensitive stomach. Do you, my friend, believe that good can come out of evil? Even great good out of very little evil? Do you, Comrade?"

Peter grinned at him.

"Do you believe that a woman can be only a little pregnant?" he said. "Or that a *chica* can lose only a little of her virginity? Or, if Jacinto of the Yellow Eyes were to shoot me, as he is clearly desirous of doing, that I should be only a little dead?"

"No," Jacinto said, "you would be dead all right. Totally."

"This is a clever statement, son," Father Pío said. "Carry it further."

"It goes no further," Peter said. "And we have tired Juan enough. How goes it, old one?"

"Badly," Juan said. "Jacinto—"

"*Sí*, Jefe?" Jacinto said.

"He—is to be released. He—and the priest. An order. My last. You have heard me?"

"But Juan!" Jacinto said.

"Order. Padre . . ."

"Yes, son?"

"Come," Juan said.

The old priest got up, went to the side of the cot.

"You," Juan said; and now, suddenly, his voice was strong. "You, Jacinto, and you, Pepe, get out. You, Peter, stay."

"Why?" Peter said.

"Because you are a Christian. Father—"

"Yes, my son?"

"I—" His voice went abruptly out of sound. Peter could see his lips move, and leaned close. The words came up to him in a fetid stink of fever-laden breath.

"Ave Maria, llena de gracia, el Señor esta——"

And he, Peter, saying it, too—in English, because that was the language he'd learned it in, as a child—trying to recapture the miracle and the privilege of innocence, the simple joy of believing in something, anything; and failing, as always; but saying it anyhow, forcing the words out over the barrier of disuse, over the mountains of doubt, the crags of intellectual pride:

"—is with Thee. Blessed art Thou among women."

And Father Pío, taking it up:

"Bendita sea el fruta de tu vientre—"

"Jesus. Holy Mary, Mother of God—"

"Santa Maria, Madre de Dios," Juan whispered.

"Pray for us, sinners—"

"Reza por nosotros, pecadores—"

"Now, and at the hour of our deaths, Amen."

"Ahora y en la hora," Juan began. And ended it there; because for him the hour was now, visible, and at hand.

"Padre?" Peter said.

"What a beautiful death!" the old priest said.

IV

They buried Juan in the middle of the campsite, piling rocks on his grave so that no animal would be able to dig him up. Father Pío made a cross of wood, on which he carved Juan's name, his dates—pitifully close together—and the notation, "He Returned to the Faith." But when he had set it up, Jacinto came out of his tent and kicked it over. The old priest set it up again. This time, when Jacinto started toward it, Pepe got in front of him.

"You will not do this again, Jacinto," he said.

"Who will stop me?" Jacinto said.

"I," Pepe said.

"And after you lie beside him, who will stop me?" Jacinto said.

"I," Peter said.

Jacinto stood there, looking at them both.

"And, finally, God will stop you," Padre Pío said.

Jacinto's gaze moved, lambent and pale, from face to face to face. Then he turned without saying anything at all, and started back toward his tent.

But, before he got there, they heard the noise of motors, laboring up the trail.

Jacinto turned. What was in his face was very simple and uncomplicated and terrible and sure. It was joy.

"Pepe!" he said. "Go tell Federico to form ranks! Now we have them! Now we will take them from both sides of the trail and—"

"How will you do that?" Peter said. "Since, from the sound of them, they are already past this place, searching for my cadaver and Juan's and those of the horses?"

"Simple! We will attack from both flanks and—"

"Jacinto," Peter said.

"Now what?" Jacinto said.

"Do you not remember the topography of the trail above the camp?"

"I do," Pepe said. "It is as bare as the buttocks of a baby six months old. Additionally, the trail follows the ridge so that we would be visible to them long before we got to the side of the road. We should have to attack uphill under the fire of fifty-calibre BARs which can kill us at a distance that these little toys of ours cannot carry; and tomorrow we would be hanging upside down for the moral edification of the populace in the Plaza of the Liberation."

"Remove your pants!" Jacinto said.

"Remove my pants?" Pepe said. "Why?"

"I wish to see what, if anything, you have in them."

"What I have in them is of both a sufficiency and an excess to make all your female relatives scream in delight and in pain," Pepe said, "but what is more important is what I have in my head. Brains—unscrambled by either hate or suffering, Jacinto. Listen, old one, you are Chief. But I am now Second in Command. And, just as Juan often listened to you, at least in those situations where valor and speed counted more than intelligence, so must you listen to me—as I will listen to Federico when they have killed you, and I become Jefe, and he Second—"

"I am listening," Jacinto said.

"Is it our purpose to display our bravery or to win this war?" Pepe asked.

"There, you have a point," Jacinto said, "still—"

"Still nothing," Peter said. "If you wish to die, cut your throat, and we will bury you beside Juan. For to attack up a slope without cover, against heavier fire than you can answer, unsupported by either aviation or artillery, is suicide, Jacinto."

"How would you know, newsvendor?" Jacinto said.

Peter opened his shirt. The great scar running from his left shoulder to his armpit was ice-white against the sun-blackened darkness of his skin. So were all the other whorls and crescents and rips and tears of shrapnel that covered his chest. He took the shirt off. Slowly he turned his back to Jacinto. The long slope of his shoulders, the trapezoidal V of back muscles, lean and powerful, were teak-colored and clean.

"Do you see anything here, Jacinto?" he said over his shoulder.

"*Madre de Dios!*" Pepe said.

"Blasphemy serves for nothing, son," Padre Pío said.

"But it is not possible!" Pepe said. "No man could take that many wounds and live!"

"As you can see, I did," Peter said. "It is not even very unusual when one has the luck to be caught on the far edge of a shell burst instead of at its center. The record, I think, was held by the writer

Hemingway, who took one hundred fifty-four pieces of shrapnel at one time, on the River Paive, in Italy, during the first world war, and survived. Which has no importance now. What does have significance is that I got these mounting an attack up a snow-covered hill against your good friends the Chinese Reds. So this of uphill attacks with insufficient firepower I know, Jacinto. I had the lesson rammed into me in ninety-three separate places—most of them, fortunately, smaller than birdshot. So forget this madness, will you? There where the slopes have the shape of the anatomies of the girls at The Blue Moon and rather less natural foliage, it cannot be done."

"All right," Jacinto said. "I am prepared to be reasonable. And to accept the advice of the heroic Comrade Gringo. What do you think should be done, Comrade?"

"I think," Peter said, "that we should get the hell out of here."

Jacinto looked at him through those flat yellow eyes. A long time. A very long time. Then he sighed.

"So be it; we will retreat," he said.

They went down from the camp on the opposite side from the trail, hearing the motors of the jeeps laboring above them. And, after a time, the noise of the motors stopped, so they knew by then Villalonga's soldiers had found the body of Peter's horse and whatever the kites and buzzards had left of the shattered carcass of Juan's. From then on it would only be a matter of time before they found the place where one left the trail to come down to the camp. So, without Jacinto's having to say anything, they all started force-marching, on the double, until Peter was covered with sweat and staring at Father Pío. The old priest went as fast as the rest. Faster than most.

Behind them, the noise of the motors started up again.

When they had put them behind them finally, faded them out of time, they could see the jungle before them. Here, where they were, they had to cross a marsh to get into it. Peter looked at the marsh mud. Then suddenly, he sat down in that sticky, black mud. It came up to his waist. He lay down in it, rolled over. Stood up again. What he looked like they couldn't put a name to.

"Now, what the devil?" Pepe said.

"Defense against insects," Peter said. "When it dries I shall be armored. I saw the water buffalo do this in Indo-China."

"Is there any place you haven't been, son?" Father Pío said.

"Yes," Peter said. "Heaven."

"Nor hell either," the old priest said.

Peter stopped smiling.

"I wouldn't bet on that one, Padre," he said.

Going through the jungle was as bad as before except that this time the bugs couldn't get at him. The sweat ran off him in rivers, plowing furrows through the mud on his face. But he stooped and clawed up hunks of fetid jungle earth and patted them back over the bare spots. He got through the jungle like that almost unbitten. Then they were out of it again and at the foot of the Sierras again, but at a place other than the old camp. Looking up, he saw they were much closer to Zopocomapetl than before. Almost at the foot of it, in fact. Where they were now the trail was very definite, worn by many years of use. When Peter mentioned that to Pepe, the second officer said:

"Yes. There is an Indian village called Xochua about an hour's climb from here. We shall stop there to rest."

"Isn't that dangerous?" Peter said.

"No. The Indians never tell anything to Villalonga's soldiers. In fact, the troops of the National Army never see any Indians."

"Why not?" Peter said.

"The Tluscola are a proud people. Unlike those dirty fisher Indians down on the coast, they do not share their women. Additionally, they do not relish having their heads cracked upon with gun butts. So now, when the troops come up here, long before they arrive, the Tluscolas have gone. And when they go, they leave not even an ear of corn in their houses for the soldiers to eat. At first, Villalonga's brigands used to throw down the houses in their rage; but to throw down houses built of stone and adobe calls for too much work. And Costa Verdians do not like work, amigo!"

"Who does?" Peter said. "They don't run from you, then?"

"No. Juan made it absolutely clear that he would shoot any man who touched a Tluscola woman. So now we have been among them many times, and they know their daughters are safe. Which is a point they are very strict about. A Tluscola girl who is not a virgin when she comes to her marriage bed is put to death in a sickening fashion. That is, if the new husband was not himself responsible for her loss of virginity prior to the ceremony. In that case, they pardon the offense, holding that the marriage removes the sin. They killed all the unmarried women of Xochunga after the soldiers of Our Generous Benefactor swept through that town. Because they were just, they acknowledged that the loss of their virginity was not the girls' fault; they killed them not as they usually do in such cases, but quickly and mercifully. The married women they merely gave a ceremonial beating and let it go at that. But the young men of Xochunga, having no girls to marry, had to leave that pueblo; and for a while, there was trouble among the Tluscolas."

"You said that they killed the young women mercifully," Peter said. "How do they kill them if *las chicas* have merely been generous and donated a small portion thereof, of their own free will?"

Pepe shuddered.

"*Hombre*—let us not speak of that!" he said.

When they came into Xochua, the Indians greeted them with grave courtesy. At least until they saw that Father Pío was with them. Then they ignored Peter and the rest completely, and clustered around the old priest, dropping to their knees before him.

Father Pío blessed them, talking to them in the harsh grunts and gutturals of their own language.

The Chief of the Indians came up to Peter.

"You new Cacique?" he said in Spanish.

"No," Peter said, "why?"

"You most tall," the Chief said. "More tall than any. The other Cacique was tall. Dead now, no? The great hawk of the thunder kill him, yes?"

"Yes," Peter said.

"Who Cacique now?" the Chief said.

"That one," Peter said. "The Comrade with the yellow eyes."

The Chief looked at Jacinto. Looked back at Peter.

"Better you Cacique," he said.

"Why?" Peter said.

"Know that one. Crazy like sick wolf. Bad. I talk you, not him."

"Talk then," Peter said.

"You stay here, four-five days."

"Now look, Chief—" Peter said.

"You stay here four-five days," the Chief said.

"Why?" Peter said.

"Many dead. No big medicine said over them to bury, *sabes?* Many *bebes* without the good water on their heads. Many young people not married in church together, girls big belly, and Padre Pío no take away the sin. Four-five days. Yes? Padre said he your prisoner. Say ask Cacique."

"Chief," Peter said, "I've got news for you. I'm a prisoner just like the good Padre. And we cannot stay here. The soldiers would come. Bad. Screw all the girls. Then you would have to kill them, no?"

"I think better we kill the soldiers," the Chief said.

"You've got something there, Chief," Peter said.

"Soldiers come, we hide you, hide us," the Chief said. "Never find."

"Look, Chief, all I can do is to ask the Jefe. Then I'll come back and tell you. Of accord?"

"*De acuerdo,*" said the old chief.

Peter walked over to where Pepe and Jacinto stood.

"What was the old buzzard talking with you about?" Pepe said.

"He wants us to stay four or five days," Peter said, "so that Padre Pío can police up the place. Seems there has been nocturnal frolicking around. Girls big belly, the old boy says. Look, Pepe, I thought that was a hanging offense . . ."

"Worse," Pepe said, "but all he means is that they've only been married by Indian ceremonies and not in the Church. Besides, you did not understand me, Peter. They do not kill young people for fornication. They make them get married. It is only when a girl is formally engaged to a young man, and on their wedding night he finds that—due to the activities of another rapid type—you could drive a jeep up it, that the poor thing is put to death . . ."

"What do they do with the male offender?"

"If they can catch him, they alter him. But usually the girls don't tell . . ."

"Jacinto," Peter said, "about our staying here——"

Jacinto turned very slowly from where he had been staring off across the village square. His yellow eyes came back from farther than that. From towering heights. Immense depths. From heaven, maybe. Or, more likely, hell.

"All right," he said.

"What!" Peter and Pepe said together.

"You heard me. I said 'Of accord.'"

That was one of the good times. After he got used to how an Indian house smelled. After he got over the shock of opening a door and having a dead man grin at him with immense yellow teeth. In spite of the fleas.

They took the dead man away the next morning, after Padre Pío had told the Indians that he wouldn't christen babies, perform marriages, hear confession, or say Mass unless they consented to bury their dead properly. The burial ceremonies were very colorful, so Peter asked

Jacinto to give him back at least one of the four cameras he had had in his saddle roll and which they had confiscated along with his carbine. Jacinto gave them all back without a word.

"What's got into him?" Peter said to Pepe.

"I do not know. Father Pío said once that he would become a great criminal or a saint. It frightens me. I prefer him as a criminal. When he is blustering about, threatening to shoot people, I know how to handle him; but this quietness, this saintly mood—*Dios mío!*—who knows what he will do next?"

The following morning they found out.

Peter came over to where the Indians stood, silent and rapt, looking at the old Chief. Slowly, powerfully, the old man was swinging a rawhide whip. It sang through the air, whistled, bit. Peter heard something that sounded like a moan. He pushed his way through the crowd. The girl was young. She was hanging by her wrists, which had been bound with rawhide thongs to a crossbar set on two forked poles, high enough so that her whole body swung beneath it. She was naked. And the whipping had been going on for some time, because she was striped and bleeding from her heels to her neck. She was thickset and not particularly pretty. She smelled of blood, and even more strongly of that nauseous odor that the gray beans they ate gave to the Indians' sweat. That and the smell of unwashed female and the stench of fear came over and took Peter in the face. He retched; but he came on, stood before the Chief.

"Why?" he said.

"She lay down for white man," the Chief said, "for him of the yellow eyes."

"You mean to beat her to death?" Peter said.

"No. Just five more. Then we sit her on the stick."

"You sit her on the stick?" Peter said.

"*Sí,*" the Chief said, and pointed with the butt of the whip.

Peter turned. There in the middle of the square a stake had been driven into the ground. It stood all of thirty inches high. It had been sharpened into a spearpoint—that is, the top of it had. He hung there, staring at it.

"Law," the old Chief said. "Man steal, cut him off hand. Lie, split him tongue. Woman do that, we—"

"My God!" Peter said. "Chief—"

"Yes, tall Cacique?"

"You'll let me call Padre Pío first? Let her say her prayers before? After all—"

"*Sí. De acuerdo,*" the Chief said.

Father Pío was something to see. He roared like a lion in Spanish and Tluscolan. He waved his arms, stamped his feet. Some of the things he said didn't come out of the Catechism.

"Savages!" he said. "Dolts! Idiots! How many times have I told you—"

"Law," the old Chief said. "She open legs for the white man."

"But she is not married!" Father Pío said. "I will fetch the white man and make him marry her."

"She engaged my son. You to marry them, today," the Chief said. "No good now. She come tell him what happen before."

"Which means she did not deceive him," Padre Pío said. "She told him *before*, Zochoa!"

"No difference. She lay down, open legs, bump bellies with the Cacique of the Yellow Eyes all night long and—"

"No!" the girl screamed suddenly, "it's a lie! A lie, Padre!"

"Son," Father Pío said, "lend me your shirt."

Peter took off his shirt and handed it to the priest. It was still mud-caked. But that didn't matter now.

Padre Pío gave the shirt to the old Chief.

"Have the favor to wrap her in this," he said, "so that I may speak to her. Her nakedness is an offense to my priesthood. Go on, cover her up!"

The Chief wrapped the girl in Peter's shirt. Padre Pío stepped up to her.

"*Hija mía,*" he began in Spanish; "my daughter—the truth, now. What passed with thee?"

She told him. But in Tluscolan. As the old priest listened, he began to smile. Then to grin. Laughter twitched about his mouth. He covered it with his hand, but the rich, dark sound of his laughter came out between his fingers. By the time she had finished, he had tears in his eyes. But they were tears of mirth, not sorrow.

"Zochoa!" he said. "Call the council of the women. Have them take her into that house there and examine her. She swears that she is virgin still. That your son did not understand—that, in his rage, he would not listen to what she was really saying. Go on, call the women!"

The old Chief looked puzzled. He looked at Padre Pío.

"Do as I say, Zochoa!" Padre Pío said.

"Very well, Padre, I call them," Zochoa said.

And now, after the girl had been borne into the house amid a great gabbling of women, Peter saw the younger Indian men coming up the trail pushing Jacinto along ahead of them. His hands were tied behind his back and one of the Indians was pointing his own burp gun at him.

"I wonder," Peter said, "how many he killed before they took him?"

"None," Father Pío said, "or else he would not be alive now. They are very good at tricks, the Tluscola. It is likely that they made him empty his weapon into a pig or a goat disguised as a man, then took him before he could reload."

Peter could see the other guerrillas coming out of the other houses with the assault guns in their hands. Pepe put himself at the head of them and gave swift orders. The third officer, the one called Federico, repeated them.

"Father—" Peter said.

"Do not preoccupy yourself, Son Pedro," Father Pío said.

The Indians marched Jacinto into the square. They stood there all around him, waiting. The guerrillas made a wide circle around them, holding the machine pistols muzzle downward, not aiming them.

Pepe came over to where Peter and Padre Pío stood.

"What has he done?" he said.

"Don't know. Fornication. Rape. Or something else. Something worse, maybe," Peter said.

They waited. The women came out of the house. They were mountains of flesh under their gray hair. The girl was with them. They had bathed her, dressed her in her wedding dress, put flowers in her hair. It was an ordinary wedding dress, bought, probably, in Ciudad Villalonga.

When they saw her dressed in white, the Indians set up a roar.

"What does it mean?" Peter said.

"That she has been vindicated," Padre Pío said.

The women, led by the girl herself, walked over to where the men were guarding Jacinto. When she was close enough, the girl leaned forward and spat into Jacinto's face.

The old Chief said something in Tluscolan. Peter didn't need to know what the words meant. The young Indians obeyed at once. They took out their knives and cut Jacinto loose.

"You see," Jacinto said, "I told you I did not touch her!"

The girl's head came back. Her laughter floated up, silvery and sure.

The sky gave it back. The mountains. She ripped out a phrase. Then the Indians started laughing. All the square was loud with their laughter.

Father Pío's face was a sight to see. He didn't want to laugh, but he couldn't help it. His old lined, seamed, gnarled face fought his laughter, but the laughter won.

Jacinto stood there. His eyes were sick. He looked from one side to another.

"What says this woman?" Pepe roared. "Tell me, what does the woman say?"

"I say," the girl said, her Spanish heavy-voiced, but clear and sure, "that he is incapable. He is guilty, your friend, of intention. Only—"

"Shut up!" Jacinto howled.

"He is not a man," the girl said. "He tried. All night he tried, menacing me with his knife. But he could not. He is not a man. He tried. But his flesh failed him."

"Jacinto!" Pepe said. "Your pants!"

The guerrillas were laughing too now, shouting that phrase Jacinto had himself invented. "Your pants! Remove them that we may see what, if anything you have in them!"

Peter didn't laugh. He was too busy watching Jacinto's eyes. He saw them change. He started moving toward Jacinto. He was too late.

Jacinto uncoiled like a spring. Snatched a Bren gun from the nearest of his comrades. Whirled, the burp gun flattened against his hip, already flaming; and he, Peter, coming in on a long diagonal, already in midair in a flying tackle, saw Pepe crumple under that blast, his uniform smoking, jerking under the impact as half a clip tore into him; but Peter's arms were around Jacinto's neck and shoulder now, smashing him to the ground, and the gun still talking—but aimlessly now, stitching a line of holes across one of the houses high up under the roof until it bucked empty, and Jacinto swinging it out and sidewise with all his force so that red fire exploded inside Peter's head; and he heard or thought he heard or even dreamed as the sudden dark crashed down, Pepe's voice, fading, dying, choking, say:

"No! Let him go— Let him go— Do not kill him for—this——"

And Father Pío moving out between them and Jacinto's flying form, his arms outstretched in the form of the cross, very small and straight there on the mountainside, saying, his old voice infinitely weary:

"No, children. There has been already too much blood."

V

Here, where they were now, there was no flatness anywhere and the mountain was honeycombed with caves. They used the caves to sleep in; but they were very damp and cold and uncomfortable so fires had to be kept going in them all night long. There was plenty of water. It sprang from the rocks in trickles and streams, ice-cold and clear. On one side of the camp a cataract foamed down for two hundred meters making a noise like thunder, so loud and so constant that after a day it faded out of consciousness as traffic noises do to one whose window opens on a busy street. Beside the big cataract there was a small one, with a fall of only three meters that made a lovely shower bath when the sun was out in the middle of the day.

Peter was under it, its icy needles making him dance and roar, while the clothes he had already washed lay drying in the sun with the rocks on them to keep them from blowing away. The four guards that Federico, the new commander, had placed over him and Father Pío lay on the ground and smoked cigarettes. And now Father Pío came out of the cave and walked over to the little shower.

"Cleanliness is next to godliness," he said.

Peter came out of the cataract and began to walk about, slapping his body with his hands. After a time the wind and the sun dried him, so he picked up his clothes, blown dry and stiff, and put them on. The old priest sat down beside him. Peter looked at that ancient gargoyle face, seeing that it was lined and sad.

"What passes with you, Father?" he said.

"I should not have laughed," Padre Pío said. "It was a sin to laugh."

"But very natural," Peter said. "He made such a thing of his masculinity. Have you noticed, Father, how often men give an exaggerated importance to what they doubt in themselves? What truly they do not have?"

"Jacinto is not effeminate," Father Pío said. "What he is is wounded."

"Wounded how?" Peter said.

"In his soul, profoundly. Tell me, Son Pedro, what do you know of psychology?"

"Nothing. Or almost. And I doubt what little I do know."

"That is your wound, Pedro. That you doubt all things."

"You think I like it, Father?"

"No. I know that no man of your intelligence would move in the cold wilderness, bemused by shadows, sickened by emptiness, if he could enjoy the warmth and comfort of Faith. As you will, one day."

"Don't make book on that, Father," Peter said.

"What did you say, son? I have no English," the old priest said.

"Nothing. A stupidity. You think that Jacinto lives?"

"*Sí*. He may even have joined one of the other guerrilla bands in another part of the Sierras. But I doubt that. He will run alone, now. He is like a crazy wolf. His capacity for survival is great. I wish I could have saved him. For his place should have been in a monastery. In a contemplative order. One where the vows are of silence, work, and poverty. Because, you see, son, he has a vocation of chastity."

"Ho!" Peter said. "You mean he has a vocation of impotency, don't you, Father? Combined with two or three more. Murder, for instance."

"A little more charity, son. I think that marriage and the begetting of sons are not for Jacinto. I think that when he approaches a woman the vision of his sister the night he found her fills up his mind, freezes his normally ardent blood. Hence, for him, a contemplative order—"

"For him the gallows," Peter said, "for having murdered poor Pepe!"

"Son," Father Pío said, "Pepe forgave him before he died."

"Pepe was a bigger man than I," Peter said. "I had grown fond of Pepe. Of them all, he had the most heart, and the highest degree of intelligence. This band is finished now, you know. Without either Juan or Pepe they have no chance. I only hope the other bands have better luck, though I wonder if it will help matters or make them worse for the Castristas to win. But speaking of bands, Father—do you know where Federico took those twelve men this morning?"

"No," Father Pío said, "but you do, do you not, Son Pedro?"

"Yes. They have gone to raid Ciudad Villalonga itself. To blow up an assembly plant of trucks that belongs to the Dictator. On the outskirts of the city. A monumental piece of folly. They will not survive it. Directly contrary to Juan's policy, which was to keep moving, trying to link up with the other bands, gather recruits until they could strike in strength, signaling at that moment the clandestine bands within the city to rise up and help them. Father—"

"Yes, son?"

"Tomorrow, if they have not returned, we must escape, you and I."

"You think it is possible, son?"

"Yes. The caves. We must go casually into the third one. It has an exit."

"Do they not know that?" Father Pío said.

"Yes," Peter said, "but they will discount it. You see, the exit comes out under the big cataract. They will not believe that you and I will risk being swept away."

The old priest looked at him.

"Is the risk very great?"

"Enormous. It curdles my guts to even think of it. I would not attempt it alone. But with you, Old One—"

"With me, what?" Padre Pío said.

"It is a thing that you have. Luck, maybe. Or the Grace of God. If there is a God—I wouldn't know. Only with you and for you, it works. With you, I shall go without fear. Without too much fear, in any event. Because it can be done, only if one is not afraid to the extent that paralyzes the will. One must not look down. One must only look up—"

"And pray," Father Pío said.

"And pray. Which is your department, Father. That's all I ask of you, that you keep a hot wire plugged in with Upstairs. Because that's not my line—my prayers are of first-class lead. And go up about as fast. Will you try it, Old One?"

"Speak of it," Father Pío said.

"The exit comes out under the big falls. Only the water does not cling to the rocks, but springs out from them so that there is a space of two meters where only the spray strikes. In that space there is a ledge thirty centimeters wide on which one can walk. That ledge is of an utter vileness of slipperiness, and is of shale rock that may crumble beneath us. Below it, there is nothing. Below it there is only death."

"For the little children of the good God there is never *only* death, son."

"As you will, Father. I have stolen two knives. I stole a pistol, too; but I put it back, because to cross that ledge even a pistol will be too heavy to carry. You will carry the two canteens—empty, because water itself weighs a barbarity, and every gram we don't have to carry will help. I will dig handholds in the rock wall which is of shale, and soft. When I take away my hand, you must put yours in the place I have left. Like that we will proceed five meters until we have come out from under the waterfall. What we will find there, I do not know. I think there is a trail of a certain vileness going down. But whether it connects up with that ledge, I do not know. The only way to tell that is to try it. Will you, Father?"

"Of course, son," the old priest said. "And, son, before I forget, it was very brave of you to try to save Pepe as you did, attacking Jacinto with only your hands—"

"Less than you think," Peter said. "I was trained to fight with my hands. I led Commando raiding parties in Korea. I can kill a man with my bare hands, Father."

"And you consider this an accomplishment?" Father Pío said.

"No," Peter said. "It sickens me. And I could not do it now. I no longer have the will."

"Good. I am glad of that," Father Pío said.

Just before noon that next day, they saw Federico and the others coming up the trail. There had been twelve of them when they started out; now there were only nine. Peter and the guards went down to meet them.

"How went it, Freddie?" Peter said.

"Of a vile vileness," Federico said.

"Then this of the truck factory—"

"The factory? That went well. That was fine. That was enormous. Only—"

"Only what, Freddie?" Peter said.

"They wounded Roberto and Martin so badly I had to shoot them. But what is worse, that idiot Jaime allowed himself to be taken. By now they know of this place. Jaime is not one to resist torture very long. But that is not the worst."

"What is the worst, then?" Peter said.

"Our people within the city, hearing the explosions, rose up, thinking that the invasion had started. As we were leaving, we could hear the firing. And the screams. They were not coordinated. Nor prepared. By nightfall, our fifth column will have ceased to exist. And it is my fault! Mine! If I had listened to you, Pedro; if I had only listened to you!"

"Freddie," Peter said, "do not waste time blaming yourself. Now, it seems to me that once again, we must get out of here, move on—"

"No," Federico said.

"*Madre de Dios!* Are you mad?"

"No," Federico said.

"Then?" Peter said.

"I weary of running. I tire of being hunted like a beast. They know where we are. Let them come and take us—if they are willing to pay what it costs, which will be dear. Wili!"

"*Sí*, Jefe?" Guillermo said.

"Set up the machine guns. There before the caves—to cover that flank. The mortars a little higher. Comrades! I will now say a thing: If any of you, despite all our indoctrination, wishes to go to the little Father to confess and make your act of contrition, you have my permission, and my promise that you will not be punished for it. Since it is likely we shall all die, take what comfort you can—"

"Freddie, you are crazy!" Peter said, watching the two or three soldiers of the band who either sheepishly or defiantly headed for Father Pío's cave.

"Now, there is no chance, Peter. I am too tired. And they have the helicopters from your Navy's Aircraft Carriers scouting for them, now . . ."

Peter looked at him.

"I do not believe that," he said.

"Yet it is true," Federico said. "Your State Department is determined that Costa Verde shall not be another Cuba. Hence they have applied the formula that worked so well for you in Viet Nam: Your forces are 'technical advisers.' Technical advisers with copters that find us, guns that shoot us, napalm to roast us alive, bombs to spatter our guts. So, there is no chance now. If we leave here, we will be taken cheaply at little cost. Since die we must, let us make them pay high for our butchered, uneatable meat, with mountains of chopped loinsteak of their own. You and the little Vasco go into the caves when it starts, and only come out again when it is over, waving the white flag of surrender. That, Comrade Reporter, is an order."

"Freddie, you are either much man or a fool. Though I wonder if they are not usually the same thing."

"And I, Peter," Federico said.

Under the falls, the thunder of the water was so great that talking was impossible. Peter hung there, probing in a crevice of the rock with his knife. The spray was ice-cold. It stung like a thousand whiplashes. Every time he moved his feet they slipped out from under him and his gut turned over. But he hung on, digging handholds fifty centimeters apart. Then he saw that Father Pío was having a hard time stretching up to reach them, so he cut them lower and closer together, which made them better for the little priest, but difficult and dangerous for him. Finally he had to compromise by cutting two sets, which took twice as long. But he kept on cutting them, like that.

He ached all over, and his muscles were jerking from fatigue. They inched along that ledge like sodden spiders, spread out in a series of momentary crucifixions. Even through the mist, he could see Father Pío's lips moving in prayer.

But he had neither the time nor the strength for praying. He moved centimeter by centimeter, dying a little each time his foot slipped, being resurrected when his grip held in the downward-slanted handhold he had cut into the rotten rock. It took them two hours to cross that five meters. Then Peter hung there, seeing the place where the ledge had come to an abrupt end and beyond that the sheer drop of fifty meters down crumbling perpendicular shale rock faces that no living thing larger than an insect could have managed, and even an insect with appalling difficulty. And across that, an obscene, unspeakable, vile vileness of an unjumpable three meters away the beginning of the trail he had seen the day before.

He hung there with the icy mist on his face mingling with the lava like sulphuric tears and a great wave of profanity choking in his throat which he had no longer had the breath to say. He looked at Father Pío. The little priest bowed his head.

"It is the will of God, Son Pedro," he said.

Going back was easier. They already had their handholds. They got back into the cave, soaked to their bones' marrow, their teeth chattering like castanets. Crawled to the fire. The water in their clothes made steam rise up chokingly past their nostrils. They lay there without talking. The warmth stole into them; the tiredness spread out, out, until abruptly it ended time. Unattended, the fire burned itself out.

What wakened them was the cough and the thump of the mortars.

Because he was first of all a reporter, Peter came out of the cave. He crawled out of it on his belly, with the Leica with the 130-mm. telescopic lens in his hands, and the Nikkon with the normal F 1.4 lens slung around his neck and resting on his back as he crawled. At his side he had the spring-wound robot camera that could shoot bursts of ten or twelve shots, making a series. He had left the Rolleiflex in the cave because it was too heavy and bulky for this kind of action.

Federico had been right. He was the last of the band who had been trained under the Russians in Cuba, and his use of the topography was masterly. They had caught Villalonga's troops in the open on the plateau below the caves and the slaughter was sickening. Peter pin-pointed the long lens on one man, caught the exact instant of his death; the expression of pure disbelief on his face as a slug tore into him. He swept their faces, caught fear forever in silver salts; immobilized a falling body in midair; froze horror, froze pain in a series of shots better than any he had ever taken before. Then, as they whirled, running, he switched to the robot, capturing the attitudes of flight; the wild antics of men trying to stretch their tiny allotment of breath for an instant longer—an hour more under the sun.

Then they were all gone. And Federico threw one more mortar shell among the grotesque sprawl and seep and twist of the bodies, dismembering them; making sure that no one of them would rise. Then he turned to Peter, his teeth flashing white amid the blackness of his beard.

"What a slaughter!" he said.

"Now will you go?" Peter said.

"No. These were bait for the trap. The rest wait below to take us."

"Comrade—" Peter said.

"*Sí*, amigo?" Federico said.

"May I photograph you—and your men? This I think is a thing for history. Such men as you and yours should not be forgot, whatever the justice of your cause. May I?"

"Of course," Federico said.

They waited. Twenty minutes later, they heard the heavy roar of aircraft motors coming in.

Peter stood near the door of the cave, looking up. The two Vought Corsairs, the Mustang, and the fat-bellied P-47, went over once; then they barreled up in a climbing turn as tight as though they had been tied together on a string. He could see them, very high now: the Corsairs blue-black against the sky, but the Mustang and the Thunderbird silver; and he, waiting, caught them in the telescopic lens, as they peeled off, started down.

He stood there, shooting his pictures, rock-solid as they came in, their props mist-silver, the leading edges of their wings aflame with the multiple spluttering jet-torch of their guns; the rockets hissing out of the racks and coming ruler-straight for the mouths of the caves; and the explosions hammering, throwing up earth and rock, and he, standing there, babbling like the fool he didn't even know he was being: "Oh, brother; what a shot! What a shot! Come on down, you buzzards! Closer! That's it! Oh, baby, what a sweetheart of a shot!"

And they, those well-trained guerrillas, who could have stood off an army, breaking now, scattering, because nothing is harder to face than being strafed from the air; nothing, not even tanks, gives a man a greater feeling of helplessness; and he, photographing them as they ran, caught the whole thing as it was, so that, afterward, he was never able to look at those photographs again.

The planes whining up, the sound of their motors thinning, then coming down again in a bellow that wracked sound out of existence; and the fat black bombs detaching themselves from under the wings and striking, bursting, sending up not the explosive shriek and tear of shrapnel but a soft *plofff* of pure liquid flame.

Peter saw the men turn into torches trailing fire behind them as they ran. Saw, and photographed them as they fell on their stomachs, or on their backs, their legs arching back, their arms flung out as they twisted sidewise in a circle like flies sprayed with insecticide; screaming with opened, blackened mouths; only their screams were lost in the bull-bellow, prop-whistle, tearing-up soaring snarl of the motors, in the hammer of the bombs; the teletype sentence of death the wing guns were dictating into the mouths of the caves.

Then, higher up, he saw the Cr 47s—the old Douglass DC 3s—open their guts and defecate parachutists across the sky. He got that picture, too; but he knew that it was time to get out of there, especially since Villalonga's pilots were calling their shots now, placing load after load of napalm directly into the mouths of the caves.

He went back into the cave to where the old priest knelt in prayer, jerked the old man to his feet and started toward the mouth of the cave; but not getting there because the explosion flattened them both and the rolling billow of flame licked above their prone bodies with a heat that had to be felt to be believed and was not entirely believable even then.

They started crawling toward the exit, toward the hopeless opening under the falls. Got there and edged onto the ledge while their burning clothes hissed and sizzled out under the spray; and, hanging there, then inching out for the second time along that ledge, and again reaching that dead end, standing there until they saw the planes heading back toward Zopocomapetl; the fighters in a tight, professional V above the transports; the transports lumbering awkwardly, fighting each other's propwash, their formation ragged; but all of Miguel Villalonga's air force heading homeward now, their job well done.

Peter and Padre Pío stayed on that ledge for two and a half hours after Peter had seen the head of one of the paratroopers thrust through the spray, hanging there until the ache in their fingers, their arms, their backs, got to be worse than their fear, then they went back into the cave. The napalm had burned itself out long ago. They were alone. The paratroopers had gone back down the trail, bearing the bodies of their own troops and those of the Castristas with them.

They didn't talk. They filled the canteens and started walking. Halfway down the trail a Navy helicopter stopped and hovered over their heads.

Peter flagged it down. The two pilots jumped out. Stood there, looking at them.

"My God, it's Father Pío!" one of them said.

"And Peter Reynolds," Peter said. "Look, gentlemen, I don't know whether hitchhiking is within regulations, but if it is, may I respectfully request permission to come aboard?"

"Why sure, Mr. Reynolds," the pilot said. "We were sent out to look for you when that fracas started. Seems your father put in a call to the Senator from Massachusetts; he blasted our Ambassador down here, and he blew the whistle on Captain Andrews. Said there'd be hell to pay if you got yours—"

"I see," Peter said. "I suppose there must be some way to convince my old man that I'm crowding forty, but I haven't found it yet. Anyhow——"

The co-pilot of the Sikorsky was staring at all the cameras that Peter was carrying.

"Did you get any good shots, sir?" he said.

Peter stopped.

"Thanks, Commander," he said, "and not just for asking. Look, Sir—I'm going to give you all these rolls. Fly them out to the carrier, will you? Because Miguelito's goon squad will confiscate them sure as hell if I try to bring them in. Tell your Captain that it would be in the public interest if he got this film to New York. Tell him he can make copies of any or all of it for Naval Intelligence, but ask him to see that my paper gets this stuff. I need my job, Sir—"

"Roger. Can do," the pilot said.

On the flight back in the chopper, Peter reloaded the cameras. Better that the goon squad had something to snatch. Because even the apehood in which their minds labored was capable of suspicion if they found the cameras empty. By the time he had finished that, they were over the town.

The refinery fire was out. The British aircraft carrier stood out to sea. The American one had steam up. There was a long white yacht tied up to the quay. *La Flor del Mar*. The *Seaflower*. The beautiful craft The Leader used on his justly famous fishing expeditions. On the last one he had broken the world's record for blue marlin taken on a regulation line.

Peter pointed at the aircraft carriers.

"Why?" he shouted above the whacking rattle of the copter's blades.

"No further need—revolution's over!" the co-pilot said.

"That's what you think, friend!" Peter said.

"What did you say?" the co-pilot shouted.

"I said it's not," Peter called back, "because even if only a certain party I know is left, he'll——"

"What are you saying, Son Pedro?" Father Pío said. He was close enough to Peter not to have to shout.

Peter said it over again in Spanish.

"What man is that?" Father Pío said.

Peter's mouth grinned, but his eyes didn't.

"Me, Father," he said. "When they knocked off Freddie, they paralyzed my other cheek. The one I used for turning purposes."

"I do not understand you, Pedro," Father Pío said.

"Don't worry about it, Father; I don't either."

The helicopter drifted downward toward la Plaza de la Liberación, black with people, in the heart of the town.

Book Two

THE CITY

VI

When it was over and they had let him go—after having held him long enough to rush those quite-blank films over to the police laboratory and confirm his absolutely untrue statement that he hadn't taken any pictures, had been too scared during the battle to poke his head out of the cave, even retaining him another half-hour after that to make him shoot up a roll of twelve with the Rollei of their triumph, which included the prize-winning shot of the Dictator, Miguel Villalonga, in crisp tropical whites, looking down at the pile of bodies in the plaza, while all unknown to him a vulture perched on the cornice above his head—Peter got into a taxi, exchanging as he did so a wave of hands with Father Pío, who was being borne away to the Archbishop's palace in a limousine whose luxury was more than a little mundane, and drove straight to the little flat he had rented a month ago, the day Judith had arrived.

He had, miraculously, his key, and the mass of sodden bills that were to have been the down payment of Father Pío's ransom; so he was able not only to pay the taxi driver but also to ease by Concha, La Portera, without her seeing him in his present bearded, filthy state. He opened the door with his key and entered that little flat, so like and so different from all the dozens of other little flats he had rented for longer or shorter periods in so many Latin American capitals; and not even too different from the ones he'd had in Europe, Africa, Asia, except that it was newer, less timeworn.

When Judith didn't come flying at the sound of the opened door, he tiptoed into the bedroom. But she wasn't there, either. So he tried the knob of the bathroom door. It was empty, too. He walked all over the flat, looking around. Her clothes still hung in the closet. The vanity was covered as always with the jars and flasks of female sorcery. In the drawers were all the bras she still didn't need, all the filmy triangular wisps designed not so much for concealment as for provocation, made, as he had sworn more than once, to be ripped off her. The perfumed mist of negligees, slips, even those nightgowns she never slept in and those stockings woven of cobwebs and mist. But Judith wasn't there. That perfume of hers, *Peut'être,* that could still knot his guts at the first whiff, hung heavy and still on the air. But no Judy—no Judy at all.

He went back into the bathroom and answered the more pressing calls of nature. Washed his face and neck, lathered his stiff, black beard, picked up his Rolls razor—which, although it was a safety razor, had a permanent blade and a mechanism for sharpening it, thus eliminating the risk, inherent in his profession, of running out of blades in places where you couldn't find any, or more frequently the places where they were impossible to shave with after you had found them—and stopped dead, staring at it, because the blade was gone.

"I wonder where the hell she's put it," he muttered. Then he frowned, shook his head. This wasn't like Judy. She was meticulous about small things. He had, of course, raised unholy hell with her on more than one occasion for using his razor to shave her legs—largely as a matter of maintaining his position as lord and master, because the silken, almost invisible white blonde fuzz on Judy's legs certainly did less damage to the blade's edge than his barbed-wire beard did—but this was the first time she had ever failed to put it back. He searched for it, but he was too tired to do more than go through the motions, especially since, because he had spent his entire life, including his childhood, traveling, he had long since learned to carry two of every irreplaceable item. So he dug out the second blade, honed and stropped it to the required degree of keenness, and shaved.

He got into the shower, turned on the water, soaped himself all over and stepped under the spray. What ran off him could have been used to fill a fountain pen; so he stepped out of the area of the spray, reached for the soap to lather himself again. But he squeezed it a little too hard, and it shot from his hand in a hard, flat trajectory to land, as far as he could judge, behind the lavabo, the basin.

Swearing, he stepped out of the shower, got down on his hands and knees, pushed his right hand behind the column of the lavabo and groped for the soap. But his fingers touched something hard and cold, smeared, his tactile sense told him, with a thick, viscous substance. He drew it out. Knelt there, holding it.

It was the blade of his razor. The safety guard had been wrenched violently aside. The blade was covered with blood.

He sat down on the edge of the tub, holding it in the palm of his hand. He sat there, looking at it; and, because he knew Judith Lovell, knew in painful and complete detail her history, the palsied shaking in his limbs rose in waves through his body until his stomach knotted and he vomited, spewing forth the yellowish bile that was all he could throw up because he hadn't eaten anything in close to forty-eight hours.

Then he dropped to his knees, contorted his wet, slippery body into the little space between the bidet and the lavabo. Looking upward, he could see the whole back of the basin—which should have been flush with the tiled wall, but, because it had been installed by Latins, naturally wasn't—dripped thick, ropy, slowly coagulating blood.

He got up. Stared at the bidet, the toilet. They were spotless. There was no blood anywhere except behind the washbasin. He stretched out a hand that shook so that he had a hard time closing his grip, took a bath towel, dried himself. Went into the bedroom, moving slowly, like a sleepwalker. Opened the drawers, took out underwear, socks, a shirt, a handkerchief. Dressed himself in the same somnolent detachment until he was clad in shirt and pants, but barefoot still. Then it hit him. He doubled in half, clutching his middle with both hands, lifted up his head and howled:

"Simple! Oh very simple, Padre! You hear me? Just like falling off a log!"

Then he was off; running toward the kitchen, and getting there, yanking the interior phone, the one that connected directly with the porteria, off the hook and screaming into it:

"Concha! Concha! Answer me for the love of God!"

"*Diga?*" Concha said.

"Concha," he said, "the Señorita; where is she? What the devil has passed here?"

"Ay, Señor!" Concha wailed. "The poor little thing! She is in the hospital! In Our Lady of the Remedies! She—"

But he had slammed the phone down and was yanking on his shoes, socks, a tie, tearing on his jacket, transferring his keys, his billfold, his passport, identity card, the sodden mass of bills, to the pockets of his lightweight suit, and going out of there, taking the stairs four at a time going down, only to meet Concha coming up them.

"Ay, Señor!" she wept. "Ay, Señor, if you could have seen her! Standing over the lavabo with your razor in her hand! And the blood! Ay, yai, yai, the blood! Never have I seen so much! Not even at the bull-fight! *Ay, Madre de Dios! Ay, Señor Nuestro!* The blood! The blood!"

He caught the fat, greasy wrists.

"Why? In God's name, Concha; why?"

"The radio, Señor! The radio! It announced the great battle, although it didn't have to, because we could hear the explosions from here and see the airplanes diving and the smoke coming up. And afterwards the announcer said—he said—"

"What, woman? What, Concha? Tell me!"

"That you were dead, Señor! That you and the saintly Father Pío had been killed by the Reds! I thought about the Señorita when I heard that—knowing how nervous she is. And I was thanking the Sainted Mother that the Señorita knows no Spanish, when he said it over again—in English!"

Peter stared at her.

"Why?" he said. "Why should he do that?"

"I do not know, truly, Señor. But Mario, my son, says it is because The Leader wished your Marines on that aircraft carrier out there to hear and come to his aid. I cannot swear he said the same words, but he repeated your name and that of Father Pío, twice—"

"Figures," Peter said. "Go on, Concha!"

"So I came up here. The door was open and—"

"Thank you, Concha," Peter said.

"I—I cleaned up. I do not know why. I thought I had removed it all, the blood. Only—"

"You did just fine." Peter edged past her.

"Señor, wait!"

Peter stopped.

"I called the hospital ten minutes ago. She is alive, but in the gravest of danger. But when she sees you, Señor, she will recover! I know it! What a great love! What enormous pride must the Señor have! To be envied by all men because of the beauty unequaled of his wife; and knowing additionally that she, this celebrity more famous than any other, this star of the cinema, this luminary of the silver screen prefers to die rather than to live without him. What an enormous thing!"

Peter stood there listening to Concha exercising the vocabulary she'd gotten out of the fan magazines, which are absolutely as bad in Spanish as they are in English, and studying her face as she said all that. Then his head came back, his mouth opened. Laughter came out of him. Ripped out of him with the sound of tearing.

He mastered it, whirled, and ran down the stairs.

"Poor man!" Concha said. "The shock has deranged his mind . . ."

He sat there beside the bed, looking at Judith. Her hair was spread out over the pillow. It and the pillow and her face, and even her lips now, were all the same color: white.

Her eyebrows and lashes were only a little darker, the palest possible ash blonde, so that to achieve the platinum shade that other actresses had to murder their hair with peroxide to obtain, Judith merely had to sit in the sun a couple of hours a day, a thing she loved to do, anyhow.

He leaned forward suddenly, staring at her throat; at that thick collar of gauze wrapped around it. Leaned back, looked at the doctor. "My God!"

"She wasn't playing games," the doctor said in perfect, unaccented American.

"I thought—her wrists," Peter said. "Usually—"

"When they don't really mean it. Your girl did, Mr. Reynolds. After the fourth transfusion—she's had five now—twenty minutes after we put the call for donors out over the radio, the line stretched all around four blocks, hundreds of people who're going to spend the rest of their lives bragging about how they gave Judith Lovell the exact drop of blood that saved her life—she woke up and raved a bit. From what she said, I gather she hasn't had a happy existence—up until now. With you, yes. Seems to regard you as her salvation. Awfully dependent upon you, isn't she?"

"She's nuts," Peter said.

"You'd better pray she stays that way," the doctor said.

"I do," Peter said. "Every night."

He went on looking at her.

She stirred a little. Said, in her normal, clipped Back Bay accent: "Pe-tah."

"Yes, Judy?" Peter said.

Her voice trailed off into a broken jumble. Peter looked at the doctor. At that type-form of the young, upper class Hispano-American, complete to the pencil-line mustache. Until he opened his mouth. Then what came out was New Yorkese.

"Doctor—is she out of danger?"

"I'm afraid the answer to that one is no, Mr. Reynolds."

"Good God!" Peter said.

"Amen. She made a beauty of a try, Reynolds. Missed the carotid by the thickness of a hair. Played old hell with a whole series of major veins. Incidentally, unless she can find an absolutely miraculous plastic surgeon, she's out of the motion pictures for good. I took nine stitches in that gash. And the scar isn't going to be exactly a joy forever."

"So now what do we do?"

"We wait, Mr. Reynolds."

"Oh, hell—call me Peter, will you? Because, if I know my Judy, once she starts talking, what you've been indulging in, listening to her, was a sort of nonvisual voyeurism. You now know more about me than my mother ever did, so why keep your distance? Besides, for saving Judy, you automatically head the list of my friends for life. Anything you ask me, if I've got it, it's yours."

"All right, Peter. Incidentally, my name's Vince. Vicente Gomez. Only the types at Harvard Med cut that down to Vince the first week. What I was going to say is that quite a lot may depend on your actions when she wakes up. I'm not exactly sold on psychiatry, but there does seem to be some there—a deep-seated guilt complex; even, I'd venture, if the term didn't sound so goddam phony, a kind of a death wish . . ."

"My slant is that Judy sort of extirpated the phoniness with her do-it-yourself surgery, Doctor."

"Exactly. And she made several half-intelligible references to a Doctor Dekov. Is that—"

"Doctor Leon Dekov, the psychiatrist? Yes, Vince. And, before you ask: She was in his clinic a year. Self-committed. Voluntarily. For nervous depression—after one of several attempts to pull a caper like this."

"All right. I'm through asking questions. But I should like to make what ought to be a completely unnecessary pitch—"

"Pitch away, Vince."

"When she regains consciousness, you'd better pour it on, Peter. Rid her of her suspicion—about this she was highly articulate—that you're tired of her, that she's a burden to you. If she's only a quarter right, it's you who're nuts, not she. Even from the standpoint of altruism toward the general public, you can't let something that looks and is built like Judith die. Let her get to sixty, boy. Let that glorious frame get to be just a memory even to her; then it won't be too bad. But now, God in Heaven, what a waste!"

Peter looked at him.

"You mean she's still in danger of dying?"

"I mean that if you don't convince her that you love the ground she walks on, she'll try this again. Or something more effective. At the moment, I believe that seeing that you're still among those present will snap her out of this one."

Doctor Gomez had a meal sent up from the hospital's kitchen for Peter, but he couldn't eat it. He got a little of it down; but then his stomach knotted up on him and wouldn't let the rest of it pass. He sat there watching Judith for the better part of two hours. One of the nursing sisters stayed with him. Vince looked in every quarter of an hour.

Still, when it happened, he was caught unaware. He was gazing out of the window; not really even listening to the sister's account of how Ciudad Villalonga happened to have this absolutely top-flight A-Number-One hospital, equipped with every piece of modern medical equipment that money could buy.

"So when the Reds shot our Great Leader," the sister said, "he was brought into the hospital we had then. Here, on the same site. But it was of an almost unimaginable badness. Señor, he came close to dying. In fact, he would have died, had not Luis Sinnombre, whom some say is his brother, conceived of the idea of putting him in an airplane and flying him up to the Clinic of the Brothers Mayo in your Great country, Señor. When he came back, restored except for that limp he still has, which will not permit him to dance—he who loved dancing so!—he had the old hospital razed to the ground and built this one. He spent a fortune! A thousand millions, it is said. Why—"

"Yes, Sister?" Peter said. "Go on. I'm listening."

But behind him there was no sound at all. He turned and saw Judith's eyes. They were wide open, staring at him. At first they were blank and unfocused. Then they cleared. A little pinpoint of light—reflected, perhaps, from the window behind Peter—got into them. It was very hard-edged, definite and bright. Then it splintered; broke into slivers like the facets of a diamond. Went molten, liquid; walling out the dead-level, still-blue smoke of her gaze behind a wash of crystal, shivering upon her lashes, trembling in fragile resistance to the whole ponderous downward pull of the world.

Her mouth came open; her snow-colored lips, whiter now than the rest of her face, made a pitiful, babbling blur that he couldn't look at, and couldn't stop looking at. He could see that what they were trying to shape into sound was his name; but they couldn't manage it.

He got up slowly, crossed to her, bent and put his mouth on them, on snowflutter, on ice, on the stench of disinfectants, on near-death. He heard the click of the sister's heels as she fled down the hall.

When Vince came into the room, he was sitting in the chair by the bed, while Judith held his big hand with both of hers to her open, uncontrollably quivering mouth, and blessed it with her tears.

When he had retrieved his hand, which he managed to do only after she had sunk back into sleep again, he left the hospital, and started toward Pam-Pam, that curious quick-lunch chain that had jumped the ocean from Paris and proliferated all over Latin America. The food there was a trifle less uneatable than it was in the other cafés, tabernas, cantinas, and restaurantes. He still wasn't hungry, but he knew he had to eat something. But, before he could order, Tim O'Rourke, *Time-Life's* Latin American man, with whom he had been engaging in absolutely pitiless warfare for close to twelve years now, came into the place, caught him by both lapels and jerked him to his feet.

"C'mon," Tim said, "we're going to Les Ambassadeurs. It's on me. Deductible. Business expense. Interviewing a celebrity."

"Put that way, you've got me, Timmy, me b'y," Peter said. "I can't afford Les Ambassadeurs. And I could use some food . . ."

"I hope it chokes you, you bastard," Tim said. "Now, come on."

"So," Tim said, "you think the revolution's not over?"

"I don't think," Peter said. "I know."

"Why not?" Tim said.

"Villalonga. You think they're going to quit with him still in power?"

"No," Tim said, "but they'd better hurry. If they want to have the pleasure of doing Miguelito in, I mean. I'd make book on some of his own friends knocking him off first."

"Why?" Peter said.

"You got all night? Ten million reasons. Finance for one. He demands and gets kickbacks from everything that operates in this monkey's paradise from a bootblack stand on up. Result? Just look in any direction. United Fruit's closing its office here, end of the month. The Verdian Hilton's losing money hand over fist; tourists don't come to a country with a reputation for using them as clay pigeons. The Shell people are pulling out because Miguelito keeps upping his share of the ante; and the Beards keep blowing up the pipelines and the refineries. Coffee and sugar plantations can't make money at the market prices and pay The Generous Benefactor his cut—"

"In short, a major screw-up?"

"Plus a few minor ones. Another thing: Your foreign editor ever give you the house rules for operating in Latin America?"

" 'Don't criticize the country, and let the dames alone?' "

"Right. Substitute *ruin* for *criticize,* and you've got what El Indomitable fractures every day. Both clauses."

"I see," Peter said.

"The funny part about it is he doesn't even like dames—not really. Just uses 'em to get even."

"Even for what?" Peter said.

"Isabel. Old Hundred Thousand. Hell of a note to have that for a mother. I think that's what kind of drove El Benefactor Generoso off his nut. You know how he came to power?"

"No," Peter said.

"The Big Fish down here backed him. Notably one Manuel Miraflores. Figgured this young, ambitious punk would be the perfect weapon against his own class. So Miguelito rose from a small-time *chulo*—pimp is as close to that as you can get in English—petty mobster, strongarm man to Head of the State. Have to admit he was a pretty smooth article, even as a kid. Knew how to ape the manners, speech, and dress of his betters. But the Big Fish forgot one thing."

"Which was?"

"Isabela. They might set up a straw dictator to operate behind, but their brides weren't starting to sit down at a table with the Ex-Star Performer of the exhibitions at The Blue Moon. So, socially, the deep freeze set in. His Nibs has never married, because my guess is he prefers little boys or even lap dogs to babes. And years ago he shipped the kid sister out of the country to keep Old Hundred Thousand from teaching her womanish tricks."

"I heard she's back now," Peter said. "At least according to that idiot Jacinto, she is."

"Yep. I've seen her once or twice. Down here they make jokes about her looks; but I think she's kind of cute. Pert and perky, if you get what I mean. Homely little phizz, but appealing. Keeps to herself—trying to avoid getting hurt, I suspect. His Nibs had her husband knocked off for plotting against him. The point is, Petie, that old Cienmil officially became First Lady. And las Damas Ilustres de la Alta Sociedad weren't having any. The result was that Miguelito got his back up, made his half-brother—maybe—Luis Sinnombre, Head of the Secret Police, and started in to be a real dictator instead of a straw one. Insulting Isabel changed overnight from being High Society's favorite indoor sport to a pastime that would make bullfighting look like croquet. Miguel has filled up three concentration camps with types who said something that even could be mistaken for a lack of respect for that wicked old broad. And the dames—the caper he figured out to cut them down to size, you'd—— Oh, hell! Now what?"

Peter turned. The headwaiter was flying toward the table, bowing from the waist from twenty feet away.

"Señor Reynolds," he got out, "there are two reporters from the national newspaper, *El Líder Glorioso*. They wish to interview you and take some pictures, if you don't mind . . ."

"You mean to stand there with your bare face hanging out and imply he could refuse even if he wanted to?" Tim said. "Horse business, Martinez! People get shot for less than that down here."

"It would be a very great honor, Señor Reynolds," the headwaiter said, "which would lend great light to our establishment——"

"Oh, hell—all right," Peter said.

When they had gone, after having taken dozens of pictures of Peter in the act of talking to Tim and the staff reporter of *The Glorious Leader,* Tim sat there, staring at Peter.

"Now you're going to get it," he said.

"Get what?" Peter said.

"The treatment. You're ripe for it. Hell, you're spoiling for it."

"Tim, what the ever-loving hell—"

"Is the treatment? Simple. It's—why should I tell you? Be more fun watching you lapping it up. Tell me, how long is Judy going to be in Vince Gomez's hemstitching emporium?"

"Vince is going to try to keep her there a month. Says he wants to build her up. Claims that if she comes out in a weakened condition, in this climate, she'll catch something godawful, sure as hell."

"He's got something there. A month, eh? Then they've got time."

"Goddamnit, Tim! Who's got time?"

"Miguelito and Company. You ever spend a longish stretch in Costa Verde before?"

"No. A week was my longest up until now. I was down here photographing the Standford's Expedition's return from Ururchizenaya. Bringing in my sweetheart, that godawful, beautiful pre-Columbian statue they call the Goddess of Death. Love that girl. Wish I could bring her back to life. Have you seen it? It's in the Museum of Archeology, here. I go down there twice a week to look into that face. Can't figure how a thing can be so beautiful and so terrible at the same time. Find myself talking to her. You have seen it, haven't you?"

"Yes—and it gives me the creeps. You've got some funny tastes, boy. But tell me, can you figure why this dump has the best press of any country in South America?"

"No. It ought to have the worst. Yet you're right. Everybody sent down here comes home raving about it. And sends home the most nauseatingly saccharine reports about it, and His Nibs. Hell, Tim—you mean he brainwashes them?"

"Something like that. But subtly. He wins friends and influences people."

"But how, Tim? How?"

"Said I wasn't going to tell you. But here's one teensy-weensy lil' hint, amigo. Five'll get you ten that before tonight some dame you never heard of will ring you up. And that just her voice over the telephone will start you climbin' up the wallpaper—"

"And then?"

"You figure it out, Peter Pan," Tim said.

VII

That night, after visiting hours—during which Judith had displayed her really considerable histrionic talent by wringing the last drop of pathos out of the role of the martyred saint, thereby convincing Peter that she was out of danger, because when Judy started acting, he was wryly aware, normalcy was once more at hand—he went back to the flat.

He let himself in with his key and sat down before the typewriter. He wrote steadily until eleven o'clock, grinding out those colorless and neutral stories he'd already found out were the only kind he could get out of Costa Verde, where there wasn't supposed to be any censorship, but where, actually, it was absolute. But, at eleven o'clock sharp—at which ungodly hour Costa Verdians, like all Spanish-speaking peoples, sit down to their heaviest, most important meal—he stopped typing or else, as he knew damned well, the people in the apartment below his would start banging on their ceiling with a broom handle. He sat there, the palms of his hands behind his head, looking out the window. Southward, the sky was strangely red, so he got up and went to the window. Looking out, he could see what the red glow was. Zopocomapetl was acting up again, sending a livid tongue of flame straight up into the night sky. This could, with only a little exaggeration, have been called a major eruption. From the photos published at the time of the last real outburst, five years ago, or at least from his memory of them, Peter judged that this show was only a little smaller than that one had been, but he couldn't really tell, because there weren't any towns like Chitimaya left for old Zopo to bury. There was, of course, the Indian village of Xochua, where Pepe had died; but it was on the far side of the volcano, the side where, up until now, lava had never been known to spill over the cone. So Zopocomapetl's capacity for destruction was limited, unless it exerted itself and took care of Ciudad Villalonga, as it had two hundred years ago, when Costa Verde was still a Spanish colony and the capital had been called Antigua. But there wasn't much chance of that, because after the volcano had wiped out Antigua, the surviving colonists had moved the capital much closer to the sea, preferring to face their human enemies, the English buccaneers, than to live under the perpetual threat of fiery death. Peter stood there watching the natural fireworks until their sinister beauty palled on him. Then he turned and started back to his desk, but before he got there, the telephone rang.

"Señor Reynolds?" the voice said.

"Yes," he said. "Speak."

"You are Señor Reynolds, aren't you?" the voice said. It didn't purr. It was curiously harsh. But its enunciation was beautifully crisp.

"Unless somebody gave my mother the wrong package a long time ago, I am," Peter said.

"Good!" the voice said.

Peter didn't say anything.

"Are you there?" the voice said.

"Yes," Peter said. "And Tim was wrong. Dead wrong."

"I beg your pardon?"

"I said my friend Tim was wrong," Peter said. "He informed me that when you called, your voice alone would melt the sidewalks. Instead you have the voice of a daughter of family, who has spent all her life under the teaching of nuns . . ."

She sighed.

"You are right and he is wrong," she said, "but I wish sincerely it were vice versa."

"Why?" Peter said.

"Because I should like for you to do a thing for me which you might if I had the kind of voice he said. Or, more securely if I were the kind of woman who possessed such a voice. But, no—if I were to try to induce you to aid me by giving you the impression I were a beautiful and sensual woman, you would only be disappointed and might even refuse to help me—"

"Then I take it that you are neither beautiful nor sensual?" Peter said.

"I—" she began, and stopped. Then, "Courage, Niña!" she whispered, apparently to herself.

"I am listening," Peter said.

"If one were charitable," she said, "one might call me plain."

"And if one were truthful?" Peter said.

"Ugly," she said. "Perhaps not repugnant; but ugly enough."

"There are differences of opinion. And of tastes there is nothing written. Perhaps I should find you lovely."

She sighed again.

"No," she said, "that is not possible. In the first place, I am very thin. If one bothers to look twice, one can see that I am a woman. I have been told that it is not worth the bother."

"Who told you that?" Peter said.

"My husband," she said. "My late husband, who is dead."

"Oh," Peter said. "And your face?"

"Have you been to the Museum of Archeology here in Villalonga City?"

"Yes," Peter said. "Why?"

"There is a female statue there, brought from the lost city of Ururchizenaya. Since we know nothing of the language of the ancient Tluscola-Toltec civilizations, we do not know what it represents. But, from its aspect of sadness, its look of emaciation, the museum authorities have decided to call it the Goddess of Death. Have you seen it?"

"Yes," Peter said. "It is absolutely gorgeous."

"Oh!" she said.

"*Oh* what?" Peter said.

"Now I cannot make the comparison I was going to."

"Why not?"

"Because now it will seem both false and vain. I was going to say that if you have seen the so-called Goddess of Death, you have seen very exactly—my face."

"Then, Señora, you are one of the loveliest women on earth," Peter said.

"No, no! Oh, but this is wrong! I start out to demonstrate to you my utter sincerity, because the matter is too important to be deranged with lies, and you—"

"I do not doubt your sincerity, Señora. I merely beg to differ with your opinion and your taste. Say my own is odd. I prefer an interesting face to a beautiful one."

"All right," she said. "I have been called that. You could legitimately call me interesting. Please, Mr. Reynolds—"

"Ah, one moment!" Peter said. "There is one other detail we must clarify."

"And that is?"

"That of your sensuality."

She didn't answer him at once. And, when she did, her voice, speaking, was very quiet. "That, Señor Reynolds, is a matter between me and my father confessor, and ultimately—my God," she said.

"Bravo!" Peter said.

"Why *bravo,* Señor Reynolds?"

"I like spirit, and you have it," Peter said.

She was silent a long moment. Then she said:

"All right. I have gone thus far; I might as well go all the way. Señor Reynolds, would you have the kindness to meet me somewhere—tonight?"

"I should be delighted," Peter said.

"Oh!" she said.

"Why *Oh!,* Señora?"

"I—I didn't expect you to say yes. I—I only tried this because I was desperate, and now—"

"And now, two final details. When and where?"

"At the end of the Street of the Fifth of May. Where it runs into the Botanical Gardens."

"That's isolated enough. Even romantic."

"Please, Señor Reynolds, do not entertain ideas. It is not my intention to—"

"I know it is not, Señora. I have lived in Latin America many years."

"Meaning?"

"That girls with cultivated voices like yours don't proposition men. They don't have to. Only one thing puzzles me: You sound extremely young, and yet you say you are a widow—"

"I married at eighteen, Señor. I was married three years. My husband was killed in an airplane crash one year ago."

"Making you all of twenty-two. Now I understand. May I belatedly extend my condolences?"

"Thank you," she whispered. "You are very kind."

"Now, where are we? I am to meet you—?"

"*Al finale de la Calle del Cinco de Mayo*—"

"Say that again?"

"At the end of the Street of the Fifth of May."

"Ah, yes. I thought that was what you said. At what time?"

"At midnight." Her voice was so low he could scarcely hear it.

He looked at his watch. "In twenty minutes, then?" he said.

"*Sí,* Señor."

"One moment! Don't hang up! How am I to know you?"

"You will take a taxi. Before you reach the end of the street get out and dismiss the cab. Walk straight ahead. A car will draw up beside you. A white convertible. I shall be driving it. That is all."

"But how will you know me?"

"I have been following you everywhere you have gone for the last few days," she said. "By now I can distinguish your walk in total darkness."

Peter laughed.

"You find this diverting?" she said.

"My dear young lady," Peter said, "I think you have been seeing too many motion pictures . . ."

"Perhaps. But this of secrecy is very necessary. You will come, won't you?"

"But of course!" Peter said.

He had no sooner put the phone down than it rang again. He picked it up, said:

"Now look, Infant!"

"You are mistaken, Señor Reynolds," a man's voice said.

"You've got something there, friend," Peter said.

"Mr. Reynolds, I am the secretary of His Excellency Señor Corona, Minister of Information and Tourism. His Excellency requests the honor of your presence at a banquet at his residence tomorrow night. Will you be able to attend?"

"Of course," Peter said. "Please convey my thanks to His Excellency. Does the occasion require formal dress?"

"To the extent of a smoking jacket," the secretary said. "The time is eleven o'clock. I may assume that you will come unaccompanied since this of the unfortunate accident of Miss Lovell?"

"You may assume that, yes," Peter said. "If it is not an indiscretion, may I know why you ask?"

"Oh, we have a very pleasant custom here in Costa Verde. When a gentleman is alone, we provide him with feminine company. Exceedingly charming company—"

"From The Blue Moon?" Peter said.

"Why, Mr. Reynolds!" The secretary's voice sounded genuinely shocked.

"Sorry," Peter said. "I just wanted to know where I stood."

"Your company," the secretary said, "will be a young married woman whose husband is temporarily absent upon a diplomatic mission. She is a descendant of one of the founders of the Republic. I do not think you will find anything undesirable in her general culture, her manners, deportment, or her morals, Mr. Reynolds. It is not our intent to insult you."

"I beg your pardon most humbly," Peter said. "I was laboring under a misapprehension."

"Quite all right," the secretary said. "Anything else you'd like to know?"

"Yes. Can she count up to five?"

"I—I'm afraid I don't understand," the secretary said.

"Don't worry about it. She will," Peter said.

He hung up the phone, and sat there studying all the things that were wrong with that second call. The hour? No, the hour was all right. Even in private homes, nobody ever ate dinner earlier than eleven o'clock at night in most of Latin America. But to call him only one day ahead of time—that was wrong. Even to call him at all was wrong. For a banquet at a Minister's house, requiring evening dress, nothing less than a formal, printed invitation fitted the circumstances. And, last of all, that pleasant custom the Minister's secretary had mentioned. That was worse than wrong; in any country where Spanish is spoken, that was incredible. A single girl—would have been barely possible. A niece or daughter of the Minister, himself, graciously offering the hospitality of the house under Papa's damned watchful eye—that, maybe, yes. But a married woman whose husband was absent? That no. The Moors hadn't stayed in Spain eight centuries for nothing. And the Conquistadores had imported their temperament to the New World, intact. To put one's bride out to pasture—and on such a loose rein? Not just *no—hell no* fitted that one.

"That one," Peter muttered, "stinks on ice!"

Then he looked at his watch and grinned a little.

"Time to start your treatment, Son," he said.

When he saw the car coming toward him, he whistled a little. It was enormous. It drew up alongside him and stopped. Lincoln Continental. The very latest model. Snow white. She had the top up. But even so, the only thing she could have possibly used to attract more attention would have been a flashing red dome light or a police siren. He opened the door and slid in beside her. When the door opened, the automatic roof light came on. But it was set too far back for him to see much of her face. But even in that brief winking on and off of the light, he had the impression that he had seen that strangely regal little head before. Then it came to him he had. In the Museum. That achingly exquisite pre-Columbian head. The likeness was startling.

"Buenas noches, Señor Reynolds," she said. Without the telephone to distort it, her voice was something. It was a true contralto. Speaking, it made interesting atonalities, like modern music.

"Buenas noches," Peter said.

She touched the accelerator. The car moved off. He saw that even the instrument lights were out.

"Would you mind telling me your name?" he said.

"I am very sorry," she said.

"That's a hell of a name," Peter said.

"Please, Señor Reynolds—it is much better that you do not know my name . . ."

"Why?" Peter said.

She sighed.

"Could you not be sufficiently gentlemanly to accept my word that there are excellent reasons for my not telling you who I am?"

"Put that way, I have to," Peter said, "but don't push my rather insufficient gentlemanliness too far, *Muñeca.* It may not be functioning well tonight . . ."

"Muñeca," she said. "Doll. Good. You may call me that. It will serve as a form of address."

"I could think of others," Peter said, "without half trying."

"Please!" she said.

She swept the big car expertly through a whole series of outlying streets. Peter could see that she was taking him out of town, but by a route that avoided every decent neighborhood, every fashionable street.

"You should have used a smaller car," he said, "of a cheaper make. Painted black."

"I thought of that. But it would have caused surprise at home. They know how fond I am of this one."

"But it does not cause surprise for you to leave the house at midnight—alone?"

"I have been married, you know," she said.

"That makes a difference?"

"Yes," and the note of bitterness was there in her voice; "since physically it is impossible to lose one's virginity twice, they are—less concerned, say. I believe they think I am engaging in a romance. And, since they would be delighted to have me marry again—"

"But you, *Muñeca,* would be less delighted?"

And now her voice became ashes and sand.

"My experience of matrimony would not incline me to repeat the experiment, Señor Reynolds. Ah. Here we are . . ."

She swung the big car off the road into a rutted wagon trail that disappeared under a black and menacing grove of trees. Brought it to a stop. Cut the ignition. It was absolutely lightless in there. He could not see her at all.

"Would you like a cigarette?" he said. But instead of saying *un cigarrillo,* which is correct wherever Spanish is spoken, he used the racier Madrid expression *un pitillo.* But she didn't hesitate.

"No thank you," she said.

"You don't smoke, then?"

"Yes, I smoke; but to light a cigarette would enable you to see my face. And it is far better that you do not know too precisely how I look. For the same reason, I ask you please not to smoke."

"I don't smoke. I merely carry cigarettes as bait."

"Oh," she said. "Señor Reynolds—you said that you had been warned that I would call . . ."

"No. I said that I had been warned that a woman would call. And that when she did, just her voice would melt rocks. A part of what is known locally, I'm told, as The Treatment."

"Your information—was accurate, Señor Reynolds."

"Look, *Muñeca,* I like you. In fact, I think you're wonderful. So let's climb down out of this Hitchcock thriller and relax. For instance, call me Peter, will you?"

"Of accord—Peter. It is a nice name. It suits you. Pedros are generally nicc."

"Is this part of The Treatment, *Muñeca?*"

"No—Peter," she said. "Please listen to me very carefully, and try to understand what I say. Because I cannot be too explicit. I do not dare."

"Shoot," Peter said.

"All right. You will receive an invitation to a party at the home of a personage high in the government."

"I already have. Five minutes after you called."

"Oh!" she said. "Did they mention an intention to provide company for you?"

"Yes," Peter said.

"They would!" she said. "Since your—your mistress was obliging enough to play into their hands by cutting her silly throat!"

"*Muñeca,*" Peter said.

"Sorry. That wasn't nice of me, was it? Strange that I dislike her so! But no matter. Did they tell you who your company was to be?"

"No—beyond mentioning that she was the wife of a diplomat absent upon a mission."

"*Oh, los cabrones! Los cerdos! Los—*"

"*Muñeca,* I felicitate you. Your vocabulary is extremely ladylike."

"I am sorry, Peter. I did not know those words until I married. I learned them from my husband. Listen, I will tell you what will happen. But first, let me say that Roberto is quite unlikely to return from that mission."

"Go on," Peter said.

"And that you will find Marisol extremely attractive. No, you will find that she is one of the most beautiful girls in all Costa Verde—"

"You're making me impatient," Peter said.

"That was what I was afraid of. Additionally, she will be most attentive. She will seem truly impressed by you, even—"

"Swept off her feet by my fatal charm?"

"Exactly."

"But the catch, I gather, is that word *seem*?"

"I do not truly understand this expression *catch,* but if you mean the *trampa,* the trick, you are right."

"Go on," Peter said.

"She will ask you to take her home."

"And?"

"Once you arrive, she will invite you in for a nightcap."

"Then?"

"Then it depends upon you, Peter. I hope you will say to her, 'No thank you, my dear; it is very late'—"

"And if I don't say that?"

She was silent for a long, slow time. Then she said:

"You are a man of the world, Peter. You know what will happen next."

"But, beyond that. Does friend husband come rushing in, waving a revolver? Or does some busy photographer pop up with a flash gun to make interesting pictures? In other words—blackmail?"

"An unmarried man with no official connection with his own government is hardly vulnerable to blackmail, Peter. You have not been discharged from your newspaper because of your liaison with Miss Lovell. And surely that is not the world's most closely guarded secret!"

"Strange how that subject offends you," Peter said.

"While I was following you about, playing my childish and silly game of private detective, I—it seems to me—came to know something about you. At first you seemed to me a hulking brute—"

"Why thanks, *Muñeca!*"

"Hear me out. Then I saw that your mouth contradicted totally your face of an old boxer, which is not so much ugly as battered. And your eyes are the eyes of someone else—of another man entirely."

"What sort of man, Infant?" Peter said.

"The sort who should never, never, never belong to women like Judith Lovell!"

"Nor to your friend Marisol?"

"My friend Marisol does not want you!"

"And you, of course, *Muñeca*—even less?"

He heard the sharp intake of her breath. Then she was silent. Intensely silent.

"*Muñeca*—"

"Yes, Peter?"

"Have I offended you?"

"No, Peter. *You* could never offend me."

He sat there without moving. Because very exactly what she said was: "No, Peter; *jamás podrías tú ofenderme.*" Switching deliberately from the formal *Usted* to that *tú* which in Spanish, on the lips of a woman like this one, has both the sound and the quality of a caress. You could render *tú* in English as *thou.* But *thou* was wrong. *Tú* is not *thou. Tú* is—warmth, and an invitation, and a challenge, and—maybe—even surrender.

"You mean—?" he said.

"Oh, I do not know what I mean! Peter, will you promise me not to—"

"Indulge in fun and games with the lovely Marisol? If you will tell me why not."

She was silent again. Those silences seemed a part of her.

"Why not?" Peter said again.

She went on being silent for a long, long time. Then she said, so softly that he had to bend forward, close to her, to hear it:

"Because I do not want you to." But she didn't say *you.* She went on saying *tú* to him. That quite untranslatable *tú.*

He could feel her breath rustle against his face. It was wonderfully pure and sweet, like a child's. And the position he was in was ridiculous. He was off balance in more ways than one. So he muttered, "What the hell," and put his mouth on hers.

She didn't move. She did not bring her hands up either to embrace him or to slap his face. She lay back against the seat and let him kiss her. Her mouth was unlike any other mouth he had ever kissed. It bloomed on his like the petals of some great, fleshy flower, adhesive, parting, warmsoft, defenseless, tender. Then he felt the wetness on her face. Tasted the salt. At once he drew back.

"I'm sorry," he said.

"Do not be. Peter—"

"Yes, *Muñeca*?"

"Why did you do that? Do you pity me?"

"Jesus H. Christ!" Peter said.

"Do not blaspheme, Peter. Tell me why."

"Does there have to be a why, *Muñeca*?"

"Yes. You have never seen me in the light. You have never spoken to me before an hour ago. Therefore it is not possible for you to love me. And yet you have kissed me—with enormous tenderness. Why, Peter?"

"I love your voice, *Muñeca*," Peter said. "That's one thing."

"And another?"

"I have been to the Museum twenty times to visit that haunting face from another world. I first saw it eight years ago on my first trip to Ciudad Villalonga. Every time I've passed through—if there were time—I've stopped to see her again. I call her my love. The museum guards think I'm crazy, they've caught me talking to her so many times!"

"Oh!" she said.

"So when you said you had her face, I had to come. Only you were wrong."

"I do not have her face, Peter?"

"No. She has yours."

"Oh!" she said again.

"Now it's my turn," he said. "Speaking of whys—why did you *let* me kiss you?"

She was silent.

"*Muñeca*, why did you?"

"I suppose it was because I wanted you to," she said.

"*Muñeca*—"

"No, Peter. You mustn't again."

"Why not?"

"Because it would be wrong. I came out here to save Marisol—"

"From the fate worse than death," he quipped.

"You make a jest of it, but it is very nearly so. Peter, you know the women of our race. Do you believe that one of us would give herself to a man she doesn't even know? Especially when she is very happily married, and adores her husband?"

"I not only do not believe it, I know she would not. Girls of Spanish blood are the most chaste women on earth."

"Thank you for that. Though it is not entirely true. Yet, tomorrow night, that is exactly what Marisol Talaveda will do. Unless you refuse her."

"And if I do refuse her?"

"She—and I—will be most grateful to you."

"*Muñeca,* couldn't you clarify this thing a bit?"

"No, Peter."

"Why not?"

"You are not stupid!" she flared. "Figure it out for yourself!"

"Hmmn—" Peter said. "I take this lovely creature home. She invites me in for a nightcap. Excuses herself to go upstairs and slip into something comfortable: a transparent negligee, say . . ."

"One can see that you have been about," she said. Her voice was tart.

"Of course. But that is, or should be, nothing to you."

"Only it is something to me. I'm sorry! I don't want to seem an aggressive female—"

"Why not? I should love it."

"I know. But I should not."

"Same question: Why not?"

"I—I had a bad marriage, Peter. I have been lonely, too long. And I do not precisely like the ways you appeal to me. They make me ashamed of myself. Now go on with your speculations, and leave me in peace!"

"At the crucial moment, according to you, we are not interrupted. No one takes photographs suitable for French post cards. I simply have a lovely evening and—"

"Go home and write about what a magnificent country Costa Verde is. How *simpatico* the people are. What a bulwark against Communism our Leader is!"

"Now I get it! Tell me, how much does little Marisol get for the job?"

"Ohhh, men! Oh, you!" she said.

"Well?" Peter said.

"Marisol Talaveda de Ruiz Mateos is one of the richest women in Costa Verde in her own right. And the Ruiz, her husband's family, are wealthier still. Hardly the type to assume the role of prostitute, Peter!"

"Then she finds these little outings diverting?"

"Peter, you cannot be this dense!"

"I was teasing you. I know The Leader commands great powers of persuasion. In that regard, would you mind telling me something?"

"If I can," she whispered.

"What has he against Marisol? Why shouldn't he have simply selected some woman of the bad life—a high-class, expensive one, say, instead of forcing a girl of gentle background to—"

She bent her head.

"No answer?" Peter said.

"No. Yes! I shall have to trust you, that's all! I—I do trust you, Peter. All right—it is *because* she is of gentle background. Because when he came to power, the aristocracy scorned him. Because of—because of—his—"

"His mother?" Peter said. "Because of Isabel of the Hundred Thousand Loves?"

"Oh!" she said. "So you know!"

"Yes," Peter said; "that's it, isn't it?"

Her voice was so low that he had to lean close again to hear her.

"Exactly. They would not receive—his mother. Nor—his sister. They said that—that they were unaccustomed to dining with—whores!"

"Isabela, all right. But the sister—is she also?"

"No! In that they were unjust. So, because he is a subtle monster, he set out to reduce their women, their wives, sisters, daughters, to the condition they accused his of. He has nearly succeeded. He *has* succeeded to the extent that now the virtue of all upper-class Costa Verdian women is suspect."

"And the men stand for that?"

"How can they help it? They are, by then, already in prison. And when a woman receives the ring finger of her husband with the wedding ring still on it, packed in cotton wool in a dainty little box, she is —unlikely to refuse her body to the visiting foreigner Miguel feels the real or fancied need of influencing, Peter. Especially since it is not merely a matter of saving one's husband from death, but from death by centimeters prolonged over weeks until usually the mind goes long before the body does . . ."

Peter's voice was very harsh.

"He has—used *you*, thus?"

She looked at him. He could feel her eyes on him in the darkness. "And if he has?" she whispered.

"Nothing," Peter said. "People who voice threats usually don't carry them out. Which is why I don't voice them."

"Oh!" she said. "Peter, about Marisol—"

"That again? You know, *Muñeca,* under these circumstances, I find myself unconvinced of the wisdom of refusing your little friend."

"And I commence to be convinced that you are as swinish as the rest!"

"*Muñeca,* you wound me. Say I refuse her—what happens to her, then?"

"They will force her to try again and again until you succumb, or until it becomes obvious she is not your type. Then they will send you another light o' love . . ."

"You, for instance?"

"No, Peter; not me. I am not considered attractive enough."

"They're nuts. But, in any event, she has to obey orders, no? If not with me, then with some other foreigner who needs softening up. So why not oblige her and get it over with? Especially if she is as lovely as you said."

"Because, afterward, she will die. By her own hand. I know her. She is the only friend I have. And surely, Peter, you have had enough of that sort of thing!"

"More than enough," Peter said. "But, perhaps you underestimate me, *Muñeca.* Perhaps I can show her so pleasant an evening that this of killing herself will become to her totally unappealing."

She didn't say anything, for a time; then she said slowly:

"I—I suppose you could. But, don't you see, that would be worse? That you would have reduced her from the pardonable category of victim to the totally unpardonable one of—adulteress? Oh, Peter, please!"

"Of accord. I will refuse her. But on one condition."

"Which is?"

"That you, *Muñeca mía,* take her place."

She bent her head. He could not see the motion, but he felt it. When she spoke, her voice was infinitely weary.

"No, Peter."

"Why not?"

"Solely because I do not wish you to die," she said.

He heard that *solamente.* Considered it. It had a lovely, lovely sound. He bent, and with only a minimum of groping, found her mouth.

This time, her two hands came up. Her long, slim fingers moved, voiceless and remote in his close cropped hair. Then they dropped to his chest, pushing.

He turned her loose at once.

"For you, *Muñeca,* it would be worth it," he said.

She turned to the wheel, flipped over the ignition key. The motor caught. Purred. When she spoke her voice was humid. He could feel the tears moving through it.

"I will take you home now, Peter," she said.

VIII

"Peter—" Judith said.

"Yes, Judy?"

"Can't you take me home now? I feel fine. I feel wonderful. I'm sick of this goddam hospital!"

"No," Peter said.

"Why not?" Judith said.

"Vince won't let me."

"Call him. I'll talk to him. I'll explain it to him."

"You'll explain what to him, Judy?"

"That I can't just lie here and look at you every day, and not do something about it. I can't. I'll go crazy."

"Judy dearest, that is pure, undiluted, unmitigated rot."

"Peter, I can't do without you; I can't!"

"Baby, you did without me a good many years," Peter said.

"But not because I wanted to. I fell in love with you when I was eight. And I never got over it—"

"Which is just another of those weird ideas Dekov should have rid you of."

"It is not! Why . . ."

The nursing sister put her head through the door.

"Señor Reynolds—"

"Yes, Sister?"

"You are wanted on the telephone."

"Peter—" her voice said.

"Yes, *Muñeca*?"

"Have you decided, truly?"

He hardened his voice.

"I told you my decision last night. You must take her place."

"Oh!" she whispered.

"*Muñeca*—"

"Yes, Peter?"

"Would that be so terrible for you?"

She was silent.

"Would it, Infant?"

"What is truly terrible is that it would not be terrible," she murmured; "not at all. Holy Mother, forgive me! What a dreadful thing to say!"

"Then you will?"

"No, Peter."

"Why not?"

"Because afterward, you would die."

"I still say it's worth it."

"And I that you are mad!"

"Over you," he said.

"And I," she said, "for you. Equally. Or worse. Only, what good is it?"

"Good is not the word. I call it great!"

"No, Peter. Because I can never have you. No matter how much I want you. Because neither could I live, knowing I had caused your death."

"Lord!" he said. "There's something morbid about this place."

"Peter—"

"Yes, Infant?"

"Perhaps I shall think of a way. *Adios!*"

He heard the click. The line went dead.

"Who called you? A woman?"

"Yes," Peter said.

"Pretty?"

"Glorious."

"What did she want?"

"What do women always want? You know I can't help it. It's my fatal charm . . ."

"Pe-tah—"

"Oh, brother! Here we go. When my baby starts calling me *Pe-tah* with that Back Bay accent, head for the woods, men!"

"Peter, is this one of those many truths, spoken in jest?"

"What do you think, Judy?"

"I think you're that barking dog who barks and barks and then takes one hell of a chunk out of where I sit."

Peter lifted the bedcovers, peered under them.

"Hmmn, looks appetizing," he said. "Tasty. You mean you don't trust me, Judy?"

"No. You look too sleek. Too contented. Why, you're fairly purring! *Pe-tah,* are you being unfaithful to me?"

"And if I were?"

"Subjunctive mood, condition contrary to fact. If you *are,* my beamish boy, I'll—"

"You'll what?"

"Cut my neck again. Only deeper."

He went over to the bed. Put his hand under her chin. She was twenty-seven years old now, but without make-up she looked like a child. A rather sweet child, timid and bashful and shy. That quality came through even in her pictures, which made the roles they gave her shocking in a way, to a degree that no other actress could have managed. They had typed her, all right. Whatever the script, what came over from the screen was the portrait of a rather sweet kid engaging in juvenile delinquency without really enjoying it or knowing quite what she was doing. Perked up jaded appetites no end.

"That," he said, "was Don Andres Corona, Ministro de Información y Tourismo. Inviting me to dine *en famille ce soir.*"

"Oh!" she said. "Did you accept?"

"Had to, Judy. You don't refuse invites from bigwigs down here."

"All right. Peter—"

"Yes, Judy?"

"Kiss me."

He kissed her.

"Hmmm—nice! Oh, if I weren't so goddam weak!"

"Good thing you are. Or we'd shock the Sister all to hell," Peter said.

He was tying his bow tie when the doorbell rang. He went to the door, opened it. A policeman stood there. His uniform differed from the ordinary one. It was subdued. Navy blue. His cap had only one thin line of gold braid. Peter had to look very close to see the bulge under his armpit.

"Yes?" Peter said.

"Señor Reynolds?"

"Yes," Peter said again.

"I am your chauffeur. Your car waits below. Don't hurry, Sir. You have plenty of time."

"All right. Mind telling me your name?"

"Enrique," the chauffeur said.

"Very well, Enrique. Wait for me downstairs. I'll only be five minutes more," Peter said.

The car was a Daimler with wickerwork side panels. Peter appreciated the subtlety. A Caddy wouldn't have been enough. A Rolls, too much. A Daimler was just right. Taste; finesse; discretion.

So was the Minister's house. It was a minor miracle as to how all that luxury always stopped one millimeter short of vulgarity.

Peter found himself surrounded. Some of His Excellency's guests tried their English out on him. But when they heard his Spanish, they stopped, relaxed. But not entirely. There was an undercurrent of unease running through that crowd that made the air whine.

Peter looked at the women. Not too directly, which would have been bad form. But they were all clinging to various masculine arms. He saw that the Minister, Señor Don Andres Corona McDowell, was watching the door. He went on watching it out of the corner of his little blue eyes for the better part of half an hour. By a quarter past eleven, he was beginning to sweat a little.

Peter touched his arm, said:

"This of my special company is without importance, Your Excellency. Surely the lady has been unavoidably detained, or even encounters herself indisposed. Tomorrow I shall send her a bouquet of roses with a little note expressing my sorrow at not having had the great privilege of knowing her. But certainly Your Excellency has no reason to be concerned . . ."

But His Excellency's red Celtic face had split into a broad smile under his bushy guardsman mustache.

"Oh, no, my deah Reynolds," he said in English. "Little Marisol is most dependable! Here she comes now—"

Peter didn't follow Don Andres in his rush toward the door. He stood back and studied Marisol Talaveda, Señora de Ruiz. And immediately revised his estimation of Miguel Villalonga. Sent him to the head of the class. Gave him top marks. Miguelito hadn't missed a trick This wasn't on the level of the Daimler. This exceeded it.

Marisol Talaveda was dressed in black. In one of those simple little black dresses that defy both analysis and copy. That defy anything on earth except the long side of five thousand dollars. Her hair was what the Spanish call *castaño*, which is actually just off-blonde, not quite auburn. She was slender. Her figure was perfect. And everything about her was innocent, almost virginal, implying a purity of mind, of spirit that must have been damned uncomfortable to live with if one were her husband. To even think of using this grown-up girl child for such a mission required a turn of thought, a subtlety, a refinement of lechery, a warped kind of sensuality that clearly stood on the other side of perversion.

Peter went on watching her until she was close enough for what was going on behind that very nearly perfect poise to reach out and take him by the throat. He saw that pale pink smiling mouth was screaming so that he could almost hear it. That those enormous, velvety blue eyes had long since eclipsed all the joy that there had ever been on earth. That she was studying him, too, but with horrified fascination. As Mary Stuart must have studied the man with the axe.

"Amigo Reynolds," the Minister said, "this is Marisol—"

"Talaveda, la Señora de Don Roberto Ruiz Mateos," Peter finished for him, "who is as lovely as I have been told. No, lovelier. And whose presence would make me the happiest of men, were it not—"

"Oh!" she said. "You do speak Spanish—and beautifully! You didn't tell me that, Don Andres. I might have said something indiscreet!"

"You, my dear Marisol, are the soul of discretion," the Minister said. "But we are interrupting Señor Reynolds. You were saying that little Mari's presence makes you unhappy? That, my deah fellow, is a hell of a note!"

"I beg your pardon, Your Excellency; but that is not what I said. My exact words were that la Señora's presence would make me the happiest of men, if she could bring herself to realize I only look like a bear. I don't ordinarily eat little girls alive—not even so dainty a morsel as you are, Señora—"

"But you could be persuaded, eh, Reynolds?" Don Andres said.

Peter looked at her.

"In this case, I think not, Your Excellency," he said.

Now she was really looking at him.

"Why?" she said.

He smiled.

"Say the bear's a curiously tender beast—with a finicky appetite. He only dines on grubworms and wild honey. Never upon terrified does, no matter how lovely they are. And that, at least as far as this particular gross animal is concerned, any relationship whatsoever must be based upon mutual consent. And that consent must be real. Don't you agree with me, Don Andres?"

"Perfectly," the Minister said. "If only a few other chaps I know felt the same way about it, what a world we'd have, my friend!"

Sitting beside her, listening to her voice, Peter began to feel contented with life. Her voice was utterly lovely. Low and soft and sweet. She seemed to have formed a genuine liking for him, because her voice was no longer taut with nerves, but rather vibrant with what must have been hope.

"Peter," she said, "you don't mind if I call you Peter, do you? It seems I've known you forever!"

"I'm delighted. But, truthfully, if I can say so without seeming vain, girls usually like me. That is, after they come back from wherever they run screaming to, the first time they see me."

"Strange," Marisol said. "You really aren't ugly, you know. I think you must have been in a car smash-up. Your nose has been broken, hasn't it?"

"Yes," he said, "but it wasn't a car."

"What was it?" she said.

"A Red Chinese sergeant in charge of interrogating prisoners in Korea. He wanted me to admit I was guilty of bacterial warfare."

"Oh!" she said. "Peter—"

"Yes, Mari?"

"You really *are* nice. Just as she said."

"Just as *who* said?"

"My friend. You've never seen her. And she's forbidden me to tell you her name. But you'll meet her soon. And when you do—"

"When I do meet her, what, Mari?"

"Be gentle with her, Peter, please!"

He grinned at her.

"I'm usually gentle with little girls, Mari. Tell me: Is she as pretty as you are?"

"She—she's not pretty at all, Peter. But I do wish you wouldn't mind that."

"Maybe I won't."

"She's not ugly. Just—just odd-looking. Exotic somehow. Her face is like a tribal mask. If I were a man, I'd find her exciting."

"I do," Peter said.

"What did you say?"

"Nothing. Go on. This of your friend interests me."

"It should. You see, she started—well—investigating you. For—for reasons I'm not free to tell you."

"I know those reasons. I find them hateful. No—nauseous. There was never the slightest danger that I would have gone along with this monstrous charade. To me, there is only one excuse for certain acts

Mari. Love. The kind of love that continues after one has resumed a vertical position. That goes on. Forever."

"Oh!" she whispered. "Oh, she's right! No wonder she's so in love with you!"

"Is she?"

"Yes. I told her she was foolish. That one couldn't love a man one had never talked to, didn't really know. You know what she said to that?"

"No, what?" Peter said.

"That when I met you, I was not to pay any attention to your shoulders nor to your rather brutal face. 'Look at his mouth,' she said; 'then his eyes. You'll see what I mean.'"

"And do you?"

"I think so, yes. Your mouth and eyes are—gentle. Peter, listen to me. She—she's not responsible for the terrible position she finds herself in. She didn't choose her parents any more than you and I chose ours. What I'm trying to say is that she's—so vulnerable. Her life has been —awful. Emilio treated her like dirt."

"Why?"

"She will tell you, one day. It is not my place to. She's so terribly alone. Surrounded by people, sitting upon a mountain of gold; with a terrifying amount of power in her hands, she's alone. Cut off from any happiness, any joy—"

"By her looks?"

"Oh no! By the walls of hate that surround her. Hate she did nothing to cause, but cannot cure—"

"Maybe I can kick those walls down for her," Peter said.

After dinner, which Peter remembered as having been absolutely marvelous without being able to recall a single thing he had eaten, they danced. Marisol was a beautiful dancer. She floated, two full centimeters off the floor. But she had gone away from him, somehow. Her small, sweet face was remote. Then abruptly, nervously, she said:

"Would you mind taking me home, Peter? I'm very tired."

He stared at her. "Of course," he said.

He saw at once that excuses were unnecessary. That everyone at the party had been expecting this. The women looked contemptuous. The men hard-eyed, grim. So he made his excuses anyhow, in person, and in form. Then he took Marisol by the arm and led her out to the car.

Enrique jumped out at once to open the door for them. They got in. The Daimler moved off. Marisol didn't say anything to Peter. She didn't even sit close to him. She seemed to have forgotten that he existed. Peter sat beside her and watched the quivering rolls of flesh on the back of Enrique's neck.

The car swept up a curved driveway under the palms, the tamarinds, the lavenders. The house was buried under dark masses of bougainvillea, hibiscus, frangipani.

Enrique got out, held the door open for them.

Marisol looked at Peter. Her smile was something to see.

"Would you care for a nightcap, Peter?" she said.

"Look, Mari," he began, "it's awfully late, and—"

But her hand came out and took his. Her nails bit into his palm. She closed one gorgeous blue eye, suggestively.

"Please, Peter," she said.

He stood there. His lips moved, soundlessly: "Must I?"

She nodded vigorously. Her face was very white.

He made up his mind, said the only thing that could be said:

"All right," and added under his breath: "Judy baby—I think my will power's up to par, but if it isn't, or if what they're holding over this lovely child's head is too goddam rough, will you forgive me, please?"

"What did you say?" Marisol said.

"A prayer. One I don't think is going to be answered. And I find I need that nightcap."

Her voice, speaking, made a flute note.

"You needn't wait, Enrique," she said.

It was beautifully planned. She poured excellent smoky Scotch over the ice cubes. Said, pleasantly:

"Amuse yourself, Peter, while I go upstairs and slip into something cool."

"Now look, Mari!" he began; but she clamped a slim hand over his mouth. When she took it away, he whispered: "The servants?"

She nodded, swiftly. Said, her voice high, taut, bright:

"Oh, I'll be right back, Peter." And ran up the stairs.

He waited. Then he saw her coming back down again. She hadn't changed. She still had on that wonderful little black dress. He had already opened his mouth to say "Now, what the hell?" when he saw that he was wrong; that she had changed totally. That the woman in that black dress wasn't Marisol Talaveda de Ruiz at all.

He stood up, watching her come down those stairs step by step by step like a dream figure, slowly. And now, seeing her in the light for the first time, everything he had guessed about her, every intuition was confirmed. She was thin. Thin enough to wear that dress like a professional model, wear it in a way that Marisol couldn't have worn it, or any other woman he had ever known. Her face was a Greco, even to the distortion along the vertical planes, even to that curiously exciting cool-toned hint of—green? blue? greenish-blue?—in the shadows. Only Bernard Buffet had brought it up to date, because El Greco would never have conceived the totally nonethereal quality of that mouth. That mouth. Too wide-lipped, full, defenseless, tender, wounded unto death for her inhollowed tribal fetish of a face. Nine men out of ten would have found her ugly, he knew. But now, here, at that instant of time, in that particular place, he, Peter Reynolds, was that lonely tenth man. He found her glorious.

He stayed there looking at her, watching the play of light and shadow over that sculptured mobile of a face as she came down those stairs in the midst of velvety silence, unbreathing still, watching him out of those enormous, long-lashed, definitely slanting eyes, turning toward him the face which—even under the short black cap of hair, a gamine's cut that on her defined the word *chic* and was actually closer-cropped than most men's—could have played Antigone or Electra or Phaedra or even Medea without a mask.

He couldn't stop looking at her. He stared at her openly, frankly, almost rudely, peering into that wonderful, haunting, tragic, tender face, at those eyes of Nefertiti, his gaze caressing the exquisite sculpture of her cheekbones, the long cool slant of jaw, that warhorse flare of nostrils above a mouth that, even smiling, both was and made a wound—until she blurred sight out of focus by too much nearness, going up on tiptoe, tilting that matchless head sidewise, and drawing every hurt he'd ever known, every disappointment, chagrin, anguish, defeat, shame, loss, along with whatever residual scattered, shattered grains of rationality, of will, he had left by then, out through his suddenly, tenderly assaulted mouth.

"*Muñeca,*" he said. And then they both heard the muted thunder of that heavy motor, the whining screech of the tires, as it tore by the window in a long blued milk flash, bottoming out with a sodden thump at the end of the driveway, slamming onto the pavement, going on.

"Marisol?" he whispered.

"Yes," she said. "In my car, my clothes, with my passport. Her picture's pasted over mine. Since so very few minor functionaries have ever seen me, it doesn't matter. With a ticket, bought by me personally in her handbag. Flight 201, which leaves in half an hour. She'll make it. There's no traffic this late—or rather this early. And no one will dare stop that car. The ticket's one-way—to New York. So now she's safe."

"And you?" he said.

"And I—I've come to take her place. Wasn't that what you wanted, Peter?"

He stared at her. Speaking now, his voice was rough:

"In every way?" he said.

She smiled. The impact of that warm red curl of lip hit him like a fist.

"In every way," she said.

She kept filling his glass. But that excellent smoky-tasting Scotch might as well have been ice water for all the effect it had. The slow, deep sickness crawling in his middle negated it, killed it, effortlessly. So now she tried another tactic. She took direct action. She came and sat down beside him. Took his face between her two hands, her long slim fingers cool and dry and slight and almost untouching along the slant of his jaw. Then she bent and clung her warm, soft, adhesive mouth to his, forcing his lips apart, exploring the limits of his resistance, his will, with that wine-scald, bitter-honey, hot, sweet, melting serpentine thrust and probe.

Angrily, brutally, he put his hand upon her secret body. She moaned a little, went on clinging her mouth to his while her long fingers worked in the close-cropped iron-gray brush of his hair.

He drew back, said:

"Why?"

Her eyes went blacker still.

"There are no *whys*, Peter," she said.

He looked at her. Said it again. "Why?"

She shrugged.

"I have been without a man too long. I am not of the temperament of a nun. You appeal to me. Simple, no?"

"No," Peter said. "*Muñeca*—"

"Yes, Peter?"

"Put an *X* beside the proper choice: Prig. Boor. Brute. Insensitive dolt. Or plain damned fool."

She laughed. A long, ice-bright glissando, with the top notes flattened into a haunting dissonance. A bar from Stravinsk, combined with Bartok, say.

"I should put the *X* beside brute," she said, "but I should be wrong, shouldn't I? Because your mouth contradicts both your jaw and your shoulders, Peter. It is so sensitive that it is practically defenseless. I love your mouth. May I kiss it again?"

"Later," he said. "Now, we talk."

"So?" she said. "What do we talk about, Peter?"

"You. Why you're doing this."

"But I told you. I am a poor starved female who is intrigued by those shoulders. By your look of—of brute male——"

"Infant, I won't buy that one. You'd better set up your stand on another corner."

"Meaning?"

"Meaning you have a motive. And motives transform love into a dirty word."

She laughed again. She was clearly enjoying herself.

"Peter. Dear Peter! For once in a lifetime, the boot's on the other foot. *I* am the hungry aggressor; you, the prospective victim of violation. So, don't call me a whore, not even by implication. Not that the word offends me; it simply doesn't fit. Tonight, *I* am buying. How much do you usually get?"

He grinned at her, said:

"Would you like a *pitillo?*"

"Yes," she said; "why yes, of course."

He took out his cigarette case, opened it. Lit the cigarette for her. Snapped the case shut.

"Don't you smoke?" she said.

"No," he said. "I told you last night I didn't. These are bait."

"Meaning?"

"Meaning, my dear little girl baby playing grown-up sophisticate, that you are the finest actress I ever met."

"Oh, come now, Peter!"

"I'll prove it to you. All night long, you've played a role foreign to every aspect of your training—even, I'll wager, to your true personality. For instance, I've spent a good part of my life in Spain. So I know that Madrileñas of good family never—"

"And who, may I ask, is a Madrileña of good family?"

"You," Peter said.

"Now really, Peter! I am a native Costa Verdian."

"A native Costa Verdian who knew instantly what I meant when I said *pitillo* instead of *cigarrillo*? Who, for our first date, invited me to meet her on the Street of the Theenko de Mayo, instead of the *Seenko* de Mayo? Who always says Theeoodad Villalonga, instead of *Seeoodad* Villalonga?"

"Bravo, Peter! My clever, clever Peter! Yet, you are wrong. I was born here in Ciudad Villalonga, however you pronounce it. I will concede you your point, though. From age eight to eighteen, I was educated in Spain. So?"

"So this. Spanish girls of your social class or Costa Verdians are the same. They don't proposition a man. They'd die first."

"Of—unsatiated lust, Peter—or of shame? Or of a combination of both?"

"That's my question, *niña.* And the answer to it is, in your case, neither. Now, I'll ask you one: What the hell ever gave you the idea that I'd consent to being used?"

Her eyes were very bleak.

"I was too busy looking at your shoulders; the set of your jaw that I didn't study—your mouth, sufficiently, Peter. Nor your eyes—"

"Oh, hell," he said. "This isn't getting either of us anywhere, so . . ." He stood up.

"Don't go, Peter," she said. And then he saw the tears were there, hot and bright and sudden on her face.

"That's better," he said. "That's much better."

And sank down beside her once again.

IX

"Peter."

"*Muñeca?*"

"Tell me about—her."

"Oh, hell! Tell you what about her, Niña?"

"Is she as beautiful as her pictures?"

"More. She is absolutely breathtaking."

"Oh!"

"Why *Oh, Muñeca?*"

"I don't know. No, that isn't true. I'm afraid I do know."

"Then say it."

"Not now. Later, perhaps. Peter—do you—do you love her so very much?"

He turned away. Turned back again.

"You want the truth, Infant?"

"Yes, Peter."

"Very well. The truth is that I don't love her at all."

She looked at him. Her gaze explored his face.

"Are you trying to comfort me now?" she said.

"No. I haven't any comfort to offer anyone, *Muñeca.* All I've got left in me is—pain."

"And some capacity for pity, I hope. Tell me, why don't you love her? You said she is beautiful . . ."

"Beauty is a state of mind. To me, you are the most beautiful thing that ever drew breath. I was meant to love a girl like you. That's part of it. The rest is too long, too dreary, too hurtful. Say that my love was a long day dying. Say it was bled out of me by watching from the sidelines what she let happen to her. What she seized, welcomed, embraced. Say it was killed little by little by—disgust. By utter nausea. That when, finally, pity gave me my heart's desire, I found it too-too hideously scarred by all too many brief encounters; that the image I'd worshiped so long was dead. Leaving—"

"What, Peter?"

"A ghost. A Pavlovian bitch going through the conditioned reflexes of passion. You ring that bell, and my Judy gives. Oh, I am sorry! That was a lousy thing to say."

She bent her head. Averted her face for a long, breath-stopped moment. Then she lifted it, said:

"Isn't the truth nearly always rotten? Peter—"

"Yes, Infant?"

"I'll take you home now. You've won."

"I've won what?"

"Your moral victory. I—I won't risk your contempt. You were right. I was playing a game. A great and terrible game which I have lost now. Totally. In so many, many ways—"

"Meaning?"

"How do I know what I mean? Say that what I'd planned to do was less sacrifice than sin. That the nobility I was giving myself credit for was—all, or nearly all—a lie. A pitiful thing, to lie to oneself, no? But now, I have stopped doing it, I think. . . . Come. When we're outside in the car—"

"What car, Infant?"

"Mine. She has probably sent it back by now. I told her to. When we're outside and in the car, I shall say a thing to you. Will you please not look at me when I say it?"

"Not looking at you, *Muñeca,* calls for will power. But if you insist—"

"I do insist."

"Then, tell me why?"

"Because it will be the truth. For the first time tonight. No! I—I've told you the truth many times tonight, Peter. Without knowing it. Believing that I lied. Now, come."

He got up. Put out his hand to her. She took it. Then, watching her face all the time, he drew her very slowly, quietly, into his arms. Kissed her mouth, gently, tenderly, with what was less passion than an aching sense of loss; less desire than pain.

She drew back, looked at him; and her eyes were crystalline, light-filled.

"Now," she said, "I don't have to wait until we are outside. Now I do not even have to hide my face. I love you, Peter. Do you hear? I love you!"

"And I—" he began, but she put her hand over his mouth.

"Don't say it!" she said. "It is enough that I love you. Because tomorrow, when you learn my name and begin to hate me, you will wish those words unsaid. Oh, Peter, *Cielo,* I–"

The telephone guillotined her voice.

He released her. She went to the instrument, picked it up. Said: "Speak?" Then:

"*Ay, no!* Do not tell me this, Doña Elena! Oh, Holy Mother of God! Oh, Infant Jesus! Oh– What? *Ay, no!* No, Doña Elena–of course I sound strange! I am not Marisol! I am Alicia. Marisol is not here. She is saved! By now she is almost to New York! Yes, Doña Elena–yes, I do know that. But it is not my fault. It is not my fault, I tell you! Yes–yes! He is a monster. Yes, perhaps you are right. Perhaps we are all monsters in my family. Because, even to save your daughter-in-law, this night I would have done a monstrous thing. That God pardon me! *Adios! Adios . . .*"

She turned away from the phone.

"Peter," she said. "He is dead. The comedy would have been futile in any case. Roberto, the husband of Mari, is already dead. I–I should have sinned for nothing, but for you! And I–"

"Alicia," he said. "That's your name, isn't it? What a lovely name!"

But she went on speaking very slowly and clearly in the flat-toned, deceptive calm of pure hysteria.

"And now I am sorry that I did not. That I did not take you into my body, into my life. Make even with you a child in your image. But then, who knows? I might have cursed it with my own–with this filthy blood I bear!"

"Alicia mía," he said. "Alicia what? Tell me the rest of your name."

She shook her head, wildly.

"No, Peter," she said.

"Why not?"

"Because you would hate me. And that would be too much. On top of all the rest, Love, that simply could not be borne!"

"Infant, nothing could make me hate you. Nothing in this world."

Her eyes flickered over his face. He could almost feel her gaze.

"Tell me."

She did not answer.

"Tell me, Alicia."

She turned her face away. The lamp was behind her. He could see that crystalline spill outlining her profile in a wash of light.

She turned back again. Faced him.

"It is Alicia Villalonga," she said.

He stood there, blessing his knees for not having given way beneath him. He took a step forward. Another. Put out his arms to her.

Wonderingly, she came to him. He lifted her chin. Kissed her throat. Her mouth. Kissed away the glitter, the salt, the wet. She clung to him, weeping.

And from every point of the compass, the sirens shrilled.

She looked up at him. But he was not looking at her. Gently he pushed her away. Walked over to the wall above the sofa. Took down quietly and carefully the ancient breastplate of a conquistador. Stood there a long moment, staring at that fine pair of almost invisible wires trailing down the wall. At the round, black, obscene mouth of the microphone.

He heard the pitiful, sobbing intake of her breath. Put up his hand and tore the microphone from the wall.

"*Ay!*" she moaned. "Now I have murdered you, too! Now I have caused your death!"

He grinned at her.

"Let's get out of here, Infant," he said. "Don't think the night air's healthy in this neighborhood. Come on! Let's go!"

"Where?" she whispered. "Where can we, Peter? Where in the world that he–"

"*Muñeca*, when necessary, I can play rough, too. Now come on!"

X

The first thing they saw when they came out of the house was the white convertible. It was parked directly in front of the door. The top was down and music was blaring. Peter leaned over and cut the switch. The music stopped.

The man who lay across the seat sat up, rubbing his eyes. He was dressed in a green-gray uniform with red collar, cuffs, and epaulettes. They could see all that because the sun was already up. On his chest was a badge. It read *Aeropuerto: Estacionamiento—Airport: Parking.*

"*Buenas días,* Guardia," Peter said.

"Ay, Señor! I fell asleep. The little blonde Señorita—how pretty she was!—gave me the keys to this enormous vehicle and told me I must bring it to this address. Whereupon, she said, the Señor would reward me . . ."

"She was right. But why did you not ring the bell?"

"Because," the parking attendant grinned, "the little blondie said I was not to. She said that since it was very late, the Señora and the Señor would prefer not to be disturbed. She said, however, to inform the Señores that she had got safely aboard the four-motor of reaction for New York."

"Your friend," Peter said to Alicia, "is not as innocent as she looks."

"Peter!" Alicia said. "We must go! Jesus y María! How can you be so tranquil?"

"Haven't seen anything very frightening yet. Come on, *Muñeca,* get in." He helped her into the car. Turned to the guard. "Here," he said, "is your reward, friend."

The guard stood there holding the thousand-peso note between his hands. They shook. It was more money than he ever made in a month. Before he could get his mouth closed enough to say thank you, Peter had slipped under the wheel, kicked the Lincoln into life. They moved off, down the street.

"Where are you taking me, Peter?" Alicia said.

"My place," Peter said.

"Your place! Dear God!"

"Yes. The last place they'd think we'd go. There're things there we'll need. A gun. Camera. Rough clothes. A sleeping bag."

"For two?" she said.

"For one. For you. I'll sleep on the ground. I'm used to it."

"But, Peter—"

"'Licia, you think we could get across a frontier?"

"No, Peter."

"Neither do I. So we head for the Sierras. Join the Castristas."

"But the Castristas are dead, Peter."

"One band. There are others. Many others."

"Peter, *Cielo,* we'll never reach the Sierras."

"We'll try," he said, and bent the Lincoln around a tight turn into his street.

"Ohhh!" Alicia said.

"*Muñeca,*" he said, "believe me, that was the sweetest lifetime any guy ever used up in one night."

The armed police were already out of their jeep, walking toward the white convertible with their Bren guns pointing. Another jeep screeched around the corner and pulled up behind him. Every window in the building where he lived was open. All his neighbors were hanging out of them. Except for Concha, la Portera. She was out on the sidewalk. For a scandal like this one, she'd risk getting shot.

They sat there, waiting. Suddenly, Alicia turned to him. She put her arms around his neck, tilted her face sidewise and kissed him. A long time. A very long time.

Concha dropped to her knees. Crossed herself. Started praying. "God forgive her!" she said.

"Get out!" the Captain in charge of the Armed Police barked. He had a Mauser pistol in his hand.

Peter opened the door; Alicia opened the door on her side, too.

"No, Doña Alicia," the Captain said. "Not Your Excellency. Only this lecherous brute of a Yanqui who has abducted the illustrious lady."

"So?" Alicia's voice was clear, ringing, carrying from one side of the street to the other. "That is your story, my Captain? You have been misinformed. I was not abducted. I went with my lover willingly. I declare this before God and in the presence of all these witnesses! And if it is your intention to save my reputation—"

"Alicia!" Peter said.

"I further declare that I spent all night in his arms. Which may be a sin, but is no crime. So now, put up those guns!"

"Doña Alicia," the Captain said, "I am very sorry; but my orders are from your Illustrious Brother, His Supreme Excellency, the Head of the State."

"Who is an assassin, a pervert, and a murderous swine. This, too, I declare before witnesses."

The Captain turned to the Sergeant.

"Arrest the people in those houses. All of them. Shoot any who resist."

"Oh, God!" Alicia said. She bent her head and wept.

"Get out, Gringo!" the Captain said to Peter.

Peter got out of the car. He looked at the Captain. Said:

"Tell me, my Captain, when you go to the *excusado,* do you also jerk out a pistol and order your bowels to move?"

The Captain brought his knee up into the pit of Peter's stomach. Clubbed him with the flat of the pistol as he doubled. Kicked him after he was down. It was a beautiful job. Very expert. The worst of it was to be taken like that, having had Ranger-Commando training himself.

Then Alicia was out of the car and upon the Captain. Ten years under the Carmelite nuns of Madrid disappeared. Eight centuries vanished. Every drop of Castilian blood, leaving only Gypsy, Moorish, Tluscola. It took four policemen to get her off the Captain. What her nails did to his face wasn't pretty.

The policemen came out of the houses, herding the people before them. They did their work with enthusiasm. With zest. They used their rifle butts, rubber truncheons, their feet. One old man fell. They encouraged him in various ways to get up. But not even reddening their bayonet points in his skinny old buttocks was effective. He wanted to cooperate, but he couldn't. The blood that was coming out of his mouth and nose was choking him. They kept on encouraging him until he turned his head to one side and vomited up his breakfast. It was mixed with blood, too, from where they'd kicked him in the stomach.

The Captain nodded. They dragged the old man to the corner. Shot him in the back of the head. Stuffed him head down into a garbage can with his feet sticking out.

After that, they didn't have to encourage the others any more.

They slung Peter into the jeep face down. Five policemen sat on him. From time to time they hit him with the rubber truncheons. A sergeant and three policemen got into the Lincoln with Alicia. The

Marias Negras came, those big black closed trucks that could pack prisoners in on a raid, drive slowly around town in the heat of the day and arrive at the jail with most of the captives dead of asphyxiation, thus saving the Everlasting State much trouble and expense. They loaded the people into them.

Then the procession started off, down the street.

Peter sat there, staring into the spotlight. He had been staring into that spotlight on and off for the better part of three days.

"Now, will you sign it?" the Captain said.

"No," Peter said.

The Captain nodded. The Sergeant hit Peter in the face with his fist.

"Now?" the Captain said.

"Look, my Captain," Peter said. "I have a thing to say."

"Then say it!" the Captain said.

"If I sign this literary masterpiece, confessing to the crimes of abduction and rape, I will have conceded guilt to acts for which the punishment is death even in many civilized countries."

"You mean we are not civilized?" the Sergeant said.

"My dear Sergeant, in a civilized country, you would be in a cage. In the Zoological Gardens. And the children would feed you peanuts."

The Sergeant hit him again. So hard the chair crashed over.

"Pick him up, fool," the Captain said. "You break his skull before he signs this and we'll all be shot!"

The Sergeant picked Peter up, chair and all.

Peter grinned at the Sergeant. His lips were like two blood puddings, but he managed that grin.

"I was mistaken, Sergeant," he said. "You are a very pretty boy. So pretty that I think—"

"What?"

"That Miguelito has enlarged your anal orifice for you."

The Sergeant's fist came back.

"Stop it!" the Captain said. "You were saying, Reynolds?"

"That goon squads are always defeated by a certain lack of logic."

"Meaning?" the Captain said.

"I sign this, and I am executed. I don't sign it and I am assassinated. Either way, I die."

"True, but by signing this you die very quickly upon the *garrote vil;* which merely breaks your neck when the Executioner turns the wheel. Whereas, if you do not sign it, I shudder to contemplate how you will die. In fact, I shall not contemplate it. I should, I fear, lose my lunch."

Peter grinned once more.

"My dear Captain," he said. "There is one other element in this equation—"

"Which is?"

"Marisol Talaveda, wife of Roberto Ruiz Mateos. No. I beg pardon: Widow of Ruiz Mateos."

The Captain stared at him.

"Who is already in New York. With a document signed by me. With certain photographs taken by me. The document is addressed to my government. It says, in brief: No matter how expertly they fake it, even if they blow me up in an airplane with fifty-three others as they did Emilio Duarte y Marin, or in a jeep crash, suspiciously close to the correction centers, as happened to Roberto Ruiz Mateos; no matter what confession I may sign, my death in la Republica de Costa Verde is *ipso facto* murder. Please take the proper steps."

"You lie!" the Captain said.

Peter grinned. It was a very tired grin, but authentic, for all that.

"Of course I lie," he said; "under these circumstances, wouldn't you? But, before we commence the waltz again, dear Captain—are you willing to gamble upon the certitude or lack of it of what I have said?"

The Captain sat there. The sweat popped out on his forehead and ran down the furrows Alicia had clawed in his face.

"Shall I hit him again?" the Sergeant said.

"No—wait. I must think—" the Captain began; but with no interval at all, the door opened, and another policeman stepped through it. This one was a Colonel—a rank existing in the Costa Verdian police because in the Glorious Republic they were a part of the Army, like the SS.

"Release him," the Colonel said.

"What!" the Captain said.

"You heard me! Release him. Don Luis wants to talk to him."

"So!" Peter said. "Even *this* joint is bugged!"

"What do you mean?" the Colonel said.

"Bugged. Implanted with various microphones which enable his superiors to hear every time the Captain scratches his balls. Or breaks wind. Or makes love to the pretty Sergeant," Peter said.

"Begging Colonel Lopez' pardon, the Colonel did appear with much suddenness at a strangely appropriate moment," the Captain said.

"That is none of your business," Colonel Lopez said. "Release him!"

"Don't just stand there!" the Captain said to the Sergeant. "You heard the Colonel! Release him!"

The Sergeant bent and fitted a key into the handcuffs holding Peter's arms to the chair. Then he knelt down and unlocked the cuffs holding Peter's ankles to the legs of the chair.

"Can you stand, Don Pedro?" he said—promoting Peter thus to the aristocracy, giving him that upper-class title of *Don,* seizing with a lackey's instinct upon flattery as a means to defend himself, to defend the absolutely indefensible: the hired thug that he was.

Peter sat there rubbing his wrists, his ankles.

"I think so," he said; "just give me a minute, Sergeant."

The Sergeant stood there. So did Colonel Lopez. The Captain still sat behind the desk.

Peter put his hands down on the arms of the chair and pushed. Came up, very, very slowly. Stood there swaying like an axed oak. Bent forward. Farther. Gathered speed. Measured his length upon the floor.

"Pick him up," Colonel Lopez said.

The Sergeant bent, put his two arms under Peter's armpits. Stopped, seeing how Peter was looking into his eyes.

"Take your hands off me," Peter said. Saying that, his voice wasn't even loud.

"But, Don Pedro," the Sergeant said.

"Take your hands off me," Peter said.

The Sergeant looked at Colonel Lopez.

"Leave him alone," the Colonel said.

Peter put his own two hands down, and pushed. They were swollen to the size of a pair of small hams. They were about that color, too. He went on pushing, while the sweat jetted out of his pores. It plowed furrows through the dirt and blood on his face. And now he was on his hands and knees, shaking his head, so that the drops of sweat and blood made a splatter on the floor. Again the Sergeant bent to help him.

"Don't touch me!" Peter said.

He came upright now. Hung there. Put his two massacred hands down on the Captain's desk, and stared into the Captain's face.

"Look, Reynolds—" the Captain said.

"I know. You were only following orders. So was the Sergeant. I hold you no ill will, either of you."

"That's damned handsome of you, Reynolds," Colonel Lopez said.

"So," Peter went on, "when I, personally, take care of both of you, it will be on behalf of the poor bastard you shot in the back of the head; the women you beat and kicked; the children you slapped around while following orders. Entirely without malice, gentlemen. As a demonstration of what a free man is."

"And what is he, my dear Reynolds?" Colonel Lopez said.

"One who never follows orders. Not from the Devil. Not from God. A guy you've got to kill. Because break him is the one thing you can't do. Well, Colonel, shall we go?"

The Colonel smiled.

"Yes—Don Pedro. The indestructible Don Pedro; we might as well," he said.

Colonel Lopez did not take Peter directly to the office of the Head of the Secret Police. Rather, he took him to his own quarters. There on the bed was a complete change of clothes, from the skin out. When Peter came reeling out of the Colonel's shower, still groggy but beginning to feel remotely human again, he found that the clothes fitted him perfectly. Then he saw why. They were his own. He looked at Colonel Lopez. The Colonel smiled.

"It became obvious to me two hours ago that Doña Alicia was winning her battle with Don Luis. Which didn't surprise me, Mr. Reynolds. Her brother's known weakness for her makes her difficult to oppose. So I had your clothes brought here. I hope you will permit me one indiscreet question—which is not inquisitiveness on my part, but simply a prudent desire to be able to trim my sails closer to the prevailing winds, if such an excessively nautical term may be allowed a soldier . . ."

"All right," Peter said. "What do you want to know?"

"You are not actually married to the lovely motion picture actress, are you?"

"No," Peter said.

"Then my tactics were correct," Colonel Lopez said. "I may even boast a bit of my skill as a strategist. May I offer you a brandy, Mr. Reynolds?"

"Yes," Peter said.

"Carlos Primero? Veterano? 103 Black Label? Or—Remy Martin? Bisquit? Heine? Courvoisier?"

"Carlos Primero," Peter said.

The Colonel poured a snifter for Peter and another for himself. Big snifters.

"What was your strategy, Colonel?" Peter said.

"To dissociate myself from your interrogation from the outset. Those who have offended the future brother-in-law of the Head of the State are going to regret it," Colonel Lopez said.

Peter sipped the brandy. It was a good brandy. The best of all the Spanish brandies. Better even than most of the French.

"You, Colonel, are an optimist," he said.

This office was different from the Captain's. Possibly because it obviously was not designed to be used for the interrogation of prisoners. It was paneled in caoba and teak. The furniture was upholstered in top-grain calfskin. The only picture was a photograph of El Indomitable. Life-size. Looking at it had the usual effect upon Peter. He felt faintly sick. But he went on looking at it. And getting sicker. Because, studied well, with due allowances made for the puffiness of lifelong dissipation; the down sag and twist of utter depravity, Miguel Villalonga did look like Alicia. When it came to the mouth, in him gone past her mouth's warm tenderness into a sado-masochistic leer, the resemblance was remarkable. There was something to be said for that "blood of monsters" remark after all.

The man behind the desk watched what was going on in Peter's face. It seemed to amuse him. He made no effort to interrupt Peter's study of El Lider Glorioso's portrait. He said:

"Why yes, Mr. Reynolds, they are full brother and sister, not half. Carlos Villalonga acknowledged them both. And since I have often had the privilege of swimming with our Great Leader, I can tell you that he, too, has a blue-moon birthmark under his left breast."

"So?" Peter said, and looked at the man behind the desk. He was dressed in civilian clothes, a perfectly cut suit of raw Italian silk. Peter had never seen him before, but he knew who he was: Miguel Villalonga's personal assistant and Head of the Secret Police, known throughout the Republic of Costa Verde as Luis Sinnombre, for the two excellent reasons that, having started life as an orphan and a foundling, Don Luis actually hadn't any name and because, without stretching the point too far, the phrase *sin nombre* could also be held to mean unspeakable, which Don Luis indisputably was.

He smiled at Peter out of what an American lady journalist had been pleased to call his jaguar mouth and turned his—phrase also the lady's—antique Toltec eyes toward one of the heavy, upholstered chairs.

"Have the goodness to sit, Don Pedro," he said. That was another of the Costa Verdian oddities. In no other country in South America are the ancient Spanish forms of courtesy—reserved, of course, to the upper class—*Don* and *Doña* used. But in Costa Verde, they come almost as naturally to the tongue as they do in Spain.

Peter sat.

Luis Sinnombre looked at his face, and made little clacking noises of sympathy.

"I fear some of the minor police have been overzealous again!" he said. "If you will give me a description of the offenders, I shall see that they are severely punished."

"No," Peter said. "I fell down the front stairs while in a state of intoxication."

Don Luis laughed.

"You know who I am?" he said.

"Yes," Peter said. "I once met a friend of yours in New York. Grace Matthews."

"So?" Luis said. "And how is dear Grace?"

"As well as can be expected," Peter said.

"What am I to imply from this curious phrase?" Luis said.

"What you will," Peter said.

"Then I shall permit myself to think that all is not well with the little Grace . . ."

"You have permitted yourself a thought of remarkable accuracy," Peter said.

"Would the great Don Pedro, journalist extraordinary, care to elaborate?"

"I don't suppose it matters. The last time I saw Grace she was in an insane asylum. Her middle-class American background had never ceased to war against the curious and unusual desires that had been instilled in her—where, and by whom, it is superfluous to say. In the war which her prim Midwestern conscience fought against the filthy, nauseous, and even painful sexual perversions she had learned to enjoy, it was her reason that lost. The psychiatrists say her case is as much without hope as its cause was—without name."

Luis Sinnombre threw back his head and laughed aloud.

"What a pleasure it is to hear a Gringo employ the Spanish language with such precision. Even to the play upon words! Don Pedro, tell me: What are your true feelings toward that skinny little she-monkey of an Alicia?"

Peter looked at him. Smiled.

"Whatever they are, they remain my affair," he said.

"And hers?" Luis said.

"Perhaps. Why don't you ask her?"

"I have."

"And what did she say?"

Luis shrugged.

"What one might expect. With her looks—which I, for one, find oddly attractive; exotic, rather—"

"That makes two of us," Peter said.

"Ah, so? Good! I shouldn't want the poor little thing to pine away of unrequited passion. In any event, I think you'll understand that the little Alicia isn't every man's cup of tea, that here tastes are rather conventional, we prefer the Goyaesque female, *Maja Desnuda* type. Or to use a totally intranslatable phrase of ours, *metida en carnes.* Do you know what that means?"

"Stacked," Peter said. "All the usual feminine equipment, but applied with a certain generosity in certain places."

"Right! What an apt translation of it! So, the poor little thing has been lonely. Her position as sister of our Glorious Leader doesn't help, either. Frightens the more desirable types away. Attracts the undesirable—the overly ambitious with no merits of their own. So, naturally, when you were a little kind to her, she rather seized upon that kindness; you, a foreigner, with obviously no desire to inherit the Presidency of Costa Verde—"

"Obviously," Peter said.

"The trouble is, Reynolds, that you've put yourself—and me—in quite a spot. Due to the excellent training that the lovely Miss Lovell has bestowed upon you——"

"I don't know what you're talking about," Peter said.

"Ah? Oh, I see—the Anglo-Saxon conception of gallantry! Touching. Oh, quite. But actually, my dear Reynolds, I was referring to the exquisite knowledge of feminine psychology you displayed, not anything more intimate—"

"I still don't know what you're talking about," Peter said.

"Oh come now, Reynolds! Your performance was masterly! All that mid-Victorian reluctance to letting yourself be seduced, on the score of abstract morality, or again, on the score of your loyalty to dear Judith, and lastly, out of your doubt as to the lady's sincerity—so put that those doubts became a sort of modesty on your part on the one hand and a delicately implied exhibition of respect for the lady herself on the other. Oh, yes, masterly is the word!"

"Thanks," Peter said.

"Took me all night to decide what your game was. Incidentally, your refusal to mention her name added quite a filip to the performance. Had I known it was merely our Alicia, your resistance would have been much less impressive. Poor 'Licia easy to resist, isn't she?"

"I may have been more tempted at another time in my life," Peter said, "but, offhand, I can't remember when."

"Now, Reynolds!"

"I mean it," Peter said.

"All right. Then let me put it to you fairly: What, actually, is your feeling toward Doña Alicia Villalonga, Widow of Duarte y Marin?"

Peter looked at Luis. Studied him.

"I love the ground she walks on," he said.

He heard the door crash open. Alicia came through it in one long blinding rush. Hurled herself upon him, curled with boneless grace into his lap, her arms around his neck almost strangling him. Then she turned him loose. Put up her slim hand and ran her fingertips over his facc, his mouth, so lightly that almost they didn't touch. Even so, they made him wince.

"*Ay!*" she wailed. "*Ay yai!* How they have hurt you!" She whirled, would have leaped across the desk if Peter had not held her. "Beast!" she screamed. "Animal! Pig! Dog and son of dogs! Ay, I will kill you, Luis! I will! I will! I will!"

"Infant," Peter said, "gentle down, will you?"

She turned and started kissing all the bruises and the cuts and the cigarette burns upon his face.

"*Muñeca,*" Peter said, "even that hurts."

"Oh!" she said, and buried her small face in the hollow of his throat.

"My dear Reynolds," Luis Sinnombre said, "either you are the cleverest man alive, or the luckiest. Pcrhaps even both. They go together, don't they?"

"You mean?" Peter said.

"That you, of course, did not know or cven guess that I had the little Alicia concealed behind that door?"

"Of course not," Peter said.

Luis sighed.

"My intention was good, Reynolds. I wanted to demonstrate to my beloved little sister—"

"My God!" Peter said. "You mean that you—?"

"That I am her brother, too? I think so. But we do not know, really. The ever-generous Isabel brought me up. At various times, in various moods, and in various stages of drunkenness, she tells various tales. Usually I am the son of a dear, dear friend of hers, who died. A fellow worker—"

"You mean a fellow whore?" Peter said.

"That sort of bravado is cheap, Reynolds. Besides, the truth does not insult me. My mother—if I had a mother—was either a street whore or the great Isabel herself. Which is a difference in class, merely. At times, dear Isabel—who is much woman, Reynolds, and for whom my admiration and my gratitude are genuine—says I am hers, and that my father was an exiled Mexican, or Colombian, or Chilean, or Peruvian—or any other republic that comes to her mind—statesman. At other times, she declares that my mother's name was Teresa, or Pilar, or Rosario, or Mercedes, or Maruja—and that my father was a billy-goat. Or a monkey. Or a big black buck nigger they imported from Cuba because of his sexual prowess. Which didn't—and doesn't—matter. What does matter is whoever my parents were, they seem to have endowed me with brains. Which inheritance—my only one, I assure you—Isabel furthered by sending me to one of your greatest, most liberal universities. . . . Oh, no; don't ask me which one! The authorities at my Alma Mater have been trying to hide the fact that my name rightfully belongs on their roster of graduates—and with honors, my dear Reynolds—ever since. An amusing point is that she used money she had blackmailed out of Carlos Villalonga for Miguel's education to send me along, as well, with the additional irony that I graduated with honors while Miguel was expelled for failing his classes and general roistering. But where were we before we entered into this detour through my personal history?"

"You were attempting to demonstrate to Alicia—"

"That, despite all my warnings, and her own exemplary behavior up until now, she has at last allowed herself to fall into the hands of a mercenary adventurer. But you have endured three really rough days and persist in saying that you love her. Almost you convince me that you actually are sincere."

"Frankly, Don Luis," Peter said, "I don't give a damn if you're convinced or not. So long as Alicia is. Are you, Nena?"

"Peter—" Alicia whispered.

"Yes, Nena?" He used that word because it suited her. Both it and *niña* mean little girl, except that *nena* is generally applied to littler girls, and is tenderer somehow.

"How can you love me? I am ugly—"

"Lord!" Peter said.

"And depraved and of a family of utter vileness. You are kind, I know; but this is too difficult to believe . . ."

"My dear Alicia," Luis laughed, "may I suggest that the smell of money surrounding you is sufficient to perfume away the odor of your family, even if you are generous enough to include me?"

"And may I suggest that you take all that money and shove it?" Peter said.

"Oh, come now, my dear Reynolds, everyone knows how you Yanquis are!"

"And everyone forgets that we are the people who have given away more money than any other in the history of the world. Say we did it selfishly. All right. But who else ever has, even selfishly? Skip that. It leads to politics and politics give me a pain in the gut. Put it this way: If it were possible for me to marry Alicia, I should insist that she use every *centavo* of her fortune to build an orphanage exclusively for the children of the people murdered by you and Miguelito. That she take off her clothes and burn them. That she come to me absolutely unadorned, and uncontaminated by anything that that money, which stinks of blood and putrefaction and has the echoes of screaming about it, has ever bought. *Only* on those conditions would I accept her as my wife. Point number two: I earn between twenty-five and forty thousand dollars a year, which works out to enough millions of your pesos to make the question of fortune-hunting on my part academic. Point number three: Miguelito would have a hemorrhage of fecal matter, faint, and fall into it, before he would permit his sister to marry a Gringo. Am I not right?"

"Perfectly. Except that Miguel knows absolutely nothing about this —so far."

"Ha!" Peter said. "You mean he missed the chance to listen in on a bugged passage at arms?"

"I mean that you, my dear Peter, would not be alive now if he had heard that tape."

"You heard it, didn't you?"

"Oh yes. And found it vastly entertaining. I gather you wonder why *I* have not had you killed? My dear Peter, Miguel and I don't see eye to eye about a great many things."

"All right. But just tell me: Why didn't he listen to it? I thought that was one of his favorite amusements."

"It is. Only, last night, his leg—you know about the attempt on his life some years ago?"

"Yes. You flew him to the Mayo Brothers' Clinic. Saved his life. Touching example of fraternal devotion. He came back and built Our Lady of the Remedies Hospital. Fine job. One of the best hospitals I've ever seen."

"Thank you. The point is, my dear Peter, that the doctors at the Mayo Clinic gave him three choices: a paralyzed, dragging leg; no leg at all, except, of course, one of the marvels of your Yanqui ingenuity, an articulated metal limb; and third, a leg which functions almost normally, but at the cost of a slow dull pain from the damaged nerves all the time, and even, some of the time, an absolutely insupportable ache. He chose number three, which was courageous but hardly intelligent, no? It accounts, I think, for the badness of his temper. Additionally, his violence and his excesses have weakened his heart. Doctor Gomez insists that he spend much of the time resting—"

"I know," Peter said. "Vince told me. An injection that puts him out for twelve hours."

"Which he hates and refuses to accept most of the time. But that night, the pain was so great, that he gave up even the keenly anticipated pleasure of determining whether even so powerful a chap as you are would be able to thaw out dear Marisol's deep-frozen little tail. Which is why I say your luck is astonishing, Reynolds. He was asleep during the festivities. My second act, after listening to that touching curtain speech of Alicia's—noble of you, my dearest; but oh so foolish, no?—was to give Miguel another shot of the sedative, after, of course, sending the police to apprehend so dangerously convincing a lover. Incidentally, that medicine is another of Padre Pío's discoveries; he has compiled a whole new *Materia Medica* from the pharmacopoeia of the Tluscolan witch doctors."

"The little Padre cured me of a tropical fever in one day," Peter said, "but I still think he did it with prayer."

"Ah, so? Charming thought. Look, Peter, I find myself forced to trust you. What's more, inclined to do so. You are a sentimentalist. I even believe you mean it when you say you have no interest in Alicia's money; the more so since my investigations show that the Reynolds of Charlestown, Massachusetts, are not exactly poor."

"My father's dough. Belongs to him while he lives. And when he dies, he can do what he pleases with it. Bury it with him, if he wants to. I make my own."

"Sturdy Yanqui independence! But your father *is* a wealthy man?"

"You could call him that. The point's irrelevant. I love Alicia. I should love her equally if she hadn't a centavo. I categorically refuse to accept even a real, a sol, or if you have any smaller coins, one of them of that money. I'm sentimentalist enough to believe it would damn us forever. On the other hand, if she too seriously cares whether I have money or not, she can go to hell. As much as I love her, she can. Do you, Nena?"

"Peter! You know I would scrub floors for you. Or"—and a flash of pure mischief lighted her eyes—"sell myself to other men and bring my earnings home to you. Would you like that, Cielo?"

"I'd break every bone in your lovely little body," Peter said. "Get on with it, Luis."

"All right. There is no point in my trying to convince you of my great love for the sovereign people. I sprang from their loins, as it were; I had to endure their manners, and their stench, far too long. Until Isabel rescued me. There's nothing ennobling about poverty, Reynolds—quite the contrary. The people are, you know, if you're not totally a fool, a disgusting conglomeration of exceedingly filthy and stupid animals. But, despite that, I fear me that Miguel's oppressively totalitarian state is an anachronism which cannot long survive."

"You've got something there," Peter said.

"So now, you, my dear Peter, offer me an out. I present Miguel, when he returns, with a *fait accompli.*"

"Returns?" Alicia said. "Returns from *where,* Luis?"

"The high seas, my dear Alicia. You know he has been threatening to leave Costa Verde to go to hell and go fishing as he does every year about this time. So when he awakens aboard *la Flor del Mar,* he will be told that I personally brought him aboard, which is true; and that he, in a moment of lucidity between profound dreams, ordered me to do so, which is not."

"Oh!" Alicia said.

"The point is, he is unlikely to return until the fishing palls upon him. Which depends upon how the marlin and the sailfish are running. If his luck—and ours—is good, he'll stay away for two months, maybe three. Time enough for me to get you two safely entangled in the bonds of holy wedlock."

"Good God!" Peter said.

"You *are* of our faith, aren't you, Reynolds?"

"Yes," Peter said.

"Simplifies matters. Wait—I'll explain. The only way for the Republic to survive is to make an opening toward the Liberal Center, if not toward the Left. We push the happy couple forward. Under the liberalizing influence of our new Gringo brother-in-law, we slacken off a bit; let the canalla breathe—if they haven't forgotten how. Peter and Alicia —the popular young lovebirds: opening orphanages, dedicating schools, visiting the peasants with gifts of fertilizer and a tractor or two, say. Having babies. Oh, swarms of babies! Starting housing projects—low-rent, of course. The new public image, until the *muchedumbre,* which is as dumb as it is much, forgets. Neat, don't you think?"

"And," Peter said, "closing the Centers of Moral Correction and Social Re-education? Taking away all arms except maybe their truncheons from your goons?"

"Hard bargainer, aren't you, Reynolds? If you insist, even that."

"Good. But I don't insist. I can't."

"Meaning?"

"That I cannot marry Alicia."

Alicia sat up suddenly, staring into his face.

"Sorry, Nena; but it has to be said. I can't marry you. As much as I'd love to, I can't."

Her mouth was visibly trembling now.

"Because of—*her*?" she said.

"No. Not because of her."

"Then why, Peter?"

"Because on June Second, 1954, I married a Miss Constance Buckleigh in Our Lady of Mercy Church in Boston, Massachusetts. That the lady later left my bed and board in the company of an advertising executive who could have bought and sold me three times over even with my father's money thrown in, and who had, additionally, a position that allowed him to come home every night, which was the chief objection that Connie had to me, has nothing to do with it. Nor that she later obtained a Nevada divorce and, at least as far as civil law is concerned, legalized her position. Nor that she has since presented him with three splendid children. Canon law is explicit: So long as Miss Buckleigh lives, she remains my wife. And in la Republica de Costa Verde, there isn't any other kind."

Luis Sinnombre sat there. Then, very slowly, he smiled.

"A formidable obstacle, I'll admit. But not insurmountable," he said.

"And how do you propose to surmount it?" Peter said.

"Leave that to me, Peter! Alicia, you may take him home, if you like. Even bundle with him a bit more, if either of you feels up to it. Betimes, I shall pay a call on the Archbishop in the Ecclesiastical Palace. Clever old boy, the Archbishop. Expert on Canon law. Might come up with a fancy new grounds for an annulment, say—"

"Oh!" Alicia said.

"Now, Dearest, you run along. Take your new fiancé home. Your Perhaps Brother will fix things up so you can marry him. But please, Dear, one thing—"

"Yes, Luis?" Alicia said.

"Try not to get too obviously pregnant too far ahead of time. You know how archbishops are. Stubborn old chaps. Always dreaming of picking up that final Cape and Mitre in Eternal Rome—"

"Good God!" Peter said.

"Don't worry about it, Reynolds. By the way, Alicia, I've already ordered all those people released, just as you requested. Except, of course, the old boy who tripped and fell into the garbage can. The garbage truck took him away by mistake. We'll compensate his family, of course. . . . What are you waiting for? Miguel is completely out of the way, unreachable except by radio; which is to say totally unreachable in this affair, since all telecommunications are controlled by the police, which I head. So run along. Divert yourselves hugely, with the proper precautions, of course. However little you may be disposed to trust me, you can trust my desire to stay alive and in power. So we have a community of interests: you want your sex bouts legalized and sanctified before God and man. So do I. What does it matter that our motivations differ? You heard me, go ahead!"

Peter stared at him.

"And, Amigo Peter—the Captain who conducted that inquisition has as of now been transferred to a highly unpleasant post in the South. The Sergeant has been broken to the ranks. They, believe me, exceeded their instructions by far—"

Peter went on looking at him. Then: "Thanks for nothing, Luis," he said.

Riding in the big car toward his flat, Peter didn't say anything. Alicia didn't either. From time to time he looked at her profile, studying it, trying to capture its unique quality. He supposed that, if you wanted to be strict about it, you could call her a homely little soul. Only he couldn't be strict about it; he was past being strict about anything so far as she was concerned. But one thing was beyond argument: he had seen men go to the firing squad with more cheerful expressions on their faces than the one on Alicia's now. He went on watching her. She went on driving. Pulled the big Lincoln up before his door. Said:

"Good-by, Peter." She said it in Spanish, using *Adios!*—"To God."

"You mean 'till later on,' don't you? Or 'till tomorrow'?" Peter said. Those forms—*hasta luego* and *hasta mañana*—are a lot less final than *Adios!*, especially the way Alicia said it then. He didn't like the way she said it at all.

"No, I mean good-by, Peter," Alicia said.

"*Muñeca*—" Peter said.

"Good-by, Peter. *Adios!* Because there are some things I know. You see, they forced Emilio to marry me, too. Oh, not what you're thinking! I came virgin to my marriage bed. They have other means of persuasion, and the situation where I could justify to myself my she-goat's blood didn't exist then. I couldn't delude myself into thinking I was trying to save a life."

"Angel," Peter said.

"Angel! Don't blaspheme, Peter! Call me what I am, my mother's daughter. Your little bitch. In any case, Luis has spoiled it now. Again. I won't watch your eyes grow weary, trying to avoid mine, as Emilio's did. I won't go through that again, Peter. I—I used to try to invent—stratagems to—to force him to lie with me—to get me with the child I wanted with all my heart. He was all man, Peter. During our three years of marriage, he worked his way through the entire chorus line of el Teatro de la Comedia! But, when he started in on La Luna Azul, I—"

"You what, *Muñeca*?"

"Screamed and cursed him and threw one of my Latin women's vile temper tantrums. He sat there looking at me until I had no more breath left, or any tears. Then he said, he said—Ohhh, Peter!"

"He didn't say 'Ohhh, Peter!' I'm sure of that, Nena."

"No. He said very quietly: 'My dear Alicia, I gave you my name, which was to sully it enough. I have no intention of begetting monsters.' Then he walked out and left me there."

"He was a fool!" Peter said.

"No, *Cielo*, it is you who are a fool. If you had any sense, you'd leave me, too."

"Alicia, if you don't cut this out, I'm going to do more than that. I'm going to beat the very hell out of you!"

"Go ahead," she said; "I wouldn't care."

"Baby—" Peter said.

"No, Peter. Luis has spoiled it now. You were—beginning to love me a little, weren't you? Lies! Deception! Tricks! Always manipulating everyone. Or murdering those whom he cannot manipulate. So hear me well, Peter!"

"Yes, Alicia?"

"I will not marry you. No matter what Luis forces that poor old frightened man in the Ecclesiastical Palace to do or say. Not because I do not love you; but because I do—"

"Nena, Bébé, Infant!"

"You won't be forced to take me, Love. You won't be tied to this—

this outcast and garbage of the world! This ugly little witch and daughter of witches! No! No! I can't, I won't, I won't!"

"All right. Romance is all over. Thanks for a lovely evening, Nena. And a few more scars."

"Ohhh, Peter!" she wailed.

"Putting aside for the moment my own feeling about the matter, answer me one thing, Angel."

"Don't call me Angel! What thing, Love?"

"Now that our wedding has become an affair of state to Luis, how do you propose to stop him, 'Licia?"

She looked at him.

"Do you not have another razor you can lend me?" she said.

"Alicia!"

"No—that's her style—isn't it? So cheap, somehow. So mundane. No, Peter, *Cielo*, I—I shall enter the Carmelites. Peaceful, what? No fear. No hate. No—no *maldito* men!"

He grinned at her, suddenly.

"Nena," he said, "I wasn't going to, but now I think I'd better invite you to come upstairs with me."

She shook her head so violently that the tears jetted from her eyes in a semicircular spray.

"Upstairs," she whispered, "where *she* has been all these weeks? In *her* bed, Peter? I may be a Villalonga. I do have Isabela Cienmil's blood in my veins. But this species of vile vileness I am not, Love. Oh, Peter, can't you see there's no hope for us? That it's wrong? All wrong? *Ay, Jesus y Maria!* I—"

But he took her small face between his two hands and kissed her mouth.

She tore her face away from his. Said:

"And when she comes out of the hospital, what will you do, Peter? Tell me! What will you?"

"*Muñeca*, we'll cross that bridge when we get to it."

"No, *Cielo*. We have crossed it already. Now get out! Leave me in peace! *Leeeeve meeee!*"

But he put his arms around her and drew her to him. His mouth hurt like hell, but he went on kissing her until she curled up against him, clinging to him and crying, and Concha, la Portera, came out of the house and stood beside the car.

"Doña Alicia," Concha said.

Alicia straightened up, blinking at Concha out of those enormous doe's eyes.

"*Sí,* Señora?" she said.

Concha dropped to her knees before the car. Her fat face was flooded. She knelt there blubbering like a bleached whale. Then she put out her two fat red paws in a gesture that must have cost her more than charging into enemy fire costs a soldier. She grabbed Alicia's little hand and covered it with great slobbering kisses.

Alicia looked from Concha to Peter, her warm mouth making a jungle orchid, blooming into a perfectly rounded *Oh!* of pure astonishment.

"But, Señora, I do not comprehend—what is it that passes with you?"

"*Ay* Doña Alicia!" Concha sobbed. "You are good! You are so good!" And Peter could measure the degree of Concha's emotion by the very forms of her speech. For not only did la Portera forget that a woman of the humble classes should have addressed so distinguished a lady in the third person, saying "The Lady is so good!" but she swept past the second degree of politeness and instead of calling Alicia *Usted,* just barely acceptable in a female concierge, called her *tú.*

Peter, who had summered and wintered with the Hispano-American aristocracy, held his breath. But Concha rushed heedlessly on: "You are so good, Doña Alicia! All the world loves you, for you have saved us all!"

Then Peter saw what there was in Alicia's face now: radiance. She put out her other hand and tugged Concha upward. La Portera lumbered to her feet. Then Doña Alicia Villalonga, Widow of Duarte y Marin, did a thing that had never been seen in Costa Verde from the day when, according to a completely lying tradition, Cristóbal Colón came ashore and unfurled the banner of Their Catholic Majesties before a group of stark-naked fisher Indians: she leaned out of the car and planted two soft, warm kisses on Concha's fat cheeks.

Concha clapped her two hands to her face. Swayed there. Then she whirled and ran back into the house. From every window on that street, the great shouted *Vivas!* roared.

"Long live Doña Alicia!" the people cried. "Long live our good, kind lady! Long live the Patroness of the Poor! Long live our Protectress!"

And now truly that warm, mobile, wonderful face was dissolved, was melted. She hid her face against Peter's chest, and lay there, crying, while the people made the heavens ring.

"Nena, I don't know whether you know it, but you've just won the revolution," Peter said.

XI

"Peter!" Judith said. "Your face!"

"Lord, Judy, I forgot," Peter said. "Should have left it home, shouldn't I?"

"I knew Vince was lying. I knew it. He swore that a big story had broken, down in the South, somewhere, and you— Peter, tell me: What was her name?"

"What was whose name, Judy?"

"The dear little creature you got your countenance pushed into that meat grinder over."

"That, baby, is a long story."

"But not a true one. Peter, if you're going to lie to me, skip it. I knew damn well that if they kept me in here another week, you'd start in to investigate the local talent! But, Lover Boy, couldn't you have picked a single gal? From the way you look, this one must be married to King Kong!"

"Judy, baby, about dames, down here they shoot a guy. This lesson was purely political. I got caught accidental, like in a dragnet-type raid. And Miguelito's Boy Scouts thought I was refusing to answer questions I didn't know the answers to. Hell, I didn't even understand the questions. This morning they released me with apologies. Risks of the profession, girl friend."

"Peter—how much of the truth are you telling me now?"

"About twenty-five per cent, Judy. The other seventy-five, I'd just as soon you didn't know in case they start getting inquisitive again. When it comes to politics, all that Latin gallantry sort of takes a holiday. Whatever else they may do to this pan of mine falls under the heading of gilding the lily by now; but nobody ever taught these goons they shouldn't play rough with girls—"

"Peter, is it true that they automatically rape all the women prisoners?"

"So I've heard."

"Oh, good! Look, Lover, if you don't get me out of this den of chastity right away, I'm going to commit a political offense—like screaming 'Down with The Leader!' at the top of my lungs."

"Judy, for God's sake!"

"Oh, Peter—just think! All those big, strong policemen!"

"Sorry, baby; but my sense of humor's way off today. I grant you that, for a healthy girl, being raped isn't all that godawful. But these types are graduate sadists. I don't think even your definition of fun and games includes having your nipples burned with cigarette butts, or your vaginal tract packed with broken glass."

"Judas!" Judith said.

"I've been trying to get into one of those correction centers to try to see if I couldn't sneak a few shots so that later on I'll be able to prove what goes on down here. But so far, no good. Latin America is one of the world's worst beats, Judy. Down here the choice isn't between good and bad, but between bad and worse. No, between worse and worst. You have a perfect demonstration of Malthusian principles, under a religious hierarchy which makes any effective birth control program impossible. You have a wealthy upper class—in Costa Verde, twenty-five families own seventy-two per cent of the arable land—whose response not only to the legitimate demands of the lower orders, but also to any slight amelioration whatsoever, is, 'Screw you, Jack!' Who, while keeping not two, but three sets of books, and managing to escape paying taxes entirely, swear at us because our contribution to their welfare isn't greater. You have no effective middle class. You have not rich and poor, but plutocrats and the starving. And, on the other hand, you have the Commies. Who promise the moon and the stars, and deliver rocket bases and the rationing of even those miserable foodstuffs formerly available to the hungry. Who, after liquidating the poor, goddam noble, deluded kids they've sucked in by their propaganda and used as cannon fodder to gain their ends—like Juan and Pepe and Federico, and even that poor bastard Jacinto—will substitute for the crude job those gorillas did to my face a subtler kind of torture, one that gets down to where a man lives, to the ultimate question: Just what the hell am I?"

"Peter," Judith whispered, "those coppers have discouraged you, haven't they?"

"Not just them. Human nature discourages me. Let's change this subject. When does Vince say I can bail you out of this Saintly Atmosphere?"

"Friday. Day after tomorrow. Peter, darling, are you in good shape?"

"Middling, Judy. Middling. Miguelito's playmates don't leave a guy feeling like the power and the glory."

"Peter—"

"Yes, Judy?"

"Kiss me. Then go home. Go to bed. Alone. Get some sleep. Eat lots and lots—of eggs. It's eggs that little boys are supposed to eat to build them up, isn't it? And oysters. Eat two dozen oysters. Because, Lover Boy, you're going to need your strength!"

When he came out of the hospital, he found Tim O'Rourke waiting for him, sitting behind a big black cigar in a rented car.

"Peter," he said, "how much of it is true, and even if it is, what sense does it make?"

Peter looked at him.

"None—to both questions," he said.

"I was going home this Monday. And then this breaks. Carloads of uniformed throwbacks arresting a whole streetful of people. And why? Our *Pe-tah's* been busy again! *Hayzus,* as they say down here, why don't you keep still, boy?"

"I do," Peter said. "Just like a mouse."

"Yeah. I'll bet. The kind of mouse that has dames screaming and pulling up their skirts. And from the looks of what's left of your manly beauty, the cats down here play awful rough when they catch friend mouse up to his mousie tricks. Look, Pete, I don't know how, or why, or with what you do it but tell me: is it true?"

"Is what true, Tim?"

"*His* sister! *His!* Cute little monkey-faced babe with lips that would keep her out of the University of Alabama. That one? True or false?"

"Tim," Peter said, "you'd better change your brand."

"Don't know why; but she sends me, brother! Just like Judy does. No, more. Is it that great minds move in similar channels?"

"Could be," Peter said.

"Then you admit—"

"I admit nothing, friend."

"You wouldn't!" Tim grinned. "But, Peter the Mouse—or rather Brother Rat—just look what's coming around the corner!"

Peter looked in the rear-view mirror of the rented Ford. The white Lincoln pulled up behind him, so close that its front bumpers almost touched the Ford's rear ones.

"Oh, hell!" Peter said.

Alicia got out of the Lincoln. She had on a white sharkskin suit. The suit was another little marvel. With her in it, it made two marvels. At least two. Maybe more. Her heels clicked decisively on the sidewalk as she headed toward the door of the building in which Peter lived.

Tim put his head out of the window.

"Señora de Duarte!" he called.

Alicia stopped; turned.

"Pardon me, Señora," Tim said, in his quite good Spanish, "but if you're looking for Peter the Rat, here he is!"

Alicia came toward the Ford. Tim got out of it at once. So did Peter. He came around the other side to meet Alicia. Put out his hand to her; but she didn't take it. She went up on tiptoe and kissed his mouth.

"Oh, Peter, *Cielo,* I have been so worried," she said. "I have been calling you all day—"

"Alicia," Peter said, "may I present a friend?"

"But of course!" Alicia said; then, seeing Tim's red, Irish face, she switched at once into English, which she spoke in musical little trills and bursts, and—probably because she had learned it in Madrid—with a marked British accent. "I am so sorry, Señor. It was not my intention to be rude; but I was so preoccupied with the *asunto*—affaire, no?—of Peter, that . . ."

"I noticed that, Señora," Tim said.

"This," Peter said, "is the Señor Timothy O'Rourke. He is Irish-American. A reporter, like me. But since he now has first cousins in the White House, he's got all the advantages."

Alicia's dark eyes widened.

"Oh, then he can help us, *Cielo!*" she said. "If he is a first cousin of your President, why—"

"Niña," Peter said, "I made a joke. A bad joke."

"Not so fast, *Cielo!*" Tim said. "Oh, brother, just wait till I tell the types on your night desk that the babes down here call you Heaven. Old Heavenly Pete!"

"You want me to laugh? Comic? Ha! I just laughed. You got something to say, say it."

"Seriously, Pete, maybe I *could* help you lovebirds. I'm going home next week. I could get a message out, if that's what you need."

Alicia looked at Peter.

"Yes," Peter said. "One can trust Tim."

"Then, *Cielo,* may we not ascend to your flat, all three of us, where we can talk?"

Peter stopped.

"I think they may have hung a few microphones in strategic locations by now," he said.

"No," Alicia said. "Colonel Lopez gave the order that you were to be removed from close surveillance. And I have an enormous desire to see your flat."

Tim looked at them both.

"Doña Alicia," he said, "are you sure you're being wise? In any country such as this, the arming of scandals necessitates very little—"

Alicia smiled. But that smile was the saddest thing in the whole world.

"The scandal has already been armed, Don Timoteo. And of reputation, I no longer have any left to lose. So let us go very quickly up the stairs so that *quiza* we may prevent crime from being added to what so far is merely the minor sin of evil thoughts."

"Crime?" Peter said.

"Yes, Love. Now come that we may speak of it."

"Wait a minute," Tim said. "Doña Alicia, don't you think it would be wise to put up the top of your car, and lock it, before we go? Why, you've even left the keys in the ignition—"

"I always do leave them thus," Alicia said, "in order to evade having to search for them amid ten thousand other useless things in my handbag. There is absolutely no danger, Don Timoteo; this car is too well known. Who would be so ungrateful as to steal the automobile of the sister of the Ever Generous Benefactor of the People of Costa Verde? Besides, in this *barrio* at least, the people love me. Don't they, *Cielo?*"

"Yes," Peter said.

He opened the door for them. Alicia walked straight across the room and picked up Judith's photograph from where it stood on Peter's desk. She stood there studying it, a long, long time. When she put it down and turned to him, Peter could see the tears in her eyes.

"Now, Nena—" he said.

"It is all right," she said; "a weakness, no? I should not have come up here. I have no right even to—to this stupid jealousy I cannot dominate. Don Timoteo, the women of your country are not so foolish, are they? No matter. I love Peter. I have no shame of that. But to share him with this faded *viciosa* upon terms of equality—one concubine is as good as another, no?—that is too shameful. And yet—and yet I am here to prevent a thing from happening that would make it possible for him to marry me and take away my shame."

"Would your brother consent to such a marriage, Doña Alicia?" Tim said.

"No. But Luis thinks to arrange it before he returns. And afterwards to convince Miguel—wrongly I am sure—that through Peter he can influence the attitude of your country toward ours—"

"Now I get it!" Tim said. "Your Old Man still pulls a lot of weight around the State Department, doesn't he?"

"I don't think you do. It's a very complicated oversimplification," Peter said.

"Peter," Alicia said, "do you know the address of your—your wife?"

"Oh, brother!" Tim said. "So you've been holding out on me again, Peter Pan! Not only has the guy got a harem down here, but—"

"If you mean my ex-wife, yes," Peter said.

"A wife can never be *ex*, Peter. Or very rarely. Then there are special circumstances which permit an annulment. Beyond that, no. That she left you, played the whore, is a matter for her conscience; but it does not dissolve your bonds, as you know very well. There is only one way that you can be free of her. The way with which Luis is occupying himself now."

"Good God!" Peter said.

"Amen!" Alicia said, and crossed herself. "Yes, Peter, Love; Luis has thought of that. You see, the Archbishop has proved difficult. He is an old man and tired and afraid. But now he has Padre Pío once more at his side, which makes a difference. Because of that, Luis has had to forego his dream that the Archbishop would grant you an annulment of your marriage. And you—"

"And I?" Peter said.

"Must give to Don Timoteo here, the address of your faithless wife. So that he may warn her, and him who calls himself her husband, and also the police of the state or province wherein she resides. Or else—"

"Nena, don't you think you exaggerate a bit?"

"Do you remember the case of Professor Hernandez?"

"Good God!" Peter said again.

"Hernandez? Hernandez?" Tim said. "Rings a bell. Saay! Wasn't he a refugee from down here, who was teaching Spanish at City College, and sort of wound up missing?"

"He," Alicia said, "was flown to Ciudad Villalonga in an airplane. After he had been taken by two thugs in the very mouth of the Metro —the Subway—on one of your busiest streets. He was drugged, brought to Flushing Meadows Airport in an ambulance. The pilot of the aircraft filed a false flight plan, telling the authorities that he was taking the sick man to a clinic in Massachusetts. Instead, he flew south. Brought the poor man here. It is said that Dr. Hernandez could be heard—screaming—for days—before they grew tired and let him die."

"Who told you that?" Peter said.

"My mother. She witnessed it." She opened her bag. Took out a pack of cigarettes—Players. Peter lit her cigarette for her.

"And where is your mother now?" he said.

"She is a prisoner. In a luxurious flat she is not allowed to leave—since this of her drunkenness and vile behavior at your embassy. Please, Peter, give him the address."

"All right," Peter said. He took out his pen. Tore a sheet of paper from his address book, and wrote on it. Passed the paper to Tim.

Tim looked at it. Folded it; put it in his pocket. Turned to Alicia. "You don't even know her," he said; "and yet—"

"I know Peter," Alicia said; "which is enough."

"Meaning?" Peter said.

"That I will not have you look at me with accusing eyes. Or see in them speculation over what sort of monsters I may bear you, fruits of a marriage based upon a murdered woman's blood. No, Peter—all that is possible between us is sin. Sin I shall one day have strength enough, grace enough to give up. But now—"

"Now?" Peter said.

She turned her face toward Tim.

"Don Timoteo," she said, "would you think too ill of me if I asked you to leave us here—alone?"

"Not at all," Tim said, and stood up.

"Tim, boy," Peter said. "I——"

"You've got it rough, son," Tim said. "Don't worry; I'll do what I can—"

She lay there on the sofa in his arms. Put up her hands and touched his battered face. Then her little head lifted. Her nostrils flared. She got up. Walked through the door into his bedroom. Stood there staring at all those flasks and jars. Pulled open a drawer. Lifted a handful of gossamer. Of silken cobwebs and mists and air. Let them fall. Turned to the closet. Jerked wide the door. The rich, insidious odor of Judith's special *Peut'être* perfume came out from the rows and rows of dresses hanging there.

"Ohhhh!" Alicia said, and bolted for the door. In it, she stopped, without even turning her face:

"Peter—"

"*Muñeca?*"

"Come with me?"

"Where?"

"Oh, I do not know. To the forest, to the swamps. To a wild place where you can take me like an animal upon the ground. But not—not here! Not in this little flat that smells of her. Not where her presence moves between us like a ghost. Oh, Peter, *amor, Cielo,* I——"

Peter got up. Took her arm. Quietly they went back down the stairs.

From where they were now, they could see the volcano. It jetted fire. The clouds above it were angry, red.

"The old gods," Alicia said. "There are times, Peter, that I believe in them."

"Do you?" Peter said.

"*Sí.* It is sinful of me, I know. But I have too much Tluscola in my veins. Zopo is amused. Now he is chuckling to himself at the sins and follies of men. One night he will laugh. And his laughter will destroy the world."

Peter looked up at the volcano.

"You just might have something there," he said.

"Peter—" Alicia said.

"Yes, Nena?"

"I—I pray for you—for us. Which is a kind of blasphemy, no? For how can one pray while in a state of sin? For to want you as I do is a sin. And such a sin for which forgiveness is not possible, since to be pardoned one must repent. And how can I repent of loving you? Oh, Peter, *Cielo,* I—"

"Don't cry, Nena. This is a great thing that you have. I envy you."

"You envy me? Why, Peter?"

"Because you have this simplicity. As though there had been neither time nor history. As though the world had stopped six hundred years ago. I envy you these wondrous, childlike things you have: Sin. And remorse. And repentance."

She stared at him.

"You have them not?"

"No, Nena."

"But, Peter—"

"Let us not speak of it. There are no words. Or too many. What they add up to is vacancy. A universe from which all gods have fled. Except perhaps Shiva."

"Shiva?" she said.

"A monster of a Hindu god. With many arms. Dancing upon the prostrate world. The Destroyer."

"Oh!" she said.

"Hell," he said. "I talk rot. Nena!"

"Yes, Peter?"

"Shall I take you back now?"

"Yes. Because it is spoiled, no? Our night. Because I cannot get the smell of that scent of hers out of my nostrils. How is it called, Peter?"

"*Peut'être.*"

"*Peut'être?*"

"Yes. *Peut'être,* which means *tal vez,* which means *quiza,* which means perhaps, which means maybe. Like life."

"Oh," she said, "if I had a perfume made, it would be for you. And I would call it *Siempre.*"

"*Siempre*—Forever. Or *Jamás*—Never?"

"Oh, Peter, *Cielo,* you are in a mood! I am sorry. Do you want me to—to—If you desire it, I . . ."

"No, Nena."

"Oh!" she said.

"Let's just sit here and look at the volcano. For one thing, I'm tired; for another— Hell, Nena; can't we just be?"

"Yes," she whispered, "only——"

But he reached out suddenly and gripped her wrist. Because something rose-white and enormous was rising behind them. It filled the rear-view mirror completely, shutting out the dark.

"Pe—" she began; but he clamped his other hand over her mouth. Turned her loose, laying a warning finger across his own lips. Opened the door. Got out. Saw that what had risen behind then was the Lincoln's trunk lid. But, by then, it was too late.

"No," the voice said; "the time for being is over, Comrade."

"Ohhh!" Alicia said.

"The time for many things is over. You disappoint me, Comrade Reporter. I had the intention to wait until you were mounted, in the saddle, and then remove you. Take your place. Let you divert yourself by watching—"

"As you did with the Indian girl, Jacinto?" Peter said.

"Oh, I'm cured of that, Amigo! Twenty nights in The Blue Moon cured me. But now there is no time. The pretty Alicia will pardon my lack of gallantry. I will teach her the delights of love another day. To-night, there are more important things to do."

"Such as?" Peter said.

"Later. First, do you feel heroic tonight, Comrade?"

"Hell, no! And point that burp gun some other way, won't you? It makes me nervous."

"Good. Then I shall not have to make the so-very-pretty Alicia twice a widow, and only once a bride?"

"No," Peter said.

"Good, again. From the looks of your face, Peter—you should be more inclined to cooperate with me by now."

"With the murderer of Pepe? Why should I trust you, Jacinto?"

"I have much sorrow of that," Jacinto said; "but trust me—you must, or die. Now listen to me carefully—"

"Wait," Peter said; "tell me one thing, Jacinto: How the devil did you get into the trunk of this car?"

"Oh, Peter!" Alicia said, "the keys! Just as Don Timoteo said, I shouldn't have—"

"Do not blame yourself, little Monkeyface," Jacinto laughed; "you did nothing more than save me five minutes. The five minutes it would have taken me to open the trunk in any event. And, before I forget, if you cooperate with me, upon your return you will find the spare tire in the hall of your building. I put it there. I needed the space."

"I see," Peter said. "Go on, Jacinto. What do you want of us?"

"You will get in the car and drive to the military air base. But slowly, Amigo. You have already given me heart failure more than three times on the way here. Of course, most of the stuff I put into the trunk of your car is plastic, which requires fire to explode. But I have not too much security about the pins of those Czech-fabricated grenades. They never fail to fire; but often they go off ahead of time—"

"*Dios mío!*" Alicia said.

"God does not exist, Comrade Sister of the Dictator. Now listen to me, while I explain it. You, Peter, will drive straight for the gate of the military airport."

"And?" Peter said.

"When the guard stops you, you, Doña Alicia, will lean out."

"And?" Peter said again.

"She will say that you, her fiancé, has expressed a desire to see the aircraft."

"At this hour?"

"At this hour. The great are always whimsical, no?"

"All right," Peter said.

"You will drive the car onto the base. Park it by one of the hangars.

Get out. I shall remain hidden between the seats. But you will remember that this Sten gun can cut through the backs of the seats quite easily."

"Then?" Peter said.

"The aviators will gallantly show you about the base. If you are wise, you will accept their invitation to drink with them. You will behave quite normally; and say nothing of my presence, here. You will leave the air base in the car. By then, neither I nor the explosives will be in it. This, if you are wise."

"And if I am stupid?"

"You will betray me. And I shall die. But the results will be the same. I shall still destroy that base. There will be only one difference."

"And that is?"

"I shall shoot Doña Alicia. I make this choice now, because I know from experience you are willing to risk your life, Peter. Somehow, I do not believe you will risk hers."

"You've got something there, chum," Peter said.

Peter looked at Alicia where she sat, surrounded by the pilots. They weren't all there, of course. Only one of the four aces who flew the pursuit planes, and nine of the sixteen others who piloted the lumbering transports which also served Miguel Villalonga as bombers were present. The rest were out on the town. Which was just as well.

"Nena," he said, "excuse yourself for a moment. I have a thing to say to you."

She came to him at once. He took her hand, led her to the door.

"We stay," he said. "There is an enormous risk; but it is better that we run it than to accept the certainty that we will be connected with the events if they occur after we have departed. When the shooting starts, fall to the floor. I do not think Jacinto can shoot us all; but—"

"Now look, Don Pedro!" one of the pilots called out, "Time! You're being damned selfish, y'know. After all, you have her company all the time."

"Should we tell them?" Alicia said.

"No. Your kind-hearted brother has bombed too many poor villages of innocent Indians with these aircraft now. Let him lose them! Why—"

"Time, Don Pedro; time!" the pilots called.

Smiling, Peter released her arm. She went back toward the group of pilots. The way she walked was something to see.

The lone pursuit pilot came up to Peter. He was smiling.

"It seems I owe you an apology, Don Pedro," he said.

"I'm sure I don't know for what," Peter said.

"Not too long ago," the pilot said, "I bombed and strafed two horsemen on a mountain road . . ."

Peter looked at him.

"Great sport, wasn't it?" he said.

"Well, of course, I can appreciate that from your end it might—"

"And I can appreciate it from yours," Peter said, smiling still. "I didn't, before. Throughout the Korean War, I was an infantryman. Saw things too close up. Since then, I've learned to fly. I hold a limited commercial ticket now. So I know how it is upstairs, Amigo. A man doesn't look human, does he? Even on horseback. The perspective plays tricks. The height, the speed. At five hundred kilometers an hour, it isn't possible to see the precise details. Only—"

"Only what, Don Pedro?"

"I was an infantryman, so I remember them. The shredded flesh. The pink coils of guts. How Juan screamed—because he had a name, you see; his mother called him Juan—and went on screaming almost until he died. I remember the spinning human insects at the vortex of a small-sized hell of napalm. I, Captain, have seen—quite recently—manflesh bubble and char and stink while that black, blistering dummy of tar twisting in the middle of your chemical holocaust had still air enough in his lungs to scream his guts out with. I know, I know; you get yours, too; you young, Jovian riders of thunderbolts. But it's over very fast for you—even when you light the day with flame. And to scribe one's end across half of heaven is different in quality from puking up one's life into the mud. Such an end is glorious, don't you think?"

"The fortunes of war, Don Pedro. I think you're being unfair to us, actually. You came out alive, so you shouldn't have any complaints . . ."

"While you do?" Peter said.

"Yes! If we only had jets! I do not see why your government is so stingy with us, Reynolds. After all, we are the number-one anti-Communist force in Latin America. And Castro has his MIGs!"

Peter turned to the window. The four pursuits stood on the tarmac. The Republic P-47 was closest to him. Then the Mustang. Then the two Corsairs. The DC 3s were in the hangars.

Peter saw the tiny figure come running out of the hangar. He turned back to the pilot.

"I beg your pardon?" he said. "I don't follow that argument. There is no quarrel between Costa Verde and Cuba."

"No quarrel!" the pilot said. "Why—"

And all the night roared. Vomited flame.

The pilots rushed through the door.

Peter raced toward Alicia.

"Get down!" he said. "On the floor! Flat!"

"Peter!" she wailed.

He caught her by the waist. Threw her down. Fell beside her.

Just outside the door the Sten gun stuttered. They could hear the pilots scream. The windows crashed in. Dissolved into powdered glass. A line of splinters plowed itself across the floor, marching toward them. Peter gripped Alicia to him, hard, rolled with her, putting his body between her and that burst. She moaned a little. The next burst went over them, clipped clods of plaster from the walls. Then there was silence.

Peter crawled toward the window. Raised his head. Saw Jacinto lob a grenade into the open hatch of the Thunderbolt. Another. The fat-bellied pursuit lifted from the tarmac. Came down in two halves. Blazed. And now the Mustang split itself down the fuselage, spewed around, trailing flame. The two crank-winged Vought Corsairs dissolved into fire. The flames stood straight up three hundred meters. The tarmac was like day.

Black figures poured out of the blazing hangars. Then the burning gasoline got to the wing guns of the wrecked planes. The fifty-caliber Brownings started talking, chuckling to one another with mindless, murderous laughter. The tracers were beautiful. They cut down the running men as though they had been aimed.

Peter crawled back to Alicia.

"Scratch one air force!" he said. "Viva Jacinto!"

She didn't answer him.

"Come on, Nena!" he said. "We'd better get out of here!"

He heard her voice. It was curiously faint.

"*Cielo*—" she said.

"Yes, Infant?"

"Kiss me?"

"Lord God, Alicia!"

Her hand came away from her side. She held it out to him. He saw now what it was filled with. What dripped between her fingers.

"Alicia!" he screamed.

"Kiss me?" she said again.

He kissed her mouth. It was very cold.

"Infant, Nena, Bébé," he wept. "Oh, Christ! Oh God, Oh Jesus—why? God damn it, why?"

"Peter——"

"Nena?"

"They laughed. The old gods. They—"

But he was up by then, had her in his arms, was racing for the door, jumping the sprawl of bodies that lay in it, pounding through that firelit hell to the Lincoln. Got to it. Saw it hadn't any windshield. The front seat was snowy with powdered glass. A line of black holes were stitched along its side. But he got into it anyhow. Laid her down beside him, her head resting on his lap. Turned the key. The motor caught.

He bent the Lincoln around in a screaming turn, racing for the gates. He saw the sentries standing there firing at the car. He ducked as low as he could and slammed the accelerator to the floor. Barreled through the wildly leaping sentries, through that gate out onto the road. Sitting there now, his eyes flooded, blind, he snaked the big car through turns it was never made to take at the speed it was going now.

She lay there looking up at him, her eyes wide, smiling a little.

By the time he got to the hospital there were four police jeeps behind him and two motorcycle police at his side. When he slammed the Lincoln to a stop, they surrounded him, pistols drawn.

He ignored them; bent and picked Alicia up. They fell back, staring at the dark, exotic flower, blooming through the white sharkskin suit at the level of her waist. Then they came roaring in. Her voice stopped them.

"No!" she said. "It is nothing—a scratch. Let us alone! Oh, Peter, Love—"

Then she fainted.

Peter was borne through the doors of the hospital on the crest of a green-clad wave. Hands came out of a white blur and took Alicia away from him. Other hands reached out and pinioned his wrists. Then one of them, an officer from his voice, said:

"Do not be fools! Look at his face!"

They stared at him. Turned him loose. Fell back. It was like the movements of a satanic ballet.

"Don Pedro," one of them said, "pardon. We did not think—"

"'Sall right," Peter said.

He sat down, suddenly. He had to. He sat there with the tears on his face for three eons and one eternity. Then Vicente Gomez came through the door, said:

"Peter—she's all right. A bullet plowed along her side. Made a furrow. Bloody mess, but not dangerous. Snap out of it, will you?"

"Thanks, Vince," Peter said. But he didn't stop crying. He couldn't.

Vince bent over him.

"Sister!" he called.

"Yes, Doctor?" the nursing sister said.

"Prepare a room. He's in shock. I'm going to give him a shot. One that will put him out until day after tomorrow."

"Thanks, Vince," Peter said again.

XII

Leaving the hospital with Judith in a taxi, Peter saw that all the streets were crawling with uniformed policemen. They were stopped four times in three blocks, and the identity cards which were *de rigueur* for any foreigner remaining more than three weeks in Costa Verde carefully examined. But the fourth time, the officer commanding the Security Police was the Colonel Lopez who had kept apart from Peter's interrogation.

"Look, Colonel," Peter said, "we really would like to get home before night, you know."

The Colonel smiled. Took a large piece of paper from his brief case. It had the Costa Verdian shield on it. Seals. Stamps. Ribbons. It was as official-looking as all hell. He scribbled on it briefly. Took out a roll of Scotch tape and stuck it onto the inside of the windshield of the taxi.

"There, Don Pedro," he said; "you won't be stopped any more. Just remember to make the *taxista* give you back that permit when you leave the cab. Remind him that if he doesn't, he'll be shot. *Adios!*"

"*Adios!*" Peter said. "Many thanks, Colonel . . ."

"This," Judith said, "is one hell of a joint, isn't it? What are they all so jumpy about?"

"They've got troubles, Judy—now more than ever."

And now, as the taxi moved off, purring past one roadblock after another, slowing just enough for the police to see all those ribbons, stamps, and seals shining through the windshield, Peter could feel the stiff square of cardboard in his inside coat pocket. The sister had brought it to the room in the hospital in which he lay, fighting to wake from that little death Vince Gomez had slipped into his veins. Only it had been in an envelope then. He had torn open the envelope and a note had fallen out of it, first. He picked up the note and read.

"For you. I did not dare give it to you last night. Your Alicia."

It was a post-card-size photograph of her. It hadn't been retouched at all, which meant, if anything, that she had finally convinced herself that he actually did like the way she looked. And, for that very reason, the photographer had produced a little masterpiece. Given the materials he had to work with: Alicia's peculiarly exquisite sculptural quality; her lack of a line-blurring excess of flesh; the haunting purity of the planes, angles, shadow-catching hollows of her tribal fetish of a face, dramatically bisected by the startling warmsoft contradiction of her mouth—and add to all that the simple fact that the essential ingredient of any masterpiece is the truth, the photographer could hardly have missed. And hadn't. Those eyes of Nefertiti, Astarte, almond-shaped, doe-tender, effortlessly resolving the antithesis of utter blackness and total luminosity, caressing his face out of that light-transformed gelatinous mass of silver salts; that imperial lily stalk of a throat swaying toward him; that regal, queenly little head, fixed in an attitude of total attention under that saucy, mocking little-bad-boy's cut of hair —all these unlive counterparts of things that, living, he loved, would, he knew, so long as sight and sense and memory dwelt in him, be able to stop his mind, his heart.

Across the bottom, she had scrawled in a tall, angular Gothic script that somehow defined her *Siempre, tu Alicia*—"Forever, your Alicia." And he had the feeling that that was nothing less than true; but instead of exalting him, it made him feel like dirt.

He could see Judith's absolutely perfect profile against the window of the taxi. He said, under his breath: "Oh, goddam!"

Judith turned toward him.

"What did you say, Peter?" she said.

"Nothing," Peter said.

"Peter—"

"Yes, Judy?"

"You have such rotten luck, don't you?"

"Judy baby, you've lost me already. Climb down off that oblique tangent, will you?"

"I lost you a long time ago, Peter. When I first started in to make a career of being a bitch."

He looked at her.

"Baby, can't we talk about something else?"

"No. It has to be said. You have such rotten luck, my poor old battered darling. Just think—if I had died, you'd have been rid of me. Left with a first-class memory: Judith Lovell died for me. Killed herself because I wasn't there—"

"Baby."

"Yes, Peter?"

"That won't wash."

"I know it won't. The truth is always nasty, brutish, and short. Who said that?"

"Hobbes. Hume. One of the two; I can never remember which. Only he wasn't talking about the truth. He was replying to Jean-Jacques Rousseau's Noble Savage concept. The exact quotation is, I believe: 'Man in a state of nature is nasty, brutish, and short.'"

"He had something there. The truth in my case is that I've tried to kill myself several times. Usually for the same reason: Life had started to taste like vomit again. That nothing anybody did or said had any sense to it, any meaning. That everything I did ended with me puking my guts up. That waking up with a hangover, or with the screaming meemies from having smoked half a pack of reefers, or with some hairy stinking naked ape beside me all produced the same effect: that this was always where I came in on the goddam picture. The fornicating merry-go-round. The life is circular. That 'the future is only the past again, entered through another gate . . .' Who said that, Peter?"

"Oscar Wilde."

"*He* would. I even tried that, once."

"Tried what once?"

"Sleeping with another dame. No goddam good. Nothing she could do that a sixteen-year-old boy couldn't do better, not to mention a man. Only, Peter, darling, will you permit me a slightly less unpleasant truth?"

"Yes, Judy."

"The only time I ever tried to kill myself, meaning it, was *this* time."

"Oh!" Peter said.

"Oh, what?" Judith said.

"Oh, hell."

"Amen. The other times, I scratched my wrists. Or took sleeping pills. But this time I picked up that cool, sweet blade and really dug it in where it'd do some good."

"Judy, please!"

"And even then, it didn't work out. I missed the big artery. I didn't die. So you're stuck with me again."

"You hear me screaming?"

"No. You're too goddam sweet. Too good. Oh, Peter, I—"

"Now, Judy—"

"When you came into my room this morning to take me home, it—

Say, Peter! I know what it is I've been meaning to ask you! What *was* all that uproar last night? People yelling their heads off over some Doña Alicia. Who is Doña Alicia? And what the hell were they saying? I heard something about Don Pedro, too. And *foo seel lah do. Tee rah tay ohs*. What the devil was all that? And policemen all over everything this morning. Why, darling?"

"Judy baby, do me a favor?"

"What kind, Lover?"

"Never learn Spanish. Promise me?"

"Oh!" she said. "Pedro—Peter. You!"

"Baby, there are hundreds of guys named Pedro down here."

"Peter—what did happen? The truth, now."

"Somebody took a shot at His Nibs' sister. Wounded her slightly. That's all I know."

"*Foo seel lah do*. From *fusil*—a gun! That was it. And the other word?"

"*Tirateos*—a volley of shots. Crossfire."

"And Don Pedro?"

"You'd better ask the lady that, if you ever meet her. I wouldn't know."

"All right. It sounds like the truth. Not very likely for you to get mixed up with the Boss' sister. The girlies at The Blue Moon and creatures like me are more your style."

"Gee, Toots, thanks!" Peter said.

"Because you're a softie. You don't know how to say no. Instead of telling us '*Screw you*, Jill!' you go ahead and do it for us—so sweetly, nicely, tenderly, that we never get over it. Ever since Madrid I've known that. Remember what I did when I got off the plane in Mexico City, after you'd stuck your neck in a sling for me again?"

"Yes, you cried."

"Do you know why I cried, Peter?"

"No," Peter said. "Besides, you're going to tell me anyhow; and at some length—"

"Right. Peter, tell him to drive around a while. I don't feel like going home yet. I do want to tell you things. All the things I've never been able to say before. Only, I'm back from the Valley of the Shadow now, so maybe I can."

"All right," Peter said, and instructed the driver, who grinned at him, said:

"Of course, Señor! With this permit we can go anywhere!"

"Now where were we?" Peter said.

"The reason why I cried. You. There you were outside the Customs stall. So big. Rock-solid, steady. So good. So goddam good. Standing up there amid all the rubble—"

He looked at her.

"What rubble?" he said.

"My rubble. The years, Peter. You know, all the wasted years. All the time I've spent helling around, collecting bodies, faces. Funny how they all run together, now. But yours never did. Maybe because you look like a bulldog or a prizefighter. So ugly. Did I ever tell you how ugly you are?"

"No," Peter said, "you never did."

"You are. Horrid. A mug to frighten children. But such nice eyes. Brown. Warm. Kind."

"Is this the latest technique, Judy?" Peter said.

"No. Or if so, it's awful. What I'm trying to say is the same thing I couldn't say when I got off that plane in Mexico two months ago, now. Still can't say it. I've misused those particular words too often. Taken all the shine off them. And now that I mean them, honestly and truly and awfully mean them, they choke me."

"What words, Judy?" Peter said.

"I can't. They sound so goddam phony. All right. When I came out that door of the Customs in Mexico, it hit me. For the first time, I mean. Harder than now. By now, I'm almost used to it. I stood there with my heart in my hand—my battered, vagrant, shopworn heart—and tears in my eyes—real ones, not glycerine—and was literally sick with the realization that all I've been doing all these years was trying to find an adequate substitute for you. A stand-in. A double. A replica. A replacement. Only there aren't any. And as phony, fake, incredible as it sounds, even to me, what I wanted to say to you in Mexico and couldn't, because I didn't think I could put the bit across convincingly is: 'I love you, Peter.' You know, L-O-V-E. The emotion that the ingenue feels for the hero. And you don't spell it S-E-X. At least not all the time. When that detail came around like a rabbit punch, I went into shock a little, I think. So now, finally, I've said it. And please forgive me for being so presumptuous . . ."

Peter didn't say anything. There was, at that moment, nothing to be said. He could feel Alicia's photo in his jacket pocket. It was growing. In a little while it was going to burst through the cloth. Through his heart.

But Judith was talking again.

"It hit me and I cried. The contrast. After all the phonies and the creeps, you. Just like I remembered you. No, better. A little uglier, a little more battered. But aged so beautifully like a good no-frills Burgundy. Did Dekov tell you how much time I spent talking about you?"

"Yes," Peter said.

"He called you my point of no return. My life's fatal divergence. Oh, Peter, why didn't you just beat the hell out of me in Madrid that time and make me stay? I wanted to! I wanted to so goddam bad . . ."

"You didn't act like it," Peter said.

"I know. I never do. If I acted the way I should, or the way I really want to— Funny. They're always the same. Did you know that? I don't *want* to do the perfectly dreadful things I do. I want—"

"What, Judy?"

"To be kept warm and safe. Protected. Told what to do. I love you, darling. Only you spell it *need.* Oh, Peter! That really takes the shine off, doesn't it? I'm being honest again. Bad habit, being honest."

"No," Peter said. "It's a good one, Judy."

"Peter—"

"Yes, Judith?"

"Take me home, now. And Peter—"

"Yes, baby?"

"When we get there, *don't* make love to me. Even if I ask you to."

"All right. Judy. But out of plain curiosity: *Why?*"

"Hard to explain, darling. Say I want to be with you. Stay with you. Literally. As in *Webster's.* To remain. To be near. Close to you. There. So that I can—love you. *You.* Peter Reynolds; you big ugly paleolithic throwback, but with such a lovely, lovely soul. Oh, Peter, why can't one say these things any more? Why does it sound so fake to say what's simply true? That you're good! That I love your goodness. That there are other things about you far more important than your abilities as a bedmate; that—"

"In other words, my soul?"

"Yes, goddamnit; and don't call it a semantic irrelevant, either!"

"I wasn't going to. I was thinking about a line from a popular Spanish song of some years back, 'Julio Romero de Torres.' That line is *'Con alma negra y con pena . . .'*"

"Meaning?"

"Meaning a soul black and with pain."

"No! That's not true! Not at all—"

But Peter had leaned forward and was touching the *taxista* on the shoulder.

"Stop the car!" he said.

"Peter," Judith said, "what on earth did I do or say—"

"You? Nothing, baby. It's that boat tied up to the quay there."

"That pretty white one?"

"Yes."

"What's wrong with it?"

"Nothing. Except that it shouldn't be there. And that it's got the wrong name painted on it."

Judith leaned out of the taxi.

"*La Flor de Mar,*" she read. "*The Flower of the Sea,* right?"

"Right," Peter said.

"And what should it be called?"

"Let's skip that bit, Judy. If I'm wrong, it won't make any difference; if I'm right, it'll make even less. Just wait here for me like a good girl," Peter said.

He got out. Walked toward the quay. At once, an armed policeman barred his path.

"The yacht of His Excellency," Peter said, "when did it return?"

"This morning," the policeman said. "Why?"

"I'm a reporter," Peter said; "the doings of His Excellency are always news."

"Your papers!" the policeman said.

Peter showed them to him.

"Pay tayrrr Rrrraynolddds. *Ay, sí!* The celebrated Don Pedro who some say is the fiancé of—I am very sorry, Sir; but it is prohibited to allow anyone aboard without a special order from His Excellency or Don Luis; but if the Señor will wait a minute, I'll see what I can do."

"Don't want to go aboard. Just want to know why they came back. Usually when the Head of the State goes fishing—"

"He stays for weeks. But this time—tell me, Don Pedro, were you not a witness of what happened last night? I heard . . ."

"Yes, I was," Peter said.

"Then I can tell you. The explosions could be heard out to sea, and the flames from the aircraft and the hangars burning could be seen even from the distance at which the yacht of His Excellency cruised. So—"

"I see. Thank you, Guardia," Peter said.

He walked back to the taxi. Got in. Gave the driver their address.

"Peter—" Judy said.

"Not now, Judy; I've got thinking to do," he said.

The taxi drew up before the building.

"Wait here, Judy," Peter said.

"But, Peter—"

"Wait here, Judy. There's no time. All I'm going to bring down is your passport, and mine. Not even baggage. So, if we are stopped, I can say we were simply going to have a drink on the airport terrace. Just you smile sweetly and say nothing, catch?"

He found the passports at once. But he stayed upstairs long enough to write:

"It is still perhaps, *Muñeca.* And even though hope is a game for fools, I cannot accept that *never.*" He signed it simply *Peter;* added his New York address and phone number, sealed it in an envelope, and wrote her name on it. Then he went downstairs to give it to Concha.

Concha was already outside talking to Judith. The fact that Judy got one word in ten troubled la Portera not at all. With delighted malice she was telling the story of how Doña Alicia, who loves much Don Pedro, had saved all the people on the street from being shot, when Peter came up to her. He smiled at her broadly.

"If," he said in Spanish, "you don't keep your fat, silly mouth shut, I personally shall see that you are not only shot, but tortured to death. Now take this, and give it to the lady whose name you have already mentioned too frequently, the next time she comes here. Have you understood, Concha?"

"*Sí,* Señor!" Concha said, and fled back into the hall.

"Peter—" Judith said.

"To the airport," Peter said to the taxi driver.

They moved off.

"Peter—"

"Judy, couldn't we just skip it?" Peter said.

"Oh, no, my beamish boy! Because that Don Pedro isn't two hundred other guys, he's you. Now tell me, what's she like?"

"What's who like?" Peter said.

"Doña Alicia," Judith said.

"Cute," Peter said.

"Come on, Great Lover, give!"

"Judy, do you mind if I save what little breath I've got left? Because much as I hate to tell you, if I don't get onto a plane damned soon, the guy who's going to be *fusilado* is me. And however you spell it or pronounce it, it comes out meaning dead."

"Oh!" Judith whispered. "Peter—"

"Yes, baby?"

"Because of her?"

"No, Judy; not because of her."

"Then why, darling? Please tell me."

"Because His Nibs and Luis Sinnombre don't see eye to eye on certain delicate matters. And I got caught in the middle. Judy baby, don't ask me questions. Let's just go eat some cherry cheesecake at Lindy's, shall we?"

"Oh—all right. Let's," Judy said.

The girl at the reception desk was stunning. But when Peter asked her for two one-way tickets to New York, she stopped smiling.

"Your passports, please!" she said.

Peter passed them over. What she was looking for took her two seconds to find. Or rather not to find.

"But you have no exit visas!" she said.

"Now look, *Cielito Lindo,*" Peter said, "we're United States citizens, remember? I know that to get out of this free and liberal organic democracy, Costa Verdians have to have exit visas with a certificate from the local police precinct that they haven't spoken out of turn in the last six months. But not us. The tickets, please, like a nice little girl?"

"Sorry," the receptionist said.

"Why not?"

"National emergency. There were—well—certain acts of sabotage."

"The military air base was blown up. All the aircraft therein contained were destroyed. Several pilots, mechanics, and other personnel were killed. The assassin escaped. After shooting, among others, Doña Alicia Villalonga, Widow of Duarte, Sister of the Head of the State. Which events I witnessed and have already filed with my newspaper by carrier pigeon. So keeping us here is ridiculous. Come on, Maja Vestida—give!"

"I am sorry, Señor; but I have my orders. You have to file a petition for an exit visa ten days ahead of time just like everyone else. With the police of the *barrio* of your residence. As of this morning, foreigners are no longer exempt from this ruling."

"I see," Peter said. "Thank you, Señorita."

"Don't mention it," the receptionist said.

"I won't," Peter said; "and Señorita—"

"Yes, Señor?"

"Be my guest. At my funeral, that is," Peter said.

"Oh, Peter! Peter!" Judith said.

"Gentle down, Judy. Just you sit in the waiting room while I do some telephoning."

"Peter, for God's sake!"

"Judy, let God take care of Himself for the moment. Right now I'm trying to take care of Peter and Judy. I'm going to try to get through to Don Luis. Convince him that perforated hides aren't being worn this year. Definitely unhealthy. Drafty, what?"

"Peter, if you don't stop being so goddam bright, I'm going to scream!"

"Baby, do it for both of us, will you? Now sit there," Peter said, and was gone.

He called the hospital first. But they wouldn't put him through to Alicia's room. They insisted that she had gone home. So he asked to speak to Vince, who confirmed what the sister had said.

"Why, yes, Peter; she's gone home. I tried to point out to her that it was inadvisable, but she simply wouldn't stay. And one doesn't say no to Doña Alicia, you know. I don't suppose it matters. I've got her wrapped up like a mummy. And if she moves about too much, it'll hurt enough to make her lie down. What's that? Why no, Peter—no one's been here asking for you. Right. I'll call you tonight."

He had no trouble getting through to Don Luis. The conversation was brief. Don Luis politely suggested that Peter drop in to see him at his office. He seemed neither troubled nor annoyed.

Peter took Judith home first. That was easy enough. What took some doing was getting her to stay there.

"My dear Peter," Don Luis said, "if you will help me by answering truthfully a few questions, I think we can smooth the whole thing over. First of all, how did those Commandos get into the airport?"

"Commando, not Commandos," Peter said. "Just one. If they had a few more like him, they'd be sitting in that chair right now, asking *you* questions."

"Don't doubt it. How did he, Peter?"

"Hidden between the seats of Alicia's car," Peter said.

"I thought so. Why?"

"He was awfully persuasive. His persuasion could run through a twenty-five shot clip in three seconds flat."

"Again, all right. I'd already assumed you were under duress. But what is going to be dreadfully hard to explain away is why, after he'd left you and Alicia in the officers' club, you didn't report what was going on."

"He said he'd shoot Alicia if I did. *Alicia,* Luis, not me. He figured that I might be willing to risk my neck. But not hers. He was right. Damned right. The proof of what I'm saying is that the bastard, thinking I had talked, did shoot Alicia. Fortunately, his aim wasn't any too good."

Very slowly, Luis Sinnombre smiled.

"You, my dear Peter, are either the world's finest liar or you are telling the truth. Which is it?"

"The truth," Peter said.

Luis went on smiling.

"In any event, it doesn't matter. Miguel has been informed that Alicia is in love with you. I pointed out to him that having a fatal heart attack would make sure that you would end up married to her, and thus stopped him roaring like an infuriated bull. He has not been informed that you were ever in a position to consummate this great love of yours and Alicia's. By the way, if—as she stubbornly insists—you haven't attended to that detail, it might not be a bad idea to do so. A little bundle from heaven on his way might make excellent life insurance for you. In any event, don't worry. Miguel is not overly bright. He tried to insist that if she hadn't been out with you, she never would have been in danger. To which I could easily reply that since he has always been exceedingly permissive about her comings and goings out of the idiotic idea that she could be trusted, she might have been in much greater danger alone; and add to that the fact that by driving that shot-up wreck of a Lincoln like a madman, you very probably saved her life. So now, he has subsided into the sulks, muttered grumbles, and ridiculous threats to beat her half to death once she has that bandage off."

"You tell him for me—"

"One moment, Peter! Let me handle Miguel. I'm good at it. All I want from you is a bit of cooperation."

"Such as?"

"First of all that you refrain from pulling any more silly stunts like attempting to leave the country as you did this morning."

"All right," Peter said. "And—?"

"You take dear Judith night-clubbing tonight. May I suggest the Obsidian Room of the Verdian Hilton?"

"All right again. Why?"

"Special performance for Miguel's benefit. He sees you being most attentive to dear Judith, who is certainly the world's most tasty dish, he'll be comfortably reassured that you have no serious intentions toward that skinny little she-monkey of a sister of his. Or maybe ours. Even he has no illusions about her looks."

"Only I do. What happens when he tells her about the performance?"

"He won't have to. She'll be there."

"Look, Luis. She's been shot. Even a grazing wound like that one hurts like hell."

"I know. But it's not my idea, Peter. It's hers."

"Oh," Peter said.

"The thought being to prevent Miguel from being nasty to you. Or finding some capricious excuse for murder. Of course, she's sure to get her tender little heart slightly broken. Sorry, but that can't be avoided. You can repair it, oh so sweetly, later."

"I'm not so sure I like this—"

"My dear Peter, I'm trying to keep you alive and functioning. I base my future on this romance of Alicia's. And Miguel is damned unpredictable. For Alicia's sake he just might risk ruining the country for the simple pleasure of having you shot. One never can tell with him. His mind functions in odd ways. I'd advise you to cooperate."

Peter looked at him.

"Luis, you just sold me a bill of goods," he said.

When he opened the door to his flat, Judith didn't come running to meet him. Instead she came very slowly, and her face was strained and white.

"Well?" she said.

"Shooting's off," Peter said. "I may be target for tomorrow; but tonight—Peace—it's wonderful. So we celebrate. City's flossiest nightspot. The Obsidian Room."

"Peter, I don't think I . . ."

"Judy, we have to. Semi-command."

"Oh!" Judith said.

"Don't I even get a small-sized kiss?" Peter said.

"No. Yes. But first close your eyes, and put out your hands."

He closed his eyes. Put his hands out. She poured something into them. Something light and powdery and dry. He opened his eyes. Looked down at his two hands. They had cigarette butts in them. Lipstick stained.

"I don't think I need to remind the Great Lover that I don't smoke Players," Judith said.

"Oh, hell!" he said.

"She also pawed my lingerie, the jealous bitch," Judith said.

Peter didn't say anything.

"All right," Judith whispered. "No scene, darling. What right have I? Peter—one question: You want me to get lost?"

"No," Peter said.

"You mean that, darling?"

"I mean it."

"Don't worry; I'm not going to ask you why you mean it. I know better than to look a gift horse in the mouth. Peter—"

"Judy?"

"I think maybe you had better make love to me, now. I know I told you not to. But, oh Judas! Now I need comforting. Please?"

"Oh, all right, baby," Peter said.

XIII

The walls of the Obsidian Room were of black glass. The lights were concealed behind plaster cupids. The orchestra members were dressed in white tuxedos with silver lapels. The instruments were white, too. The trick was to cut all the lights except a couple of ultra-violet rays. Then the instruments seemed to be floating in midair held by white suits with nothing in them. Even the girl singer disappeared, leaving only her vastly overstuffed white-spangled dress wiggling on the dark without any visible means of support.

"Big deal," Peter snorted.

The waiter guided them to the table with the aid of a flashlight. Slapped the menu down on the table. Disappeared. The lights came up again. Things grew edges. Tables blossomed all around them. People.

Peter began to relax. Then he saw what was standing around the walls. Behind all the columns. He said: "Ugh!"

"Why *ugh!*, darling?" Judith said.

"Ever noticed that apes in tuxedos look more like apes than they do in the raw?" Peter said.

"Oh!" Judith said. "Peter, why are they here? Following you?"

"No. Means that some bigwig is going to put in his appearance. The situation is a trifle uncertain since the Commies washed out the Costa Verdian Air Force. The Minister of War is already in Washington, pleading for jets. Their pitch is that Fidel is all set to invade."

"Is he?"

"No. He's got troubles enough in Havana. Don't know why, but I enjoy seeing these types sweat. Remember how the streets were crawling with coppers this morning? Everybody watching everybody else?"

"Your order, Sir?" the waiter said.

"Champagne," Peter said. "Piper Heideseick, Forty-three."

"I'm sorry, Sir; but—"

"Veuve Cliquot. Same year. Or Mumm. Brut. Or any goddam thing. As long as it's not pink or sweet."

"Very well, Sir," the waiter said.

"Peter!" Judith said. "Just look who just came in!"

"No," Peter said, "I don't want to. I can't. Not so soon. Not without a drink in me."

"But, darling, it's Doctor Vince. With a girl. A very pretty girl. Probably his wife. He does have a wife, doesn't he?"

"Yes. But as a general rule, one doesn't go pubcrawling with one's own frau in Costa Verde—"

"Oh," Judith said. "Peter—I do think they're coming over here!"

"Oh, God!" Peter said.

"But why, darling? I thought you liked him?"

"Judy, tonight I don't even like me."

Vince was standing by the table, smiling at them. Peter got up.

"Peter," Vince said, "may I present my blushing bride? That is, she used to blush. By now, she's forgot how. Paloma love, this is Peter Reynolds."

"Enchanted," Peter said; "and this—"

"Oh, I know who she is!" Paloma Gomez said. "She's why we're here. I insisted brazenly that Vince bring me. I was just dying to meet her. Am I forgiven, Miss Lovell?"

"Of course," Judith said, "though I fail to see what you've done that requires forgiveness. I like being flattered!"

"Join us?" Peter said.

"Try and stop us," Vince said. He signaled to the waiter. The waiter came flying, followed by a busboy with two more chairs.

"Vince," Peter said, "how'd you know?"

Vince leaned close. Dropped his voice. "That you two were going to be here tonight?" he said. "Simple. Luis called me. We're window dressing. My Dove doesn't know that, though."

"Oh," Peter said.

"You're in a spot, Peter. But anything I can do to help, I will."

"Son, you got your sewing basket with you?"

"Lord, Peter; why?"

"To put the pieces back together," Peter said.

"I've seen all your pictures," Paloma was saying to Judith. "I don't think I've missed even one—"

"How could you stand 'em?" Judith said.

"Now really, Judith," Vince said, "you've done some fine things."

"Yes," Judith said, "two. One was to leave Hollywood. The other was to come crawling on my knees to Peter. Only things I've done in my life that made any sense—"

"Judy," Peter said, "drink your champagne. Generally speaking, people cry into their cups after, not before."

The trouble was, she took him at his word. But instead of making her morose, it made her gay. Peter stopped holding his breath after a while. Because, now, clearly, she had set out to please. And, when Judy deliberately decided to be charming, what happened to the people around her was worth watching. They melted. Under the hypnotic, loving, tender, total attention of her gaze, the soft, liquid caress of her voice, they turned wax, helplessly waiting to be molded into the shape of her whimsical heart's desire. There was something a little terrifying about it. Because you never could be sure she wouldn't suddenly whirl and rend the creatures she had made. All the time she spun yarns about the motion picture industry—already moribund and half a ghost by the time she had come to it, so that her career had mounted upon the great final wave of its dissolution—Peter kept watching her out of the corner of his eye, listening to her voice playfully combining lies, damned lies, and goddamned lies for Paloma's especial benefit with such stark, utterly simple sincerity that even knowing how most of it had really been, he found himself half-believing her.

"So," she was saying, "all I had on was about five pounds of beads—you know, the costume department's concept of how a Byzantine Empress dressed—"

"You mean their concept of how to titillate the suckers," Peter said.

"Right, darling! Right as rain! But anyhow, Paloma dearest, I was supposed to wear a few things under all that dime-store jewelry. The essentials—Peter, can I tell her this? You know Spanish girls are so modest . . ."

"Now you've got to!" Paloma said.

"All right. So along with the beads they gave me a sort of half-bra and a *cache-sexe*. That sounds nicer than a G-string, doesn't it, Peter darling?"

"Judy, for God's sake!"

"Anyhow, it was ohhh so ohh hot in Madrid. I went to sleep in my dressing room. So when they called me, I jumped up, put on the beads, and forgot the essentials. I thought that the cameramen and the grips were sort of staring at me; but in that costume, they would have anyhow. Besides, all I had to do in that scene was to sit on a throne. I suppose everything would have been just fine and dandy if Peter hadn't chosen that moment to drop in. I hadn't seen him in years. And, of course, I've been in love with him all my life—"

"Judy, please!" Peter said.

"Oh, leave her be, Peter," Vince said.

"So I got up from there, and ran to meet him. Well, one smart cameraman kept right on shooting. Made himself a fortune selling bootlegged copies of that take!"

"How awful!" Paloma said.

"You've got something there, my dear," Peter said. "It was even worse than that. You want to hear the really horrible part?"

"Of course!" Paloma said.

"The real lowdown is that not one word of this yarn of Judy's is true," Peter said.

"Now *Pe-tah!*" Judy said.

"She had on a thing like a Mother Hubbard. Acres and acres of cloth. Gold lamé shawl. A crown. She was so damned covered up that—"

"Peter," Judith said, and her voice made him stop dead; "just who *is* that girl?"

"What girl?" he said.

"That one. That little dark creature. Stunning. Looks like she belongs on a barge on the Nile."

Peter didn't turn.

"Why?" he said.

"Well, from the way she's staring at you," Judith said, "I'd say that all she needs to make her perfectly happy would be a knife and a fork. And you on the plate, darling. That gleam in her eye is positively cannibalistic."

"Judy," Peter said, "you're imagining things again."

"No, I'm not. Peter, darling, would it be badly seen in polite Costa Verdian society if I went over there and belted her one?"

Vince laughed.

"I'm afraid, Judith, that if you belted that particular little creature one, you'd end up in front of a firing squad. That little girl happens to be the sister of the Head of the State."

"Not Doña Alicia!" Judith said.

"The same," Vince said.

"*Pe-tah—*" Judith said.

"Oh, Lord," Peter said.

"Now, darling—all I wanted to ask you was: Do you think the orchestra knows 'Frankie and Johnny'?"

"Hell, no!" Peter said.

"Why, Judy?" Vince said.

"Want to sing it. To celebrate being done dirt to. Or by. Really give out with that punch line, 'He was my m-a-a-a-n; but he done me wrong!"

"Now, Judy," Peter said.

"Well, haven't you?"

"No," Peter said.

"Then you're a fool. She might have taught you something new. With hot sauce and chili peppers on it. Vince, which one is His Nibs?"

"The one on her left," Vince said.

"Oh!" Judith said.

"You're among friends, Judy," Vince said. "Speak your piece. I'm curious."

"He'd set a new style in heavies," Judy said. "Subtle. Delicately cruel. The kind who'd have to have a violin sonata played to him while he watched a man being tortured to death. Right?"

"Absolutely," Vince said.

"Look how listless he is. Bored. Like Nero. Or Caligula. No, Nero's better. Caligula was just plain nuts. But this one is crazy in devious ways. Twisted. He'd kill his own mother for amusement. Say, Doctor Vince, who is the other one?"

"Luis Sinnombre," Vince said.

"Hmmm," Judith said; "that I like. That I'd buy a portion of. He looks like—he looks like—Paloma, please forgive me; but he looks like horizontal fun!"

"Judy," Peter said, "I've the damnedest feeling that the one who's going to get belted is you, Baby. And by *me*, if you don't cut this line of chatter out."

"He looks as lower-depths as a slum brothel," Judith said. "Appeals to all the ways I'm not a good girl, darling. You know, Peter, you're so goddam wholesome. But that Luis! Oh, brother!"

"You know," Vince said, "it's curious what a chasm separates the sexes. Women never have the faintest idea why we find certain little creatures exciting. Nor vice versa. I know that Luis is enormously successful with the girls, but I'll be damned if I can see why. Dreadful-looking creature, isn't he?"

"That Toltec eye," Peter said; "that jaguar mouth."

"Why, Peter! What a poet you are!" Paloma said.

"I'm only quoting one of Luis' ex-girl friends," Peter said.

"I," Judith said, "do see what *you* see in *her*, darling."

"That hot sauce and chili pepper?" Paloma said. "You know, Judith, we *Hispano-Americanas* get a bit tired of that conception you Nordicas have of us. We aren't at all—"

"I wasn't being serious, Paloma," Judith said; "I was only plaguing Peter. Fact is, I don't think that at all. I think she's cute. Ugly cute. But interesting. Such a soulful face. She probably wouldn't be worth a damn in bed, but–"

The champagne Peter was drinking went down the wrong way. He choked.

Judith looked at him.

"So," she whispered, "you already have!"

"Now, Judy–"

"Oh, Peter!"

"Baby," Peter said; "you see any holes in me?"

"Oh, no! Don't give me that one. She's a sly little number. She'd never be so stupid as to–"

She stopped dead, because the headwaiter was already bowing over their table.

"–get caught," she said, staring at him.

"Señor Reynolds? Doctor Gomez?" the headwaiter said.

"Yes?" Peter said.

"His Excellency requests the pleasure of you and your ladies' company at his table," the waiter said.

It wasn't the first time Peter had seen Miguel Villalonga. But it was the first time after he had met, had got to know Alicia. And now, looking at him, the effect was disquieting. It was as though someone had held that exquisitely sculptured head of hers into a flame, and let it melt a little. Let it run to flesh. Those full lips of hers became negroid in her brother's face, a trifle bluish–the result, perhaps, of his heart condition. They pulled down at the corners under a sparse, mongoloid mustache. Their expression was feline. The sleepy look of a well-fed tiger. But of one that was perfectly willing to kill for pleasure, even after the more normal appetites were sated. His eyes had the same Tluscolan slant as his sister's. But where Alicia's were luminous, Miguel's were lightless. The blackness of the pit showed in them; the night of ice-cold hell. He was only a little corpulent, probably because of an enforced lack of exercise. He was dressed in white, as always; and his dinner jacket was of an excellent cut. He was smoking a long, pencil-thin cigar, letting the smoke curl up past those ice-black eyes. His nails were delicately manicured, tinted with a soft rose-colored polish. On his finger he wore a massive ring of gold.

Looking at Peter now, his nostrils flared in a gesture that was an exact duplicate of Alicia's. So exact that it stopped Peter's breath. And he saw one thing clearly and absolutely and perfectly: Luis Sinnombre was wrong. He might enjoy playing Gray Eminence to Miguel Villalonga, but he didn't manage him. Or deceive him. Or conceal anything from those black ice-floe eyes that they really wanted to see. The boot was on the other leg. Here was greatness. Great evil, of course. But greatness. The one quality which throughout human history has always been totally independent of morality.

Miguel didn't get up, even to greet the ladies. He sat there studying them, until every nerve they had was screaming.

"Miss Lovell," he said at last, "Costa Verde is honored by your presence."

His voice was light, dry. It sounded like the rustle of oiled silk.

"Thank you, Your Excellency," Judith said.

"This," the Dictator said, "is my assistant, Luis Sinnombre. That means, in your language, Miss Lovell, Louis Without A Name."

"Oh," Judith said. "How do you do, Don Luis?"

Luis bent over her hand. Raised it to his lips. Kissed it instead of making the formal gesture of merely pretending to, which was what good manners demanded.

"Doctor, Doña Paloma, please be seated," Miguel said. "And you, too, Mr. Reynolds. Over there, next to my sister. I believe you've already met?"

"Yes, we have," Peter said.

"But *I* haven't met her," Judith purred, "and I'm just dying to! You see, I've heard so much about her—from Peter."

Alicia's doe eyes were stricken things. Wounded unto death.

"Have you?" the Dictator said. "I didn't know they were so well acquainted. But then, you know how it is, Miss Lovell; nobody ever tells me anything . . ."

In the resulting little flurry of laughter, they all sat down.

"Peter, darling, may I have a cigarette?" Judith said.

"Of course," Peter said, and offered her a pack of Chesterfields.

"Oh, not those!" Judith said. "Don't you have any Players?"

Alicia looked at her.

"I do," she said, and held out her gold, monogrammed cigarette case.

Miguel Villalonga raised an eyebrow.

"Odd that you have similar tastes in cigarettes," he said.

"We have similar tastes in a great many things; don't we, Doña Alicia?" Judith said.

Luis Sinnombre laughed.

"Women!" he said.

"Don't we?" Judith persisted.

"I wouldn't know," Alicia said. "In men—perhaps, yes. I think Peter is—very nice."

"He is," Judith said. "Oh, he is! You have no idea how—"

"Miss Lovell," Luis said, "may I have this dance?"

Judith smiled at him.

"Well," she said, "I was looking forward to dancing with His Excellency first—if that isn't *lèse majesté*. Is it, Your Excellency?"

Villalonga smiled.

"Not at all," he said. "But, unfortunately, Miss Lovell, thanks to the badness of a would-be assassin's aim, I find myself a cripple. Dance with Luis. He is quite good at it."

"Of course," Judy said, and stood up. Luis took her arm. They moved off toward the dance floor.

Peter could feel Alicia's gaze.

"Peter—" she said.

"Yes, Doña Alicia?" he said.

"Oh!" she said; "don't be so formal. I don't care about my arrogant and stupid brother. Call me Alicia, as you always do."

"Certainly, Nena. Better?"

"Much!" she said. "May *I* have this dance, please?"

Peter looked at Miguel Villalonga. Looked back at Alicia.

"Delighted," he said, and took her arm.

"You know," Miguel Villalonga said, "I have the distinct impression that I have been lied to, about a number of things—"

"You have, dear brother—oh, but you have!" Alicia said; and moved off with Peter toward the dance floor.

The orchestra was playing a cha-cha-cha. Peter wasn't very good at that; but he managed. Then they switched to a slow bolero. He smiled. At boleros, after his years in Spain, he was very good indeed.

He drew her close. Then he felt her wince. Released her.

"God, Nena, I forgot!" he said.

"No," she said; "hold me, Peter. It hurts a little. But not as much as your not holding me does. Oh, Peter, *Cielo,* I—"

"Nena," he said.

"I have never wanted to kill anyone before. But now I do. Oh, how I hate her! Oh how I should love to claw out her eyes!"

"Nena," he said again, "hate's such a futile emotion. Haven't got time for it. Nor the space. Too full of its opposite at the moment. Overflowing."

"And I," she whispered. Her voice went ragged. "If I could only kiss you now," she said; "if I only could!"

"That makes two of us," Peter said.

But she didn't answer him; and, looking down, he saw that she was crying. He froze.

"No," she said; "go on dancing, Peter."

She danced the way he had known she would. Totally. She was the music, the rhythm, the slow beat, the lazy guitar strumming.

The music stopped. He took her arm.

"No!" she said; "don't take me back! He knows I love you. And he might as well accustom himself. And she. Because now I am going to take you away from her. Oh, Peter, *Cielo,* you cannot belong to such a horrible woman! I will not permit it!"

"*Muñeca*—" he said.

"I will not, Peter! Why—"

The next was a tango. He drew her to him the way you have to if you mean to dance a tango, not fake it. She fitted into him like a second skin. Under the thin stuff of her dress he could feel the gauze and the tape of the bandage. He drew his hand away.

"Put it back, your hand!" she said.

He could feel her trembling. But she didn't miss a beat. He was aware that Luis and Judith were still dancing, and that Vince and Paloma were, too, now, floating hazily and out of focus on the lateral margin of his gaze. But then he forgot they existed, forgot Miguel Villalonga and the ice-cold menace of his gaze, forgot time in the long slow quiver of her clinging to him, the contact unbroken, from below the throat to just above the knee through all that potent sweep, halt, side break, follow-through of the tango, moving trancelike through steps so intricate, so spectacular that the dance floor emptied, Judy, Luis, Vicente, Paloma, and all the other dancers forming a ring watching them, and the orchestra playing one tango after another until finally he noticed it, and quit. The spectators applauded loudly.

"Kids," Judith said, "the management ought to pay you. What an act! Peter, darling, you've been holding out on me. I didn't know you could dance like that!"

"Perhaps he cannot—with you," Alicia said. "It requires a certain—Peter, *Cielo,* how does one say *compenetración* in English?"

"Don't bother," Judith said, "though I must say that a dance floor is hardly the place to indulge in it. A trifle daring don't you think, Doña Alicia?"

"Oh," Alicia said, "you distort my meaning—but no matter. Peter,

Amor, we must go back now. I had better start persuading Miguel not to have you shot!"

They all moved back to the table where the Dictator sat, smoking his thin black *puro* and watching them out of his flat basilisk eyes.

"Ah, Reynolds," he said, "you have hidden talents. And so do you, Alicia, my dear. Quite a show. Quite a show. I suspect there have been others I didn't witness. For instance, for Marisol Talaveda to have got aboard the jet for New York, she could hardly have complied with orders. Which leaves me with the unlikely supposition that Luis became sentimental and allowed her to defy me—or—"

"Or what, Miguel?" Alicia said.

"Or— Nothing, my dear little sister. Some suppositions are far too unpleasant to pursue, don't you think, Miss Lovell? One finds oneself in the position of the tired husband who always telephones his home rather than return unexpectedly. Wise, don't you think?"

"Very," Judith said; "especially if my Peter is in town!"

They all laughed. Sat down.

"Tell me, Reynolds," Villalonga said, "aren't you pro-Communist? A bit of a fellow traveler, say?"

"No," Peter said.

"Why not?" the Dictator said.

"Because they push people around," Peter said.

Miguel Villalonga laughed. Pleasantly. Wholeheartedly.

"And that, of course, is a terrible crime?"

"The most terrible," Peter said. "Too hard to stop. Starts with a few broken heads in Munich. And ends up in Dachau—"

Villalonga drew in on his cigar. Studied Peter.

"And what, my dear Reynolds, do you think of *my* government?" he said.

Peter smiled.

"I'd rather not say," he said.

"Why not?" The two words were a whipcrack. Peter smiled, even more slowly.

"Because there are ladies present," he said.

Miguel Villalonga looked at him. A long time. A very long time. Then suddenly, abruptly, the Dictator threw back his head and roared.

"My dear Reynolds, a man with your nerve deserves to live," he said. "I like you! Damned if I don't!"

He turned in his chair, his hand raised. Five waiters, two of whom crashed into each other, converged upon their table.

"More champagne," El Indominable said.

"Miguel—" Alicia said.

"Yes, sweet sister?"

"Hear me well," Alicia said. Then she said, very fast, in a kettledrum roll of pure beautifully precise Castilian: "I love Peter. If you kill him, I shall not survive him one hour. No matter how you try to prevent it. Even if you set guards over me, as you have over our loved and respected mother. There is no way you could stop me—any more than you could have stopped me from doing what I have already done."

Miguel's face darkened, congested.

"With him?" he said.

Alicia smiled.

"With—various," she said. "Am I not your sister, brother mine? Daughter of your mother? Have I not blood of a hundred thousand loves in my veins?"

Miguel sat there looking at her. His face slackened. He looked very tired, suddenly, very old. He turned in his chair. Looked toward one of the policemen standing beside a column. The man hurried over.

"Call my car," the Dictator said. He turned back to the others. "You will forgive a tired old man, won't you? Time I was abed, eh, Doctor? Alicia—"

"Yes, Miguel?" Alicia whispered.

"Would you come with me? Or would you prefer to stay?"

Alicia got up slowly. Took his arm.

"I'll come with you, Miguel," she said.

XIV

Now again, when they had got there together—when with one last arrogantly demanding, prehensile, unspeakably expert, long scalding twist, she had hollowed him out from the base of his throat down to his tight-curled toes, drawing the life out of him into the savage thrash and broil and undulant heat of her, achieving total fusion that included not only the red murder in her teeth and nails but her willful and willing self-destruction, rising through the rhythmically mounting chain of chanted prayerful obscenities to the feral, anguished, demented cries that clung in his ears like the negation of all joy; and it (the act of what they both euphemistically called love) over and done with—he returning to life through the slowing breath-storm heart-hammer, saw that she was propped up on one elbow staring at him, the whole of her glistening in the morning light with the rivers of sweat that poured out of her, still staring at him and fighting for breath, and her face tightening suddenly with something he couldn't recognize until he said "Judy?" and she brought her free hand whistling around to smash open-palmed across his face.

And even then he didn't recognize it. But he had been around a good many years by now and his lessons had all been well learned the hard way; she, Judith, having been one of the first and certainly the best of his teachers, so that he knew one thing with absolute certainty: If you let a woman get away with a rebellious or a humiliating act for as long as five seconds flat, you are done.

Knowing that, not having to even think about it, he responded without anger or heat or any emotion whatsoever, simply rolling her out of the bed with a slap whose crushing, overwhelming force was designed to end the matter forever, and did.

He lay there watching her come up on hands and knees, shaking her head from side to side to clear it, jetting the tears from her eyes in a fine spray by the motion; but when she looked up at him finally, tugging that long, livid, rose-silver scar that was his brand upon her, taut by her throat's lifting upcurve, she was smiling.

"So you're a big boy, now," she said. "Took you one hell of a time, but you've learned. Who's been teaching you things? That little mouse?"

"You, among others," he said. "Come on, Judith: give. Why the Pearl Harbor-type sneak attack?"

She got up then, stood there looking at him. She was still something. The packaging remained unmatched. What was inside was a different matter. Then once more her face came clear, her eyes bleak with sudden hurt.

"Again," she said.

"Again what?" Peter said.

"That's the second time you've put her head on my body. That's why I hit you. After being so goddam reluctant to play house with me, you top it off by closing your eyes and pretending it was she you were doing it with! Deadly insult, Peter! There's nothing worse. Absolutely nothing at all. I won't be used. I'm me, darling. Judith Lovell, remember? Not a substitute for your little mixed-blood mouse. Though I have to admire your imagination. Because even if you have played indoor games with her—which I doubt, because in spite of leaving those crummy Players all over the place on purpose so I'd find them, and pawing in my things, I happened to notice the bed was completely unused—you ought to realize she isn't even in my league . . ."

She stopped still, peering into his face.

"Oh!" she said.

"Oh, what?" Peter said.

"Oh, hell. Same bit. We've been through this routine before. Does that untidy smile on your exceedingly unlovely countenance mean what I think it does?"

"Depends upon what you think it means, Judy."

"That she *is* good. At this sort of thing? Better than I, Peter?"

He grinned at her.

"I wouldn't know, Judy," he said.

"You're lying!"

"Say I'm being a gentleman . . ."

"*Pe-tah!*"

"Put your most charitable interpretation on it, baby. A gentleman doesn't speculate about a girl's abilities in a horizontal position. And if he knows, he doesn't admit it—not even to God in prayer. So since there's no way on earth you, or anybody else, could get me to confess to unlawful carnal knowledge of Alicia, any more than I'd ever own up to ever having seen your nicely rounded little tail uncovered by those invitations to rape you usually wear, why not just assume I'm telling the truth when I say I don't know? I could be. Ever think of that?"

She didn't answer him. She clawed in the box on the table, looking for a cigarette. But it was empty.

"In my side coat pocket," Peter said.

She walked across the room toward the clothestree on which he had hung his jacket. He lay there watching her moving in all the barbaric splendor of her nakedness, the burnt-gold sculpturing a little faded by her long stay in the hospital but still unmarred by any white, showing that her body's yielding to the sun had been as total as all her surrenders—and as wanton, surely.

She put her hand into his coat pocket. The wrong one. As she drew it out the pull tilted the clothestree a little. He saw her stare at something. Then her hand moved. But she had the long, singing curve of her back to him, so he couldn't see what she had done. She put her hand in the other pocket and came out with the cigarettes. She shook one out of the pack, stuck it in her mouth with her left hand, all the time keeping her right hand out of sight, pressed, it seemed to him, against the inhollow of her waist. She moved sidewise to the table. Picked up the table lighter, lit the cigarette. Walked over to the window, unfurling the pale gray banner of the smoke behind her.

"Judy, come away from there!" he said. "People can see you!"

She turned now, and he could see the iridescent crystal and sapphire wash that hid her eyes. She came back toward the bed, holding Alicia's photograph in her hand and walking with that tensioned stride of hers that brought "The War March of the Priests" instantly to his mind.

She didn't say anything. She sank down beside him. Lay there holding the photo and staring at it.

"Oh Judas!" she said.

"Now, Judy—"

"She's—absolutely gorgeous. It's what was bothering me last night. Only I was half-drunk and bitchy jealous so I couldn't see it. Takes a long time to see it, doesn't it? She's—so—so unconventional. How long did it take you, Peter?"

"No time. But then I'd known this face for eight years before I ever saw it."

"Now, Peter!"

"God's truth. Remember the National Museum of Archeology? That statue I showed you?"

"My God!" Judith said. "She could have posed for it, couldn't she?"

"A grandmother of hers, forty-nine greats removed, probably did. Judy, please. I'm awfully tired and—"

She looked at him and let that star-sapphire mist become a crystal spill; a luminous steeplechase down the contours of her face.

"Don't worry, Love. I'm not going to behave like a jealous ingenue. I'm not jealous, really. What I am is scared."

"Scared? You?"

"Yes. You're all I've got, darling. And a girl with a face like this could take you away from me. I hate to admit it, but she could. Notice I said a face. The rest of her equipment's merely incidental. If it were only that, I'd send you off with her for a weekend to get it out of your system. Only it's more than that. Much more."

"More?" Peter said.

"Yes. That was the main thing that was bothering me about her, last night. Not the fact that she was committing dry fornication with you on the dance floor—dry, hell!—say clothed. But that hungry look she has when she looks at you. I don't like it, Peter. It's such a total hunger. This lovely little witch wouldn't be contented with merely the occasional loan of your body. She'd want your soul as well. More than your manly talents. She's probably not much good in that department; but very, very long on soul. Peter—"

"Yes, Judy?"

"What would you do to me if I tore this up?"

He looked at her.

"Don't try it, Judy," he said.

She sighed.

"I thought that. All right, I'll put it back in your coat pocket. But keep it out of my sight, will you, please? All tortures aren't physical . . ."

She got up, went over to the clothestree. Put Alicia's picture back into his pocket. But she didn't come back at once. Instead, she stopped by the radio, switched it on. Stood there waiting until it boomed into sound. A man's voice said:

"*Government forces in Orense Province successfully counterattacked the Communist invaders who landed yesterday, proceeding from the Island of Cuba. Although vastly outnumbered, the superb training and self-denying heroism of our forces enabled them to—*"

Judith switched it off.

"No, baby; for God's sake leave that on!" Peter said. "He's talking about the War . . ."

She switched the radio on again.

"Oh, Peter," she said, "I'm so sick of wars and killing and . . ."

"So am I, Judy. So is the world. But this is important. This is *here*."

"Oh," she said, "not again!"

"It's never stopped, Judy," Peter said.

"Oh, hell," she said. "Mind if I turn it down a bit, Love? You listen to it. I'll keep my attention fixed on other things."

"What things?" he said.

"The invaders suffered numerous casualties," the announcer said.

"This," she whispered, and came back to him; sat slowly and carefully on the edge of the bed with the studied grace of motion that came from having had a battery of cameras trained on her ever since she was seventeen years old, so that the conscious avoidance of the awkward, the ugly, had become unconscious and a part of her; then she fitted her mouth to his with the camera angles uncalculated but right, because she did it now from habit even after the need for it was gone, turning her right profile, the better one, to catch the light, and kissing him with a slow tenderness that pushed a probing blade into his vitals, seeking (perhaps consciously) his known and fatal weakness; the pity that always and dependably unmanned him.

"The Indians of the town of Xochua . . ."

Peter took his mouth away from hers. Sat there listening, all attention, now.

"Peter," she said reproachfully.

"Ssssh!" he said; "I was in that town once. It was there that Jacinto—"

"Under their Chief, Zochao, have flatly refused to leave the village, threatened on three sides by the renewed flow of lava from the volcano. Although the approach of the lava is very slow, government geologists believe—"

"Peter, turn that goddam radio off! It distracts your attention too much. And I—"

"You what, baby?"

"I—need you, Peter. To comfort me. Cure my sicknesses. Heal all the various places where I hurt—"

"That," Peter said, "is a very large order, Judy."

"I know. Huge. Immense. And terrifying. You aren't afraid, are you?"

"Baby," he said, "I'm scared spitless."

"Our representatives in Washington," the announcer boomed, *"indignantly deny—"*

"Oh, Judas, Peter! Please stop him from jabbering!"

He got up. Started toward the set. Stopped. Stood there. Seeing his face, Judith said:

"Peter!"

He didn't answer her. He was looking at the radio. Judith listened now, heard:

". . . *que el brutal asesinato de la Señora Crosswaithe fuera llevado a cabo por agentes Costa Verdeneses. Esa acusación tan ridícula procede de una fuente poca fidedigna, el Señor Timothy O'Rourke, Corresponsal de* Life *en America Latina, expulsado de nuestro país por . . .*"

"Peter!" she screamed.

His knees doubled. Then he was kneeling before the set, whispering "God! God! God!" so low she could scarcely hear him.

She got out of bed. Ran to him.

"Oh, Peter, Love, what is it?" she said. "What is he saying? What could he say to upset you so?"

"Nothing," he muttered. "Nothing that concerns you, Judy—"

"Tell me!" she said.

"They—they just killed somebody I was fond of, once," Peter said.

"But, Peter, I still don't get it," Judith said. "Why should they want to knock off poor old Buckteeth?"

"Judy, please!"

"Constance Buckleigh. Your ex-wife. Divorced from you. Married to H. Rodney Crosswaithe. Mother of his three kids. Why should anybody——"

Peter went on knotting his tie. Said, without looking at her:

"Because that's the only kind of divorce that counts in Costa Verde. Because Padre Pío got the Archbishop's back up and he wouldn't cooperate. Because Miguel Villalonga happened to see the fire burning up his nice, pretty airplanes and turned back. Because Luis couldn't, wouldn't, or hadn't time to call off his thugs. Or maybe even forgot—I wouldn't know. Because there are people big enough bastards to use even love——"

"Peter!"

"Yes, Judy?"

"You aren't making much sense, you know . . ."

He looked at her.

"Does anyone, ever, in this world?" he said.

"Peter—where are you going?"

"Out."

"Out where?"

"Out of here. Now stop asking so many questions. I've got things to do."

"Oh, no you don't, my beamish boy! Where you go, I go. You know, the latest thing: togetherness."

"Judy, you can't. I've got to see Luis. Got a couple of things to say to that boy. I've let what his goons did to me slide, so far; but this—"

"Peter—"

"Yes, Judy?"

"Think. You know, T-H-I-N-K. With that big head of yours. Which even has brains in it. Which even upon occasion, you can use."

"Damn!" Peter said.

"So you go to see that sweet, simple rattlesnake. You talk things over with Don No-Name Jive. He extends his regrets for knocking off poor old Connie. Or he denies it absolutely. And where are you?"

He looked at her.

"Nowhere," he said. "So?"

"So get back out of your things, darling. And let me comfort you. My turn now. I'm good at it."

"Baby," he said, "I'm in no mood for country comforts."

"You never are, with me, any more," she said.

And then the bells rang. The doorbell. And the telephone. Both of them, at the same time.

"You get the phone, baby," Peter said; "I'll attend to the door—"

"Why?" she said. "Afraid I'll shock somebody?"

"Judy, for God's sake!"

"Oh, let them ring, Peter! I—"

But he was gone in one long stride, out of the bedroom, closing the door behind him. It was a good thing he did; because when he opened the front door, Father Pío stood in it.

"So," Peter said, "you want me to use my good offices with Alicia to see that the penal system is modified?"

"Yes, my son," Father Pío said. "I do not know whether you know it, but it is of a vileness and a cruelty unimaginable. To be sent to one of the so-called Moral Correction Centers is simply a slow death sentence. The Social Re-education Centers, where the political prisoners are kept—though that distinction is not always observed—in them, the sentence is not even slow. Most do not live out a month. They are literally tortured to death. What I ask of you, son, is that if the day ever comes when you can marry Doña Alicia, you inspire her to—"

"Padre—" Peter said.

"Yes, Son Pedro?"

"I can never marry Alicia. Especially not now."

"Why not?" Padre Pío said. "Nothing is impossible with God. He may see fit to call your wife to a reckoning, or . . ."

"Padre, He already has. Constance is dead. I am a widower."

"Then," Father Pío said, "it is as I told the Arzobispo! Why should we be forced into mortal sin? Leave all matters up to the Good God! He—"

"Padre, I have absolutely nothing against your God—not even the fact that He's nearly always guilty of criminal negligence. I just don't like some of His self-appointed assistants. Luis Sinnombre, for instance."

"Son Pedro, what do you mean?" Father Pío said.

Then Peter told him.

The old man's face was very still and sad.

"You have much right, my son," he said. "There are many things upon which a marriage may be based, but never upon a murdered woman's blood. Strange. You would deny your faith; yet all your moral instincts are sound."

Peter glanced toward that closed bedroom door.

"Are they, Father?" he said.

"Yes," the old priest said. "Now I must go. Bearing with me, I must admit, the burden of a heart heavier than when I came."

"Father," Peter said.

"Yes, Pedro?"

"Do you believe that God has forgotten the use of men of valor? That if a Gideon were to rise now—a Samson, a David, a Saul—or, best of all, a Joshua—to blow down the walls behind which freedom dies, would God condemn his anger? Or, more—if he were to stain his hands with the blood of the wicked, would God turn away from him? Is there forever a condemnation set upon human wrath, however just?"

"I do not follow you, my son—"

"Nor do I follow myself, entirely. A vagrant thought, Father. Perhaps an idle one. Shall we leave the clarions of liberty, the trumpet calls against the oppressors of the people to los Castristas, Padre? Leave the Reds to use men's hunger, anguish, need for their own dirty ends? Or shall we——?"

The old man stood up.

"I cannot answer that, Son Pedro," he said. "I am not wise enough."

"But there must be an answer, somewhere, Father."

The old man smiled.

"There is. Oh, there is. In your own heart, my son. If you were to spend the whole of one night upon your knees, you would be surprised at the illumination there!"

"Peter," Judith said, "we're in for it again."

"In for what again?" Peter said.

"A party. At Doctor Vince's house, this time. Only it's going to be more of the same. His Nibs is going to be there."

"And Luis?"

"Yes. And your sweet Alicia. Oh, it's going to be just ginger-peachy, Peter! Jolly. Bully. Top hole. You know any more outmoded slang?"

"It all is, as far as I'm concerned. Look, Judy, go take a shower and get dressed. A shower, not the tub; I've got things to do, and I don't have two hours to wait."

"What things?" Judith said.

"Feeding you, for one; you're getting downright skinny—"

"Judging from Alicia la Dulce, I thought you liked 'em like that."

"Them, not you. You I like *llenita,* which means well covered. Get going, Judy—"

"Peter, what other things do you have to do?"

"Buy a swagger stick."

"A *whaaaat?*"

"A swagger stick. You know, a little cane, too short to walk with. You tuck it up under one arm. Use it to smite the insolent members of the lower orders. Veddy, veddy U. Or something."

"Peter—come again?"

"Judy, I just told you . . ."

"Oh, no. 'Cause I know you, Lover. You don't smite the lower orders. You're fairly dripping with liberalism, democracy, and brotherly love. Not to mention the milk of human kindness. Come on, Peter, give!"

"Believe it or not, Judy, I'm actually going to buy a swagger stick."

"I heard you the first time. What I want to know is why."

Peter frowned.

"Hard to explain, Judy. Say it's a symbol. No, a reminder."

"A reminder of what, Peter?"

"The day old Grandpa Ape picked up a stick and thereby became—man."

"Pe-tah!"

"The tool-bearing animal. A short extension of one's hairy paw. A stick's a useful object, Judy. You can use it to point with. Or to root out vermin. Judy, will you please—"

"Peter, you're going to do something foolish! I just know . . ."

"When haven't I? Now, will you go bathe? You smell like Saturday night at Susie's."

"That's why I love you, darling. You say the nicest things!" Judith said.

Doctor Vicente Gomez-García's house was in that district of Ciudad Villalonga known as Puerta de Oro. The district was exactly what its name indicated. The people who lived in this section didn't actually have golden doors on their houses; but they probably could have had, if they had wanted to. When he saw the line of Chryslers, Lincolns, Cadillacs, Mercedeses, Rollses, Bentleys, Daimlers lined up before Vince's door, he took a long slow look at the battered Ford he had rented for the occasion.

"Speaking of the Lower Orders," he said, and pointed at the Ford with his new teak-and-ivory swagger stick.

Judith laughed. Tucked the stiff shawl of tulle higher up around her neck.

"Nick the Greek," she said, "and his scarred-up moll. Tell me, Peter —does it show?"

"A little," Peter said. "Don't worry about it, baby. Besides, that scar is the best advertising I ever had. Now all the little creatures just line up, their *bragas* already off—"

"Bragas?" Judy said.

"Panties. Scanties. Culottes. Minimum essentials."

"I'll bet. And it may even be true. The way your little Alicia—"

"Judy, can't we kind of, sort of stay off that subject tonight, please? I've got troubles enough."

"Oh, all right, darling," Judith said.

Through the ironwork grille of the gate they could see the lights on in the garden, and the men in white dinner jackets and the women in Paris creations, sitting or strolling around the swimming pool. Actually, the lights were superfluous with Zopocomapetl growing angrier (or, if you accepted Alicia's version, more amused) every night. But they did serve to counteract the baleful red of the volcano's glare. Before he touched the bell, Peter took a long look. Saw the uniformed policemen standing in the shadows. Saw, too, from the width of shoulders of some of the men in dinner jackets, from the paleolithic heads sitting on those shoulders like a boulder on a wall, unseparated by anything remotely resembling a neck, that there were detectives among the guests. Then a little farther off, he saw Miguel Villalonga surrounded by a little group of most respectful men. And Luis Sinnombre turning his fine black subterranean perverse charm on a group of women. But there was no sign of Alicia. No sign at all.

Judith grinned.

"Chickened out on you, darling?" she said.

"Could be," Peter said, and touched the bell.

A uniformed manservant opened the gate for them. They went in and pole-axed all conversation. Every woman in the garden was staring with frank curiosity at Judith, while Vince led the concentrated rush of males toward the gate. For a long moment they were surrounded. Peter had met most of the men at Señor Corona's house. In fact, the Minister of Information and Tourism was among them now. They all laughed, joked, and presented each other to Judith. Then they bore her off, presumably to introduce her to the women, calling back to Peter:

"Take your pick, Don Pedro! There are many girls—"

But Peter reached out and caught Vince by the arm. Leaned close; said:

"Alicia?"

"Inside the house. With Paloma. And my mother. She looked so ill when she came that they took her in hand. Dreadfully upset over something, which I gather is connected with you—right?"

"Right," Peter said.

"Want to tell me what it is?" Vince said.

"No," Peter said.

"Oh," Vince said. "Look, Peter; I didn't mean to pry—"

"You're not prying. And I could tell you. Only I think this particular item is dangerous. The kind people get killed down here for knowing."

"Oh," Vince said again.

"Alicia," Peter said; "any way you can arrange for me to see her?"

"Later," Vince said. "*After* you've chatted with our Glorious Leader."

"Hell," Peter said.

"I agree; but one doesn't say it, Peter. Bad form. And dangerous. Incidentally, you've done wonders for Alicia's public image."

"I?" Peter said. "How?"

"That stunt of getting her to make Luis turn all those people loose."

"I didn't get her to do a damned thing. She did it on her own."

"She would. Sweet little thing, really. And she's won over the Social Register by saving Marisol Talaveda. Part of it's bitchy curiosity, of course. The girls are dying for you—or her—to confirm the current rumor that she took dear little Mari's place."

"I'll send flowers to their funerals," Peter said.

Luis Sinnombre stepped out of the shadows, suddenly, and took Peter's arm.

"My dear Peter," he said, "what on earth is this?"

"A swagger stick," Peter said.

"May I see it?" Luis said.

"Of course," Peter said and passed it over.

Luis stood there, holding the slim, wandlike stick with the ivory head. He gave the head a tentative twist.

"It doesn't have a blade in it," Peter said.

Luis laughed.

"I didn't think it did," he said, "but I preferred to make sure. You just might have heard that broadcast this afternoon."

"I did," Peter said.

"I feared, dear Peter, that you might have jumped to conclusions. Erroneous conclusions—just as the New York police did, thanks to your friend O'Rourke."

"Look, Luis," Vince said, "I'd better go see to my guests—"

"No, stay, Vince," Luis said. "I prefer to have this particular conversation witnessed. For Peter's sake. And, truthfully, for mine. Peter, do you believe that I, through agents of mine, had your ex-wife killed?"

"*Dios!*" Vince said. "So that was it! La Señora de Crosswaithe was—"

"My ex-wife. Yes. To your question, Vince. And also, Luis, to yours."

Luis smiled. Handed Peter back the little swagger stick.

"So, believing that, you went out and bought—this?" he said.

"Yes," Peter said.

"Which, as you've allowed me to prove, contains no hidden weapon, and is too small and light for beating a man?"

"Yes," Peter said again.

"Might I ask why?"

"Doesn't conceal weapons. It *is* a weapon. A magic wand. You point it at assassins, and they disappear. Only it doesn't work yet."

"Why not?" Vince said.

"Haven't had Padre Pío bless it for me. That's one of the essential ingredients. One of the two essential ingredients."

"And the other is?" Luis said.

"Truth," Peter said.

Luis laughed easily, gaily.

"Peter," he said, "do you know the details of how Constance Buckleigh Reynolds Crosswaithe died?"

"Yes," Peter said. "I called my paper in New York. And got through. Which meant that you wanted me to know those details, Luis."

"I did. And they were?"

"The killer entered her home during the day. While her husband was at work, her children off at school. He shot her with a Luger. He was a bad shot. The bullet went through her right shoulder. He tried again, and the Luger jammed. Apparently he was unfamiliar with that type of sidearm."

"Go on," Luis Sinnombre said.

"He couldn't get it to fire again. So he hammered her head bloody with the butt. Broke off one of the plastic grips, which is why the police know it was a Luger. But Connie is a tall, strong woman. Ex-tennis champion. He dragged her into the bathroom and tried to drown her in the tub. She revived, got away from him. He followed her into the kitchen and broke a carving knife off in her throat—"

"*Dios mío!*" Vince said.

"But she still got away from him. Ran, walked, crawled to the nearest neighbor's house. She died with her finger on the bell."

"You are very accurate, Peter. Now may I ask you another question?"

"Go ahead."

"Is there anything you know about me—anything you've heard, that would make you imagine I'd hire a clumsy idiot butcher like that one?"

Peter stood there.

"La Señora Crosswaithe lived in the outskirts of Great Neck, Long Island. Daily she drove her husband to the station to catch the Commuter's Special. This, of course, after having deposited the children at school. And your superhighways, my dear Peter, are hideously dangerous. At any intersection, a heavy truck, with its brakes out of commission, say, might have crashed into her Plymouth Valiant Compact, white, matricula 356 GN 175; turned it over; reduced it to one of those lamentable masses of twisted steel and splintered glass one sees so often in the newsreels. That, my dear Peter, would have been the intelligent method of assassinating la Señora Crosswaithe, don't you think?"

Peter stood there. Ran his tongue tip over bone-dry lips.

"Then *who?*" he said.

Luis shrugged.

"How should I know? A psycho, likely. You have so many of them," he said.

XV

The party, as parties do, was gathering speed. Vince had the big glass doors thrown open and people were wandering into the dining room and coming back with plates piled high with cold cuts, salads, shellfish, chicken. Only the serious drinkers lingered in the garden. Among them, Peter saw worriedly, Judith.

He heard her voice soar above the general rumble of male conversation, the glissando ripple of female laughter, glass tinkle, the clicking of silver against fine china.

"Oh no, Señora Corona! I don't worry about Peter—" she was projecting a good line over, getting it past the footlights, her tone not exactly ringing, but full, strong, deceptively effortless—"at least I haven't, up until now . . ."

The dramatic pause, the timing right, perfect, until Sara Martinez de Corona, the Minister's wife, broke it, coming in exactly on cue.

"But now you do?" she said.

"Yes," Judith said; "you Latin American girls are so sexy! I kind of, sort of, suspect that down here my Peter has been had."

"By whom?" Sara Corona said.

"Oh, no!" Judith laughed; "that would be indiscreet, Señora! Especially considering present company . . ."

Then Peter saw that Miguel Villalonga was sitting beside her. Luis had moved a little way off. Out of prudence, likely.

"And you, my dear Judith, are the soul of discretion, no?" the Dictator said.

Peter started moving toward them.

"Oh, come now," another woman—a girl really, not long in her twenties—said: "Surely you *know* who she is."

It was all wrong. Wrong and incongruous. Then he looked at the girl. Recognized her. He had been introduced to her at Señor Corona's party. Carmen—Carmencita Miraflores. Daughter of a man he'd interviewed once—Joaquin Miraflores, Costa Verde's richest citizen. Industrialist and rancher. One of the backers of the Standford Expedition to Ururchizenaya. And, if rumor were telling the truth, as rumor quite often did, the man who had financed Miguel Villalonga's rise to power, having seen in him a bulwark against the same hungry masses from whom he sprang. But even so, it was only a little less wrong. Carmencita should have known better. The Leader had long since proved his capacity for biting the hand that fed him. For, in fact, chewing off the entire arm. It was he who used the rich and idle aristocracy who had planned to use him; throwing sons, husbands, fathers, into those prisons from which no man emerged alive; converting daughters, sisters, wives into reluctant whores to avenge, surely, their very knowledge of what his own mother had been and was. Then Peter saw that The Leader was drunk. Or pretending to be.

"Oh, yes! I know all right," Judith began.

"Judy!" Peter said.

"Have the goodness to leave her in peace, Reynolds!" the Dictator said. "This is, after all, a Republic, an Organic Democracy. Free speech is permitted."

"For how long?" Peter said.

"As long as it takes to offend me," Miguel said. "And tonight I am in a complacent, even a permissive, mood. Good food, good wine, excellent company. Go on, Judith. Tell us who it is that has had your friend Reynolds."

Judith looked at him. Smiled.

"Your little sister," she said.

Nobody spoke. The silence hummed, smoke-blue, spark-shot, electric. Everyone within reach of Judith's voice had ceased, quite literally, to breathe.

Miguel Villalonga's heavy, bluish lips spread. He smiled.

"Are you now going to define the verb *had,* dear Judith?" he said.

"Are you?" Alicia's voice whispered through the dead-stopped air. "Can you, Judith?" She came toward them out of the shadows by a little door that must have been a service entrance. Now she stood there where Peter could see her, and her face was ravaged. "Can you, Judith?" she said again.

"Judy!" Peter said.

"Don't interrupt, Reynolds! Free speech and women's rights!" The Leader said.

"Had," Judith said, her voice a feline purr. "To have possessed—as physically. To have indulged in boudoir acrobatics, horizontal gymnastics, indoor sports, fun and games. All right?"

"No," Alicia said, "not all right."

"Then you deny—?" Miguel said.

"Nothing!" Alicia said, and her voice was quiet. "Nor admit anything either, Miguel. What may or may not have passed between Peter and me is a matter that concerns only us, our consciences, and our God. I say simply that the Señorita Lovell's definition of *had* is not all right; that if she defines possession thus, I pity her. Peter, *Cielo*, I should like to talk with you—away from this panting pack. Would you?"

"Of course," Peter said and took her arm.

"Wait," Judith said. "'S not fair. How would you define it, Doña Alicia?"

Alicia stopped. Her eyes were luminous.

"How?" she said. "How does one describe white to a blind man, Judith? One says snow, and he thinks of cold."

"Cold, babydoll, is the last thing I'd think of in connection with you," Judith said.

Alicia nodded.

"That I grant you," she said. "But we waste time. Talk between people so different as you and I amounts to the concealment of thought. In my case, now, not even intentionally. I simply cannot say it. It comes out wrong."

"Try," Judith said.

"No," Alicia said. "The effort is too painful. And the subject itself not to be profaned by mouthing over in public, Judith. To me, so total a tenderness was, and is—a sacred thing."

"Alicia." Miguel's voice was heavy, tired.

"Yes, Miguel?"

"You realize that those words amount to a confession?"

"Do they? I still say white is white and you are blind. You and all the rest. Come, Peter, Amor. I have things to say to you."

"No!" Miguel said. "You will say them here, Alicia!"

She stood there looking at her brother.

"Very well," she whispered; then suddenly, wildly, blindly, she whirled and clung to Peter, went up on tiptoe, and kissed his mouth

"Well, I'll be goddamned!" Judith said.

Nobody else said anything. They didn't even gasp. Instead they measured their breaths out on the dead-still air.

"That, *Cielo*, is the first of the things I have to say to you," Alicia said. "That I love you. I tell you so in the presence of these witnesses and before my God. The second is that I shall go on loving you for the little time I have left before I die."

"Nena," Peter said. "You shouldn't. I—"

"The third is that this ends here and now. You will never see me again after this night. Oh, Peter, *Cielo,* that that poor woman had to die that way! That she should die like that because of me, never having heard my name!"

"It was not your fault, Nena," Peter said.

"Wasn't it? At least by cowardice, my Love? If I had made it clear beforehand that I should respond to the murder of Señora Crosswaithe by a public immolation, by an auto da fe in the Plaza de la Liberación, like those Buddhist monks in Saigon, then—"

"They would have prevented you," Peter said.

"They could not have! Any more than they can prevent . . ."

"'Licia," Peter said.

She hid her face against him, crying.

"Luis!" the Dictator cried. "Do not move, my friend. Remain where you are!"

Luis Sinnombre stood there. Looking at him, Peter saw he showed no sign of fear.

"Reynolds," Miguel said, "what was la Señora Crosswaithe to you?"

"My wife. Ex. Separated. Divorced. Which is, of course, entirely meaningless in the eyes of the Church, and before God."

"My dear Luis," Miguel said, "what a sentimentalist you have become. Furthering young love! Though to call Reynolds young is rather stretching the point. And I—I had gone fishing. Normally, I should not have returned for weeks. Whereupon you would have presented me with—"

"A *fait accompli,*" Luis said. "Or, more accurately, an opening toward the Left, Italian style. With a charming, popular young couple for you to hide behind. To lull the canalla into a sort of contentment. And thereby, dear Miguel, avoid the fate of being hanged beside you like the good thief. Though I seriously doubt that either of us shall ever see Paradise."

"Luis, dear brother," Miguel laughed, "I love you. I love the deviousness of your mind. But best of all I love the clumsiness with which you have operated in this case. I was beginning to be a bit apprehensive of your Machiavellian turn of thought. But this crude and ugly butchery is unworthy of you. Ugh! You've put us in quite a spot with Our Great Sister Republic to the North, you know."

"I have not," Luis said. "Someone anticipated me, Miguel. Somebody liquidated the dear lady for reasons of his own. Accuse me of what you will, but this sort of stupidity—no, Miguel. You know me better than that."

The Dictator looked at Peter.

"Reynolds," he said, "is it not possible that you grew impatient?"

"Your Excellency," Peter said, "is it not possible that you and Don Luis have already talked too much in the presence of too many people?"

"Ha!" Villalonga said. "You suffer from the poverty of spirit that comes from living under a system where noses are counted instead of brains and will. I, and to a lesser extent Luis, can say what we will, wherever we will. Who, my dear Reynolds, would dare gainsay us?"

"I might," Peter said. "One day I may point this little stick at you and—"

"Oh, don't talk rot, Reynolds! Tell me, did you purchase your ex-wife's death?"

"No," Peter said. "The season's permanently closed on females, so far as I'm concerned. Besides, what would I have done with Judith, here?"

Alicia tightened her arms about his neck. Peter turned his face away from Judith's eyes.

Miguel looked at Luis.

"Now that's a thought," he said. "Luis, once your matrimonial agency had achieved its object, what did you propose to do with our lovely screen star?"

Luis came over to him. Bent close to his ear. Then the two of them rocked with laughter.

Judith stood up.

"Peter! Will you turn that woman loose and take me home!"

"My dear Judith," Miguel said, "please do not desolate me by leaving. You will pardon our bad manners. Unlike these gentle people here, Luis and I are plebeian, and we have had little home training. Alicia, dear, be so kind as to turn Reynolds loose. Give him back to his rightful owner. And hurry, or I shall borrow that silly little cane of his and beat you with it, in public!"

Alicia released Peter. Stepped back. Then she saw Judith's eyes. Went up to her, took her hand, said:

"Forgive me. I do not like to cause pain—even to you. And I was never a threat, even when I thought I was. I should have known that they would spoil it for me. As they have spoiled everything, all my life

They even grow cleverer. Now they don't even need to blow up airplanes . . ."

"Alicia, dearest," Paloma Gomez said, "I'm afraid you talk too much!"

"What does it matter now, Paloma? Cannot the dying speak the truth? And in one form or another, I am already dead. Since"—she made a wry little gesture with her hand toward Peter's face—"this image will forever blind my eyes to any other, I end tonight."

"Now look, child, don't be a fool," Judith said, not unkindly.

Alicia put out her slim hand, let her fingers stray along the scar on Judith's throat.

"Were you, when you did that?" she said.

"Hell and death!" Miguel said. "I tire of hysterics, histrionics, and melodrama. Alicia, go lie down somewhere. Paloma, dear, put her in a spare bedroom and lock the door. If she weren't my sister, I'd have her shot for spoiling my evening."

"Why don't you, Miguel? I should thank you," Alicia said.

Paloma got up, took her by the arm.

"Come along, Alicia. I really do think you should lie down; don't you?" she said.

"Judy," Peter said, "how about a little food to weigh down some of that Scotch?"

"Oh, all right," Judith said, and got up at once.

"Wonder of wonders!" Miguel Villalonga said. "You don't mean that an enlightened North American woman is actually going to obey a man!"

"Oh," Judith said; "Peter's different. You see, he beats me."

"Bravo, Reynolds!" The Leader said. "A pity to have to shoot you, really!"

"Peter," Judith was saying, as she put a pinch of this and that on her plate from the magnificent buffet supper Vince had spread on the immense table, dating back at least to the reign of Juana la Loca, "You think His Nibs means it?"

"I know he means it," Peter said, "only he won't dare."

"I think he's beginning to like you as a brother-in-law. Oh, damn your fatal charm!"

"Which I don't have," Peter said.

"You've got me," Judith said, "and you've got her—and still you say—"

"That's why I say it," Peter said.

Judith looked at him now. From the way she did it, it was probable she saw at least three of him.

"Meaning?"

"Meaning that maybe you can judge a guy by what he attracts, Judy. And I'm getting a little sick of playing snug harbor to shipwrecked dames."

"Oh!" she said. "Y'know what, Peter?"

"No, what?" he said.

"That's the filthy, rotten, nasty, stinking, lousy—truth. So help me, it is! C'mon, let's go back outside, shall we? I'm parched. I need another little drink . . ."

"Judith baby, I wish you wouldn't—"

"Do I sound like a drunken female, darling?"

"No. But you're getting there. Your speech has retreated back to Boston. You're murdering your consonants."

"Am I?" Judith said. "Poor consonants! Come on . . ."

But he had no sooner brought her back to that empty chair than Vince's *ayudera de cama*—valet—came up to him and whispered in his ear:

"Pardon me, Señor Reynolds, but you are wanted on the telephone."

As he moved away from the little group composed of Miguel, Luis, Paloma, Carmencita, Vince, Sara, Don Andres, he could see they were all very gay. Judith was gayer than anybody. He could hear her talking much too loudly. Her voice was blurring fast now.

He walked through the big glass doors.

The phone was in the oak-paneled library. Peter glanced at the periwigged and goateed portraits of Vince's ancestors, at the rows of books, leather-bound, handsome, the dull gold of their titles glowing softly in the subdued light. He picked up the phone.

"*Camarada*?" a man's voice said. "Camarada Reynolds?"

"If you cut that Comrade bit, you've got it right," Peter said. "Speaking."

"I am a friend of him of the yellow eyes," the man said.

"Fine. Great. I'm so happy for you," Peter said.

"I do not jest," the man said. "Do you like the artificial fires, Amigo?"

"Fireworks?" Peter said. "Where?"

"In the Barrio de la Negra. At the warehouse belonging to him whose company you must endure this night. After that, at the Archbishop's place. We war on oppression and superstition both!"

"Look, friend, I wish you'd lay off the Archbishop. He's a friend of a friend of mine."

"You mean Padre Pío? For that very reason, his life will be spared. And the other?"

"*De acuerdo.* That one I'm for—that one I'm with you. In twenty minutes, friend."

He turned and saw Alicia standing behind him.

"Take me with you, Peter," she said.

"And get you shot or blown up again? Not on your life, Nena!"

"Then take my car. The white Jaguar outside. It replaces the Lincoln. There is a pistol in the glove compartment. It is loaded. But please take me with you, Peter . . ."

He took the keys from her outstretched hand.

"I mean to take you with me, permanently. But not this trip," he said.

He knew where the Barrio de la Negra was. It was a poor district crowded with slum dwellings and small factories. Also warehouses. Like the one belonging to His Nibs. The Barrio was called *of the Negress* because it had a jet-black Virgin in its oldest church. Tradition held she had been washed up from the sea. She hadn't been designed to represent a Negress; it was just that she had been carved of ebony, which naturally left her dark. Once Tim O'Rourke had tried to buy her from the church with the general idea—inspired by an overdose of Scotch—of trying to enroll her in the University of Mississippi. He had his lead already written: "Ole Miss Rejects the Mother of God!" but the people of the Barrio had a genuine devotion for La Negra. Tim had had to drop the idea and even leave the Barrio in some haste.

Peter did not go straight there. Instead he turned the Jaguar into his own street, went upstairs and got his Rolleiflex and his strobe. He was coming down the stairs when it hit him. He had got out of the side gate of Vince's house, walked through an army of chronically suspicious policemen, and nobody had stopped him. He had got into Alicia's new white Jaguar which, if anything, was even more conspicuous than the Lincoln had been, and the Armed Civil Guard, who automatically should have been watching the parked cars, had been nowhere to be seen. To go farther back, Alicia's behavior, sufficient in itself to have caused any Costa Verdian whatsoever to have shot him dead on the spot, had been accepted by Miguel Villalonga with bored complaisance. Or had it? And, worst of all, Alicia herself had given up far too easily to his refusal to take her with him. He sat there at the wheel of the white torpedo and stared out into the night. Then he gunned the car, roaring through the empty streets, through which that darkest hour drifted with no faintest promise of the dawn.

Looking at his watch, he saw he had time. So he rammed the Jaguar through a series of power-skidded turns, and approached the Barrio de la Negra from the south, in the direction directly opposite from that anyone waiting for him would have expected him to come. When he was close enough, he did still another thing—he stopped the Jaguar, got out, locked it, and started to walk in the general direction of The Leader's warehouse.

He got there. Found the warehouse alone and unguarded. "In this country where they'd put an armed guard in front of a pit privy if it belonged to a VIP," he muttered. Then he moved away from it, walking almost on tiptoe. Even so, his own footsteps were loud in the empty street. He moved back. Stopped. He had the battery pack of the strobe draped over one shoulder and the Rollei hung around his neck. For some idiotic reason—half superstition, really, he had that damned fool swagger stick hung around his left wrist by the little strap it was provided with. And, now that he was still, he could hear noises. They sounded like breathing.

He moved off, stopped. The sound of breathing came from still another place. And with it, the hard clink of metal. There was no doubt about it, the whole square was surrounded by hidden men. So well hidden that even though his eyes were accustomed to the darkness now, he could not see them. So beautifully concealed that this *coup* must have been planned for days.

He started edging away toward what is called in Spanish *una boca calle,* a mouth street, that is, a street opening into the square. But, before he got two meters from where he had stood, he heard those footsteps coming on. He stopped, pointed the Rollei in the direction from which the sound came. Focused it by guesswork and feel, racking the twin lens all the way out, then back again so that a reasonable depth would be acceptably clear.

He waited. The footsteps came on, heavy and slow, obviously burdened. Then he did something that is the kind of thing called genius when it works and idiocy when it doesn't. He opened his mouth, yelled "Halt!" at the top of his lungs. Then he punched the shutter release of the Rollei.

The strobe murdered the dark. For one instant he saw the man standing there, his mouth a round black cavern in the frozen white terror of his face.

Then Peter cranked the Rollei and shot, and shot again, the white repeated lightnings building up recognizable images in his mind.

"Well, I'll be damned!" he murmured. "The pretty sarge who——"

But that was all. The blue-stained dawn coolness broke apart into shattered fragments, flame stabbed, borne in upon him on a rush of air grown solid, impenetrable, the sound a physical impact that rocked him like a double punch to both ears, so that he lay there on the ground with the smoke rising from his singed clothes, where the vortex of the whirlwind that followed or accompanied or even preceded the sound had smashed him down, in the midst of a silent, glare-washed world that dissolved very slowly into renewed darkness, echoes and a stench he couldn't recognize.

He got up from there. Reeled toward the middle of the square, forgetting that it was very probably surrounded, and stood there looking down through the thinning darkness at the Sergeant who had been the active member of the interrogation team, or rather what was left of him. A pair of trouser-clad legs lay in the square; hips, buttocks, a part of the abdomen. Above that nothing, except the slow seep of blackness draining out of what was left. He raised his eyes toward the shattered shop windows. Saw, in the deep-blue fading of the dark what dripped from every wall within a radius of twenty meters.

He could hear the frightened cries starting from all the houses, see the lights come winking on, so he brought the Rollei to sharp focus and washed that shattered, bloody debris of what had been a man in sudden lightnings, cranked the Rollei and fired again, and still once more, hearing the shrill babble of women's voices from the window, the stride of many men, heavy, purposeful, racing in; and lifted his head, making his bitter, irrevocable decision, his choice between evils, crying:

"No, Comrades! The square is surrounded!"

And, whirling, got out of there through a dawn gone hideous with siren scream, racing miraculously unstopped, unarrested, unshot, toward where he had left the car, and getting there, slowing, stopping, coming on with his hands raised above his head now, straight toward the muzzles of those Czech-made machine pistols he had seen before, and recognized from another time.

"No, Comrade, put your hands down. You are among friends," their leader said.

XVI

He had been in the makeshift prison a long time. It was the boiler room of an abandoned factory filled with machinery rusting away in the tropical damp. They had placed two guards over him, youngsters in their late teens, armed with the inevitable Sten guns, clearly middle-class by their looks and behavior, which didn't surprise him, because never in all of history have revolutionists sprung from the ranks of the proletariat, for the very simple reason that to upend the world, envy is a more potent weapon than despair. The two guards had sat by the door, looking stern and grave and threatening for almost an hour after the others had gone, making the controlled, underplayed gestures of menace they had learned from old Hollywood gangster films, before they gave it up and started to ask him questions about his adventures in the Sierras; about the now-legendary Jacinto of the Yellow Eyes; even—with an indirection and delicacy that proved they belonged to the University-student class—about his relations with Alicia. He told them what he could, and also what they wanted to hear—which was usually, but not always, the same thing. He evaded the questions about Alicia with a half-chuckled *"Hombre—"* and a widespread gesture of his hands that left them with the delighted belief that they knew everything, while in sober fact they knew nothing. And they ended up laughing and joking with him, smoking his cigarettes, and winning most of his money from him at poker, which he let them do in the interest of good will.

But now they were both asleep by the door that not merely didn't have a lock on it but whose bolt was rusted solid as well, so that the officers hadn't been able to fasten it with that and had given up trying and left the teen-agers to guard him when it finally occurred to them that the bolt was on the inside of the door anyhow, and hence useless for keeping a prisoner in. He looked at the two youngsters where they lay, sprawled out bonelessly on the damp cement floor, their young faces slack and untroubled. Then, lifting his gaze, he could see through the little iron-grilled window at street level the pale, washed-out, yellowish light of another dawn, convincing himself at last that his big military-type chronometer with the luminous dial hadn't been lying when it indicated that nearly twenty-four hours had slipped over the rim of the world since they had brought him there.

"Baby boys," he whispered in the general direction of his guards, "it's not simple. It's not simple at all. But don't find that out, yet. Enjoy your youth. Go on believing it."

Then Martin, the Second in Command, came through the door. Stood there looking at the guards.

"Look at them!" he said. "Idiots! Dolts! Why——" Then he drew back his foot and sent it thudding into their ribs. They jackknifed, snatching up their burp guns. Then they saw who it was and put them down again.

"You are a brave man, Amigo," Peter said.

"But you, Comrade Reporter, are not, or else you would have been twelve kilometers from here by now!" Martin said.

Pablo, the Commander, stepped through the door.

"I think that is open to various interpretations. Why did you not escape, Comrade Reporter?"

"I like it here. It's kind of cozy," Peter said.

"All right," Pablo said. "We developed the pictures in your camera. You are a remarkable photographer, Comrade. Would you like to see the prints?"

"God, no!" Peter said.

"As you like. You will be pleased to know that the negatives are already on the way to your paper in New York. This publicity is in our interest. That fool even wore his uniform."

"How did you get them out?" Peter said.

"Martin, here, is a skirt-chaser of the first class. One of his latest conquests is a Gringa airline hostess, who now walks spraddle-legged down the passage of the airplane because he keeps her so sore, that she can no longer close those long, beautiful thighs of which your women seem to have the exclusivity. She will deliver them personally to the office of your paper."

"I hope she can get a taxi," Peter said.

Martin laughed.

"Comrade Reporter," Pablo said, "I thank you for warning us that the square was surrounded. But for that, we should have been slaughtered. Another group of Comrades, who, hearing the explosion at the Archbishop's palace—an explosion from which the little Padre Pío escaped by a miracle, for clearly they wished to murder him and blame us for it—rushed out, and all were killed but three. And those three were captured."

"Don't you boys ever learn?" Peter said. "The same thing happened when Federico blew up the truck factory."

"I know. But we are betrayed both by impatience and by hope. In any event, I thank you. But for you, we should all be dead now, or like the three before the Archbishop's Palace, taken."

"Those three are the unlucky ones," Peter said.

"I know. Two of them are friends of mine. I do not like to think about what is happening to them now."

"Nor I," Peter said. "Comrade Chief, would you like to do something about—that?"

Pablo looked at him.

"Why do you ask?" he said.

"I stayed here to ask it," Peter said. "I did not escape in order to ask it."

"Careful, Pablo!" Martin said. "Take care!"

"Comrade Martin, have you ever read the English writer Maugham?" Peter said.

"No," Martin said.

"He wrote something about you once. Or about somebody very much like you. He said: 'He was very suspicious, and therefore an easy dupe.' Think about it."

"I have thought," Martin said. "And it makes no sense."

"What does?" Peter said.

"What could be done about those who have been captured?" Pablo said.

"If you will release me, I will return here at midnight with the information concerning the exact location of the Moral Correction and Social Re-education Centers."

"Why?" Pablo said.

"You have those little Czech-made popguns. Also, doubtless, a supply of Hexogen—or RDX, if you prefer, mixed with TNT in a rubber-compound base. Or, to put it more vulgarly, plastic. I know of no other edifices in all Costa Verde I'd rather see plasticized."

"Why?" Pablo said again.

"You see these scars upon my face? The new ones? The ones that are still pink?"

"Yes," Pablo said softly, "I see them, Comrade."

"I still say it is a trick!" Martin said. "Just as they sent *agents-pro-*

vocateurs to blow up their own palaces and warehouses in order to gain sympathy abroad, and to have an excuse to root us out, they could have scarred him thus in order to—"

"He called out," Pablo said. "He warned us. Else we would have been killed."

"All right," Martin said; "but have you not learned with what a subtlety the mind of this *cabron* of a Villalonga works? Tell me a thing, Comrade Chief of the Band: Why did they not shoot him, afterwards? Or even arrest him? Why did they let him go?"

Pablo looked at Peter. And now he, too, was frowning.

"Have you an explanation for that, Comrade Reporter?" he said.

"No. It puzzles me as well," Peter said, "except that—"

"Except what?" Martin said.

"Their officers may be among those who are laboring under the misapprehension that my friendship with Doña Alicia Villalonga has the approval, even the consent, of The Leader."

"Hasn't it? People in the *barrio* where you reside say that she visits your apartment openly, and that you are her lover," Pablo said.

"People in my *barrio*, like people everywhere, have an excessive fondness for speculating over things they do not know," Peter said.

"They also say that you are influencing her in favor of the humble classes," Pablo said.

"I did not have to influence her. Doña Alicia is a very gallant woman, Amigo."

"Yet," Martin said, "before you came, she did nothing!"

"Before I came, she felt herself alone. Now she feels supported by me."

"So," Martin said, "you would have us believe that The Leader does not approve of your pretensions toward his sister?"

"I have no pretensions toward Doña Alicia; but no matter. The Leader does not approve of me—period."

"And yet you live?" Martin said. "Ha!"

"Amigo Martin, have you ever seen a cat with a mouse between his paws? Do you know what he does?"

"Yes. He releases it. Lets it run. Catches it again. Turns it loose once more. Until he tires of the sport, and then—"

"Exactly," Peter said.

"But to leave you free to walk the streets—"

"In this one enormous prison that your country is, what difference does that make?"

"And Doña Alicia," Martin said; "what are her feelings toward *you*, Comrade Reporter?"

"*Hombre*," Peter said, "the feelings of a woman toward a man are always a matter of speculation, even when they are married. Let us say she does not dislike me excessively."

"She," Pablo said, "kissed you on a public street in the full sight of hundreds of witnesses, including three jeeploads of police. She declared in a loud voice that she had spent the night in your arms. What do you say to that, Don Pedro, Friend of the Poor?"

"That she lied," Peter said. "She was trying to save my life. As I told you before, she is a very gallant woman, Comrade."

And now Martin was looking at him in a new way, a way that was hard to define; then, turning to Pablo, said, with what sounded curiously like joy:

"Ay, yes, Comrade Chief; let him go! You are right. He will return to us. I guarantee it!"

Luis was not in his office. So Peter asked to see Colonel Lopez. He already knew where Colonel Lopez stood. The Colonel was laboring under that very special misapprehension—that now exceedingly useful misapprehension. When Peter walked into his office, his astonishment was plain.

"My dear Reynolds," he said. "I have my entire force scouring the earth for you, and you walk into my office!"

"As big as life, and twice as ugly," Peter said. "Mind if I sit down? I'm tired."

"Of course, of course! Tell me, where on earth have you been?"

Peter grinned at him.

"That information's classified, Colonel," he said.

"Ah, romance!" the Colonel said, "I wish I had your gifts, my friend!"

"So do I—at least those I'm popularly credited with having," Peter said.

"The evidence would indicate—" Colonel Lopez began.

"Nothing. Like all evidence, it is circumstantial and inconclusive. I seem to have a fatal affinity for either the hurtful—or the hurt," Peter said. "Look, Colonel—is there any reason why you couldn't tell me the location of the Moral Correction and Social Re-education centers?"

Colonel Lopez studied him.

"So far as I know, none," he said slowly. "That you're alive still, and walking the streets would indicate . . ."

"Love that phrase, don't you?" Peter said. "To be honest, Colonel, I'm not at all sure they indicate a goddamned thing. But I would like to know where those torture factories and murder camps are . . ."

"Why?" the Colonel said.

"Life insurance," Peter said. "Want me to make you one of the beneficiaries of the policy?"

"I'm not sure I get your meaning, my dear Reynolds," Colonel Lopez said.

"Fighting fire with fire, Colonel. I should like to take a few dirty pictures. French post cards of what goes on in those places. Thereafter, I get my negatives to a trusted friend in New York. Until such time as I can do something constructive about Alicia, or Miguelito starts to do something destructive about me, those pictures don't get printed in any newspaper. But I want my alleged future brother-in-law to know they exist and what will happen if he starts playing rough. If you'll cooperate, I'll earmark five or six for your protection as well . . ."

The Colonel looked at him. Then very slowly he closed one eye in one long wink. Pointed at the swagger stick Peter was still carrying. Put out his hand toward it.

Silently Peter passed it over.

Colonel Lopez walked over to the wall map of Costa Verde hanging behind his desk. Lifted his hand. Pointed to a place on the map with the stick.

"Why no, Reynolds!" he shouted. "You dare ask me to betray Our Glorious Leader! You dare!"

Peter took out his notebook. Scribbled down the name of the town the Colonel had pointed to. The Colonel moved the swagger stick. Pointed to another place.

"Thing of bad milk!" he screamed. "Son of the great whore! If you did not have the protection of the gracious lady Alicia, I should shoot you myself, and now!"

Peter wrote that name down, too.

"Take it easy with the hard language, Colonel," he said; "I'm only trying to save my skin."

"You've come to the wrong place!" the Colonel roared and pointed for the third time. "Now get out of here, before I forget myself! Forget the protection you enjoy! Save your skin, indeed! You are lucky I do not have it removed from your filthy gringo carcass in strips!"

"Why, thank you, Colonel, I think you're sweet, too," Peter said, and put out his hand for the stick. The Colonel passed it back to him. Peter shifted it to his left hand, put his right hand out. Colonel Lopez gripped it, hard.

"Never try a trick like that again, Reynolds," he said. "You have tried my patience, sorely!"

On the way back to his flat, Peter studied those three names. They were all to the south, in the jungle country. Xilchimocha, Chizenaya, which was said to be near the ancient Tluscolan-Toltec ruins of Urur-chizenaya that the Standford Expedition had found nine years ago but which was lost again now, so quickly had the jungle growths covered the trail that the expedition had hacked to it; and Tarascanolla—all three of them Indian villages forming an isosceles triangle whose legs were approximately twenty kilometers apart. The Costa Verde section of the Pan-American Highway would put them within a reasonable distance of Chizenaya, if they dared use it. But the safest way to go that far south would be by air or sea—if there were a plane or a boat available. Of the two, the boat seemed far more likely . . .

Then, suddenly, he saw Alicia's white Jaguar roaring toward him, coming from the direction toward which he was going. She was driving it. Obviously the police had found it where he had left it and returned it to her. As she poured that sleek torpedo past the cab, he could see her face. Even in that fractured instant he could see the anguish in it.

"'Licia!" he called, but she didn't hear him. Seconds later the Jaguar was a white toy in the distance, murdering space and time, going on.

"Señor," the taxi driver said, "I fear we have not speed enough to apprehend a vehicle of such velocity—"

"I know we don't. Take me to the address I gave you, Amigo," Peter said.

The flat was a shambles. All the ashtrays were full of cigarette butts and the sodden ends of cigars. So was the floor. The drawers of his dresser had been pawed through. The lock on his desk had been broken and all his notes were gone. He grinned. "Don't think you'll be surprised at how much I love you, Miguelito," he said. But he didn't worry about that detail. Any serious reporter knew better than to refer to his sources in writing, even indirectly or in code, when his beat was a dictatorship or the Communist states. He worried about quite another thing: In all that disorder there were no signs of Judith.

He picked up the cigarette butts one by one from the floor; examined those in the ashtray, but none bore lipstick stains. Her clothes hung in the closet beside his own—except the simple, black-sequined, low-waisted imitation of the 1920s she had worn to Vince's party. The cosmetic jars and flasks of feminine allurement stood on the vanity, untouched. The mute rows of slippers beside his vastly bigger shoes. And in the drawers, the diaphanous wisps of negligees, slips, those silken triangles, so tiny that he wondered how even a girl as slim-hipped as Judy got into them, had been disturbed by clumsy hands, of course, but were, so far as he could tell, all there. The plastic envelopes filled with stockings. Garter belts. Bras. All her intimate, personal things. There was no doubt about it. Judith had not come home at all.

He sat down in the big chair and stared out of the window. He sat there a long time, not thinking but rather consciously trying to reject a long list of things he knew about Judith Lovell. Knew beyond the tender mercy of a doubt.

But it had been a long, rough go, and he was, after all, thirty-seven years old. He sank down, down into the black depths of slumber, dreamless and remote. He escaped memory, drowned anxiety, buried fathoms deep under soundlessness the refrain that had haunted him into sleep.

"What am I going to do, now? What am I going to do now? What am I——"

He beat upward through the mindlessness, thrashing the black water into foaming rage; he clawed for breath, for life, for meaning, crying: "Oh, no, Father! I will not call upon You! I will not. I am not beaten yet. I cannot yet bow down, enter the temples of unreason, nor surrender my thinking mind without murdering my integrity—whatever the hell that is—"

He surfaced, wildly, into light. Saw that the pale amber glow washing the windows was another sunset; and turning over, he lay there staring at the winking orange-red of her cigarette's end, brightening, darkening, flaring, as she ate up the smoke in convulsive gulps.

He put out his hand and switched on the lamp by the chair. The light washed over her in a cruel wave. He saw her hair's poorly, clumsily, half-heartedly rearranged disarray; the smear of lipstick that descended a full half inch beyond and below the corner of her mouth; saw her eyes blue-ringed, deep-sunk, lightless, dull; saw the flutter at the base of her throat. Saw the mouth tremble, the lips so swollen as to look negroid; the bruises on her shoulders; and as he raised himself from the cramped, muscle-twisting position he had sunk into in the big chair, he caught full in his nostrils that last intolerable detail: the wild, fetid, feral stench of sweat; not hers, male. He said:

"Which one, Judy? Miguelito? or Luis?"

She giggled senselessly. The sound of it ended in a hiccup.

"Which one of them, Judith?" he said.

"Both. His Nibs is no damn good. Likes to watch. But that Luis!"

He stood up very slowly; what there was in his face got through to her, penetrated the whiskey fog, the long, dull, slow ache.

"Please, Peter!" she said.

"Please what?" he said.

"Beat me," she whimpered. "Break all my bones. Put me in the hospital for a month . . ."

He looked at her.

"No," he said. "You can find your dirty pleasures elsewhere, Judy."

She came to him, her eyes colorless behind a scald of tears. She put her arms around his neck. He brought his hands up and broke her grip. Stood there looking at her, his face utterly weary.

"Go take a bath," he said. "You stink."

"Peter!" she said. "Don't leave me! Oh, Peter, don't leave me, please!"

He stood there.

"I'll die!" she said. "I'll kill myself. I will, Peter!"

His face didn't change. He said:

"This time, Judy, use a gun."

"Peter—" she whispered. She was rapidly becoming sober now.

"Yes, Judy?"

"I won't kill myself. I'll do worse."

"There is worse?"

"Yes, Peter."

"Such as?"

"I'll live."

"Riddles, Judy?"

"No. I'll live and let Luis make of me what he's already trying to."

"He can make something of you that you aren't already?"

"Oh, Peter!" she wailed.

"Oh, hell, Judy. Go get in the tub."

"You won't sneak out on me while I'm in there?" she said.

"Judy, have you ever known me to sneak about anything—ever?"

"No. You're so goddam honorable that you're almost atavistic. Anyhow, come sit on the edge of the tub. Talk to me—"

"We have something to talk about?"

"Yes," Judith said. "Please, Peter . . ."

"All right. But beyond that I make you no promises, Judy."

"Just listen to me. That's all I ask," she said.

When he saw her body, saw the marks of all the various things Luis and maybe even Miguel had done to her, he wanted to puke. But he mastered the impulse. He sat there watching her lolling in the hot, perfumed water, and contemplated the idea that she not only hadn't resisted the nauseating, painful, unnatural acts inflicted upon her, but that she had probably enjoyed them. The idea fitted. Perfectly.

She saw his face. Whispered:

"Please don't be mean, Peter."

"Oh, no," he said. "I mustn't, must I? I must be nice enough to sit here and be buried in it. Up to the eyes. Go on, Judy, speak your piece."

"All right," she said; her voice was very bleak. "You're nobody's fool, so you'll recognize the truth when you hear it. I was drunk when that happened, but drunkenness had nothing to do with it. If Luis were to walk in that door right now, he could take me to bed, here, before your eyes. All he has to do is to beckon, and I'll come running. Any act he demands of me I'll perform, no matter how unspeakably vile."

Peter didn't move.

"Then, Judy, one question: What the hell are you doing here?"

"Simple," Judith said. "I love *you*, Peter. I don't love him."

"And yet?" Peter said.

"And yet, what I said before still goes. All he's got to do is to crook his little finger and . . ."

"Let's skip the recapitulation, shall we? Seems to me that this pure love you feel for me, and not for him, is hardly an article of value, Judith. Since it wouldn't prevent, or cure—"

"Prevent?" Judith said. "Cure? What can be prevented, cured in this world, Peter? Life itself is an incurable disease we always die of. Yes, I'm quoting you. Shall I give you back a few more of your bright remarks? 'There are no answers to anything.' 'No problems whatsoever can be solved.' Like your own pearls of wisdom, sage?"

"No," Peter said.

"Yet you're right. Let's put it another way: Life is a long nausea that starts with a leaky diaphragm and ends up in a maggot's belly. Is that better?"

"No," Peter said.

"No, of course it isn't! There aren't any good or better. There are only bad and worse. And worst, superlative, like me."

She climbed out of the tub. Dried herself with the big towel. Applied a deodorant spray to her armpits. Took down a flask of that hideously expensive *Peut'être* and began to rub it into the pores of her skin. All over.

"Now does my aroma please you, my lord?"

"No," he said.

"Why not?"

"The way you smell now won't wash off, Judith. The decay's internal. Involves the soul."

She laughed.

"That semantic irrelevant!" she said.

"Quoting me again?"

"Quoting you again."

"Then I was a goddam liar. A loud-mouthed idiot. And a fool. Judith—"

"Yes, darling?"

"Put some clothes on. Tonight I don't like you naked."

"Why not, Peter?"

"You look like a Krafft-Ebing case history. Or something out of Havelock Ellis. Say I find the marks left by your excursion into sado-masochistic sexual gymnastics a trifle unbecoming. In fact, they make me sick."

"Oh!" Judith said.

He got up. Walked out of the bathroom. She came out behind him. Dug into the drawer. Put on panties. A bra. Slipped a thin housedress over her head. Sat down in a chair, looking at him.

"Peter," she said, "tell me something."

"What, Judith?"

"The truth. Look me straight in the eye and tell me: Have you ever slept with her?"

"The best defense is an offense, Judy? Then you lose. I never have."

"Oh!" she said. "Are you going to—now?"

"Apart from the fact that it's none of your goddamned business, I don't know. And it would depend upon her, anyhow. But you can make book on one thing, Judy: One way or the other it will have absolutely nothing to do with you!"

"Oh!" she said again.

"Besides, that's not the question at hand."

"'There are no answers to anything,'" Judith quoted again. "What is the question at hand, Peter?"

"You. What the hell do I do with you now?"

"Peter—"

"Yes, Judy?"

"May I get up from this chair and come close to you? What I have to say can't be said coldly and from a distance."

"No," Peter said. "Stay where you are, Judith."

"Why? Afraid I might be able to convince you?"

"No. Even though I haven't eaten in God knows when, if I threw up, it still wouldn't be pretty."

"Is it ever? You mean I disgust you that much?"

"Yes, Judith," Peter said. "You disgust me that much."

She bent her head then and started to cry. She cried soundlessly, without any visible motion of throat and shoulders. She sat there and let a flood of tears chase one another down her face. She made no effort to wipe them away. She just sat there like that, crying.

"Oh, hell!" Peter said.

She lifted her head and faced him. Said:

"You're right. It's better that I say it from here. Dead still, without making an act of it. Without even gestures. If I went down on my knees before you, as I want to, that would reduce this to a bad Class B quickie, wouldn't it? And what I'm aiming for is—"

"A sleeper," Peter said—"your Lotus Eaters' term for a picture that unexpectedly achieves great success with small means, reasonable outlay. Right?"

"No. What I'm aiming for is the truth, Peter. So I oppose your question with another one: Do you refuse to save me?"

"Save you?" Peter said.

"Yes," she said. "As Grade B as that dialog sounds. The truth often lacks style, doesn't it? Only you can, Peter. Save, rescue, heal, cure. Maybe even resurrect. In all my life you're the only man who has meant enough to me to be able to work that miracle. To gather up the pieces of me that are scattered all over hell by now. To erase the scars of all too many brief encounters; wash me till I'm whiter than snow like that hymn says. This is very hard. I don't know how to say it. I don't even know the words."

"Huh!" Peter snorted. "So far you're going great, Judy."

"If you leave me, I won't kill myself, Peter. Because I can't lay that burden on your conscience. You do have a conscience, don't you?"

"Yes, I suppose I do," Peter said.

"If I did that, it would be your fault. The rest doesn't matter. It would be because *you* left me; because, having let me glimpse heaven, you kicked me downstairs again. The backstairs: the ones they let muddy female canines creep up from time to time. Wiggling on their bellies, imploring. So I can't depart this vale of wrath and tears leaving you holding a sack full of moral responsibility. No—only half full. But even so, you see what I mean, don't you?"

"Yes," Peter said.

"I thought you would. Peter, may I please, please get up now?"

"Why? Are you stiff from sitting there?"

"Yes. But mainly because I want to come close to you. Awkward to beg for my life sitting way over here. If this script is *nouvelle vague*, Franco-Italian neorealism, I don't like it. I'm old-fashioned. I want to scream, tear my hair, roll on the floor, chew the carpet. You know, like Theda Bara in the silent flickers a million years ago. Only it wouldn't work, would it?"

"No," Peter said.

"So I have to do it your way: quietly. With restraint. But however it's done—any way at all—I'm still begging for my life, Peter. And I don't necessarily mean life as opposed to death. There are other alternatives, you know."

"Such as?"

She got up from the chair and came to him. Stood there very close to him but not touching, not even trying to.

"Such as life opposed to horror," she said.

He stood there, looking at her.

"What am I supposed to do, Judy?" he said.

"Just take me away from here. Just—love me, without even thinking how little I deserve it. I don't. Not at all. I deserve to be beaten into a bloody, unrecognizable pulp and left in a ditch to rot. Think, if you must think at all, of how much I need you. I don't ask justice of you, Peter. What I ask is mercy."

He didn't move.

"And if I consent to wear my horns with complacent grace, there'll be no more—of this sort of thing?" he said.

She looked at him. When she spoke, her voice was bleak. As bleak as truth usually is.

"I don't know. I can't promise you that, Peter. You would have to prevent it. For now. Maybe for years. Until I'm cured. If I ever am. Will you take me on that basis, Peter? On nothing more than my awful, helpless need of you?"

He went on looking at her. Then he said it—voiced what was the victory of pure compassion or his own utter, abject, irrevocable defeat:

"Yes, Judy."

And stood there, wondering which of the two it was, as he held the long, slow tremble of her body against him; not only knowing, but knowing he would never know, until the hour he ceased to breathe, think, feel pain.

But she was talking again.

"You won't be sorry, darling! I promise you you won't. . . . Peter, I know you love her. And she, poor thing, she is dying of wanting you! Only you can't have each other, can you?"

"No," Peter said.

"Why not?" Judith said.

"There's a grave athwart our path. With Connie in it," Peter said.

"Oh!" Judith whispered. "I——"

And then they heard the thunderous knocking on the door.

Peter opened it. Luis Sinnombre stood there, surrounded by a herd of policemen. Judith shrank back, all the color draining out of her face. But Luis didn't say anything. Instead he turned to his uniformed Piltdown men.

"Search the place!" he said.

They fanned out, tearing open doors. All the rooms. The closets. They even looked under the beds. Then they came back, saluted, said:

"She's not here, Don Luis!"

"I didn't think she would be," Luis said. "My dear Peter, are you going to be stupid and gallant and Anglo-Saxon and force me to take unpleasant measures, or are you going to be reasonable and tell me where she is?"

"Where who is?" Peter said.

"As if you didn't know! Your little Alicia, who has disappeared. Miguel is most upset. And when Miguel is upset the results compare with Zopocomapetl when it's upset. I hate to be stern, Peter, but with *this* caper, you've put *my* neck in a sling. In the charming Gringo phraseology of our charming Judith here—how are you tonight, my sweet?—come on, Peter—*give!*"

Peter walked up until he was very close to Luis. Stood there looking at him.

"I wouldn't give you the time of day, now, Luis," he said.

"My dear Peter, you don't have to give me anything," Luis said. "What I want, I take. Or hadn't you noticed?"

Peter didn't say anything.

"Come on, Peter, don't be tiresome. Speak your piece like a good boy."

"No," Peter said.

"Why not?"

"Don't like this script. Too Hollywood. No, TV. Anything I could say now would come out wrong. Make me sound like the male lead in one of Judy's pictures. The kind of thing you can't say now without laughing, or wanting to puke. Or both."

"Why don't you have a try at it in your own inimitable style? Your dispatches are first-rate, everyone gives you that."

"All right," Peter said. "I don't know where Alicia is. But if I did, I wouldn't tell you. I was in the hands of your goons for three days before, remember. It's possible, given time, you could break me, Luis. Hell, it's probable. You took a good bit out of me that trip that I haven't been able to put back. That was maybe irreplaceable. But now you'd better kill me, Luis, because, if you don't—"

"If I don't?"

"I am going to kill you. Do you mind if I say that again?"

Luis smiled, said:

"Of course not. But why do you want to?"

"Because I want to say it right, with the proper lack of emphasis. Not because of what you did to Judy. Not because of my previous, or any future, sessions with your persuasion squad. But because noxious insects and poisonous reptiles have to be eliminated. For the general good of society. Because at heart I'm a Boy Scout. My good deed for some future day, Luis."

Luis laughed.

"I don't think I need worry about that, do you?" he said.

"No, but there is one thing you had better worry about," Peter said.

"Which is?"

"Time. The time you could use, tracing Alicia. The time you're going to waste on me until you finally convince yourself that the only reason why what the cleaning woman will carry out in the slop bucket didn't talk while it was all in one piece and could was because it didn't know. So why don't you take your Neanderthals out of here and go do something useful?"

Luis looked at him.

"You know, Peter, you almost convince me—" he said.

"Luis, I don't give a two-peso crib-girl screw about your convictions. What I'm worried about now is 'Licia! Why—"

"Oh, hell," Judith said. "I wish . . ."

"What, my dear?" Luis said.

"That whoever has got her now would feed her to the crocodiles. Or the fish," Judith said.

"Oh, come now, Judy; you'll have *me* to console you," Luis said.

"But I don't want you, Luis; I want him."

"You said that last night, remember? But we waste time. Peter, aren't you—"

The doorbell rang. Loudly. Demandingly.

Luis nodded. One of the policemen went to the door. A telegraph messenger stood in it.

"A telegram for—" he began; then his voice died.

The policeman put out his hand. The messenger put the telegram into it. He didn't wait for anybody to sign anything. He went down those stairs at a run.

"The Organic Democracy," Peter said.

The policeman brought the telegram to Luis. Luis smiled.

"With your permission, dear Peter?" he said, and ripped it open. Read it at a glance. Stopped smiling. Looked at Peter.

"So you were telling the truth!" he said. He extended the telegram to Peter.

Peter took it. Read it. From somewhere very far away, he heard Judith's voice. It made a hateful noise in his ears.

"Oh, Peter!" she said. "What's wrong?"

Peter didn't answer. He started for the door.

"Peter! Where are you going?"

Peter stopped. But he wasn't looking at Judith. He looked at the Head of the Secret Police.

"Luis," he said, "do I have to ask you not to have me followed?"

Luis looked back, and now his dark face was absolutely grave.

"Of course not, Peter. These boys mean business. And they never heard of the Marquis of Queensberry."

Peter stood there, looking at him.

"You could never get there quickly enough, Luis. Never in this world. And even if Miguelito let you off the hook—"

"What, Peter?"

"I wouldn't," Peter said.

XVII

As soon as he came out on the street, Peter heard the police sirens. They came from every direction, loud on the warmsoft, feathery, tropical night air. So he knew that Luis Sinnombre was making good use of his telephone, which meant that the Head of the Secret Police would be too busy to occupy himself with Judith tonight. The comfort was small; the choice, like most of life's choices, ugly. It was no comfort to reflect that whatever might happen to Judy (through his now deliberate, conscious abandonment of her) did not involve her death; because, considered coldly, it did involve the destruction of her identity; the annihilation of those thousand, thousand quirks of personality that made her the individual she was, and that individual, to him, in spite of everything, curiously dear. That is, if she were not as a person already destroyed. Was she not, even now, one of the walking wounded? How much more was required to force her into the ranks of the living dead? Of that army of Zombies which was the one unique byproduct of the twentieth century; the people who went on living after too much *Angst, angoise,* anguish, *angustia* had stunned their minds into abject dullness, stopped a little above the minimum requirements of vegetal, inert existence, what they had been once pleased to call their hearts?

But he had no time for that. His choice was already made. Any half-stopped heartbeat now, some blundering ape of a policeman might stumble upon that black hole, cellar, stairwell, closet in which they held bound and gagged his life, his joy, his shape of things to come, his hope of heaven—and one short, tearing burst of Sten gun fire would rip out and end time for him, end the remotest possibility of his continuing to support what was very nearly insupportable now.

So he stepped to the curb and flagged down a taxi. The driver's face was frightened. He said: "To where, Señor?" And Peter answered him: "Anywhere—as long as it's the hell away from here!"

Before they had gone two blocks, they saw the police setting up a barricade across the street ahead of them. "Take another!" Peter said; and the taxi driver: "Do not preoccupy yourself, Señor! I have lived fifty years now by avoiding these animals in uniform!" Peter saw that what the police were doing now was to begin a massive, street-by-street, house-by-house, flat-by-flat search. But in a city of nearly half a million inhabitants, their chances of finding one small, frightened, tender, haunting girl-woman, before it was too late, were nil.

But, even so, he didn't go straight to the warehouse. For, although so far he had seen no signs that Luis Sinnombre was having him followed, he knew the Head of the Secret Police too well by now to accept his word about anything whatsoever. He told the taxi driver to take him downtown. Got out, paid his fare; dismissed the cab. Entered Pam-Pam. Came out the back entrance. Took another taxi and directed the driver to The Blue Moon. Got out and went in. The taxi driver would remember that destination as sure as hell.

The substitute madam wanted to stage a parade of naked girls for him.

"I don't like girls," Peter said.

"Well, it is a little early for boys," the madam said, "but if the Señor cares to wait, I'm sure I could procure him a pretty *niño* in no time at all."

Peter sipped his drink. It was strong.

"Haven't time," he said. "Besides, I don't like boys either."

"Then *what* does the Señor like?" the madam asked.

"Horses," Peter said.

"Horses?" the madam said. "Well, that is a little more difficult—"

"And it has to be the kind that sits on grapefruits," Peter said.

"Now really, Señor!" the madam said.

"I make a jest. A bad joke. The kind that are called in my country tales of hirsute canines. Shaggy-dog stories. Truly, Madame, I have no need for any sort of sexual fare. I simply have to kill a certain amount of time. And in a place where it will be remembered that I was there at this hour."

"Oh!" the madam said. "Please don't tell me any more about it, Señor!"

She sailed out of the door like a dreadnaught.

At once a girl came through it. She had been beautiful once. She was still beautiful in a way. But now she looked like what she was. She put her hand out to Peter.

"Come upstairs with me," she said.

"I am sorry, amiga," Peter said.

"Why not?"

"I have not the desire."

"I will awake it."

"Nor the time, so do not bother," Peter said. Then: "Haven't I seen you somewhere before?"

"No. You have only seen my eyes. But in the head of my brother," she said.

"My God!" Peter said.

"Jacinto has told me much of you. Come and we will talk. Upstairs in my room. For you there is no charge. And all the filigrains you may wish. À la Italienne. À la Française. In any position; making use of whatever you will . . ."

"Look, Teresa—"

"How did you know my name? Did Jacinto tell you?"

"Yes," Peter said.

"Poor Jacinto. He comes here often. And always I take him to my room."

"Your brother?" Peter said.

"Why not? Oh, not what you think! You were in that Indian village with him, no?"

"Yes."

"And you witnessed what happened?"

"Yes. You mean he is still like that?"

"Yes. The other girls do not know he is my brother."

"With *those* eyes?"

"They do not look at men's eyes very often. They look at the bulge of their billfolds. They think he is my lover. When he is in my room I scream and shout and beg him to do this and with that and like this. So that they will not know. You see? So that he can maintain his pride."

"Poor Jacinto," Peter said.

"He is very fond of you. He says you are his only friend."

"Odd," Peter said. "I thought he hated me."

"No. Come with me? I would give you great pleasure."

"Thank you, Teresa, but I have to go now."

"But why precisely now?"

"Because I have just seen the detective who was tailing me leave his post, under the impression that I will remain here all night. Believe me, Teresita, it is my only chance. You know how the police are . . ."

"*Do* I? The billygoats! The malformed abortions of filthy mothers! The—"

"Girl-child," Peter said, "not even Spanish has profanity enough. You'd have to invent a new language. *Adios!*"

She bent and kissed his mouth. She was very expert.

"Now you will come again," she said. "I am sure of that."

"Amiga, so am I. In fact, you can depend on it," Peter said, and went out of there wondering if she had a disease and if he had a cracked place on his mouth and if he did whether the disease were the kind one could catch that way. Then he went down the stairs onto the sidewalk and hailed another cab.

He made the taxi driver zigzag over half of town, under the pretext that he could not remember the name of the street where he wanted to go but only how the house looked. He got out several blocks from the factory and walked the rest of the way. But when he got there, he found only Martin waiting for him.

"Pablo would not grant me the privilege of guarding her," he said; "he declares I am not to be trusted around women. He is right. For, although she is of a terrible skinniness, and also of a certain ugliness, the whole of her adds up to a strange sort of excitement. I have known beautiful women who moved me less. No wonder you are so in love with her, Comrade . . ."

"If she has been hurt or molested in any way, you'll see how much I love her," Peter said.

"Oh, do not preoccupy yourself about that. Pablo is worse than an old woman, or a priest," Martin said. "Now come."

They had her in the back room of a country roadhouse just off the Pan-American Highway, in plain sight of every police jeep that went shrieking past. The Edgar Allan Poe principle. The Purloined Letter technique. Hide the body where nobody'd believe you'd dare to. Not that this place looked like a roadhouse, despite its magnificent location. It looked like the Supreme Parliament of all the flies and filth on earth. And probably was.

She was in a back room, her hands and feet tied to the chair they had her in, and a gag in her mouth that just looking at was enough to make a goat heave. She was being guarded by a hundred kilos—roughly two hundred twenty pounds—of mustached, dark-skinned female whose sex could have been discerned by a blind man from fifty meters away. She had her eyes closed—and was trying to close her nostrils too, against the monstrous stink of her monstrous guard.

"Turn her loose," Peter said.

Her eyes came open. Blazed. The way she looked at him hit him in the gut, going through the scar tissue some of the Chinese mortar fragments had left there, along with the nervous stomach that was largely allergic to food.

Pablo nodded. The She Monster moved with surprising deftness, even a certain grace. Then Alicia came up out of the chair and would have fallen if he hadn't caught her, because they had shut off the circulation in her hands and feet by tying her too tight.

The way she kissed him removed any lingering doubts her captors might have had.

He pushed her away. Said:

"Have they hurt you, 'Licia?"

"No," she whispered, "they have been polite, even kind. They explained the necessity of binding me up thus, for fear I might make some involuntary sound. I bear them no ill will, Peter."

"I do," Peter said. "Pablo, the deal's off. I gave you my word I would come back. But you had to use coercion—'Licia—Nena, what's wrong?"

Her small face went scarlet. Then she smiled.

"You are my man, no? Then why do I have shame? I have been sitting there tied up for hours—and— Oh, Peter, do you suppose that they have an *excusado* that is not of a horrible dirtiness?"

"They have, Doña Alicia, but it is broken, and there has been no water in it for three months," Pablo said; "and if you were to enter it, you would probably faint. I suggest you go for a little walk with Chiquita, here . . ."

When he said *Chiquita,* he nodded in the direction of the female mountain.

"Excuse me, *Cielo?*" she said, still blushing. "I'll be back immediately."

"All right," Peter said, "but don't hurry. I wish to say a few gross words, unlovely expressions, profanities, and even an obscenity or two, to my good friends here."

"Peter, Love, do not be angry with them. They had reasons for what they did. They explained them to me . . ."

"Nena, you go make *pipi* and let me handle this!" Peter said.

"Oh, Peter!" she wailed and fled.

"Look, Peter, I am very sorry, but from sad experience we have learned to trust no one," Pablo said.

"All right," Peter said, "don't trust me. I see you have a telephone in this flyblown Ritz. I will make you one more proposition, my last!"

"Which is?" Martin said.

"That you let Alicia get into the Jag and—"

"Can't. One of our girl comrades, who is about Alicia's size, delivered the Jaguar to the back door of the Villalonga residence before the police were aware that your beloved was even missing. It was too conspicuous, Peter; we couldn't afford . . ."

"All right. That's only a detail. Put it this way: When you let me take her into town, I'll—"

"No, Peter."

"Goddammit, Pablo! I told you I'd come back!"

"I know. And I trust you, Peter; but will you live long enough to be able to?"

"They won't lay hands on me," Peter said. "Why—"

"As of last night they might. Your country's military "technical advisers," with their helicopters, airplanes, and expensive weapons designed to train Villalonga's 'Defenders of Democracy Against the Red Menace,' have been withdrawn. One of our friends among the police —for we have friends even there—states that your dispatches, and those of your Irish friend, are credited with causing your government's change of heart. So——"

"I'll take the chance," Peter said.

"But we cannot allow you to, Comrade. We need you, need the information you possess."

"All right. Then have someone else take her home. When she herself phones me here, and tells me that you have delivered her to a place of safety, I will tell you the location of those prison camps, as I promised."

"And you, *Cielo*?" Alicia whispered, as she came back through the door.

"I go with them, Nena; I have to. Part of the bargain."

"Then I go with you!" Alicia said.

"Now look, Nena—"

Martin grinned.

"It would be safer, Comrade," he said; "trying to take her back into town involves risks of a certain vileness—even to her."

Peter looked at Pablo.

"That is correct, Peter. The police are excessively nervous with firearms, as you know very well."

Peter went on looking at him. Said:

"But the camps are far away. And once we reach them the attacks will be of a perilousness viler than the milk of a witch—"

"Ha!" Martin said. "That is a new profanity! Is it from the English, Comrade?"

"Sort of," Peter said. "'Licia, Nena—"

"Take me with you! You know I am unhappy apart from you! Oh, Peter, *Cielo,* please!"

"Nena—" Peter said. "You might get killed. Hell, we both might."

"I could ask no greater happiness," she said, "than to lie beside you forever."

"Nena, there is too much risk of precisely that," Peter said.

"Is it not better to die quickly of gunshot wounds than slowly of grief? Look at me, Peter! Since I have known you I have lost six kilos. Six kilos I could not afford to lose. You would like me to end up in a madhouse, locked in a strait jacket, raving and calling your name? I know we can never be married; but I can be yours, and I will! I accept the sin! What pain, what punishment, what hell could be worse than what I suffer now? Oh, Peter, I—"

He held her to him. Said to Pablo:

"How do we go?"

"In trucks. The truck drivers, because they are all cruelly exploited, support our cause. In an hour they will begin to arrive. They will hide us among the merchandise."

"And when we reach the post of control that the carabinieros of the Civil Guard have always along the highway?"

"Then they *are* in the South!" Martin said.

"At Xilchimocha, at Chizenaya, and at Tarascanolla," Peter said.

"All near the highway! Did you hear, Pablo? Stupendous! Marvelous!"

"And when we reach those posts of control?" Peter said.

"They are fixed," Pablo said. "We know where they are. Three kilometers before each one we descend, walk through the jungles until we have passed them. The trucks will wait."

Peter looked at Alicia. She had on a chic sort of a cocktail dress. Her arms were bare.

"Martin," he said, "send one of the sleepy boys into town on the motorbike to buy a mono, a coverall. No, two. One for me, large. And the other of the smallest size they have, for Alicia. Even so, I fear it will be too big."

"Oh, *Cielo, Cielo,* I am so glad!" Alicia said.

Martin looked at his watch.

"I am afraid it is too late for that by now," he said. "All the stores are closed. Still, you are right. That little dress is not suitable for this trip. Let me see—let me see . . ."

"Do not preoccupy yourself, Comrade Second Chief!" said one of the teen-agers who had guarded Peter. "I will procure monos for the Comrade Reporter and his lady."

"How, Joaquin?" Martin said.

"I will steal them!" Joaquin laughed. "I am a thief of the first class!"

"Don't be a fool, son," Peter said, "the streets are crawling with police."

"Ha! You do not know me, Comrade! I will take along Mario to stand watch. When I return I will present the Comrade with a pistol stolen from the very belt of a policeman! And the monos. Is there anything else the Comrade desires?"

Peter looked at Pablo.

"He is crazy, this *niño,* no?" he said.

Pablo shook his head.

"No, Comrade. He does not even exaggerate. He is the best thief I have ever seen. We have found this talent of his very useful in the past. Since he is going to steal the monos, I suggest that you give him a list of other things you may need."

"Just two," Peter said; "a Commando's knife—and a radio. A transister radio of several bands. But especially of the six-to-eighteen-meters bands, which includes the police broadcasts to their patrols—"

Martin looked at Peter.

"Now that," he said, "is what I call an idea of a certain intelligence!"

And now, men began to arrive. They came on foot, carrying heavy packs. Peter hoped they'd keep some of those packs out of the truck he and Alicia would have to ride in. He knew that the only thing that would make the hexagon-TNT combination, stirred into a thick rubber foam that looked like chewing gum and smelled like marzipan, explode was a spark. He knew that you could hit it with a hammer, drop it, mold it, play ball with it, and nothing would happen; but in Algiers he had seen what it could do when it went off, so his respect for *le plastique* was profound. They had other things, too; knee mortars of Russian manufacture; long tubes that seemed to be bazookas; Sten and Bren guns; even a few heavier, tripod-mounted weapons. So extensive and excellent was their material that Peter turned to Pablo and said: "How?"

"The major offensive will be mounted any day now. We have profited from your Navy's vigilance of Cuba. Now the Russian ships debark material in a cove near the southern tip of the Republic. We have promised to transship it to Cuba, Peter. And we will—once we have used it ourselves!"

"What are you waiting for?" Peter said.

"The Indians. They are becoming more and more dissatisfied with their lot. Almost they are ready to come over to us. They would have before now, if it hadn't been for Padre Pío. Which is why that swine of a Villalonga tried to blow him to bits the other night."

"This I do not understand," Alicia said. "If my brother—and I grant you he is a swine, Pablo—more swine than you know—killed the little Father, would not that throw the Indians automatically into your camp? I speak Tluscola, and I know them well. They are very devout . . ."

"It would, Doña—no!—Camarada Alicia, since you have joined us—but for the fact that your clever brother had it arranged so that the Indians would think it was we who had murdered the little Vasco. Only, he escaped . . ."

"Thank God," Peter said.

"I am grateful, too, though I do not believe in your God," Pablo said.

"*Dios mío!*" Alicia said. "Look at that!"

They looked. And now they saw that Zopocomapetl was vomiting fire, sending a tongue of flame straight up into the heavens for three hundred meters or more.

"Good!" Pablo said. "They will have other things than us to occupy their minds with, this night!"

Then they heard the roaring of the motors on the road. And saw the first of the trucks stop before the roadhouse. The silent men began to load it quickly, but with great care. They took out what the truck already had in it, at first, then loaded their supplies. Put the innocent merchandise back on top of that.

Peter stepped up to the truck driver.

"This of the volcano," he said, "has it caused much damage in the city?"

"No," the driver said. "But the Indian town of Xochua has been wiped out. Very few escaped."

Then, before Peter could say anything, Joaquin and Mario roared up on the motorbike. They had the coveralls, called in Spanish *monos azules*—blue monkeys—with them. The knife. A policeman's pistol. And the radio. It was a damn fine radio. It had FM, AM, and three shortwave bands. It would be very useful.

Alicia lay in his arms inside the truck. The truck was loaded with sacks of cement besides the other material Pablo's band had now added. The sacks were dusty. They made Peter sneeze. But they didn't seem to affect her at all. She had been kissing him everywhere she could reach ever since they'd left the roadhouse.

"Nena—" he said.

"*Cielo*?"

"Cut it out, will you?"

"Why? Do you no longer love me?"

"Yes. Too much. But if you make me explode, I might also set off the grenades that Martin has in his pocket."

"Oh!" she laughed softly. "Peter—"

"Nena?"

"Would you that I do a thing to ease you? A thing smaller than the great thing, I mean?"

"Such as?" Peter said.

"I could touch you. With the hands. Shall I?"

"Hell, no! Who's been teaching you these childish, filthy tricks?"

"My husband. When he was being faithful to me. Because he did not wish to give me a child. Peter!"

"Yes, Nena?"

"Give me a child! Oh, Peter, please!"

"Now?" he said.

"Now! Tell Martin to turn his back!"

"He still has ears."

"I do not care! I will be very quiet. I will not cry out. I promise you."

"Nena—no."

"Oh, Peter, *Cielo*—I want you so!"

"And I you. But in privacy. And, if possible, in a bed. Because if we ever do make another little Sinnombre, I should prefer him born with hands and feet instead of wheels and a horn and headlights and—"

"Peter, you are crazy, you know? But I am glad you are. Because if you were sane, you could not love this quarter of a kilo of bones with a face like a little monkey's—"

"*Hola*, Monkeyface!" Peter said, and kissed her.

"*Cara de Mona*. Strange, when *you* say it I like it."

"That makes two of us."

"Peter—kiss me."

"Nena, let's not start *that* again!"

"I won't. Only kiss me good night. I have a desire to sleep. In your arms. For the first time. Where I mean to sleep all the rest of my life."

He kissed her. But she drew away quickly. Said:

"Oh, Peter, what is wrong?"

"Nothing."

"Tell me!"

"No. It will spoil it."

"It *has* spoiled it. So tell me!"

"I thought about—her. Sleeping alone, forever. And her three children without a mother. And her husband without——"

"*Ayeee!*" she wailed. "But this is not our fault, my love! All my life I have suffered for other people's sins. Ay, great and vengeful God! At least allow me one grand glorious sin of my own to suffer for!"

"Nena, I don't think you need worry about that at all," Peter said.

Book Three

WITHDRAWAL AND RETURN

XVIII

From where they were now, lying on their bellies in the thick, sticky mud of the mangrove swamp, they could see the camp. It wasn't at Tarascanolla at all, but twelve kilometers away in the jungle itself.

"Like it?" Pablo said.

"Very much," Peter said. "They have given us all the advantages."

"Meaning?" Martin said.

"Because they wanted to conceal these obscenities from the eyes of the tourists, they have placed them in the jungle. Which is excellent for hiding a prison camp, but even better for those who have to attack it. We can approach to within three meters of that murder factory without being seen."

"Come then," Pablo said, "let us go back to the *albergue,* that we may speak of it."

"All right," Peter said.

They moved through the swamp on their bellies. When they were far enough away from the concentration camp, they stood up, started walking back toward the inn.

"I do not understand you, Comrade Reporter," Martin said.

"What is it about me you do not understand, Amigo?" Peter said.

"Your wanting to lead this attack. If I had such a woman as you have waiting for me at the inn, I should develop such a desire for life that my cowardice would be enormous!"

"You think mine is not?" Peter said.

"Yet you insist upon leading the attack," Pablo said. "Why, Comrade?"

"The reasons are various. And of a nature both simple and complicated—"

"Start with the simple ones," Pablo said.

"Very well. In the first place, your band, Amigo Pablo, unlike that of the brave Juan, afterwards of Jacinto and last of all of Federico, with whom it ceased to be a band at all and became food for the buzzards, is untrained. Of you all, only I have seen warfare. I have seen too damned much of it; but no matter. I do not propose to watch you being slaughtered through your ignorance. You are very brave and very ignorant, which is the worst of all possible combinations. Lacking knowledge of tactics, it would be better if you were cowards . . ."

"Go on," Martin said.

"I used Commando tactics against the Chinese in Korea. I propose to teach you what I know. I propose to take this camp as a demonstration to you of how it should be done. It is not my intention to lose a single man. Thereafter, you, Martin, will take the one at Xilchimocha; while you, Pablo, with me again as Second, will take the one at Chizenaya last of all."

"Why leave that one for the last?" Martin said.

"Because after this one the element of surprise will be gone; and each attack will be more difficult than the last. That is one reason. The other is that the Moral Correction Center at Chizenaya is where they keep the women prisoners, who afterward will be a burden," Peter said.

"Ay! That they be many, and I will burden them!" Martin said.

"Wait until you see what they look like by now," Peter said.

"Comrade Reporter—" Pablo said.

"Yes, friend?"

"You have not said it all. I want to hear the complicated reasons as well."

"I do not know how to say them," Peter said. "I am not even sure I know what they are . . ."

"Try," said Pablo.

"All right. I went into the Korean War unwillingly, unconvinced that there was anything to be served by killing. Or even that there were any principles to life at all. I came out of that war a little changed . . ."

"How?" Martin asked.

"I had discovered a principle or two."

"Such as?" Pablo said.

"That a man ought to have a house. With a garden around it. And a fence around that garden. And a gate to that fence."

"These are principles?" Pablo said.

"Yes, Amigo. Because on that gate should be a sign that says *No Trespassing*. And at that man's side a gun to permanently remove any creature whomsoever who tries to collectivize that garden, or make that man go to church, or interfere with his simple pleasures such as getting drunk on Saturday night and enjoying the woman he has inside that house. Took me a long time to get to those principles. If you want to befoul them with big words, you might say that the state is made for man, not vice versa. That man comes first. That his cooperation on weighty matters must always be respectfully asked, not required. Or, as Old Abe put it: *of*, *for*, and *by*. Catch?"

"Yes," Pablo said. "I catch that you're a reactionary, Comrade."

"Yes," Peter said. "A reactionary who is going to help you win this football game. But who is going to kick hell out of you, the first time you start fouling up the things I got into this mild disagreement over."

"Which are?" Martin said.

"I told you. That little house. That little woman in that house. That little vine and fig tree. And that gate that you, the Prime Minister of the Soviet Socialist Republics, the President of the United States, or Fidel Castro can't come into unless I do the inviting. Which I would, of course. Give you a drink. Talk about baseball, bullfighting, fly fishing. Let the little woman trot out a home-baked cake. Make you very welcome, friend. As long as you are—"

"As long as I am what?" Pablo said.

"A friend. Which adds up to enjoying my company and leaving me the hell alone."

"Those," Martin said, "are very rare principles, Comrade!"

"Aren't they?" Peter said. "Men have been dying for ten thousand years, trying to make them stick."

When they came out of the jungle, they could see the inn. It was a very pretty inn, and almost new. There weren't any tourists in it now because it was summer, and the tourists only came this far south when it was winter and the climate became endurable. The trucks were all parked in the inn's parking lot, under the split-bamboo sunshades. The sleepy-headed teen-agers, Joaquin and Mario, were painting signs. The signs read CLOSED FOR THE SEASON. When they had finished, they would put the signs fifty meters down the road in both directions, and another larger one outside the door, just in case. So far, absolutely no cars had passed, but you never could tell.

Downstairs in the basement, they had the innkeeper and his wife locked up. The wife was a pretty Indian girl of about twenty. She took being locked up with the resignation of the Tluscola to everything. But the man was a heavyset, powerful mestizo of fifty. From his looks, his Indian ancestors hadn't been Tluscolan; they had probably been the dirty, degenerate fisher Indians—who swapped their wives, slept with their own sisters, mothers, aunts, or cousins when female; or when hard up, in the immediate absence of females, with their brothers, fathers, uncles, and cousins, being one of the most completely ambisexual bunches who ever lived. He, Peter saw, wasn't resigned a good goddam. He was ugly. He wasn't to be trusted.

When Peter came up the stairs he could hear Alicia singing. Her singing voice was between an alto and a contralto, though, when she wanted to she could push it up through the coloratura, through the mezzo, and peak it well within the lyric soprano's range. What she sang now was a love song. The words went:

"*La primera vez que te vi, me enamore locamente de ti . . .*" "Which came out clumsily in English as "The first time I saw you, I fell madly in love with you," thus losing all the lilt and magic it had in Spanish and proving again that translation was a thing you should never do, unless you absolutely had to.

Peter came into the room and saw that Alicia had taken off the coverall, and was wearing the cocktail dress. It looked as though she were going to a party.

"How'd you manage that?" he said. "You look so fresh and cool."

"Oh, I am, *Cielo!*" she said. "I had a shower and washed all my things and lay on the bed naked, hoping you would come in so that I could tempt you. Only all my clothes dried within ten minutes, so I put them back on, because there is no lock on the door . . ."

"Nena—" Peter said.

"Oh, Peter. You're covered with mud!"

"I know. I'm going to take a shower now," Peter said.

"Then hurry! And when you're all nice and clean—"

"Nena," Peter said, "no . . ."

She looked at him and what was in her eyes was very hard to look at.

"Peter," she said. "Tell me why?"

"Because," he said, "I did not know you would be with me, and I have brought nothing, no means of taking precautions. And—"

"Peter," she said, "I told you I want a child. Your child."

"Little Peter No-Name. Hell of a thing to wish on a kid, no?"

"*Cielo*, you are too complicated," she said.

"We can't remedy it, you know," Peter said, "unless you are willing to accept murder, as the price of a husband. I cannot accept it as your dowry, Nena. It would dirty our lives forever."

She continued to look at him.

"Go take your shower, Peter," she said.

When he came out of the shower, she was sitting by the window. It was already dusk and the sun was flaming down the sky. In a little while it would be dark, the abrupt, no-transition dark of the tropics. And when it was, he would have things to do. He didn't like even to think about those things now. He was wrapped in the big towel; when he looked for the only shorts he had, to put them back on, they weren't there.

"I washed your shorts for you, and your socks, and your shirt," Alicia said. "Ugh! They were of a filthiness unimaginable. So now they are all wet, and you have no clothes to put on and hence are at my mercy—"

"Nena," he said, "there is one other thing—"

"Which is?" she said.

"What we will do at dawn tomorrow is extremely perilous. I must not lie to you. This of your hunger for a child is one thing, but to inflict bastardy and fatherlessness upon him simultaneously is another. Let me then finish this of tomorrow. And that of the next day, and of the day after. I no longer have any faith in my luck. I have used up too much of it."

She sat there, looking at him. Then, very slowly, she got up and came to him. She put her two hands up and let them lie cool and remote along the slant of his jaw. She went up on tiptoe, kissed his mouth.

"If you are killed at dawn," she said, "you think that by noon I shall be still alive? How little you know me, Peter!"

"Nena—you couldn't; you mustn't! I—"

"I could. And I will. Except——"

"Except what, *Muñeca*?"

"Except that—that you leave your life in me. Your image. Your replica, to grow tall and strong as you are and as ugly as you are, and as beautiful. Can you deny me this, *Cielo*? Deny me the only thing that would save my life?"

"Nena," he groaned.

She opened those almond-shaped eyes very wide. Stared at him. Let him peer into the heart of darkness. Then with a brusque, harsh, angular motion that suited her, she bent her head and cried. Angrily. Terribly. Her whole body shook.

He put out his arms, drew her to him.

She hammered at his chest with both her fists.

"You leave me nothing, not even pride!" she raged. "Must I beg you on my knees? Must I? Oh, damn you, let me go!"

He turned her loose. She backed away from him, held him with the black fury of her gaze, executed a swirling veronica of silk and nylon and lace upward and away, hooked thumbs into that triangular wisp she had on beneath, made a brief, curiously graceful contortion through silken downward slither into suddenly renewed bifurcation and stood there, lifting, swelling, puckering, poised, inhollowed, trembling, under the wonder and the worship of his gaze. He saw that she was slender rather than thin. What in French is called *une fausse maigre. Trim* was as close as he could get to it in English. Her breasts were small and high and conical. Her body was champagne-colored, pale golden, except for the wild strawberries tipping the breasts, a tiny blue half-moon under the left one (What was it Luis had said?), and the startling black plume of her sex. And now, bending forward, cringing a little, surrendering to shame, she came to him with a skip and a scamper like a child, plunging into his arms, burying her face to the rough, scarred hollow of his throat.

He lay there, kissing her slowly, gently, tenderly. But she tore her mouth free, said angrily, harshly:

"Do not waste time! Can't you see I want—"

"What, Nena?"

"You. All of you. And without gentleness. That this may hurt enough to kill my shame."

"Nena," he said. "You're talking about a couple of other guys, aren't you?"

"Peter, please!" she said.

He moved a little. Carefully. But she arched all her body like a bow, and lunged forward and upward, closing around him, holding him achingly, sweetly, tenderly, screamingly, scaldingly in an abrupt shunting of his breath, his life into an oblique tangent away from time, before releasing both for him with what was less a motion than a long, slow, unspeakably total caress.

Her voice was at his ear but he couldn't hear what it was saying for the surge and thunder of his blood; then he felt her nails bite into his back and all the gigantic swelling surfpound mounted up, hung poised unbearably through the long, long, slow-crumbling dikes of will control being existence sense, going now, caving in, being swept away, exploding into utter dark through which there crashed the sudden, sun-bright cymbal of her cry.

She lay with her arm across his chest, crying. Then she sat up, looking at him with startled eyes. She let her fingertips stray over the whorls and rents and puckers with which his body was covered, lingering longest over the great silver ridge looping around his shoulder into his armpit.

"*Dios mío!* How you must have suffered!" she said.

"I was out most of the time," Peter said. "But I admit it was no fun."

She bent and kissed his mouth.

"Peter—" she said.

"Yes, Infant?"

"Do you—can you—love me? Love a woman so depraved and of such a vileness?"

He smiled at her.

"Tell me," he said, "how many hundreds of lovers have you had?"

She twined her fingers in his hair.

"No hundreds, Peter. In all my life: two. My poor Emilio—and you."

He raised his head and kissed her. When he tried to draw away, her head came downward with his, clinging mouth to mouth; and the sparkle of her crying was cold upon his face.

"Please?" she whispered.

Then crashingly, shatteringly, terribly, they heard that scream.

He was out of bed in one long leap. Snatched up his shorts, nearly dry now, from the edge of the lavabo, and put them on. From the top of the dresser he took the pistol Joaquin had brought him, but then he put it down again; knowing that the one thing no one could do this close to the concentration camp was fire a shot, and picked up the Commando knife instead.

"Peter!" she cried out.

"Quiet, Nena!" he said. "Don't move!" And raced down the stairs.

As he had known there wouldn't be—for Pablo and Martin and the rest had gone, on his orders, to plant those charges of plastic at the places he had indicated around the walls—leaving only Mario, one of the drowsy teen-agers, to guard the innkeeper and his wife—there was no one there.

And, he saw, not even Mario; because what had been Mario, all that gaiety, spirit, courage, had departed, leaving only the broken flesh that had housed him, lying there before the opened door, staring up into the dim bulb in the basement passage from sightless eyes; having now two mouths: his own, opened wide in terror, in pain; and the other, the new one the innkeeper had slashed across his throat, converting the sleep he was so fond of into that deeper dreamlessness from which no man ever wakens.

It was the woman who had screamed. And now she crouched there, staring at Mario's body with eyes filled with tears and horror; lifting up her head, she screamed again:

"Beast! Assassin! Killer of babies!"

Peter slapped her then, hard, across the mouth. Pushed her back into the room and closed the door. But there was nothing to lock it with, because the innkeeper had burst the bolt from the wood, in his bull-like surge through it. Only there was no time to search for a substitute means of locking it. And the woman had hated her husband —he knew that now—was, therefore, no threat. Peter came out into the dark, hearing that gross animal laboring through the brush some meters ahead, Mario's Sten gun in his hands. The innkeeper was no woodsman. He was already floundering, lost. Peter moved in on a long slanting diagonal; closing his eyes, holding them shut even as he ran, until they were accustomed to the darkness.

He saw the man ahead of him now, heard him puffing like a steam engine; but the innkeeper was now only three meters from the road that ran straight to the prison camp, and, once on it, there would be no stopping him. Even now, one burst from the burp gun, one great shout could end it all for them, bring the prison guards pouring out to gun them down, divided as they were, scattered, unprepared. So Peter closed in upon him, did in one unbroken chain of linked motion the things he had been trained to do: hooked his left arm around the innkeeper's throat, tightening it in ferocious jerks until there was no breath in the man with which to cry, at the same time slamming his right knee into the small of the man's back so that it served as the fulcrum of the lever against which he bent the innkeeper in one unbelievably swift motion, so that the spinal column snapped, producing so instantaneous a paralysis that the man's beefy fingers opened, and the Czech machine pistol thudded to the ground; but Peter, having no time to appraise the already fatal results of his attack, brought that long blade in and down in one swift sweep, feeling it bite flesh, sink through that nothing which is a man to reach that quivering bundle of unquiet flesh, his heart; then, drawing it out again, feeling the hot spurting jet follow it; and bringing his left hand up to clamp over the innkeeper's nose and mouth; put the edge of the blade behind the man's left ear and slashed down in one long slant, twelve centimeters long, severing the carotid, making absolutely sure, because that was the way he had been taught to do it; because what a trained Commando does in hand-to-hand combat is overkill his man, massacre him.

He left the innkeeper lying where he fell, pausing only long enough to pick the Sten gun up, but not wasting time searching for the blade the mestizo had used to kill Mario—surely a switchblade and surely concealed about his person now, and surely employed while Mario slept. Automatically, he wiped his blade clean on the dead man's shirt, and started back toward the inn.

The woman was still in the basement room, weeping and praying. She seemed unaware of the smashed lock. But all the same, Peter entered that room, jerked loose a length of electric wire, and bound her hands and feet with that, biting it cruelly into her flesh.

Then he went back upstairs and into the bathroom. He washed the blood off his arms with cold water. Stood there staring at his own face in the mirror, bent his head and vomited, the sound of it a long, long racking tearing sound that went on and on until the toilet bowl was filled with yellowish bile streaked through with blood. He pulled the chain and flushed it down. Then he sat down on the edge of the tub. He sat there until Alicia came through the door, and saw how his great shoulders shook, saw that his eyes were blind.

She knelt down very slowly until her slim body was between his knees. Put up her arms, wound them around his neck.

"Don't cry, Peter!" she said. "Oh, please, my love, don't cry!"

She took him by the arm, led him back to the bed, lay down beside him, kissing his eyes, his throat, his mouth.

"Don't!" he said, "for God's love, don't!"

"Why not?" she said.

"I killed him," he said. "I gave him no chance. I killed him like a dog."

"As he killed Mario," she said.

"You went downstairs! You saw!"

"Yes, *Cielo*. You are much man, but your heart is as tender as a woman's. Sometimes a man must kill. His death was just."

He stared at her.

"You!" he said. "You are—"

"What, *Cielo*?"

"Miguel's sister. After all. With his face. His mind. His heart. Leave me! I cannot bear you now! I cannot."

But she brought her right hand across his face open-palmed, with a sound like a pistol shot, then caught him by both his ears, furiously assaulting his mouth, pushing him over backward, and sprawling atop him, her lips on his—devouring, ferocious, feral, her small hands coming down from his ears to rake along all his body, and now, gripping, biting in, lifting him in a taut bowed arc from the bed, and mounting in one swift equestrian motion, widespread and over and down so that the act was not penetration but engulfment, she dissolved his bones' marrow, melted his flesh, his nerves, his life into the wild thrashing undulant cauldron of her loins, his senses into the sweat-steamed air, made vibrant by her voice rising through a whole minor appoggiatura into what was far more ululation than a cry.

And when the residual heart-hammer breath-storm had subsided, the anguished and agonized fight to drag enough air into laboring lungs to sustain life had been won, he—raising his head and seeing her where she sprawled across him still, boneless and supine like a rubber doll, the whole of her silvered and glistening with the cooling rivers that poured still out of her every pore, her sculptured Assyrian Astarte's head turned sidewise and her mouth blue-bruised, swollen into a negroid caricature of its former warm fullness, opened like an idiot child's—was torn by pity at her aspect of helplessness, despair. He put out his big hand, gone gray and trembling, and stroked the close-cropped black cap of hair, dripping wet now, glued to her skull by sweat, and whispered:

"Nena—"

She came upright then, staring at him. In the lamplight the tears on her face were a golden flood.

"Nena," he said, "I love you. You have taken it away. It is gone."

"Oh, Peter, *Cielo!*" she wailed, and clung to him, shuddering. Then she lifted that wonderful, tragic, tender face, and smiled, all gamin now, her wide soft mouth bisected by her tears.

"We shall name him Mario, this son that we have made," she said. "Do you not find this just?"

"Yes, Nena," he said. "If we have a child. And if it is a son, agreed."

"Oh, Peter! Have you no faith at all?" she said.

First thing in the morning, Joaquin came up to Peter with Mario's machine pistol in his hand. He held the little weapon out to Peter. His voice was rough when he spoke:

"He would want you to have it, Comrade!"

"No," Peter said. "I thank you, Comrade; but no—"

"Why not?" Martin said.

"Because it is a gun," Peter said, "and a gun is useful only for killing people. Hence I have no further need of it."

"You do all right with a knife," Pablo said, "though even that was unnecessary. He would have died of what you did with your hands. You broke his spine."

"Let us not speak of it," Peter said. "Are you ready?"

"Yes, Comrade Temporary Chief," Pablo said; "but one favor, Commander!"

"Which is?" Peter said.

"Let me drive that truck!"

"No," Peter said.

"Comrade, the man who drives the truck will die. And if you die, the little Alicia will go mad. I am sure of it."

"You are sure of many things," Peter said. "Now hear me, so that we do not make a bad motion-picture script of this. I will drive that truck, because of you all, only I can do it and *not* die. I have a great wish to live now. But I have no desire whatsoever to see one of you killed trying to do what only I know how to do. Now let us put all our watches to the same time like motion-picture Commandos, because it is necessary, not to make heroic gestures."

They synchronized their watches.

"We have found it takes twenty minutes for every man to get into position," Peter said. "By then, there will be light enough for you to see to shoot them, instead of each other. You are not to fire until you hear the truck blow up. And then you are to shoot them in the belly, from as close a range as possible, trying not to kill the political prisoners. And speaking of the guards, you are not to allow even one to escape; nor will you accept the surrender of any."

Pablo's face whitened a little.

"I do not understand you, Peter," he said. "Last night, you wept for the man you had killed. And now—"

"I shall weep for these, after we have killed them. But kill them we must," Peter said.

They lay in the brush and waited. They had blackened their faces with burnt corks taken from the wine bottle in the cellar of the inn. They lay there without moving until the truck came down the road with Peter driving it. It came on very slowly until it was abreast of them. Then Peter reached down and laid the heavy, flat stone on the accelerator, double-clutched, slamming the truck into high. As it roared forward, he opened the cab door and leaped. He hit the ground already rolling. The brush swallowed him.

Five seconds later the truck crashed through the main gate and blew up inside the prison yard.

They left the freed prisoners—except, of course, Pablo's two friends, captured before the Archbishop's Palace, whom they took with them—to butcher the wounded prison guards, and roared away in all the trucks to Xilchimocha. They took the Social Re-education Center there in a sharp fight that cost them seven casualties and would have cost them more if suddenly the Tluscola hadn't swarmed out of their sacred town, formed ranks beside them, and carried the walls of the prison camp in mass frontal attacks that cost them more than fifty dead, swarming over those walls and into the camp in one long screaming red mass of fury.

When it was over, Peter sent for Alicia, whom they'd brought with them because he hadn't dared leave her at the inn with the jungle around it filled with brutalized, starving ex-prisoners. They had left her out of range with Joaquin, who had been slightly wounded in the Tarascanolla massacre, guarding her to see that she didn't do anything foolish. But now they needed her, because she was the only one among them who could speak Tluscolan. Here in the South, the Indians' contact with the Spaniards, either as Conquistadores or colonists, had been slight. None of them spoke comprehensible Spanish.

"Camarada Alicia," Pablo said, "ask them why they helped us! Ask them what it means! Because if all the Indians have come over to our side—"

Alicia turned to the Cacique. She made a series of gurgling sounds in her throat, a very pretty drum roll of grunts; a group of clicking noises; a nasal snort or two.

The Cacique returned the compliment.

Alicia turned to Peter, her eyes wide.

"He says that Miguel defiled their dead!" she whispered. "I do not know how or why—nor, I fear, does he. The message came by the drums. You know how that works? They beat a drum in one village and the sound of it—"

"Yes, I know, Nena. What else does he say?"

"That the Tluscola are at war. That they have lifted the hatchet against Miguel, against the government. And that they will never stop until he, and it, are destroyed. Oh, Peter, how terrible!"

"It is," Peter said. "Now, Infant, you go back to the truck. We've got one more camp to take. The women's camp at Chizenaya. And we'll need you there. . . ."

They did not have to take the camp at Chizenaya. When they got there, they saw the white flag flying above the gate. But, in a certain sense, what they had to do was harder. There were only thirty women prisoners left alive, and some of them had to be carried to the courts-martial on stretchers to give their testimony. Martin argued that the scrupulosity that Pablo and Peter insisted upon was a waste of time. Practically speaking, he was right. When the trials were over, it took the firing squads the rest of the day to finish up the affair. There was not one among the guards who could have been acquitted by the most lenient civil court on earth.

And, to make it worse, with one or two exceptions, they died very badly, screaming and cursing and crying and begging for their lives. The Commander of the Camp had to be carried to the wall. When Peter saw who he was, he stopped the proceedings long enough to walk over, stick a cigarette in his mouth, and light it for him.

But when the Commander looked up and saw who it was offering him this last courtesy, he swallowed the smoke and started to cough and the tears ran down across the faint but still visible scars of the furrows Alicia had clawed into his face the day he had beaten Peter up in the street before his house. Perhaps he remembered that. Or the three days of interrogation he had conducted.

Peter bent closer.

"Would you like to give the commands to the squad?" he said. "It is an honor I offer you for old times' sake—"

"No!" the Captain screamed. "Oh damn you, Gringo! Give them yourself!"

"No," Peter said; "in me it would be unbecoming. In me, it would seem vengeance. Comrade Martin!"

"Yes, Comrade Pedro?"

"Take over," Peter said.

But Martin didn't give any commands to the firing squad. Instead, he walked over to where the Camp Commander sat tied to the chair, with his back toward the squad. He saw how the Commander was crying and straining at his bonds. He smelled the odor arising from the fact that the Commander has lost control of his sphincter and defecated upon himself in his fear. He watched the yellow pools of urine gathering around the Commander's feet.

Then he drew his Mauser and shot the Camp Commander through the back of his head.

The Cacique of local Tluscola knew where the lost, found, and lost-again city of Ururchizenaya was. So they all went there, as a more or less conscious release from the things they had had to do. Peter took pictures of all of them among the ruins. The ruins were very beautiful. They made Peter wonder if, when the Conquistadores came with the cross and the sword, the world had gained or lost. He was studying the intricate hieroglyphics when Alicia came up to him.

"Let us spend the night here, *Cielo,*" she said, "for if the God of my Spanish ancestors is too stiff-necked to bless our union, perhaps there is here another god of my Indian forebears who will!"

So they requested permission—and got it (there was nothing Pablo, and very little Martin would have refused Peter by then)—to spend the night in the ruins of Ururchizenaya. But, at supper, before the others had gone back to the regular camp, Peter caught her looking at him with what was either horrified fascination or fascinated horror.

"Nena," he said, "what passes with you?"

"Peter, will you forgive me if I say a thing?"

"Say it, *Muñeca.*"

"The—the executions. You, you commanded some of them!"

"Yes, Nena."

"Why, Peter?"

"I requested the privilege in two or three cases. Where your brother's goons had been especially rough. This disturbs you, *Muñeca?*"

"Yes, Peter, it disturbs me. Not that it had to be done. But that *you* should do it!"

"And yet, the other night, that of the innkeeper—"

"With your hands! With only a knife. And he with a machine gun that could have riddled you with bullets! Oh, but you were much, then!"

"And now I am not?"

"No, Peter. Men tied to posts—I did not watch it; but I know how it is. And I could hear. A silence that stopped my heart from beating, then your voice, *yours!*: '*Fiiirrrre!*' And all the world breaking in half with the crash of the shots! Oh, no! Oh, no, Peter! This is ugly! This is cruel! Others can do these things, but not my Love! Not ever you!"

Across the fire from them, Pablo's young face darkened. He stood up.

"Comrade Alicia!" he ripped out.

"Yes, my Commander?" Alicia said.

"You volunteered for this mission. You are under my orders. And now I order you to come with me!"

"Now look, Pablo—" Peter said.

"I shall return her to you, Comrade. And you will thank me, for if you wed a woman so sadly lacking in discipline, in respect for you, you will regret it. I propose to end this problem now."

"How?" Peter said.

"There is a thing I want the Camarada Alicia to see. I think it will improve her progressive indoctrination immensely. Now, Comrade Sister of the man who caused these things to be done—come!"

When Pablo brought her back again, she came flying to Peter's arms and cried and cried and cried beyond the hope of speech.

"Now I will leave you," Pablo said. "That you rest." Then, to the others: "Form ranks! Forward march!"

"Nena—" Peter said.

"Oh, Peter! Oh, Peter! Ohhhhh! That you had done other things to them than shooting! That you had cut them all over as the Indians do, smeared them with honey, and tied them down upon a hill of ants! That you had burned them alive! That you had killed them by millimeters! Ohhhhhh!"

"Nena—" Peter said.

"The beasts! The savages! Animals! Assassins!"

"They are dead, Nena."

"I know. Peter, *Cielo*—"

"Yes, Nena?"

"Forgive me! Forgive your stupid one, your idiot, your little fool!"

"My little angel from the sky," Peter said.

"Know what they did?" she wept. "Do you know?"

"Yes, Nena. Let us not speak of it. Let us not spoil this night."

"Ay, no! I shall never forget it; but I will not speak of it. Instead I will take away all the pain I have caused you, and you must take away what I have seen . . ."

So they spent the night in the ruins of Ururchizenaya. Peter took flash pictures of her lying naked in the arms of a hideous idol, pretending to be a human sacrifice. Bathing in the Pool of the Maidens. Kneeling before the statue of the unknown goddess she looked like. The statue was much bigger than the one in the Museum, which was why it was still here. The Standford Expedition had had to settle for the smaller one. This one was too big to haul away.

In the morning, Pablo himself came to fetch them, calling out from a discreet distance. It was a good thing he did, because they were both stark naked and fast asleep in each other's arms. When they had dressed, Pablo told them the news. All night long the radio that Joaquin and poor Mario had stolen at Peter's request had been filled with messages in code on the higher bands. But the government radio hadn't even bothered with such refinements; it was screaming to the four winds for help, crying that Ciudad Villalonga was surrounded by the Fidelistas and their Indian allies.

And, as if to compound confusion, Zopocomapetl had split itself open halfway down one side.

So they got in the trucks, throwing out the useless goods to make room for the liberated prisoners, leaving those too sick, too hurt, at the inn, under a swearing medical corpsman and two Indian brush nurses, and started north again.

XIX

They roared north without being stopped at all. There were no longer any uniformed *carabiñeros* of the civil guard upon the roads. There was nothing on the road, nothing at all. Even the service stations were closed and locked. They had to break into them and work the pumps by hand in order to get the fuel oil into the tanks of the trucks. Over the radio came a confused babble of orders, commands, and prohibitions, depending upon which band it was tuned to. Generally, Martin kept it synchronized with La Voz de Costa Verde, the national radio or Radio Villalonga, the principal broadcasting station of the city itself. The longer he and Pablo listened, the wider their smiles grew. What was going on inside Ciudad Villalonga was barely controlled panic. Strict martial law reigned. The number of offenses for which a civilian might be shot on the spot passed twenty. The Toque de Queda—curfew —had been imposed. Last night, the radio announced, five badly intentioned ones had been shot dead for violating it. Miguel Villalonga's voice, high and hysterical, came over Radio Villalonga, screaming threats to push the barbaric red invaders into the sea. Martial music boomed. There were appeals to patriotism, admonitions to remain calm, but, beyond that, nothing.

Then, suddenly, Miguel's voice came over the air again. The hysteria was gone from it. It was controlled. Perhaps a little too controlled.

"*Due to the vigorous action of one of our patrols,*" he said, "*we have conclusive proof that the Red barbarians plan to exterminate all citizens of the United States of North America who are found within the capital, once they succeed in forcing an entry. This, of course, is entirely in line with the other barbarities they have committed against the people and the holdings of Our Great Sister Republic all over Hispano-America, notable in Venezuela . . .*"

Peter looked at Pablo.

"It's a lie!" Pablo said.

"I know it is," Peter said, "but can you figure out the reason for it?"

"Therefore, since the situation is admittedly grave—" Miguel's voice went on.

"Oh, Peter!" Alicia said.

"Quiet, Nena!" Peter said.

"—my government has decided to put at the disposal of the United States Embassy several of the city's autobuses, withdrawn from the municipal transportation system, to take the personnel of the Embassy and the numerous North American tourists caught here by the unhappy turn of events to places of safety outside the capital."

"Still don't get it," Peter said.

"Each bus will be provided, of course, with an armed escort to protect—"

"Ya! Ya!" Martin said. "You get it *now,* do you not, Comrade Reporter?"

"Poor devils," Peter said.

"Peter, *Cielo,* perhaps I am of an enormous stupidity," Alicia said, "but I confess I do not understand this. Not at all."

"Your sweet brother," Peter said, "wants to make sure that somebody'll save his neck. So, he collects a few hostages. Bargaining points. Either the Marines come in, or——"

"Oh, Peter!" Alicia said.

"They'll be all right," Peter said. "He won't dare really do anything to them. He needs us too badly for that. This cute caper doesn't bother me. What bothers me is—"

"What, Comrade?" Pablo said.

"That your boys haven't taken the city by now. Before we left Ururchizenaya, it was already surrounded."

"He has tanks," Martin said.

"Very few," Peter said. "Five or six which cannot be everywhere at once. And he no longer has an air force, thanks to Jacinto. And your boys have bazookas."

Martin looked at Pablo.

"He is right, the Comrade Reporter," he said; "they should have taken the city by now. Something has gone wrong."

"I hope not," Pablo said.

"And I," Peter said. "But something always does. It is like my stick."

"What stick, *Cielo?*" Alicia said.

"*Muñeca,* do you recall the little stick I had with me at Vince's party?"

"Yes, *Cielo;* but what I do not see is the connection."

"There is a connection. That little stick—it is called a *swagger stick* in English—was a kind of symbol for me. I intended to march into battle with it, like a British officer in the first world war. Directing my men with it. Carrying no other weapon. Being cool and jaunty under fire. Big deal."

"So?" Alicia said.

"I lost it. First trip out. I think it was when I rolled out of that truck. And I didn't even remember it until now . . ."

"Does it matter?" Alicia said.

"Hell, no. It's just funny, that's all. Life has the damnedest way of cutting a man down to size. And men. And nations. And political institutions."

"Meaning?" Martin growled.

"I mean nothing. I simply repeat what I said in the first place: Something has queered the deal."

"A question of luck," Pablo said.

"Don't believe in luck. Do you?" Peter said.

"Well—" Pablo said.

"Look, Comrade, can you remember any important event in your life that was arranged by luck?"

"Well . . . no," Pablo said.

"But you can recall numerous occasions in which luck pinned a fornication on you of the very first class?"

"Peter! Your language!" Alicia said.

"Sorry, Nena. And now I know you'll make a wife. You're already learning how."

"Luck does arrange things," Martin said. "For instance, we cannot have bad luck without Miguel's having good."

"True; but over the long haul it cancels out. And most of the time it's as impartial as all hell. Dirties everybody."

"Peter! Have you no respect for me?" Alicia said.

"None," Peter said. "I only respect women I don't love."

And now, when the volcano came in sight, he could see that the split through which that moving wall of lava poured was on the side away from Ciudad Villalonga. He didn't know what that meant at first, and it wasn't until two hours later that he found out. The line of trucks stopped, ramming together like a stiffened snake; and, as they piled out of them, they could see the long lines of Communist guerrillas reeling past with handkerchiefs over their mouths and noses, and on their flanks, the Tluscolas who had joined them, with nothing over their noses, crying and coughing, too, and farther out, pushed off the road itself by the retreating army, a crowd of civilians with all their goods in ox or donkey carts or on their own backs and heads, crying in the same bitter grief, although some of them at least occasionally had on the uniform of the national Army with the buttons and insignia torn off to show that they were deserters. The donkeys and the oxen cried too, great asinine and bovine tears that looked like blood. And it came to Peter then that what the Fidelistas and their Indian allies and the civilian refugees were retreating from wasn't Miguel Villalonga's all-but-nonexistent army but the volcano itself, so he threw back his head and laughed.

"What passes with you, *Cielo?*" Alicia said.

"Want to bet that if you started downtown on a hot, deadstill day, and forgot to put your panties on, a high wind wouldn't come up?" Peter said.

"Peter!" she said.

"Say that again," he said, and kissed her. "I love you when you say my name in that tone of utter severity."

"*Joder!*" Martin said, and Peter saw that it had hit him, too.

"Now you see my point?" Peter said. "In the cinema of which you Costa Verdians are so fond, things would be arranged differently, no? In the great pictures in technicolor, Zopo would blow his top all right, but he would bury Miguel Villalonga and Luis Sinnombre beneath a mountain of lava for their sins. But this is not cinema and I hesitate to call it life, for life consists of more than marching up and down and killing people. Yet, here you have your luck, Comrades. And it is both of a vile vileness and of an utter immorality!"

"Oh, Peter!" Alicia wailed.

When she said his name like that, one of the refugees stopped. He had a pack on his back, and was a good bit better dressed than the other civilians. There was something familiar about his face.

"Don Pedro!" he said.

"You've got the advantage of me, Friend," Peter said.

"Your guide, Señor! Do you not remember me? I am Tomas, he who led you across the lava beds up there, the time you were searching for Padre Pío—"

"Now, I remember," Peter said, and took his hand. "Tomas, do you think you could do it again? I, and this lady, must enter the city."

Martin's eyebrows came together.

"Why?" he said.

"Later, Comrade," Peter said. "It is a thing that I and the Comrade

Alicia discussed last night. When things are arranged with Tomas, I will discuss them with you."

"I heard the discussion of last night," Martin said; "it made me to achieve an erection."

"Ohhhh!" Alicia said. "How filthy are men!"

"Can you again, Tomas," Peter said, "or has that big crapper up there defecated across all the paths?"

Alicia stamped her foot.

"Peter, if you do not also stop it, I . . . !"

"I have stopped it, Camarada," Peter said, and kissed her. "Can you, Tomas?"

"Well—" Tomas said. "I think so—yes! We should have to procure horses; and perhaps to search out new trails; but, beyond that—"

"Would it be too dangerous for the lady?" Peter said.

"Can she ride?" Tomas said.

"I won the woman's equestrian championship three years in a row," Alicia said; "and I won it fairly, despite all the lying gossip!"

Tomas' jaw dropped.

"Then you are—then the illustrious lady is—" he said.

"Yes. I am Alicia Villalonga," she said. "I suppose by now my carcass is worth twenty thousand pesos so that your troops may have the pleasure of staring at my legs as I hang upside down in the Plaza de la Liberación, no?"

"That will never happen, Camarada!" Pablo said. "I guarantee it!"

"How can you guarantee it, Pablo?" Peter said.

"I am known to all the important members of the Party. I will write her out a safe conduct, detailing her great services to the cause—"

"Services rendered exclusively to the Comrade Reporter, which, if he were a true Socialist, he would share," Martin said.

"Pay him no attention; he is obsessed," Peter said to Tomas.

"I will write this for her on official Party Stationery," Pablo said, "because it seems to me that she and you, Comrade, can become the means of reconciliation among all classes—"

"Shades of Luis Sinnombre!" Peter said. "Write it, then, Comrade."

"No," Martin said. "First the Comrade Journalist must tell us what he discussed with the Comrade Sister of the Ex-Head of the State, besides whether ten or twelve babies comprise an adequate family."

Alicia looked at him.

"I think you are a good boy, Martin," she said; "a good little boy who, to prove he is a big boy, must write dirty words on walls. And I think that when one day you truly fall in love, you will learn there are no dirty words. That, my friend, there are no words at all."

"Then what did you discuss? Besides the babies, I mean?"

"No. First the babies. For, until someone invents a world where idiots like you Communists and savages like my brother have no control over matters, I wish to have twelve babies with Peter. So that even in this universe of monsters, assassins, and madmen, it will be difficult to kill them all."

"I have no wish to kill babies, Camarada. It is more interesting to make them," Martin said.

"Very well. Pablo and Martin, what I discussed with Peter was a way of saving my brother's life."

"What!" Martin said.

"You heard me, Martin!"

"That, no!" Martin said.

"Comrade Pablo," Alicia said, "will you listen to me? You are older than Martin and cooler of head—"

"Speak of it," Pablo said.

"What if I offered you the surrender of the city? To you, personally. And to Martin, as your Second in Command?"

"It is a trick!" Martin said.

"What is today? The fourteenth of August? Ah, yes! There will be a new street in the city. The Avenue of the Fourteenth of August. And at the head of it, a great bronze statue: Pablo and Martin, the Heroes of the Fourteenth of August, receiving the surrender of Ciudad Villalonga from the hands of the Junta of Influential Citizens to whom the Dictator, Miguel Villalonga, entrusted it when he abdicated and fled. A plaque reading: 'By their noble, wise, and generous action in permitting Villalonga and Sinnombre to leave the country in exchange for an unconditional surrender, Pablo and Martin saved the lives of hundreds of brave Socialist soldiers who would otherwise have had to sacrifice themselves in the final struggle—'"

"Boys," Peter said, "I think we better make *her* President. Or at least head of the diplomatic corps."

"Because I can do this thing, Comrades," Alicia said. "He will listen to me. Give me a safe conduct into the city and I will persuade both Miguel and Luis to get aboard a plane. They have money in various banks abroad. And once they have gone, the hard core of murderous swine who support Miguel because they know that they will be killed along with him when the people take over, will run like rats. And when all these other bands of parvenus, Johnnies-come-lately, last-minute revolutionists march into the city they will have to treat with Acting Head of the State, Pablo, and Acting Civil Governor Martin. Because I will make sure that the city is surrendered only to you who are my friends. And thereafter, they *must* accord you the honor and the respect that is your due."

Pablo looked at Martin.

"This makes much sense, what the Camarada Alicia has said."

"*Sí,*" Martin said; "still, there are many thirsting for his blood."

"Look!" Alicia said. "See the people weeping as they pass! Even the soldiers weep! Shall we not, Comrades, put an end to blood and tears?"

"They weep because the vapors from the volcano get into the eyes and–" Tomas began.

Peter kicked him in the shin—hard. Hissed into his ear "Shut up, you fool!"

"And those who have suffered much at his hands may blame us for letting him go," Martin said. "Still—"

"Still, do you want revenge, Comrades, or a new deal?" Peter said. "A chance to build that brave new Socialist world you're always talking about? To prove to me I'm wrong? That Marxism can work? That it is not as much against human nature as I think it is?"

Martin looked at him. Grinned.

"*Se acuerdo,*" he said; "now that the so very clever comrades have played upon our vanity and our sporting instincts, both of accord! Let the bastard go! We have more important things to do. And, frankly, Camarada Temptress, with more guile than the Serpent of the Nile, I should like the various children that I have in all the various streets of the city to read in the history books that their father was a great man. We will do this thing!"

"Fine," Peter said. "Comrade Pablo, write out a safe conduct for three people. Better still, write out three separate safe conducts; because once we are in the city, our ways must part, at least for a time."

"Oh, Peter, *Cielo,* why?"

"You don't think you'll be able to talk any sense into Miguelito with *me* there, do you?"

"No," Alicia said, "but—"

"But nothing! Tomas, this of the horses?"

"There is a ranch near here where we might be able to rent or buy some nags, especially if you have some dollars," Tomas said, "but we had better start out at once, before this Socialist Army encamps itself, forgets it is Socialist, and starts acting like an army."

"Meaning?" Pablo said. Tomas came to attention. Saluted. Barked:

"Your identification, Comrade! What, you have no pass from General Mierda? Nor even one from Colonel Pedo? What is this, a pass from Teniente Jodido? Never heard of him. Comrades, take the Comrade out and shoot the Comrade, *por favor!*"

"You've got something there, Tomas!" Peter said.

"I will write you one from our great Russian Adviser the Generalski Ivanovski Gilipollas Maricon," Pablo said. "No, we will come with you to see you catch the horses. You'll come, Martin?"

"Why not?" Martin said, "since this vileness of a volcano has stopped the whole vile war."

They started out, leaving Joaquin in charge. They left the trucks parked on the shoulder of the road and followed the narrow, winding trail that Tomas pointed out.

"This of the Indians, Tomas," Peter said; "how did they happen to come over to the revolution? I thought Padre Pío had them sewed up."

"He did," Tomas said, "until the illustrious brother of the august lady made a mistake—"

"Oh, come off it, Tomas! We are all comrades now!" Alicia said.

"Very well. Miguelito made an error. But the fat one. The mother and father of all mistakes. You know what reverence the Tluscola have for their dead?"

"Yes," Peter said.

"It started with the volcano. It has been nasty for weeks now. First it buried Xochua."

"We heard that on the radio," Peter said. "No—a truck driver told us."

"And when the rescue teams dug into the ruins, they found that the dead had been transformed into statues by the ash—"

"This is not possible!" Martin said.

"Yes it is, Martin," Peter said; "I have seen it before."

"Where?" Martin said.

"At Pompeii, in Italy. I have seen bodies two thousand years old, perfectly preserved by the ash. Changed into statues. Gruesome sort of thing."

"It is," Tomas said. "But the cadavers of the Indians were so lifelike that the brother of Doña Alicia—"

"Camarada Alicia," Alicia said. "I am a Red, too, now. Aren't I, Peter?"

"Yes. Red as all get-out. Red as lipstick. Which reminds me—"

He bent and kissed her.

"More discipline, Comrades!" Pablo said.

They all laughed.

"Your brother, Comrade Alicia," Tomas said, "decided to put them in the Museum of Archeology for the edification of the tourists. That did it. In the face of such blasphemy, the Tluscola declared war. Which means the dictatorship is doomed. Not even old Zopo can stop that for very long. Miguel's troops are deserting him—except for those who have committed so many crimes that their lives depend upon his protection. When the volcano cools down again, he will be in a worse position than he is now. Therefore I think he would be wise to take the advice of the Comrade Alicia, and flee—"

"Oh, he will!" Alicia said. "I am sure of that."

Watching her now, where she rode, picking her way across the barely solidified flats of the lava, the steam coming up around the great clumsy bundles of wet rags they had wrapped around the horses' hoofs to protect them from the heat, it came to Peter that she was of those who would do everything beautifully, perfectly, from dominating a skittish horse to holding an infant in her arms. And the way he felt about her rose up and thundered in his chest, and an ice-cold blade of terror entered him slowly, probing for his breath.

Because this was wrong; it contradicted thirty-seven years of experience. For, if there were any one item life didn't provide, it was flawlessness. Or, when it did, on a strictly temporary basis, as if to make more bitter the flawed residue after flawlessness was gone; to increase the insufferability of memory. Of emptiness. Of cold.

He jammed his heels into his nag's flanks. Brought the ugly beast abreast of hers. Reached out and clawed away that mask she had made for herself, with another for him, and another for Tomas out of the torn strips of her heavy Italian silk half-slip. Dragged her into his arms, and almost broke her mouth before the residual terror drained out of him, allowing tenderness to return.

"Oh, Peter!" she said. "Oh, my Love! *Cielo mío*—My Own—what was that for?"

"Because I love you so much I think I shall die of it," he said.

"And I, you," she said, looking at the guide. "Oh, if he were only not here! Oh, if there were only some place where . . ."

"No," Peter said; "not like that, now. I looked at you, and suddenly I saw our son in your arms. Or our daughter. It was so little I could not tell."

"What was it like?" she said.

"Well, it had lots and lots of hair. Black."

"It could hardly be blond, *Cielo*—"

"And you were feeding it. And I was angry with it and jealous of it for putting its greedy little mouth where only mine has been—"

She bent her horse's head about with one swift, beautifully, perfectly executed pull on the bridle, bringing him around until he was across the would-be, half-eroded memory of a trail, so that her back was turned squarely toward where Tomas rode. Her hand came up, clawed at the topmost buttons of the mono.

"Kiss me there now," she said, and her voice was ragged. "I want you to. I——"

"No," he said. "Tonight. When it is dark. I will order him to sleep apart."

"Oh that it were night now!" she said.

And then, finally, it was night, but it was not dark. Zopocomapetl washed all the sky with orange-red. He sent down little trickling rivulets of fire nosing into their camp. He blinded their eyes, tore at their throats with his noxious vapors.

Nevertheless, they made love.

With a hungry, desperate urgency—as though they knew what was going to happen tomorrow. As if they could read the front page of a newspaper still unprinted.

"I can," he whispered. "Goddam it, I can!"

"You can what?" Alicia said.

"Read tomorrow's newspaper," Peter said.

"What does it say, *Cielo*?" she whispered.

"No," he said, "I can't. I'm not clairvoyant worth a damn. Can't read—"

"What does it say, Peter!" Alicia said.

"It's—it's blank. No. It has the usual things. Movements of armies. Alarums and excursions. Wars, threats of wars. People mucking up their lives. Only—"

"Only what, *Cielo*?"

"We aren't there. I don't see us there at all."

She looked at him. Then she locked her slim arms around his neck. He bent and kissed her mouth, her breasts.

"No," she said; "no preliminaries, *Cielo*. I do not need them. I am ready now. Enter me. Come into my body. Into my life. And then there will be a tomorrow. In one way or another; there will be."

And, when he had done her bidding, when he had entered that wonderful, warmsoft interior tremble, had been caught and held by that absolutely unbearably adhesive cling and scald, which nonetheless had to be borne if he were not to spoil the occasion with too much haste, she was entirely still, completely silent, so long that he did not know when it was that she began to move. But when she did, it was like temple dancers worshiping creation, beginning, life, in slow, sweet, undulant rhythms, so slow, so gently tender that all urgency left him, and they lay together entwined, penetrant, encompassed, making not the usual evasive euphemisms for ugly fact, but very truly love; achieving so complete a sublimation of the basic sexual hunger that the sky was graying above Zopocomapetl when she said:

"Now, *Cielo*, now."

And even then without urgency. He felt her long, deep, internal shudder begin and waited quiescent until it rose to vibrant, quivering near-peak before racing to join her in that momentary shattering of the very stuff of being, that little death, that instant of fusion when they twain became one flesh, when the awful loneliness to which each child of man is born is for that tender instant stilled.

And looking down, he saw her eyes awash, but she was smiling.

"This time, yes," she said. "This time surely!"

It took them all the next day to cross that ravaged stretch where no trails had survived the old gods' wrath, or their laughter. Four times they were stopped by Red patrols; but Pablo's passes were as effective as he had said they would be.

But, coming into the city in the dawn, after another night that had duplicated the one before and, if anything, surpassed it, they were not stopped at all.

The reason they were not was both a tribute to Tomas' skill as a guide and evidence of to what extent Miguel Villalonga had lost his grip on history. From the trail above, Tomas had studied the approaches to the city through a pair of new and powerful glasses. He handed them to Peter. Pointed.

"Down there," he said, "on that side, the eastern side, nearest the sea. Do you not see the gap, Comrade?"

"Yes," Peter said, "but what I do not understand is why there should be a gap precisely there—"

"That sector was occupied by the company of Ernesto Guttiérez. A friend of mine. They were all badly disaffected, so I suspected they might desert. I was correct. They have."

"There are other gaps," Peter said, looking through the binoculars.

"There is much disaffection," Tomas said. "For now it is the volcano and not his army which is saving Our Glorious Leader's mangy hide. Oh, I beg your pardon, Comrade Alicia!"

"It is all right," Alicia said. "I have scant love for my brother, Tomas."

So they had gone down there and passed through the gap in the blue light of dawn. Alicia gave them a lesson in horsemanship by jumping her mount over the barbed wire the troops had left. But when Peter tried it, his nag got so tangled up that Tomas had to cut him loose with wirecutters.

"Which," Peter said, "you just accidentally happen to have, eh, Tomas?"

Tomas grinned.

"To live, I must move about. And there is barbed wire everywhere, these days," he said.

But, once inside the city, it was he again who made the obviously, sensible suggestion that had occurred to neither of the others.

"You will dismount," he said, "and take off those coveralls. That is, if you still have clothes on under them. Do you?"

Alicia looked him straight in the eye.

"And what, Comrade Tomas, makes you think we might not have?" she said.

Tomas grinned.

"I thought perhaps you had left them off for the sake of quickness and convenience," he said.

Alicia turned to Peter.

"That we may have a house one day. That we be able to cease making public exhibitions!" she said.

"We have our clothes on, Tomas. Why?" Peter said.

"Because a man and a woman in *monos azules* on horseback in the city would be—rare, Comrade. But a pair of sleepy lovers, in normal clothes, walking hand in hand, are not. Even if the man does have three days' growth of beard. That only indicates their ardor. That they have not wasted time on nonessentials—"

"Tomas, you're a smart man," Peter said, and took out a five-thousand-peso note.

Tomas frowned.

"Do you not have any dollars, Comrade?" he said. "That backnote will not buy a pack of cigarettes, now."

So Peter gave him twenty dollars, which caused him to grin happily. With twenty dollars he could buy almost anything. Including one of the hundreds of luxurious automobiles stalled on the streets because there was no longer any gasoline to run them with, and whose owners' need for hard currency to further their escape was desperate. To such a pass had the Eternal Republic come.

They left Tomas and the horses and went walking hand in hand like children through the city. There was no one else in the streets. No one at all. The silence was eerie. It crawled along their nerves. Their footsteps were gunshot-loud in all that stillness. Alicia stopped.

"Oh, Peter, look!" she said.

A *buitre* was sitting on the cornice of a building looking down at them. Then he saw that there were *buitres*—buzzards—sitting on the roofs of all the houses watching them out of those flat, lightless eyes, without moving those obscene, scaly, bluish-red heads. Others circled above Ciudad Villalonga and above them the *bijiritas*—kites—and immensely high, infinitesimal black crosses against the blue wash of the heavens, the condors. Yet in the streets, there were no dead.

"They know!" Alicia shuddered. "Oh, Peter, *Cielo*, they know!"

Peter saw another thing: Miguel Villalonga was not planning a street-by-street, house-by-house, suicidal defense. There were no barricades, no barbed wire in the streets. Nor any trenches. All the defenses were peripheral.

Then, abruptly, there was sound. It blared from the loud-speakers of a sound truck that crossed an intersection several blocks away. They heard a snatch of words: "*All United States citizens are urgently requested to go to their Embassy in order to be conveyed . . .*"

"So that caper's not working so good, eh, Miguelito?" Peter said.

"*. . . to a place of safety.*" The mechanical, tinny voice came over to them, more faintly now, as the intervening buildings cut off the passage of the sound. They could hear it for a while longer. Then it died.

"Come on, *Muñeca*. We've things to do," Peter said.

They parted in the Plaza de la Liberación. Or started to.

"I will persuade him," Alicia said, "you can be sure of that."

"Only I'm not," Peter said.

"Trust me, *Cielo*," Alicia said. "Peter—"

"Yes, Nena?"

"Where will you be, this night?"

"In my flat. Why?"

"Oh—" she said. "Must you stay *there, Cielo*?"

"I will go to the Hilton. Is that better?"

"Very much better. If I can, I will come to you—"

"And if you cannot, Nena?"

"I will try to telephone you."

"All right," Peter said.

And loud in the silence, they heard the clatter of running feet. But, fast as they whirled, they saw no one at all.

"How rare, no?" Alicia said.

"Very rare," Peter began; then he heard her whisper:

"Santa Madre de Dios!"

He turned, followed the lightlocked pointing of her gaze. Saw the two women—the fat female dreadnaught who was the acting madam, since Miguel had locked his mother up, and another nondescript, rather skinny whore—come down the stairs of La Luna Azul with that burden in their arms. Shuffling under its weight, they went around the corner into the Street of the Martyrs of the Faith, which was a narrow blind alley opening on the square. Then they came back again, empty-handed, running. They pounded back up the stairs of The Blue Moon. Even from where Peter and Alicia stood, the snorting, whistling, panting of their breaths came over clearly.

"Oh, Peter, no!" Alicia said, and clung to him. But he broke free of her grasp, and entered the Calle de los Mártires de la Fe. She stood there, trembling. Then she followed him.

He was kneeling there with the woman's head cradled on his arm. She was completely naked, and now Alicia could see the blood pumping out of her through a line of little blue holes that stitched her slim, young body diagonally from left to right, starting from the left shoulder and slanting down across her right breast, which had two holes in it, one of which had destroyed the nipple, almost to her waist. She was trying to tell Peter something, but the blood kept coming out of her mouth and choking her. Peter wiped it away as best he could with his handkerchief.

"Was it Jacinto, Teresa?" he said. "Tell me! Was it Jacinto?"

She stiffened in his arms. Opened her mouth. Vomited up a great rush of blood. Got it out. Said, "*Sí,* Peter, *cariño*"—and died.

Walking together the rest of the way to the palace, because he did not dare leave her now, Alicia said nothing to him. She simply moved beside him, crying without motion, without sound, her face wet all over by her tears.

Before they were close enough for the guards before the door to distinguish who they were, he stopped. Said:

"Alicia—"

She looked at him.

"*Sí,* Peter, *cariño!*" she said.

He did then what he had to do. Drew back his hand and slapped her stingingly across the face. She stood there, looking at him. Then with a little broken whimper, she came to his arms.

"What right have I?" she sobbed. "What right at all? Who am I but one more whore among all your whores? I have not even the strength to forego my little share of you. Perhaps one day you will allow me, too, the privilege of dying in your arms . . ."

"You want me to hit you again, 'Licia?" he said.

"Why not? I have given you that right, have I not? I have become such a thing as a man may beat, no?"

"Nena," he said, "that was for two things: debasing what you are by doubting me. And for mocking the dead."

"Ohhh!" she said, and looked up at him. "Peter, *Cielo,* you mean that you have not—"

"Played indoor games with that poor slaughtered piece of commercial goods? Hell, no! I'm nobody's Tenorio, God knows; but so far I haven't been reduced to buying it. At least not yet. I knew her, yes. Her name's Teresa. She's Jacinto's sister. You know, our pyromaniac friend with yellow eyes. And the only reason I knew her at all was because I had to hole up in that dump to shake your brother's uniformed apes off my tail . . ."

"Peter, I—now I have too much shame. One day you will tire of forgiving me for this debility of mine, no? Only I cannot dominate it. I have such a fear of losing you! I think— Peter! What's wrong? You look . . ."

"Get! Go to those goons over there. Lock yourself in your room. Stay there till I tell you he's dead."

"That who is dead, Peter? I do not understand—"

"Jacinto. He said first her, then you."

She smiled at him then.

"I am not afraid, Love," she said.

"But I am! Goddam it, 'Licia—*go!*"

"*Sí,* Peter. *Sí, Cielo. Sí, cariño* of all the wicked, sensual women. Which includes your little Alicia. Who could devour you, now. Who could take you here upon the street. Who—"

"Nena, I've got it rough enough now," Peter said.

XX

When he opened the door of his flat, he saw that he need have neither worried, nor hoped. Judith wasn't there. The flat had been swept bare of her things. The only reminder of her presence was the perfume, *Peut'être,* lingering on, faint but persistent, on the air.

He walked across the room to the mantel over the fake fireplace his landlord was so proud of. In the grate it had a group of electric-light bulbs, concealed behind plastic logs. If you flicked a switch, some of the lights came on, but the others didn't; then, after a few seconds' interval, the ones that had been on before went out, and vice versa, with the result that the flickering on and off of the red bulbs made a remarkable imitation of fire. Only Peter, whose hatred of fakery was the nearest thing to a religion he possessed, never flicked that switch. Now, he ran his fingertips over the quite real slabs of flagstone of which the chimney was made until he found the one he sought. He pulled it out, put his hand inside the cavity he himself had chopped behind it, and drew out the Walther 6.5-mm. P–38 automatic that had been the official sidearm of the Wehrmacht's officers in World War II.

It was wrapped in oilskin. He unwrapped it, sat there in the big chair, and cleaned it, although it was already quite clean enough. He slammed home a clip of bullets and set the safety. Then he dropped it in the side pocket of his jacket and sat there thinking about poor Jacinto, whom he didn't hate at all but whom, sometime during the next few hours, he was going to kill. Or be killed by. But it wasn't a thing that thinking about did any good at all; so he turned to the consideration of Judith's absence; what it meant. But what it meant was nothing, or everything. So he got up from there and switched on the radio. The newscaster's voice blared out:

"His Excellency, the Head of the State, this afternoon made a direct appeal to the President of the United States of America, requesting intervention by the Armed Forces of Our Great Sister Republic, due to the extreme gravity of the situation. Previous appeals, made to the

useless and cowardly Organization of American States and the Red-dominated United Nations, having been summarily rejected by those groups, Our Glorious Leader decided–"

"Boys, you've had it, haven't you?" Peter said.

"His Excellency pointed out to the President that in view of the known atrocities committed by the Reds, and their open threat to exterminate every North American citizen found within the confines of Ciudad Villalonga when they enter the city, such intervention is entirely justified. Omnibuses of the Public Transportation System are being readied to take United States citizens residing in our capital, as well as the numerous tourists caught here by the revolution, to a place of safety. But Our Generous Benefactor insists–"

"Horsecrap," Peter said, and turned off the radio.

There was no hot water; but, considering the temperature outside, the cold water was more than warm enough. He shaved, bathed, and changed into clean clothes. He stood there holding the Walther and wishing he had a shoulder holster; but he didn't, so he cut a flap of oilskin and lined his hip pocket with it and put the automatic in that. He had already started toward the door when the door bell rang.

He opened the door. Tim O'Rourke stood there, grinning at him.

"Now I know I'd better change my brand," Peter said.

"*Hola*, buzzard's breakfast food!" Tim said. "C'mon, let's go drink to the demise of the Everlasting Republic."

"With pleasure," Peter said; "let's go to Harry's."

"Hell, no!" Tim said. "Too far. No taxis. No gas to put in 'em."

"I know that," Peter said, "only I have to go to Harry's, Tim."

"All right. I can stand the Marine-type fitness hike if you can. But why do you?"

"Because we can see the Official Residence from there."

"I've seen it before. Haven't you?"

"Yes. But today I've got a hankering to look at it some more."

"Why?" Tim said.

"To see who goes into it. Or tries to."

"You're sick, you know, boy; sick!" Tim said.

"There you've got something, Timmie lad; now come on!" Peter said.

They sat at a table in front of Harry's. Peter kept watching the Official Residence and fiddling with the Rolleiflex which he had brought with him in case whatever variety of hell that broke loose would be worth a shot. There were guards all over the place. But guards hadn't stopped Jacinto from blowing up the airport. He tried to put himself in Jacinto's place. Figure what he'd do. Then it hit him. Tonight. When she comes out to join me. If they let her.

He relaxed. Sipped his drink. Grinned at Tim.

"Timmie boy," he said, "how'd you get back down here?"

"Jet," Tim said. "From Miami. You go up, and you come down, and you're here."

"You know what I mean. Aren't you *non grata* and all that sort of thing?"

"Aren't you dead and all that sort of thing? That's what's being said in New York. Little Mari cried her eyes out. Took me all night to console her."

"Come again?" Peter said.

"Just did. Two days ago."

"Tim, let's start all over again. Were you or weren't you kicked out of this country? Declared *non grata,* et cetera?"

"Why, hell no! They love me down here. I respond to The Treatment. Besides, if I were *non grata,* they wouldn't have let me back in, would they?"

"You've got a point there. So you're *grata.* You've come back to help bury the Eternal Republic?"

"Exactly. And to see if the reports of your demise weren't a trifle exaggerated. I thought they were, what with His Nibs' little sister in there pitching for you. By the way, how is she?"

"Great," Peter said.

"And Judy?"

"Don't know. Haven't been seeing much of her lately."

"Thought not. You know, I've been studying your method. Works. Damned if it doesn't! That playing it cool. That, 'Oh, no, dear! I'm not a bit interested in getting into your lacy little scanties. I'm hard to get. *You* make *me.*' Only it works too good."

"Meaning?"

"I've acquired myself a Missus. Legal. In the Church, yet."

"Well, I'll be goddamned!"

"You are, you canine's son. 'S all your fault. But thanks anyhow. Mari was practically a gift from you to me."

"What Mary?"

"Not Mary, *Mari.* Marisol Talaveda. You and Alicia got her out of this Unhealth Resort. I finally dragged out of her how. Little 'Licia took her place in a bugged bedroom. In which old Great Lover performed in his own inimitable style—"

"Tim, believe it or not, that's just not so."

"All right. I'm gallant, too, now. Learned it from you."

"Oh, hell, skip it. So you married Marisol! You lucky bastard! Sweet little thing. I liked her."

"She liked *you,* brother. Main hurdle I had to get over. You were chivalrous. You were gallant. You were a gentleman. You nobly refused to take advantage of her. So I sez: 'Why don't you forgive him for that? He'll make it up to you the next time, or I don't know Old Ginger Pete!' So she was terribly insulted with me, like dames always are when you hit 'em with the truth. The trouble is they want to turn on the virtue and refuse you. But when a guy turns *them* down, they get anxious. Begin to worry whether they've really got it all and if it's stacked up high enough in the right places . . ."

"Tim the philosopher!"

"'S God's own truth. Anyhow, she cooled off after a while and let me start squiring her around, mainly because she was lonesome as all hell, and kind of lost in the Big City. Though that helped. Her being up there, I mean. Down here she'd have felt like a Blue Moon babe if she hadn't mourned for that poor bastard Roberto for at least three years. Incidentally, they didn't get along all that hot together—a detail she sort of hid from everybody, including your lil' Monkeyface. Besides which, I speak Spik. At first, all she would talk about was you. But I finally convinced her I wasn't half bad myself, mainly by keeping me paws off her, no matter how much I was tempted. And you know these Latin dames, brother. Invented the word *sweet.* Make all our broads seem like battleaxes. Seem, hell! How'd we manage to grow so many witches, boy?"

"Forgot the first lesson: 'A gong and a woman sound better when hit.'"

"Truth. And all those deep-frozen tails!"

"Tim—out of line, and off the record. You can even poke me one for asking, but I thought that little Mari . . ."

"Was a frosty little number herself? So did I, chum; so did I. And brother, was I ever wrong! So we got hitched two weeks ago. And then Miguelito goofs again, and I draw this caper. Anyhow, thanks, Chum. I promised to find you if I could. Give you what she sent you. So pucker up, Petie! Here's where you get bussed by remote control—"

"Sorry. You know: I use that well-known soap. So I'm lovely. And engaged."

"To Alicia?" Tim said, and started pulling photos out of his pocket and laying them down on the table.

"I think so," Peter said.

"Don't you know?"

"No. Not exactly. . . . My God, Tim, what are those?"

"Oh, these? Hell, I was looking for our wedding photo. Brought you a copy, signed by us both. Must have left it in my other suit."

The sound truck crawled around the corner, blaring. That same old announcement. Tim looked at Peter.

"You think what I think, boy?" he said.

"Depends on what you think, Tim."

"That anybody who takes Miguelito up on that one ought to have his head examined."

"Likewise. He'll get them up in the mountains someplace and then politely inform our State Department that their continued safety requires a little friendly cooperation on the part of the Atlantic Fleet—especially the Marines. But I don't think any of the local contingent of our noble compatriots have suckered in. And there aren't any tourists to speak of. But these pictures, Tim!"

"Took 'em in the Museum of Archeology. Dead Indians. Hence Good Indians. Great, aren't they?"

"They look like they could speak!" Peter said.

"They could, once. Before all that nice thick volcanic ash petrified 'em. You want some prints of these?"

"Lord, yes!"

"Then c'mon over to my place. Got a suite at the Verdian Hilton. All they've got these days. Suites. No tourists." Tim paid the check. In dollars. And almost started a riot, because all the other waiters wanted to force the lucky one who had waited on them to divide. The argument was loud. It was apparent the Costa Verdian peso wasn't exactly being held in high esteem at the moment.

"So you're going to marry His Nibs' sister?" Tim said.

"Wish I could," Peter said. "But there's one damned rough obstacle. You know: that business about Connie—"

"Connie? Who's Connie? Do I know her?"

"My ex, Tim. Luis Sinnombre had her killed."

"Oh, that! Look, Pete; you've got it all wrong! It wasn't—Holy Mary, Mother of God!" Tim said.

Peter followed his gaze. Saw what he was looking at. Said:

"So long, Tim. Be seeing you."

Then he crossed the street to where she sat. At a table. On the sidewalk. In front of a rather dingy bar. She was alone. He saw that she was crying. Looking at her now, that was exactly what he felt like doing himself.

"Judy baby—" he said.

She didn't answer him. She went on crying. Her hair was wild. There was a dried trickle of blood at the corner of her mouth. The flesh along one side of her jaw had purpled. There were other marks upon her throat, her bare arms. Looking down, he saw that one of her stockings had fallen about her ankles. She looked like the great-grandmother of all the whores on earth. He put his hand under her chin, raised her bleary, tear-stained face. Her breath reeked of whiskey. Yet, Peter saw, she wasn't drunk.

"Please," she said, "will you order me a coffee? I haven't had any breakfast. In fact, I don't think I've eaten in four days. Maybe five. And I can't make them understand. Besides, I haven't any money . . ."

"All right," Peter said. He clapped his hand. The waiter came. He looked relieved to see Peter there.

"A big orange juice," Peter said. "Two coffees. One with milk, the other black. Toast. Butter. Marmalade. Eggs. Bacon."

Judith shuddered.

"I couldn't, Peter," she said.

"You're going to," Peter said. "Why don't you go into the ladies' room and comb your hair? Wash your face. Pull up that stocking. Here—take my comb."

"All right," Judith said.

When she came back, she looked almost human. Peter held the chair for her. She sat down.

Across the street a *buitre* flapped heavily down from the roof. Came to rest in the road. Sat there staring at Peter, then at Judith.

"Make your mind up, you scaly-headed bastard!" Peter said. "The tender cut, or the tough? Or is it both?"

He picked up a glass from beside his plate. Threw it at the vulture. It rose slowly. Flapped back up to the roof. Sat there, still staring at them.

The waiter came with the breakfast. Judith drank the orange juice. The coffee. Nibbled at a piece of toast.

"Eat, goddam you!" Peter said.

She took a piece of bacon. It was damn good bacon. But she masticated it as if it were crawling with maggots. She forked up a bit of egg yolk, ropy, dripping. That did it. It wasn't pretty. Peter wiped her mouth and eyes with his handkerchief. Threw the handkerchief away. Stood up, put a bill under a saucer; took her by the arm.

"Where're we going?" she said.

"To the hospital," he said. "So Vince can give you the care you need—"

"All right," Judith said. But then she stopped.

And he, turning, in the midst of siren whoop, brake screech, horn blare, heard Luis Sinnombre's voice rising, scream shrill, saying:

"You dirty little daughter of this and that; you thing of bad milk. I this upon the grave of your father. I that into the face of your mother. Take her, Mateo! Throw her into the *coche!*" Then dropping, smoothing, purring: "And *you,* Reynolds? Ah, glad to see you back, Amigo! Juanito! Throw this lump of gringo filth in beside her!"

Peter put his hand down, edging it toward his hip pocket. Then he took his hand away. A Walther was a good gun. Excellent. But it wasn't equal to a twenty-five-shot Bren machine pistol, which could burn through a clip in three seconds flat. And when seven of those burp guns were pointing, as they were now, the odds weren't even calculable. In fact, there weren't any odds. Luis had it made. He put his hands up very slowly. But he had forgotten one characteristic of the police of dictatorships. A lack of resistance didn't change their procedure at all. Behind him, one of them lifted up a blackjack, brought it crashing down on his head. And, sagging slowly through a sunbright blaze, through a red sear of pain, Peter heard, as he dimmed out of time and space and conscious being, the soaring, delighted lift of Judith's laughter.

He was on a bus, and his hands weren't even bound. Which made no sense at all. The Walther was gone, though. That made sense. But nothing else did. Especially not that they had left the Rollei slung around his neck. He was aware that he was not dreaming. That the bus was real. It and the people on it. Judith, who was sitting beside him. Tim O'Rourke, a little farther away. Then Padre Pío. Then the American Ambassador and his wife. Then a huge woman whose face looked like Luis Sinnombre's. Looked like Miguel Villalonga's. Looked like Alicia's.

The splitting pain in his head wouldn't let him think. But he didn't need to. The armed guard beside the bus driver eliminated any necessity for thought. Miguel's radio announcement had failed. His sound trucks. So he had gathered up his hostages by force.

That was all right. That made sense. But even his bloody, aching head could get to one highly rhetorical question: What man on earth would Villalonga *not* hold as a hostage when the circumstances permitted murder—as they did now? Now they permitted anything. And the answer, requiring even less stirring of the quivering, doughy mass they had beaten his alleged brains into: One Peter Reynolds, foreign correspondent. Since he was clearly out of his mind, stark raving mad, Peter closed his eyes again.

The bus groaned on. Up a mountain road. The driver was in uniform. He had a pistol in his belt. He wasn't very military, though. He had his shirt open almost to the top of his belt. Peter could see a big hammered-silver cross on a chain nestling against the mat of sweaty black hair on his chest. It was a singularly beautiful cross. Of Tluscolan making, surely.

The bus was filled with people. Most of them American Embassy staff members. They looked worried and angry. The Costa Verdians didn't look worried. They looked like people already dead.

"Judy—" Peter said.

She didn't answer him. She sat there staring straight ahead.

Peter's head ached worse than hell. He closed his eyes. But nothing changed. The bus kept right on grinding up that road.

"Judy—" he said again. Then he saw what she was doing. She was winking at the bus driver. Not at the armed guard, who had his back turned and was already fast asleep. The driver was looking at her in the rear-view mirror. He had it adjusted so he could see her legs instead of the road. The bus driver grinned at her. She grinned back. If you could call that macabre grimace a grin. Then very slowly she pulled her skirt up, inch by inch, opening her legs wide. She didn't have on pants. Peter could see the little golden tuft between her thighs. So could the driver. He was sweating. He braked just in time to keep the bus on the road.

"*Idiota!*" the armed guard said, and went back to sleep again.

"Goddam it, Judy!" Peter said, and jerked her skirt down again.

Then he heard the roar, and that long white flash poured past them in a scream of wind, exhaust blast, motor snarl. He looked at it dully, forgetting Judy, forgetting the bus driver. It took the curve ahead of them in a four-wheel power drift and was gone. The bus driver was still staring at Judy's legs. She was inching her skirt up again. She saw Peter's face.

"It's so hot!" she whined. Then all the air went shrill with the sound of brakes, the driver fighting the wheel trying to keep the bus on the road, and the armed guard swearing at him. There was nothing beyond the edge. Nothing at all. A thousand meters farther down there was a broken jumble of rocks. But they didn't go over. The driver was fighting for his own life. For maybe a chance at what Judy was now showing him again.

He stopped the bus one meter from the white Jaguar drawn up across the road. Leaped out, pistol in hand, screaming curses. The armed guard jumped out, too, his rifle ready.

"Put up your toys, *niños!*" Alicia said.

She got out of the Jaguar. She was dressed in a blouse and skirt. Her long, beautiful legs were bare. Her dainty feet were thrust into sandals. Respectfully, the bus driver helped her aboard the bus. She stood in the front of it, arguing with him. He kept spreading out his hands and shaking his head. Then he shrugged. Put up his hand with two fingers uplifted. Just two. Alicia came down the aisle. Knelt down beside the fat woman. Talked to her, begging and pleading with her from the expression on that tribal face, from her gestures. They were both crying now. The woman stroked Alicia's head.

Tim O'Rourke was sitting in the seat just behind the fat woman's. Tim leaned forward, listening to what went on between her and Alicia. Then he got up. Walked to the door of the bus. Got out. Started to run—upward into a pine wood.

The armed guard knelt in the road; took careful aim with his rifle.

"Stop it!" Alicia said.

The guard lowered the gun.

"Yes, Doña Alicia," he said. "As the illustrious lady wishes!"

Alicia went on talking to the fat woman. The fat woman shook her head. They kissed each other tenderly. Alicia got up. Came on down the aisle. Stopped beside Father Pío. Spoke to him. The little priest got up. They both came to where Peter was. Took him by the arms.

"Come, *Cielo,*" Alicia said.

Peter looked at Judith. She was leaning back against the seat with her eyes closed. Tears stole from under her lids. But her mouth was still fixed in that macabre grin. Peter saw that her legs were bare again. Up to her hips.

"Judy—" he said.

Alicia's face darkened.

"Leave that filthy exhibitionistic bitch and come on!" she said.

But the road, like all mountain roads, looped back upon itself two dozen times. Peter could see the bus getting smaller and higher up each time the straight stretches paralleled the place they had left it. It wasn't moving. It seemed to be waiting for something. That bothered Peter. Alicia had the Jaguar's top down, and the icy blast of the air was clearing Peter's head now. He slung the Rollei from around his neck, handed it to Father Pío. The old man put it down between the seats.

Then Peter saw the pigmy figures swarm down toward the bus from the heights above. Saw what they had in their hands.

"Stop the car!" he said.

"No! No, Peter!" Alicia wept. "I cannot! I must not! I—"

"Stop this heap, Alicia!"

"Peter, no! Oh, *Dios mío!* I—"

He reached down, hauled up on the handbrake. The Jaguar bucked like a living thing. Skidded broadside the road. The motor strangled itself as Alicia's foot slipped off the clutch. In the abrupt, dead-stopped silence, they heard the shots. The ripping stutter of machine-gun bursts. The flat, slow, deliberate *c r a a a a c k !* of rifles. The lighter, spitting bark of hand guns. A scream. Another. Then nothing. Nothing at all.

Peter looked at Alicia. She cringed under his eyes. He put his tongue out. Licked bone-dry lips. Said: "You knew."

"Daughter," Father Pío said, "if you knew this, and did not tell me, the sin—"

"You knew!" Peter said.

She sat there, crumpling behind her eyes. Said nothing. Peter went on looking at her. Said:

"That fat woman. Your—mother?"

She nodded dumbly. Then he hit her. Open-palmed across the mouth. So hard that he brought blood. Again. And again, his big hand making the sound of a volley of small-arms fire, jerking her head from right to left to right again until he felt hard fingers bite into his shoulder, hauling him back, and as he whirled, a fist crashed into his face.

He bent, ready to leap. Then he saw who had hit him.

"Father—" he whispered; "pardon—I—"

"Beast!" Father Pío roared, "savage! And what is worst, fool! Look at her! Look what you have done!"

Peter looked down. Alicia lay across the seat. Her face was a mess. She was crying without motion, without sound, in a way he couldn't look at because the loss of hope is a kind of death, but that he couldn't stop looking at either until his own eyes went blind, blotting out her face.

"Nena—" he whispered. "Infant, I— Oh, Christ, 'Licia!"

But she was smiling at him now, her swollen, broken lips bisecting the crystal spillage.

"It is nothing, *Cielo*," she said. "We both have so much to forgive each other for. Yet what is love but forgiving? Since angels and saints don't marry, we must—"

"Skip the rest of this until another time, Nena," Peter said; "we've a couple of rough chores to do right now. So come on!"

She straightened up at once, took the wheel; the motor kicked into life. Headed back up that road.

"My son," the old priest said, "there is a law that fits this case. It says: 'Forsaking all others—' "

"I know," Peter said; "but, Father, I couldn't accept—"

"Who are you to reject Heaven's gifts? Sometimes you anger me," Padre Pío said.

The soldiers were still there, busily engaged in robbing the bodies of their prey. They tore rings from inert fingers, necklaces from still necks. When the Jaguar roared around the bend, they stopped it, raised their guns. But they lowered them again at once. Turned. Got out of there, running—twenty-five well-armed men running from an unarmed, battered man, a girl, and a priest.

Then Peter saw why. They were dressed as guerrillas, but they weren't. He had seen some of those faces too many times now not to recognize them. He looked at Alicia.

She had her head turned. Away from that slaughtered pile, from that boneless sprawl, from that slow blackening collective seep. The shudders raced through her slim body in tidal waves. But she saw his look.

"Yes," she whispered; "what you are thinking, Peter. So that your government would have to intervene. Your Ambassador. His wife. The embassy staff. Judith—who is famous. You, who are too, now. Father Pío, whom all the world loves. And—"

"Your mother," Peter said. "*His* mother!"

"*Ay, sí!* That was the master stroke, *Cielo!* Our poor, bedeviled mother! Who—tell me who, Peter—will believe it was not the Castristas, when The Leader's own mother is found among the dead?"

"Jesus!" Peter said.

"I tried to save her! Peter, Love, I tried! The driver agreed I could save two. I was going to save her—and you. Forgive me, Father, for making you a second choice . . ."

"You were right, daughter," the old priest said. "Your choice was wise . . ."

"But she wouldn't come, Peter!" Alicia wept. "She said she would only spoil my life with you! She tried to put me off by saying horrible things: That it was evident you had a pair well hung, and she could see I already knew it from experience! And that I must keep you worn out in the bed so that I need not fear the blonde vicious one, nor any other, and—"

"Daughter!" Father Pío said.

"She spoke truth, Father! As even you must know! And now—"

"And now let us face a sadder truth, my daughter. Let us go pray for our dead . . ."

"No! Wait! Hear my confession, Father! I am equally an assassin! Because I wanted the blonde one to die! I willed Judith Lovell's death, Father! 'As a man thinketh in his heart, so is he!' And a woman, no, Father? So I am damned, am I not? Am I, Father?"

"What you are, Nena, is hysterical," Peter said. "Now pipe down, will you? I don't have the heart to hit you again."

They knelt beside Isabela Cienmil's body. The dead woman seemed to be smiling a little. Father Pío said the prayer for the dead, then added in Spanish, and aloud: "Receive, Oh Lord, thy servant Isabel—as Thou received the Magdalene, the Woman at the Well, and her about whom Thou wrote pity on the ground, as Thou received her who washed Thy feet with tears and dried them with her hair. Her sins were great; but greater is Thy mercy. For that, and for this her daughter's sake, receive and pardon her, oh Lord!"

"Oh Peter!" Alicia sobbed. "Oh, Peter, *Cielo,* He will, will He not? She was kind, you hear me, kind!"

"*Sí,* Nena," Peter said. "Now come . . ."

They moved down that sickening row. Said a prayer above each one. But when they came to the end of it, one thing was clear: Judith Lovell's body was not there at all.

"Peter—" Alicia said. "You think—she escaped? Oh, I hope so! I have enough upon my conscience now!"

"Yes," Peter said, "little Judy got away all right."

"But how, *Cielo*? How?"

"The driver," Peter said; "the guard. Or both. I think she bribed them with the only coin she had left to offer. And, used and shoddy as that was, it worked. Father—"

"Yes, son?"

"We'd better go back, now. Send someone up here for the bodies."

"You go, son—and you, daughter. I will watch here with them yet a while."

"But, Father," Alicia said; "the soldiers might come back and—"

"I have God's protection, daughter. Is that not clear by now?"

"Yes, Father, it is," Alicia whispered; then: "Oh, Peter, *Cielo*—Tim! Don Timoteo—your Irish friend! He—"

"Is one of the finest alpinists and woodsmen you ever saw. We'll pick him up later—if he doesn't pick us up first. Now, there's no time . . ."

Alicia reported the massacre to Luis Sinnombre while Peter waited for her at the hotel. She was careful not to mention that anyone had escaped.

"I'll send up after them tomorrow," Luis said. He sounded bored. "Don't worry, little sister, cold as it is up there, they'll keep—"

Then he turned and looked at her.

"Tell me," he said, "just what the devil has happened to your face?"

"I—I—fainted when I saw them, Luis," Alicia said. "Fell—rolled down a slope. I—I could have been killed. And I wish I had been!"

"Ah, so? Now where do you think you're going?"

"To church," she whispered. "Peter was on that bus, Luis. And my mother. You find it ill that I want to pray?"

"No," Luis laughed; "pray for me, will you? And for Miguel. I suspect we need it!"

"I shall," Alicia said. "I shall pray that you both burn in hell!" Then turned, already running, and left him there.

Peter was beginning to feel much better, now. Alicia had cleaned and dressed the wound on his head. Fed him cold cuts, cheese, wine, fruit. Lay in his arms while he slept. But the whole time, she continued weeping.

What woke him up was the roar that Zopocomapetl made when it finally committed suicide by blowing itself apart.

Even that steel-and-concrete modern hotel reeled drunkenly under the impact. They could hear above old Zopo's bull bellow, the crash of a hundred thousand windows blowing in at once. The tongue of fire split the sky open. They got up and went to the window. The volcano was gone, leaving only a low truncated hump out of which poured a lake of fire, spreading down toward the jungle, toward the sea.

They saw the jungle take fire, the sea explode. Great geysers of steam rose up. Waves raced outward toward the rim of the world. Then the winds came howling back, bringing the smoke, bringing that lung-tearing vapor.

"Come on, Nena!" Peter said. "Let's get out of here!"

But when they reached the streets, they saw a curious thing: Appalling as the catastrophe looked, it had killed almost nobody. Here and there, a house burned. Farther out, some adobe huts of the poor had collapsed. The greatest number of casualties was among the loyal units of Villalonga's army, guarding the approaches of the city against the Reds.

Who would be months in coming now—if they ever did. Because to take Ciudad Villalonga under those abruptly altered circumstances, they needed the one thing they didn't have—a fleet. All the landward approaches were cut off by the burning jungle, by that lake of fire.

"Nena," Peter said, "I don't know whom your brother knows Upstairs; but whoever it is, he sure takes damned good care of Miguelito!"

She turned to him, caught at his arms, clung to him, shuddering.

"Nena, Infant," he said; "what's wrong?"

"My mother—those people on the bus—they're dead, of course," she said; "but up there, so close to Zopo—" Then she stopped. "Oh, Peter!" she wailed. "Padre Pío! Your—your Judith! Tim!"

"Good God!" Peter said. "Come on!"

She drove the Jaguar expertly up the road that so far was still open, probably because the already opened split in the far side of the volcano had spilled out the major lava flow. Still there was no valid ground for hope—smaller eruptions than this one had wiped out teeming cities within fairly recent history; and up there where Tim and Judy and Father Pío had been—

He put it from his mind, refusing to think about them, about the way they had probably died by now, because it wasn't a thing to think about, because thinking about it was too much, comparable in a way to suffering it, or maybe even worse, since the dead are forever exempt from grief, from remorse, from memory. So, he turned to Alicia, seeing her face bruised, swollen, a dried trickle of blood in one corner of her mouth, which she had been too occupied with him, too oblivious of self to wipe away; but what she was, what she meant to him, combined with the probability of his losing her, so great as to be indistinguishable from certainty, wasn't to be borne either, so when he spoke, all he said was:

"Strange—"

"What's strange, *Cielo*?" Alicia said.

"I have never met a man of Spanish blood who was wanting in filial love. No matter who that man was. No matter who—or even what—his mother was. Never."

"You are right, *Cielo*. That's what makes it so terrible—"

"Meaning?" Peter said.

"That Miguel loves Mama. As much as I do. No, more. There you have a rarity, Peter! My mother, who was a woman of outrageous behavior—who all her life had been a wanton—was lovable. I have loved her all of the little time I have known her—"

"The little time?" Peter said.

"Since I came back from Spain. Before that, that she was my mother was concealed from me—"

She was silent then. And, because where they were now the road was of a vile vileness—in the popular Costa Verdian phrase—he didn't say anything to her. Instead he looked down and behind to where Ciudad Villalonga lay white in the sun. From that height, it appeared untouched. Here and there, smoke rose from burned-out houses, but that was all. Except that between it and the truncated volcano, a lake of fire lay. Beyond that, the jungle burned. The lava still poured down into the sea, exploding it into snowy geysers of steam. The whole thing was weirdly beautiful. Peter reached for the Rollei to take a picture of it, but Alicia bent the Jaguar around a curve and it dropped from sight.

"Nena," Peter said, "you say that Miguel loved your mother, and yet—"

"He has murdered her. Yes, Peter. I think it is because he is no longer entirely sane. And because he has been corrupted by Luis, who never really was. They have, both of them, come to believe their own propaganda. That the Republic could not exist without them. That they are the only bulwark between the people of Costa Verde and complete disaster."

"I agree that changing them for the Castristas will only be swapping the devil for the witch," Peter said. "Still—"

He saw another thing now: that the road was going to be open all the way up, that the already opened split on the other side of Zopocomapetl had taken the pressure off, so that except for several meters of ash, drifted in places as high as snowbanks, there was nothing to block the road. Except for a trickle or two, the major lava flows were away from the road, sliding down the eastern side of the volcano, or what was left of it, toward the sea. And since no major road ran east from Ciudad Villalonga for the simple reason that that was where the ocean was, this road, like all the roads north and west of the city, was safe. But all the roads to the south had been wiped out, effortlessly negating the Communists' very clever strategy of striking from the one point of the compass nobody expected them to, and reinforcing Peter's belief that the basic quality of life was irony—when it wasn't meaninglessness. And then they came around one more curve, and he saw that he was right.

The bus stood there by the side of the road. All the paint had been seared off it, leaving it rust-red and silvery bright. But they could still see the line of holes that had crashed into the side of it, see the spiderweb tracery of the shot-up windows. Beyond, sullenly, fiercely, the pine wood burned, crackling with unholy laughter. The bodies still lay beside it in long rows, where they had been gunned down. And yet, Peter saw, old Zopo had granted them an accidental or maybe even a deliberate, benediction. He had covered them with white ash, had formed them into statues.

"Oh, Peter! Oh, *Cielo,* look!" Alicia said; and he turned, staring at her, because that note in her voice was joy. Then he looked back again and saw Padre Pío stepping gingerly down from the bus itself. His clothes were gray with ash, but he was unhurt. Peter was out of the car at once, gathering the old man in his arms in that great back pounding bear hug that Spanish-speaking peoples call *un abrazo* and which permits men to show a deeper and truer emotion for each other than is possible among colder races; and when he had turned him loose, Alicia, forgetting in her joy that the old man was a priest, kissed him on both cheeks, as she would have her own father.

"Children!" the old man said severely, but his eyes were misty.

"Now will you say that you cannot work miracles, Father?" Peter said; "now do you dare?"

The old man smiled.

"I say only that God still has work for me here below," he said. "The truth is much duller, son. I hid under one of the seats of the bus and prayed. And since I have not enough fat on my bones to roast, I only cured a bit more, making me even tougher and more unpalatable. Now this of the truck, children?"

"Tomorrow, Father," Alicia said; "Peter—"

"Yes, Nena—"

"It was not as bad as we thought, up here. Perhaps . . ."

"We can look, 'Licia; but if we don't find them close to here, we'll have to go back, organize a true searching party if such a thing is possible. What we really need is an airplane. Or a helicopter. Still—"

"Father, wait for us here, will you?" Alicia said. "We shall not be too long . . ."

They walked on up the road, past the burning forest. The heat was unbearable, the smoke clawed at their eyes. And it was no good. This wasn't the way to do it. Even if hope existed, which—considering how rapidly the situation deteriorated with every meter they climbed above the bus—was one big *if*, this was not the way to search for Judith and Tim. What that way was Peter didn't know. He suspected that at the moment, with the woods on both sides of the road burning like the hinges of hell, the way didn't exist. And that when rational search became possible it would be too late. Forever too late. If it weren't already.

"Hell, let's go back," Peter said, but then he heard her gasp:

"Oh, Peter, look!"

A flow of lava had cut the road; five meters farther on, another. Between the two, the soldiers' bodies lay. Their only way out had been into the woods, but the pines had surely already been afire by then.

Alicia clung to him, shuddering. Peter looked across to the low hump that was all that was left of Zopocomapetl. Then back at the bloated tarry horrors that no drop of ash had touched.

"I know they had it coming, but did you have to play *that* rough?" he said.

Then they both heard that faint, feeble voice.

"Petie, boy—"

They turned. A scarecrow reeled toward them. An all-but-naked scarecrow, fluttering charred rags behind it as it came, fluttering strips of skin.

"Tim!" Peter said; "my God, Tim!"

"Mr. Reynolds, I presume? And Doña Alicia? Honored—honored—" Tim said. They caught him between them as he fell.

Alicia knelt there, cradling Tim's head in her arms, and watching Peter's face as he made that choice. The choice he had to make now. The one choice that she less than anyone else on earth could help him make. All she could do was suffer acutely and damnably and agonizingly while he made it. And silently.

She saw his eyes clear; heard him say, his voice rough with pain:

"Help me pick him up, and get him to the car. We've got to get him down faster than all hell—"

Now she was released. Now she could say it.

"And—and Judith, *Cielo*?"

Peter's eyes went sick.

"We *know* he's alive, Nena, and that he won't be long, unless we really pour it on. So what choice is there? Gamble Tim's chances against what we *might* find? Hell no, 'Licia. Now come on!" he said.

But once they had Tim in the car—having had to leave Padre Pío once more because the sports roadster just wasn't built to hold four people comfortably and couldn't hold four at all now that Tim couldn't sit up—and Alicia was slamming it down that road, while Peter held Tim in his arms, Tim woke up and started to talk so slowly, gravely, sadly that it took them some time to notice he wasn't making sense.

"So maybe I was wrong about her. So maybe it didn't matter that she was the easiest lay in the Western Hemisphere and that her heels were shaped like ball bearings and she had calluses on her back from going over on it any time anybody pushed. Pushed, hell—waved. The breeze was enough to send her over. So what? So nothing. So I'm Paddy's Pig from Ol' Malarkey if I know a goddam thing any more. Jesus and Mary! God bless us all. Never a cry. Never a groan. Just that look. All lit up. Like candles on an altar . . . I tell you, Petie boy, she—"

"Tim, will you please for God's sake pipe down?" Peter said. "You're going to need that breath—"

"What on earth does he mean?" Alicia said.

"Who knows? Who even cares? Nena, can you get a little more speed out of this thing?"

"Yes, *Cielo;* but I am not sure I can keep it on the road if I do—"

"Stop it, then," Peter said. "Let me take over."

"All right, Love," Alicia said.

She sat there holding Tim. It was characteristic of her that she wasn't afraid. After her first startled questioning whether any man could do to and with a car what Peter was doing now, she sat there and listened to her heart; and her heart said that Peter could do anything—anything at all. So she sat there smiling while Peter leadfooted the accelerator, slamming the Jaguar into those mountain hairpin turns wide out; power-skidding them, cutting the wheel in the opposite direction from the one he wanted the car to go; and gunning it as they broke loose; showering the very treetops with pebbles from the road; trailing a hundred-meter-long cloud of dust and volcanic ash behind them; double-clutching, dropping into second with a snarl that threatened every instant to tear the guts out of the gear box, then stroking it up again, knifing through the shifts without dropping a revolution on the tachometer, barreling into the straights in one great fine lovely cacophony: exhaust blast, tire scream, motor thunder, and the wind's long, long tearing.

Then they were down again, and he was pouring the Jaguar through the all-but-empty streets toward the hospital, and getting there, chopping the ignition, jumping out, reaching into the car and dragging Tim out, and carrying him, big as the Irish reporter was, into the emergency entrance in his arms.

While they were waiting for the results of Vince's and the other doctors' examination, the sister who remembered Peter from his daily visits to Judith there babbled away until it came to him that there were justifiable reasons for murder, after all.

"Even now, in the Cathedral, His Excellency prays, alone. And then, within the hour, the procession will come up the street with Don Luis leading the Escort of Protection; and then the Archbishop and then the Image of Our Lady of Compassion, and the Jesus of the Great Power, and then—"

Vince came through the door.

"He'll make it, Peter," he said. "He has fifteen per cent of his body covered with second-degree burns. He'll probably be laid up here two months. But with the new techniques of burn treatment, he'll go home almost as good as new—"

"And then," the sister went on brightly, "they will say a *Te Deum* in gratitude for the salvation of the city, and—"

Peter looked at her.

"Hermana," he said, "who told you this city was saved?" He turned to Doctor Gomez. "Thanks, Vince," he said; "now we'd better go send a telegram."

"To relatives of his?" Vince said.

"To Marisol Talaveda, who just married the lunk," Peter said.

XXI

When they came out of the hospital, Peter went to the Jaguar and retrieved the Rolleiflex, which still lay between the seats where Father Pío had put it after Peter handed it to him on the mountain road. As he pulled it out, it came to Peter why they had let him keep it. He wasn't to have been the first of Miguel's victims, but the last. He could hear the announcer's voice now, as clearly as though the man were actually speaking: *"Films found in the camera of one of the victims, the famous North American journalist, Mr. Peter Reynolds, conclusively prove that the attack was carried out by Communist guerrillas, as their uniforms can be clearly seen in the photographs. The government plans to release copies of these remarkable pictures to the international press at the earliest possible moment. This dastardly crime . . ."*

"Son of a bitch!" Peter said.

"What did you say, *Cielo*?" Alicia said.

"Nothing, Nena; come on . . ."

They started walking across the Plaza to the cable office. Then they saw the soldiers. Alicia stopped, her fingers gripping Peter's arm.

"Keep walking," Peter said.

"But Peter, *Cielo,* they—"

"They nothing. They're soldiers, not police. And I'm dead, remember? At least as far as Luis is concerned."

He could feel her trembling; but she moved beside him, head up, staring straight ahead. And more and more soldiers came out of the Avenida McDowell, which led to the Plaza de los Mártires Concepcionistas, where the Cathedral was. From their uniforms, Peter could see that they were units of the crack Escolta del Caudillo, the Leader's Special Guard; but they weren't displaying any of the snap and precision for which they were famous—at least not now. Now they straggled across the Plaza in disconnected groups, talking to one another in low voices; and, in their faces, their puzzlement was plain.

"Peter!" Alicia said; "they should be at the Cathedral, guarding Miguel! I wonder—"

"Ask them," Peter said.

"Oh, no!" Alicia said; "*Cielo,* I—I don't dare!"

"Then I will," Peter said.

"No, *Cielo!* You, no! I will ask them. After all, I am his sister and—Peter, Love, wait for me in that bar. Have a beer. Have two beers. Do not preoccupy yourself. I'll be all right."

He kissed her quickly. Released her arm. Crossed over to the little bar under the archway. Sat there with a cold beer in his hand, almost untasted, watching her talking to the soldiers. He saw one of them indicate her battered face. He could see from the flustered gestures of her hands that she was lying nobly, trying to explain that. They clearly didn't believe her; but, being who she was, they had to take her word for it. Then he saw her coming toward him, downed the beer at a gulp, and stood up.

"Oh, Peter, *Cielo,* they—" she said.

"Gentle down, Nena. Have a beer," he said.

"Peter, he sent them away! He says he no longer needs an escort since he is clearly under divine protection! And when their Captain argued that there were subversive elements loose in the city, he said: 'When the time comes that I must die, I shall die, with you or without, Captain. Who can gainsay the will of God?'"

"He's nuts," Peter said. "A beer, Nena?"

"Yes. But Peter, he has them half believing it. He pointed out to them how hopeless the situation was before Zopo blew up. And now the Reds cannot enter the city at all!"

"The Reds can't. But the typhus can. Malaria. And that new virus infection that causes hemorrhages. In fact, they have. Vince is mobilizing all the medicos. He's afraid we're going to have a triple epidemic on our hands—"

"Why, Peter?"

"Oddly enough, old Zopo seems to have blown his top for his own reasons, not for any special interest in the affairs of men. . . . Ah, here're our beers. Down the hatch, Nena—"

"Peter, I don't understand."

"I know you don't. It's simple: The eruption blocked the Reds and gave your lovely brother a new lease on life. But it also took out the aqueduct that brings the water from the big reservoir high in the mountains to the little one just behind the town. The water supply is diminishing alarmingly. Some of the poorer districts don't have any water now. Vince isn't worried about the hospital, which has its own supply from three artesian wells in the basement, but he is worried by the already noticeable increase in the type of diseases that come from pollution."

"How awful!" Alicia said. "Haven't our poor people suffered enough?"

"Maybe they're all sinners and have got it coming. Now drink your beer like a big girl and come on," Peter said.

"Peter—what about Father Pío? He's up there alone, with nothing to eat and—"

"That's taken care of. I told Vince, who is going to send an ambulance up after him. The problem is finding a truck for the bodies. But now they can wait. Volcanic ash makes a wonderful preservative . . ."

"Now what will we do, *Cielo*?" Alicia said as they came out of the cable office.

"Hole up somewhere until I can figure what the next move is—and if it makes any sense to move at all. I vote that we check into some fleabag. Both Miguel and Luis know where I live and the Hilton's too goddam conspicuous. They're sure to find out I didn't get mine, any minute now. So a cheap hotel, *Muñeca*. In a way, I've given you a perfect disguise. Even a desk clerk who's seen you before would never believe that you're you with *that* face . . ."

"Peter—" she said solemnly.

"Yes, Nena?"

"You mean to go on beating me up every time you get mad?"

"And if I did?"

"I—I'd just have to endure it, then. Because being without you is worse. And you don't get angry very often, do you?"

He drew her to him.

"Nena," he said, "if, as long as we both shall live, I ever lift a hand against you again, I pray that God will strike me dead!"

"No, Peter! Don't say that! I can be terribly exasperating, you know, and—"

"Nena, from here on in, you've got it made. You've got carte blanche to exasperate the living hell out of me twenty-four hours a day. Anyhow, come on. I'd take you to the country, if there were any way of getting out of town; but—"

"But there is not," a third voice said; "so now, Comrade Reporter, the place where you are going to take her is the Cathedral."

"Look, Jacinto," Peter said, without even turning his head.

"Shut up!" Jacinto said. "Be quiet, Peter! I know Teresa died in your arms. And you know I killed her. But do you know why?"

"No," Peter said.

"Just keep walking ahead, toward the Cathedral—both of you. We have a little rendezvous with your August Brother there, Illustrious Lady! I have a little score to settle with Miguel—a score that requires your cooperation."

"Jacinto—" Peter said.

"I told you to shut up, Peter!"

"You will have to kill me first," Peter said. "Pointing that firecracker at me won't be enough. You'll have to kill me."

"You think I wouldn't?" Jacinto said.

"Make sure you don't miss," Peter said.

Alicia didn't say anything. She walked along beside him so close he could feel her taut, fine body trembling.

"Why did you kill your sister?" Peter said.

"Because she was a whore," Jacinto said.

"That wasn't why," Peter said.

"Because it was time to kill her," Jacinto said.

"Nor that," Peter said.

"Because she set out to demonstrate to me that the debility which sometimes comes upon me . . ."

"That always exists within you. Do not lie, Jacinto!"

"That always exists within me," Jacinto said. "Yes, Comrade, I must not lie—did not that night exist, or could be cured by a vicious one of her skill—"

"And did she?" Peter said.

"She died, Peter! You saw that, didn't you?"

"Yes. In my arms. But why? For having proved your weakness could be cured, or for not having proved it?"

"For having proved the time is now," Jacinto said.

"The time is now?"

"Yes!" Jacinto said; "yes, Comrade Reporter! The time is now! It has all terminated for me, so it is now. The time to kill. The time to die. You heard me, it is now!"

Inside the Cathedral it was dark and cool. They walked up the center aisle with Jacinto behind them pointing the little machine gun at their backs. The silence swallowed their footsteps. Peter looked at the massive walls, built by Indian slave labor three centuries ago. They would die here and not even the beggar woman sleeping before the door would know it. From within this mass of stone and leaded glass the sound of a cannon would reach the square as a gentle murmur. No one would hear the faint popping of Jacinto's murderous toy.

And then, suddenly, they saw Miguel Villalonga. He wasn't at the main altar. He was at a little side niche dedicated not to the Holy Virgin but to Mary Magdalene. They moved closer, and then they saw the reason for his choice. The good, pure little Mother of God could not be expected to understand or succor a whore's soul—so his reasoning, or his madness, must have gone—but La Magdalena, who had been herself of the bad life, could and would have compassion upon the soul of the departed Isabel, would comprehend this whore's son's, matricide's monstrous grief, accept indeed his monstrous penance—

That penance which held them there, unbreathing.

He knelt before the altar. He was rigid as stone. He had his two arms stretched out in the form of a cross. At his right side and his left two huge candles burned. They were more than a meter tall, and as big around as a strong man's arm. And Miguel Villalonga knelt there unmoving, with both his hands puffed, ballooning, charred black, resting without the slightest tremor in those candle flames.

"*Dios!*" Alicia wept. "*Oh, Dios mío!* Ay, Santa Madre Querida! No, Miguel, no!"

"Miguel!" Jacinto howled.

The Dictator did not move.

"Miguel Villalonga!"

The Cathedral threw back the echoes from nave to crypt.

"*Meeee gwel llll Veeel ya lonnng gaaaa!*"

Still the man kneeling there did not move.

"I am going to violate your sister now! As you did mine! I—you hear me? I am going to . . ."

The candles sizzled from the blood and grease dripping into them. The smell came over and took them in the nostrils. Peter retched.

Jacinto caught Alicia by the arm.

"Lie down, bitch!" he howled. "I—"

Peter moved in, very quietly.

Jacinto hooked a heel behind Alicia's legs and pushed. She went down. He sprawled atop her, clawing at her skirt.

Then Peter was there. He lashed out with his foot. The kick caught Jacinto in the face, rolled him off and away from her. But he kept his grip—in part, and with only one hand—on the gun. But a Sten gun cannot be controlled with one hand.

At his first burst, Peter threw himself flat, down, and under its flare. He heard the tinkle of glass as the lens of the Rollei broke. But Jacinto had both hands on the Sten now; it spluttered, bucked, chattered like a maniac thing. Peter saw those flat yellow eyes. Saw the insane joy in them. But they were not looking at him.

He twisted, looking back in time to see Miguel shudder under the multiple impact; see the black line of holes stitching the back of the white uniform. Miguel bowed to La Magdalena very slowly. Lay at her feet, under her doll-like, vapid smile.

Peter tensed the muscles of his legs. Jacinto smiled at him above the smoking muzzle of the gun.

"No, Comrade; I have no wish to kill you, now. Nor to avail myself of your woman. What good is it now? I have no hatred of you, and he who might have enjoyed the show is dead. So come—"

Alicia sat up, pulling her skirt down over her slim legs.

"Where?" she whispered.

"Outside in the square. At the bar in front. I feel devout. I have a desire to see the procession."

"Jacinto—" Peter said.

"Comrade, one word before you do another foolish thing. I know how brave a man you are. So Doña Alicia will walk at my side with the muzzle of this little headache-, heartache-cure pressed against her breast. You hear this?"

There was a harsh, grating click. Another. Louder. The sound of metal being slammed home.

"Yes," Peter said.

"Know what it means?"

"You just put in a fresh clip."

"Correct. Now walk with me like good children across the square and have a pleasant drink with me. Who knows? I may even let you live. At least a little while."

And then they were sitting there at the table with Jacinto between them, and Alicia was holding Peter's hand and looking into his face as though she were trying to memorize it, as she maybe even was. And now the square was filling up with the people come to watch the procession, so many of them that they got between their table and the square, blocking the view. Seeing how Peter was watching them, Alicia leaned forward and whispered:

"Please, *Cielo!*"

He didn't answer her.

"What will it be, Señores?" the waiter said.

"Beer," Peter said; "the blond, not the dark."

"Very well, Señor," the waiter said.

They sat there, drinking the beer. Peter had a hard time making it go down. Then they heard the motors of the motorcycle police come roaring into the square. They stood up. But they still couldn't see anything. There were too many people between them and the Plaza.

Then, in one easy bound, Jacinto was up on the table. He stood looking over the heads of the people with the Sten gun dangling from his hand. No one paid him the slightest attention. In the Glorious Republic, people were all too used to seeing uniformed thugs with machine guns in their hands.

Peter wrapped his fist around the straps of the Rollei's carrying case, eased it from around his neck. Let it dangle. A Rolleiflex is not the lightest camera in the world. And swung well—

Jacinto lifted the burp gun. Fired a short burst over the heads of the crowd. At the first stutter, all the people between forty and fifty years old, all those who had lived through the last revolution, the one that had brought Miguel Villalonga to power, hit the street face down. The younger ones stampeded, running.

And now, clearly, Peter could see the square. See motorcycle patrolmen throwing their machines flat and diving behind them. See the squad car in which rode Luis Sinnombre, as head of the police, brake to a stop; see the frightened face of the Mayor, who was dressed for the occasion in top hat, frock coat, and hickory-striped pants; and with him the Archbishop in his gorgeous robes; but the Archbishop's face was even more frightened than the Mayor's, which didn't speak well for his faith, and behind them the Mayor's wife in black with the traditional mantilla raised by a high comb in her hair, and at her side the Mother Superior of the Convent, barefoot as her order demanded, and behind them all the Virgins and crucifixions and Saints on the shoulders of the invisible bearers hidden beneath brocaded-velvet-covered stands, quivering as though they were living things.

Luis Sinnombre was shouting at his chauffeur, his mouth a great red cavern in his face. Then coolly, expertly, Jacinto opened fire.

Peter saw the gun stitching holes in the patrol car. It was very curious to watch: there would be a little puff of something, not vapor, not smoke, and the paint would scale off around the point of impact, leaving a little bright silvery ring of bare metal around the inky spot where the bullet had gone in; and the lines of the holes rising, rising until the windows crashed and shattered into intricate spiderweb traceries with holes in their exact middles and the door tearing open and Luis Sinnombre falling out of it, clawing at his holster for his automatic, and the stitching stopping, reversing itself, centering on the man, tattooing into him so that he jerked like a rag doll, slammed back against the car, and held there by the trip-hammer blows of that half a clip that was making ground meat of his belly, almost cutting him in two; and it was then that Peter swung the Rollei.

The camera caught Jacinto on the side of the head and knocked him off the table. He hit the sidewalk and rolled, still keeping his grip on that machine pistol and coming to rest against the overturned table which impeded very seriously his field of fire, making it impossible for him to swing the Sten to the right.

Then, knowing he was going to die if he didn't, and also if he did, the difference being that if he didn't a hell of a lot of other people were going to die with him, having time only to shape in his mind "Forgive me, Nena" but not to say it, Peter raced for Jacinto, slanting to his own left, Jacinto's right, in the desperate, forlorn, idiotic hope that the reduced swing of the gun in that direction would let him get there alive, seeing the flashes linking themselves like the splutter of a newly lighted blowtorch, hearing the sound become one continuous roar; and he, slanting in, clawing for Jacinto's legs, felt a jackhammer hit him in the left shoulder and side and upper left thigh all at the same time, with no appreciable interval between the blows, and he going on, not feeling the pain or the shock yet because they hadn't had time to register, slammed into Jacinto, sending him down, smashing his right fist into the Commando's face again and again, and Jacinto rolling, kicking free of him and diving for the machine pistol he had dropped when Peter crashed into him, and Peter coming up on his knees and Alicia's screams ripping the fabric of sound apart, and Jacinto grinning through the blood and dirt on his face and swinging the machine pistol around toward Peter—

And Peter hanging there on his knees, trying to get up, and Jacinto, out of his vast and icy reserves of pure cruelty, perhaps—or maybe because, being Spanish, being Tluscola, he understood, sympathized with, even respected whatever it was that made a man expend the last of his strength in the effort to die on his feet, to treat death with both the dignity and the contempt it deserved, easing his finger off the trigger and watching while Peter struggled there, the sweat popping out on his forehead, his veins bulging visibly in his temples, forcing himself to get up, to stand upright, to die not in an attitude of supplication or of resignation, but rising tall in whatever shreds of valor he had left, whatever tatters of pride, which was a gesture, he knew, maybe even a ridiculous one, but a gesture that had nevertheless to be made because the why and the when of his dying having already been taken care of, there remained only the how to give meaning to it, to give—and now he could think the words without choking over them—honor and grace to his taking leave of a life that had had very little grace, small honor, and absolutely no meaning at all.

So he struggled to get to his feet in the midst of a silence that had the texture and the feel of the collective horror of all the people who watched it, held there frozen by that horror which had, as horror usually does, a hypnotic quality of fascination about it, making them, those who had not already fled, who were picking themselves up out of the gutters into which they had flung themselves, forget their own danger, their own fear, until finally he made it, and hung there swaying, but on his feet, his left arm dangling, smashed in three places by the first burst, a section of his small intestine perforated, a bullet lodged in his thigh; the blood coming out of him in little spurting tendrils, watering the sidewalk with red, and Jacinto still smiling his ice-cold maniac's smile, raising the muzzle of the gun a little; then curiously spinning, whirling as the ball from the Mauser pistol of the chauffeur, who had been driving the now quite dead and even in death nameless Luis, tore into him; and caressing the trigger of the machine pistol which spat just twice before it quit, missing the chauffeur both times, and Jacinto running now, trying to fit a new clip in place of the empty one he had yanked out and thrown away, and the motorcycle police, lying on their bellies behind their fallen mechanical mounts sighting on him and holding down the triggers of their own Bren guns until they bucked empty, and the dancing rag doll caught in that murderous crossfire not so much falling as splattering upon the cobblestones, riddled, cut to pieces, hashed out of humanity even before he fell; and Alicia catching hold of Peter as he, too, started at last to sag, to give, and a dozen other hands helping her, easing him down into a chair beside the table.

And the sirens beginning to shrill along all that street and Alicia crying in a way that was absolutely insupportable, impossible to listen to, the sinews of her throat cording and those cries of more and less than human grief tearing out of her past the hand she had thrust into her own mouth and bitten to the bone, rising shrill and terrible like the scrape of glass on stone, like the splintering planes of anguish, like the final loss of hope, vibrant, naked, demented, wild, until by pure contagion every woman in the crowd was shrieking along with her, the sound of that collective hysteria racking hearing out of existence until Peter's big, gray, trembling hand came out and quivered on her face and his equally gray all-gone less-than-soundless voice stilled in an instant all their screaming as he said:

"Don't, Nena—please don't cry."

And she, Alicia, dropping to her knees and crossing herself, her contralto warm as sunlight and as deep, soaring up:

"Mother of Jesus, save him! For his life I promise Thee my life in service, in silence, in poverty, among the barefoot ones. I pledge it. I pledge Thee my life. I don from this hour the gray robes of Thy slaves. If Thou wilt save him—Oh please please please—dear little Mother of God! The sin was mine! All mine! I sought him out! I tempted him! Oh, Holy Mother do not take away his life I beg Thee, I beseech Thee, I supplicate Thee—Oh most sacred Virgin, please!"

And some of the women dropping to their knees beside her and praying with her. And some of the men looking at that bloody, terrible hulk still upright in the chair and saying, "*Que cojones!*" which is not quite equivalent to saying "What guts!" in English, but is close enough; and somebody else: "Make way for the Archbishop! Do not let him die without a prayer!" And he smiling then, thinking, and maybe even saying:

"Yes, pray for me, for all the defeated, the lost, the hopeless, the afraid—"

Then, quite abruptly, nothing. Neither time nor place nor even pain.

XXII

First, again, there was pain. It awoke somewhere deep inside him and began to grow. As it grew it whirled in bright-colored concentric circles like a pinwheel at a fireworks display. And all the colors of that pain were tones of red and yellow, whirling there from their epicenter in his middle, then widening, not into a bigger circle but into a parabola, an ellipse that included the whole left side of his body from his shoulder to his knee. The colors grew brighter, and with them the ache, the sear, the bite, the white-hot multiple stabbing. He went rigid, stiffening, his mouth opening, opening.

And hands gripped his right arm hard; there was a slight, tiny, piercing sting, noticeable only because it was so far away from the epicenter of his pain. The whirling ellipse of agony went on. But it had lessened, because he no longer had that overwhelming desire to scream. And now it lessened still more, dimmed very rapidly, the colors fading, the toothed ellipse rounding into a circle, leaving more and more of his body free of anguish, sinking finally to one white-hot coal low on his left side, which dimmed, faded in its turn into a long, slow ache, and through the onrushing dark he heard the staccato trill of a soprano voice saying in Spanish:

"Believe you he will survive all this, Doctor?"

And Vicente Gomez' voice drum-deep, slow-rolling:

"What I believe or what you believe, Sister, has no importance. What is important now is to continue the penicillin and the terramycin against infection, and the plasma against the shock. In about two hours, we will have an analysis of his blood type, which will make it possible to give him the transfusions he needs. Doctor Martinez is working on that now. Since the wrong kind of blood will kill him; and since, among the members of our staff who have not yet fled, Martinez, slow as he is, remains the only one I trust to do even so simple a thing as determining his blood grouping without making fatal errors, we have to keep him alive until that information arrives . . ."

Also, there was place. It was characterized predominantly by tones of white. The vague, featureless beings who inhabited it wore white, too. They came and went, drifting in and out of the timeless fog in which he existed. They did things to him. Many things. It wasn't very clear to him what those things were except that they were all unpleasant. He had the indistinct impression that they were torturing him. Once, in a flash of clarity—which, in his state of timelessness, may have lasted seconds or hours; afterwards he could never tell—he was sure of it. There was a tube in his right nostril. Another dangled from a bottle hanging from an iron stand, downward to his right arm, into which it disappeared through a needle big enough to disembowel an elephant. Various other tubes were attached to his body beneath the sheets, connected to him by a wildly complicated sort of harness. Then mercifully he faded out of clarity once more into dark.

Last of all, there was time. He became aware that his sensations had duration. That the aching of his arm, his leg, but especially of his middle went on and on. He realized that there were periods when the fluorescent lamp over his bed was out because enough light came through the window, and other periods when the windows were black, and the fluorescent lamps made their singing. And now the routine of the things the beings in white were doing to him changed. Other beings dressed in different colors: black or gray or blue or even vivid mixtures of tones were brought into the room and linked to him through pain.

He was not exactly sure how the linking was accomplished, but on his part it involved a hurtful piercing of his right arm. This happened several times. The last time it happened, time and place and pain all meshed, locked into clarity, into awareness; and Alicia's face stared at him with great and brooding tenderness from the opposite bed. He looked at her, tried to smile, gazed down to where her bare arm extended, saw the red flood pumping out of it through a transparent tube which entered a bottle then came seeping down another tube to enter his own through that elephantine needle. He raised his eyes to her face, seeing that she was wearing a curious kind of a headdress, a coif and veil exactly like the ones the nursing sisters wore, except that hers were gray; but, before he could occupy his tired mind with that detail, her warm, tender, wonderful mouth puckered into the shape of a kiss, and she, raising the fingers of her other hand to it, made the gesture of tossing it to him. And then, quite suddenly, it was all right. He was alive, with her warm, gay, youthful, renewing blood singing in his veins like wine.

But when she got up, he saw she had on the absolutely damnedest kind of dress. It was gray and shapeless, and belted around her waist with a piece of rope.

And, oddest of all, her feet were bare.

It took him until the middle of the next night to discover that *all right* was an exaggeration. A gross exaggeration. *All right* meant he was going to live, that he had time ahead of him, a future of sorts. But now the lesson that Luis' goons had begun was extended in depth; and he was forced to apply to his continued existence the same logic or illogic that had made him fight his way to his feet in order to die standing tall. Only now it was infinitely harder. Because it was no longer a grand gesture, one brief emotional clawing deep into himself to find the roots of atavistic valor; now it consisted in a long, slow, deadly contest with what is any man's cruelest adversary, himself. He lay in the hospital bed, alive now, fully conscious, staring at that dangling electrical push-button called in Spanish, because of its shape, *una pera*—a pear—which would ring a bell and light a lamp to summon the night sister. He lay there ten minutes, twenty, half an hour; then he pushed it.

Because, if he hadn't, he was going to scream his guts out. The sister came, saw without questioning his pain, eased that needle into his arm, and dropped him very swiftly through the bottom of the world into the gray hell of delirium of formless, morphine-bred dreams. The next time he held out for an hour, lying there staring up into the great white eye of naked agony, all his body licked about with flame. He lay there for that hour thinking or not thinking, forming in his brain and with his silent lips a chant that had no words, and that was and was not a prayer which afterwards he could never remember, but which got him through one hour, three minutes, and four seconds, before he pushed that bell.

That night pain came and sat upon his chest. It had weight, an odor—of ether, of disinfectants, of medicines, of various indefinable hospital smells—but it had no form. Silently he continued his fight with it, retreating into that wordless chant of the night before, calling Alicia's face to mind, thinking precisely and profanely upon the details of her body, feeding the feeble flame of sensuality; but that was no good, although it got him through two hours and a half.

He had already reached for the bell when Padre Pío walked through that door with that serene disregard for rules that didn't mean anything—such as visiting hours (aided and abetted in his stubborn effort to do God's work twenty-four hours a day by the nursing sisters on night duty who, defying Vince's orders, let the old priest come and go as he pleased)—that was as much a part of him as his respect for those that did, such as truly loving his neighbor as himself and maybe even a little more.

All night long the old man sat there holding Peter's hand and talking to him gravely, tenderly so that all the air was filled with his raspy, breathy "*Hijo mío*"—"My son"—until Peter fell into a sleep both healing and profound, whereupon Father Pío left him with a whispered blessing and hurried out to visit some other sufferer, some heartsick, grieving widow, some family all too desperately poor. In the morning, to his own intense disappointment, Peter could not recall what they'd talked about, what the old priest had said.

The morning came graying in through the windows and the day sister's rubber-soled shoes came whispering down the hall. She came into his room and stared at him, gave a little choked-off scream, fled.

When she came back, Vince was with her. He stared at Peter in his turn.

"Had a bad night, didn't you? Why didn't you call?" His voice was rough, angry, concerned, armed against his own pity.

"No," Peter whispered; "no calls."

"Why not?" Vince said.

"Oh, damn you!" Vince said, lapsing back into Spanish, which proved if anything how greatly he was shaken: "I will never accustom myself to it—never. If it served for anything, perhaps. But no. It is foolish and wasteful and maybe even bad; but it moves me much. And in my profession, Friend Peter, it is not useful to be moved. Oh, you son of the great whore! Oh, you Yankee unsayable of bad milk, spare me this. I am tired of witnessing useless valor—if valor is ever useless—if it can ever truly be deprived of meaning—"

Peter smiled at him; said:

"Vince—"

"Yes, Peter?"

"Let me keep it. Don't befoul it with words. Say I had—a great night. Great, marvelous, fine, enormous. Yes, an enormous night . . ."

"Why enormous, Peter?" Vince said.

Peter went on smiling, feeling the pain sinking down, down, fathoms deep, withdrawing now, maybe even vanquished.

"Because," he said, "because I won."

Doctor Gomez went on looking at him. And, usefully or not, he was moved. His voice came out harshly, angrily, filled with pain.

"Did you? Does any man, ever?" he said, and walked out.

"Now what the devil?" Peter said; and, probably because they had been speaking Spanish, he said it in that language, so the day sister understood.

"Oh," she said brightly, "he is afraid that when you find out—" Then she stopped, clapped a hand over her own mouth; whispered: "*Madre mía!*"

Peter looked at her.

"Say it, Sister," he said.

"But—" she quavered.

"Say it!"

Her head came up. Angrily. Proudly.

"Why not? It is, after all, the Will of God, and Doctor Vince, for all his skill, and despite his criminal denial of the teachings of the Mother Church, is but a man; and so are you, even though you were brave; and—"

"Say it!"

"Doña Alicia has—entered the convent. The gray sisters. The Barefoot Ones. She made a vow that if Our Lady would save your life, she would give up her own to the service of the Sainted Mother of God. And in the humblest of the Orders: The Barefoot Slaves of Our Lady. So—Don Pedro! You must not! *Ay, Madre mía!* What have I done?"

"Murdered him, no doubt!" Vince said, stepping through the door. "If I had my way, all you silly religious bitches would rot in hell!"

He bent over the bed.

"Peter—" he said.

Peter didn't answer him. He had turned over, his face to the wall. His eyes were closed. But the tears came out under their lids. Soaked his pillow until they had to change it. They had to change the next one, too. Sometime during the afternoon, the nursing sister noticed that he had vomited up the little food she had been able to get down his throat. By then it was already too late; he had lapsed back into unconsciousness. They had to feed him intravenously. That night, Vince called Padre Pío.

"Look, Father," Vince said; "he is going to die unless we do something. Something that lies outside of my training. You think the Mother Superior would let Alicia come to see him, if you intervened? Do you?"

"Of course, son. I am sure she would," Father Pío said. "The Mother Inez of Jesus is a very intelligent woman. She knows well when a rule must be bent a little, say in the interest of values that transcend all rules. But speaking of transcendental things, when are *you* going to find time to have a long talk with me, son Doctor? It seems to me that we should examine this atheism of yours scientifically, no? I will borrow your microscopes, flasks, test tubes, and the like to weigh and sort out the reasons you say there is no God!"

"I will give you one," Vince said. "In there, on that bed. That a man like Peter should be dying because of utter nonsense. Sort that one out, Father—but later on, please! Now what is necessary is that you leave this of my conversion for some other time and go talk sweet words to that baldheaded old witch at the convent. Father, believe me; there is no time!"

Father Pío smiled.

"With God there is always time, but in deference to your anxiety—I go," he said.

Two hours later Alicia was there. In her novice's robes, flanked on both sides by two stern-faced sisters of the order. Vince looked at their feet, which were exceedingly dirty from having walked all the way across town to reach the hospital.

"There is a bathroom down the hall," he said; "go wash your feet."

"Doctor," the oldest of the sisters said; "God will protect us and your patient."

"God?" Vince said. "Never heard of Him. Go wash your stinking, filthy feet before you track a whole epidemic into my hospital!"

"Doctor!" the sister said.

"Or get out," Vince said. "I have a dying man on my hands now because of your irrational tommyrot! I am not of those who suffer fools gladly. You heard me—go wash!"

Alicia's voice was almost under sound.

"Doctor Vince," she said, "is he—is he—?"

Vince looked at her.

"Yes," he said, "he is. When I had him saved. When he was out of it. What we need, my dear Alicia, is a new law, in which murder by superstitious cant is added to the list. Then I'd at least have the pleasure of seeing you hanged for what you've done!"

"Doctor," Alicia said, "I——" Then her voice drowned.

"Oh, hell, Alicia, I'm sorry! But I had grown fond of Peter. Do not listen to me. Listen to your heart. Listen to your God. Your cheap little God you can strike bargains with!"

Then he turned on his heel and marched out of there.

"What a wicked man!" the sisters said.

"No," Alicia said; "he is very good. Many nonbelievers are. Now come."

"Where?" the oldest sister said.

Alicia looked at her.

"To wash our feet, just as he said. Who knows? Perhaps microbes are unbelievers, too."

She spent the night on her knees beside Peter's bed. She heard him raving, heard the things he said. The other sisters left the room lest their very ears be corrupted by such blasphemies. But just before sunrise he quieted. He seemed to be talking to someone.

Alicia got up, went to the bed. Leaned close.

"Judy—" Peter said.

Alicia whirled, her bare feet whispering against the floor. But in the doorway she stopped. Stood there. Bowed her head.

"All right," she murmured. "This, too. All right. Do not take it away. But along with it, a little strength, for favor? What is needful for bearing it. Is it wrong to ask that?"

She went back and knelt beside Peter's bed.

"Judy," he said. "Dead. You're. So stay. Go back. Can't stand—"

"Peter—" Alicia whispered.

"Your eyes. Dead. Ends. All. You said. In a maggot's belly. Dirt clotting on your mouth. Back. Nothing to say now. All said. Useless. Down there. In the dark. The wet. The ooze. Dead."

"Peter—" Alicia said.

"Back. Leave me. What do you want? In God's name, what? Save me? You? Laugh. Don't make me. Hurts. Hurts like hell. To laugh—hurts. Hurts to cry to cry to cry. For you. Jesus, yes!"

"Oh, Peter, please!" Alicia wept.

"For you. Sure, baby, sure. Sure, Judy—anything. Say it. Yes. Make a doormat out of. Intellectual pride. For wiping. Feet. Say it. Hail Mary, full of Grace, the Lord Our Father Who art in when you come into Your kingdom remember—"

"Please!" Alicia said.

"—one hurt sick lost—idiot baby girl—remember—heal, bind up, shelter, save—"

Alicia bowed her head, whispered: "Yes, I pray it, too. Yes."

"—and wash. It off. All that stuck from twenty-seven years of rolling in it. Wallowing. Sometimes with me. Yes. In the Name of the —— In peace, yes. Rest, Judy, rest. Leave me in peace in peace in peace don't torment me with your new-washed angel's face, your strange saint's eyes! No! Let me die let me die you're gone and blessed and beatified and I couldn't love you hadn't love enough what I had left to 'Licia—"

And now, kneeling there beside him, Alicia ceased to breathe.

"—took it all. So don't. Save. A life I don't want. Can't bear. Don't!"

Alicia leaned close to him.

"Peter, *Cielo,*" she said, "she wants you to live, your Judith. And I—I cannot, unless you do. Please, Peter. It is so small a thing. Even though I can never be yours again, nor you mine—don't leave me! Don't empty the world!"

His eyes were closed; but slowly, painfully, he smiled. And his voice, speaking, had a hint of consciousness about it now, of thought.

"'S all right," he said. "Outnumbered. All the heavenly hosts. One barefoot angel. One soiled, made-over saint. Too many. Give. Uncle. Towel's in."

Alicia put out her hand and touched his forehead. It was cool. His pulse seemed normal.

She touched the bell. The night sister came. She called Vince. Vince examined Peter.

"Yes," he said at last, "the crisis is past. He will live. And you, what now, Alicia?"

She looked at him. Her eyes were awash, but she was smiling.

"My cheap little God keeps His cheap little bargains, Doctor," she said, "even when they are made on His behalf by His little Mother. So I must keep mine. *Adios!*"

Then, very quietly, she walked away.

Two hours later, Peter woke up. He was very weak, but he was both conscious and sane.

A week later, they rolled Tim O'Rourke into his room in a wheel chair.

"Petie boy," Tim said. "Goddammit, you had me sweating! Couldn't do that to me, you know!"

"Do what to you, Tim?" Peter said.

"Cash in your chips. Mari would kick me out of the flat as sure as hell. Blame me for it. Swear I hadn't taken good enough care—"

"You did your best, Tim," Peter said.

"And so did you, son. Thanks, boy. They told me you made Stirling Moss look like me auld grandmither, bringing me in. Down that road. That road where if you *walk* too fast, you fall off. Alicia told me you never got under a hundred an hour, even on those hairpin bends!"

"Kilometers, Tim. That's only sixty miles. You said that—that Alicia—"

"Yep. She looked in on me before she went back to the convent that night she prayed you back out of your grave. Sorry she took that plunge. Damfool trick. I'm a bead-counter myself, but—"

"Let's not talk about it, Tim."

"All right. Have it your own way. I said a prayer or two myself. Of course they probably went up like a lead balloon, but—"

"Thanks, Tim," Peter said. "That chair. That doesn't mean—"

"Hell, no! Tendons are a little drawn, that's all. I'm having baths, massage, and exercise every day. That Doctor Vince of yours is an ace. Harvard Med School. Did you know that?"

"Yes," Peter said.

"Talkative little fellow, aren't you? Fairly running off at the mouth. Diarrhea of the jawbone. Now, look, Petie boy, there're other dames—"

Peter shook his head.

"No, Tim," he said, "not for me there aren't."

"Pete, they just don't take a babe into a convent right off the bat. You know that, don't you?"

"Yes. She has to be a novice for a year before she takes her final vows. So what?"

"So you've got time! During her novitiate, you get notes to her—by the gardener. By the gal day students. Hell, there're a thousand ways—"

"No, Tim, there aren't any ways at all. That was Alicia, and she gave her word. Her slant is that Our Lady of the Mercies, or of the Remedies, or of the Good Happening, or something, came through. Saved this shot-up hulk. So now she has to keep her part of the bargain. And she will, brother! You don't know her . . ."

"Know her well enough to realize you're probably right. You damn fool, you should have married her two months ago."

"Couldn't."

"Why not? Because of Judy?"

"No. Not because of Judy. Tim, tell me—did they ever find her body?"

"No. And they've quit looking. Funny thing . . ."

"What's a funny thing?"

"I've got the damnedest feeling I *know* something about that. That I saw something, heard something— Hell! Probably the DTs . . ."

"You saw or heard something that—?"

"It's tied up with poor Judy. Only it's gone, boy. I must have been playing Joan of Arc at the stake when it happened. Because it's all mixed up with—with fire. With hurting. The trouble is, I'm not sure I saw it at all."

"Saw *what* at all, Tim?"

"Dunno. Judy. She was doing some crazy thing. Not crazy. Odd. Unlike her. Then—"

"Then?"

"Bang! The mountain cut loose. What was that line that Robert Oppenheimer said the first time they pushed that button and dumped the A-bomb on us?"

"'I am become Death, Shatterer of Worlds.' Shiva. My favorite deity. Because he makes sense. From the *Rig-Veda*, I think. No, the *Bhagavad-Gita.*"

"He had something there. That was what it felt like. I lay down and rolled. But even the ground was on fire by then, so it didn't do much good. It's all mixed up now. I don't even know whether it was before, or after, I heard those shots—"

"After. The lava caught the soldiers who did the job, Tim."

"Say! I remember that! They shot themselves. They were being roasted alive so they took the easy out. And Judy—"

"And Judy?" Peter prompted.

Tim's eyes went blank.

"Damned if I know, chum," he said.

"Tim, if you get out of here first, will you wait for me?" Peter said.

"Sure, Peter! I was planning to anyhow."

"Help me find Judy's body. Give her decent burial. I owe her that much. I—I deserted her, Tim. To go after Alicia. Who didn't need me. Who, as she's proved, was strong enough to go on without me. And now I've lost them both."

"Peter, being saddled with Judith Lovell all your life isn't the sort of thing I'd wish off on a friend of mine. You talk about saving her, protecting her; but, hell, boy, you aren't God Almighty! She'd have gone off the deep end someday, in spite of you. Like I said, what you should have done was to marry little Alicia—"

"And, as I said, I couldn't. Not because of Judith, Tim; but because of Connie—my ex-wife, in case your memory is still as bad as you claim. What kind of life would 'Licia and I have had, when that poor bitch had to get murdered so that . . ."

"She got murdered, all right; but you and Alicia hadn't a goddam thing to do with it. Or very little. The real cause was his secretary. Little blonde bundle of toothsome tail he was shacking up with. So poor Connie was in the way. So he hired this cheap punk. This hophead. The punk got the chair. They gave friend hubby life. Because of the kids. Not to make 'em orphans. Fat lot of good he'll do 'em in the clink."

"You mean that—that Connie's husband——"

"Yes. There was a curious little overlapping of responsibility, though. You and Alicia thought Luis Sinnombre was going to knock poor Connie off. So you could get hitched. Not that he was sold on marital love, but reasons of his own. Goddam crooked reasons, if I know anything about the late, great Luis. Maybe he was, but he never got around to it. And, anyhow, if he had been that character, the gas stove would have blown up or a brick would have fallen off a chimney as she passed by or she would have had a real fatal car smash. Slick. No evidence. No clink. Nobody fried. But you two were being so frigging noble that you sent me up there to warn her—"

"And gave friend husband the idea!" Peter said.

"He'd been entertaining that particular idea for one hell of a long time, Peter. All he had to do was to figure out an excuse. And I handed him this ready-made one on a silver platter. Even made the papers. So he hires a bodyguard to protect little wifie. And it was the bodyguard who—"

"Now you tell me!" Peter said; "*now*—"

"Tried to tell you before, but you wouldn't let me. No—it was because Judy showed up and cut us off, wasn't it? Anyhow, he'd have killed her himself, sooner or later. Comes out at the trial that your ex-beloved was a first-class pain in the ass. So this big, bloody obstacle of yours just didn't exist. Connie didn't cross over Jordan to let you chillun go. As I said, you should have married 'Licia two months ago . . ."

"Tim, will you please shut up? Or at least change the subject?"

"All right. Your beardy boys finally got over the volcano, did you know that?"

"No!" Peter said.

"So far they're on their good behavior. Only three anti-Yankee-Imperialist meetings this week. Our embassy hasn't been stoned but twice. Waste of rocks. Zopo busted all the windows out of it anyhow. And it's closed. What with the Ambassador and his wife dead and no recognizable government in sight, I doubt we'll open it. They're dividing up the haciendas. All the peasants are drunk, so nobody's farming anyhow. Food's rationed. Water's rationed. Hell, everything's rationed, except tail. And that might as well be with all the babes from The Blue Moon in uniform with burp guns in their arms playing she-soldiers. Brother, what goes on at night! The whole Red army's got the clap by now. Only us poor civilians are left out, Tomas tells me, or we would be, wasn't for all the hungry little babes who know what the only thing is they've got to sell. Some of 'em from good families, too. Seems Miguelito got that lesson across, if only posthumously—"

"What lesson?" Peter said.

"That most dames are whores at heart. Anyhow, at its worst the Everlasting Republic wasn't in the shape it is now—"

"In other words, a major screw-up?" Peter said.

"You ever see the Reds do anything else?" Tim said.

XXIII

The first week after he came out of the hospital he wasted; which, actually, was the only intelligent thing to do. But he didn't waste it out of intelligence: he let it slip by in a mood of melancholy, of lassitude; derived doubtless from his body's abysmal weakness but also from too close a contemplation of the appalling emptiness stretching out before him, now. He went daily to the Archbishop's palace to talk with Padre Pío. But the talks did him very little good. Now that the distance between him and death had widened again, the first thing that returned to Peter was the resilience, the toughness of his mind. Try as he would, he could not accept pious platitudes, even from so extraordinary a man as the old Basque priest. He respected Father Pío. Loved him even. But, as he put it: "I can't, Father. It's still the witchdoctor's cave, no matter how pretty it is. And—if you will allow me a couple of big, solemn, two-dollar words—I cannot surrender my intellect without murdering my integrity. Whatever the hell that is . . ."

"Nothing," Father Pío snorted; "words!"

Peter smiled.

"And the things *you* say, Father?" he said.

Physically, however, his daily walk to the palace was good for him. Since the Communists had come to power, not unsurprisingly none of the oil companies, had stepped forward with an offer to rebuild the refineries the Castristas themselves had dynamited. So there was no gasoline in Costa Verde. Everybody walked. And the distance between Peter's flat and the palace was great enough for him consciously to resist measuring it, for fear that it would discourage him. The walk strengthened his legs, improved his wind. That he was not hungry like everyone else was due only to the fact he had no appetite. The fleet of trucks—which, being Diesel-powered, could run on unrefined crude oil and therefore were not immobilized by the lack of gasoline—went daily into the country and returned almost empty. To the *campesinos* what winning the revolution meant was that they didn't have to work any more. In the provinces around the capital, the young Fidelistas like Pablo and Martin immediately put into effect Chapter One, Verse One of the Revolutionary doctrine: Agrarian Reform. The haciendas were divided up among the *campesinos.* The results were disastrous. Sixty per cent of the peasants lost their crop for the lack of the *hacendado,* or the *haciendado's* overseer, to tell them what to do, the simple things they had been told every day of their lives without ever bothering to think about, remember, or assimilate. Twenty per cent decided to take a holiday in town before settling down to work; and the remaining twenty per cent, the shrewd, intelligent minority, produced almost exactly what they needed to feed themselves and their families.

In Ciudad Villalonga—on the agenda, of course, was a change of name—the water tasted like gasoline because the tank trucks formerly used to carry the now nonexistent gasoline had to be sent up to the big reservoir to bring water into town. On the agenda, too, was a project to repair the aqueduct. There were rallies, meetings, parades without end. Yankee imperialism was denounced morning, noon, and night, until people actually began to believe that there were American-owned businesses in Costa Verde, which, in sober fact, apart from United Fruit—which had closed its doors and sold its holdings long before the Revolution—the Verdian Hilton, and one or two smaller hotels, there never had been; because as a general rule Yankee businessmen are too pragmatic to shovel fleas into a barnyard, which was what investing in Costa Verde (under any of its various caudillos, military juntas, and the rare civilian who reached the presidency in the elections in which each candidate usually polled more votes than the entire voting population), had always been. Even the oil refineries had been Dutch- and British-owned.

These details Peter got from Tim O'Rourke, who was everywhere, happily gathering the materials for a book about the Revolution. They dined together every night. So far, nobody had denounced them as imperialist spies—probably, as Tim had said, because even Costa Verdian ingenuity wasn't up to figuring out what they could find to spy on in a country without an air force, a fleet, or any army beyond a militia armed with light infantry weapons.

"Exploitation!" Tim roared, slapping his knees in pure delight. "Now they're talking about exploitation! Pete boy, you tell me: How're you going to exploit a bastard you can't even get to move? But, speaking about moving, *we'd* better, chum. Stateside—and fast."

"Why?" Peter said.

"Rumor has it that they're going to import Ernesto 'Rubles' Ramirez from Fidel-land to help 'em get organized. And you know what Rubles' idea of organization is, don't you?"

"Yes," Peter said. "The one thing on which the Extreme Right and the Extreme Left see eye to eye: shooting people. Purges. Spectacular trials where everybody confesses to sleeping with his own eighty-five-year-old grandmother—"

"Funny thing: they've been downright mild. The score's only ten so far; and that damn well had it coming."

"Pablo's influence," Peter said. "Good Joe, Pablo."

"Our good friend Tomas picked up any leads about—Judy?" Tim said.

"Yes. He's supposed to see a type who knows another type who is supposed to have two or three of those ash statues on his place. If one of them is a woman, I'll go have a look."

"Better make it fast, Peter."

"Why?"

"A hunch. You and me, chum, are made to order for Camarada Ernesto. Hirelings of the capitalistic press. Bent on corrupting the workers' innocent little old minds. When that boy gets here, I want to be among the absent."

"All right. If what Tomas says is promising, it only means one more day. If not, we ship out. I ought to check in at Doctor's anyhow for physical therapy to re-educate this arm—"

"Not much good, is it, boy?"

"It's seventy-five per cent paralyzed. I couldn't even squeeze a girl with it."

"Saaaay! Speaking of dames, I saw Alicia today; and she had on clothes! I mean her own, like she used to wear. And make-up. Cuter than all hell . . ."

"Did you talk to her?" Peter said.

"Yes. She asked about you."

"And?"

"When I suggested that she come along and *see* how you were, she said a funny thing—"

"I'm listening."

"That she'd better not. That since there was nothing you could do about her anyhow, she'd rather not face you. That it would only make both of you feel rotten—"

"Tim, did you tell her about—Connie?"

"No! Damn my stupid hide! That never occurred to me!"

"The next time you see her, do. You think she's broken her novitiate?"

"Looks that way. When I asked her, she smiled kind of sad-like and said: 'They decided I was—too naughty to belong to that club, Tim . . .'"

"Meaning?"

"How the hell do I know? That's all the lady said . . ."

And then, in the morning, when he was dressing himself with painful slowness to go look for her, the bell interrupted him. He opened the door with his good hand. Both Tim and Tomas stood there. And just from looking at them, he knew Tomas had found Judith for him; but the expressions on their faces seemed to be more than the occasion called for.

"Tell me," he said, "is she alive?"

"No, Señor," Tomas said.

"Then what the hell? I've already got used to the idea that poor Judy was dead. All things considered, it's probably best. So—"

"Look, Peter," Tim said. "There's one kind of funny detail that—"

"Meaning that she didn't make a pretty corpse?" Peter said.

"Ay, no, Señor!" Tomas said; "she is most beautiful! As in life. The ash—"

"I've seen ash statues before. They're a hell of a lot better than the usual embalming methods. So come on!"

"Pete," Tim said, "about that detail—"

"Well?" Peter said.

"Father Pío's outside in the car, waiting for us. You're a tough-minded old son; but I was—well—kind of hoping that this time you——"

"What, Tim?"

"That you won't spoil it for him. Brother, he's got it made! Like a kid before the tree on Christmas morning. He's already arranged for a glass-sided coffin, set in solid silver and—"

"Tim, you aren't making much sense, you know."

"How can I, when *this* doesn't? You see, Pete—she died in a church. No, in a little roadside chapel. Zopo had knocked the roof off it the same time he buried the town of Xochoa, so she hadn't any protection.

She died at the altar—on her knees. And you know these types down here . . ."

"Not to mention a certain son of th' Auld Sod who can swallow his share of mumbo-jumbo if it smells of incense and candle grease and is properly solemn," Peter said.

"So all right. I plead guilty. Call me stupid, but what she looks like right now is what saints ought to and generally don't. Her face—Jesus, Petie—when I kick off, I'd like to have a little of that—that whatever it is, she's got there now."

"Okay," Peter said. "Get on with it, Tim. Time's a-wasting. What's your pitch?"

"Just you keep still, Peter Pan! I'm getting there. Seems one of these weatherbeaten Indian broads up there got separated from her kids—five or six or eight—depends on who's telling it. Wandered into that chapel while looking for 'em. Swears Judy smiled at her. Left, and as soon as she gets outside, her brats sing out, 'Mama!' All twenty dozen of them. Nary a blister among the lot. That started it. So all the Tluscola up there started going to the chapel to pray first—pray to Judy, Pete! Can you tie that one?—before searching for the missing. And since very few people up there got it—"

"The split was on the other side of the volcano, Tim. Ninety per cent of the lava went down the eastern side."

"You see? There you go already. Lord, Pete, didn't anybody ever tell that you mustn't go around unwinding miracles? Bad form, oh, very! The point is that Father Pío and his Indians have got themselves a new saint, boy. La Gringa, they're calling her. Peter, can't you muster up a little charity, Christian or otherwise, and not foul up the deal for them?"

Peter smiled.

"You mean, like lying to them or something?" he said.

"Or like keeping your big fat mouth shut for a change, eh, Petie? I'm for the truth when it adds to the sum total of happiness, boy. Or when it props up that kind of shaky article, human dignity. But when it doesn't—the hell with it, I say! Besides—"

"Okay. You've sold me a bill of goods, Tim. Besides—what?"

"I *saw* her die, Peter. I didn't remember it. No—that's not right. My mind sort of reneged on remembering it. Call me a superstitious lug from the peat bogs of the Emerald Isle, but it's not *all* hokum, boy. The way she took it—head up, smiling—Jesus and Mary, Pete—I—"

"All right, Tim. You've done your good deed for today," Peter said.

Outside in the street there was a jeep waiting. Or rather it was a British Land Rover, which is a four-wheel-drive car considerably bigger than a jeep. It had a covered truck body replacing the original.

"Courtesy of Comrade Pablo," Tomas said. "And the tank is full, Señor."

"Bless him," Peter said.

Father Pío was inside the truck bed. He was on his knees, a rosary in his hand. Peter could see his lips move. So he didn't say anything to the old priest, then.

Again, they went up that road. The bus was still there, bright red with rust now, but the bodies were gone. The Land Rover groaned and whined over the lava flows where the soldiers had roasted alive. They were cold and solid now. That particular danger was over forever.

They went on up, past the stumps and skeletons of the burned pines, until suddenly Tomas, who was driving, wheeled the truck into a trail he had to know was there to see.

They came up to the chapel. Got down from the Land Rover. Father Pío led the way. He knelt down beside—that. Started to pray. Peter moved up the ash-drifted aisle behind him. Stopped. Stood there. When he could see again, he studied Judith Lovell's face.

She had fallen forward, toward the altar. But her head was lifted a little, her chin resting on her left arm. In her right hand she had a cross. The curve of her hand had kept the ash off a part of it, and Peter could see that it was of hammered silver. His mind reconstructed it whole from that detail: an antique, hammered-silver cross, singularly beautiful, clearly of Tluscolan making. Peter looked at that cross. At her face. Said: "My God!"

"See what I mean?" Tim said.

Father Pío went on praying.

Peter put out his good arm toward Tim. Said:

"Get me out of here!"

Tim helped him outside into the clearing before the chapel.

"Pete boy—" he said: "You want to lie down someplace? You look—"

"No," Peter said. "Call him."

"Call who?"

"Father Pío. Tim, I can't. This is too much. I can't."

"Take it easy, boy. Tom—get the Padre, will you?"

"*Sí*, Señor," Tomas said.

"Yes, son Pedro?" Father Pío said.

"Father," Peter said, "you cannot. It would be a deception. You must not! She was a very wicked woman, Father. Besides the husbands of whom I already told you, there were lovers without number, and vices, and nameless practices and—"

"I know, son. And so does God," Father Pío said.

"But, Father!"

"God has chosen such instruments before, son. You have seen her face?"

"Yes, Father."

"And what is there now, does that not to you outweigh whatever evil she has done, or been, or thought?"

"Father—I am not a believer. Her face—"

"Yes, son Pedro?"

"I cannot accept her face. I'd go mad. Deny my reason—"

"Then deny it, Pedro! And save your soul!"

"Father, I cannot—"

"You, son, are a fool," the old priest sighed; "but, one day—"

"I'll wait, Father!"

Father Pío smiled.

"You think that you can outwait God?" he said.

Peter went down the slope toward the burned-out pine wood, following the way she must have come. And then he heard the footsteps behind him and turned. Tomas and Tim had followed him. But Father Pío was still inside the roofless chapel.

"Look, Pete, you're in no shape for hiking," Tim said.

"Not hiking," Peter said. "Looking."

"For what, Señor?" Tomas said.

"Charon. His three-headed pup. Or both of them."

"Señor?" Tomas said.

"I get it," Tim said. "The ferryman of the river Styx. The helldog guarding the gates. Right?"

"In modern guise, Tim. Read bus driver. Read armed guard. Call me the original illegitimate child, but I can't buy sanctity. Too rich for my blood."

Tim stood there, looking at him. A long time.

"All right, Peter," he said. "Come on."

They found them in the little stone-and-adobe hut, roofless like the chapel. The three of them stood there looking at the ash-covered bodies of the guard, the bus driver.

"Charon," Peter said, "Cerberus. Pretty, aren't they?"

Tim found his voice. It was very harsh.

"So," he said, "you win, Peter Pan!"

Peter shook his head.

"No, Tim, I lose," he said.

"Señor—" Tomas said.

"Go get your jeep, Tomas!" Peter said.

"But, Señor—" Tomas said.

"Go get it, Tom," Tim said.

"*Sí,* Señores, I go," Tomas said.

When they had them in the truck, and were winding up the steep slope toward the chapel, Tim said:

"Look, Peter, there's no proof she shot them. Maybe they killed each other—fighting over her—"

Peter shrugged.

"Peter, for the love of God!"

"All right, all right. So she didn't. So they were struck by lightning. After they stripped down—to take a shower, say. So all she did was rob the dead."

"Rob the dead?" Tomas said.

"That chain around the bus driver's neck. Last time I saw him, he had a cross on it. Hammered silver. Tluscolan."

"The one she's got in her hand now," Tim said. "Peter, goddam it!"

"You think I like it, Tim? You think I couldn't use a nice long-bearded Father God? Some pie in the sky? A shining miracle or two? You think I like ugliness? Hell, boy, I—"

"Sorry, Pete. Only—"

"Only what, Tim?"

"It's so goddam crazy!"

"What isn't? Tomas!"

"*Sí,* Señor?"

"Turn this heap around!"

"Around, Señor?"

"Yes. Away from that chapel. Away from that sweet, simple-minded old coot up there. Who's got it made. And who's going to keep it, if I've got anything to say about it!"

"But, Señor—" Tomas said.

"But nothing, Tom!" Tim said, beginning to grin now. "Turn it around!"

When they had got up there, when they had come to that place that

Tomas had told them about, where the road edged a precipice one thousand seven hundred meters high, dropping straight down to the sea, and the sea beneath it indigo, the color it takes when it is absolutely bottomless, they lifted the statues down again.

"Hell," Tim said, "seems a pity not to say a prayer—even for these bastards . . ."

"To whom?" Peter said. "Aphrodite? Astarte? Eros? Pan?"

Then he put his good hand, the right one, against them, and pushed. He wasn't strong enough. The others had to help him. They stood there looking down. But he didn't; he turned his back to the precipice, to the sea, to the sky.

He did not hear the sound they made striking the water. The fall was too great. And had begun—since even he had to grant them humanity—and maybe even ended long ago, anyhow.

All the way back to the city, he didn't say anything. But once they were riding through the streets, he said:

"Drop me off at the cemetery, Tomas."

"The cemetery, Señor?"

"Yes. Want to have a little talk with a friend—"

"You," Tim said, "want to talk with a friend in the cemetery, boy?"

"Well, maybe not a friend. With Miguelito, Tim. Who understood sin. And repentance. And expiation. And maybe even sanctity. But then, maybe Judy did, too. And maybe great sinners make great saints. I wouldn't know . . ."

When he had got down from the Land Rover and walked through the big gates, Tomas turned to Tim and said:

"It is better that we wait, no?"

"The hell with that noise, Tom! You take me wherever Doña Alicia lives now," Tim said.

He was still there, sitting by Miguel Villalonga's grave, when she came. She walked very quietly up to him, and put her hand on his shoulder. He turned, stared at her, whispered:

"Nena—"

She was crying so she could not speak.

He got up slowly, lifted her chin with his one good hand. Bent and kissed her mouth. Drew away. Said:

"You—you've come back to me, 'Licia?"

"Yes," she said.

"Mind telling me why?"

"Because you are free, Peter. Tim told me. And I also—"

"You decided there were already saints enough, Nena? There are. Some very rare ones. Especially here of late. But, anyhow—"

She smiled at him impishly, through her tears.

"No, *Cielo,* I did not decide that. They—they—oh, what is that gringo phrase? Since I am to become a Gringa, I must learn to talk like one, no?"

"No. Talk like my 'Licia. My Nena. You were saying?"

"They indicated to me the door. Kicked me out. Almost literally, they were so mad!"

"Mad at you, Nena? For what?"

She smiled again. But now her mouth trembled. The tears on its upturning corners danced.

"A matter of esthetics, *Cielo.* The great curve of felicity that a woman pushes before her as a token of her lover's esteem is most unbecoming beneath the cassock of a nun. Especially with the enemies of the Church in power. So the Mother Superior thought it best—"

"Good God!" Peter said.

"Already I have no dress I can wear. This one is borrowed. If you were only a little as goatish as other men, and would look at me as they do, you would have seen it by now. But no matter. Come on, *Cielo.* I have to help you pack. Tim talked with Pablo by phone. It is all arranged. Pablo thinks it best we leave now before this terrible one arrives. I agree. I have much envy to see New York. Does one walk much, there?"

"Walk?" Peter said. "Walk?"

"*Sí, Cielo.* My feet hurt, now. I have not worn shoes in so long that—"

He mumbled something so low she could not hear.

"What did you say, *Cielo?*" she said.

"Nothing. Yes. A verse. 'How beautiful art thy feet with shoes, oh Prince's daughter!' I don't remember the rest of it. And it doesn't matter. Come."